MW01223168

OUT of the DARKNESS

SUE ADAIR

 FriesenPress

Suite 300 - 990 Fort St
Victoria, BC, V8V 3K2
Canada

www.friesenpress.com

ISBN
978-1-5255-9311-6 (Hardcover)
978-1-5255-9310-9 (Paperback)
978-1-5255-9312-3 (eBook)

1. *Fiction, Romance, Suspense*

Distributed to the trade by The Ingram Book Company

I Would Like To Thank

everyone who helped me accomplish my dream.
Thank you, RC and DL. You have proven that through tragedy and life experiences, both good and bad, you can accomplish anything if you put your mind to it. You both have inspired me and given me the courage to take the plunge into writing again, something I thought I'd lost the ability to do...

Thank you all for helping me make this book a reality.

1

......

Cassandra woke up to a beautiful, sunny day and knew that the nightmare she had been living for the past five years was finally over. She could finally see a light at the end of the tunnel and knew that now the possibilities that lay ahead for her were endless.

Though the time had been hard both mentally and physically, she'd felt she had no other choice but to live with the cards she had dealt herself.

Being married to Tom was so far the hardest thing she had ever done, but it was finally over. She lay there thinking how much time she had wasted in her life with a man who wanted nothing more than to get drunk and abuse her. She wondered why she would allow this to happen, but deep down she knew the truth. She had gone through this just to keep a house she had worked so hard for and was about to lose, due to the lost of her job.

Cassandra lay there thinking of all the things she had lost because of the choices she had made in life, but she knew that everything happened for a reason and one of the biggest reasons was to learn something. She'd learned the biggest lesson of them all: that worldly possessions mean nothing if you are unhappy trying to keep them.

She wondered if this was what life truly was all about, giving everything you have to someone and then finding out it was all a lie.

Tom had claimed to love her. He'd married her and promised to love her and stand by her through the good times and the bad. He'd said these vows in the house of God, and the biggest lie of them all had been that he truly couldn't make these promises. He hadn't even gotten his divorce from his first wife.

Thank God for Liliana and Grant, for allowing her to store the remainder of her belongings in their garage and giving her a roof over her head, until she could find a place to stay and get her feet back on the ground.

Cassandra decided she'd thought enough about this. She said to herself, *You have two days to pack up what is left, which isn't much.* Tom had cleared almost everything out one day when she was at work. She didn't care as long as he was out of her life. She was good with it.

The movers arrived on time and had everything loaded on the truck in less than two hours.

Cassandra stood and looked at the empty house and didn't recognize it as the place she fell in love with just five years before. It was now just a place where terrible things happened. She hoped the next family could fill it with love and joy, something she wasn't able to do during her time there. She knew it wasn't the house's fault, after all it was just a house.

"Well, are you unpacked?"

"There wasn't much to unpack, everything is stacked neatly in your garage. I don't need much other than what I need for work. Liliana, I just want you to know I really appreciate you and Grant helping me out."

"Cass it's fine. We're just glad we were in a position to help you; we both have been worried about you. Your life with Tom was toxic. We both just wanted you out and safe. We were all scared that Tom was going to become unhinged and physically harm you."

"He wouldn't have done that."

"You don't know that."

"I do. Deep down he is nothing but a drunken coward."

"So, any thoughts on what you're going to do now that all of this is done?"

"Well, last night I was looking at job postings on the internet and came across a job right up my alley."

"Really? Doing what?"

"Taking care of an elderly lady with some medical issues. The job is in Lethbridge Alberta. I think it's time for a change of scenery, someplace where everything is new and different, including the people."

"I think that's a great idea, you should go for it."

"Holy crap Lil. I just moved in and you're already trying to get rid of me?"

"Why yes, yes I'm," Liliana chuckled.

"You know you can stay here for as long as you need to?"

"I know, I appreciate it more than you know. I'd have been screwed if it weren't for you and Grant."

"What are you two talking about?"

"Not much, just that I'm going to take my time to find a place. Six to eight months or so should do it."

"SAY WHAT?!!"

Liliana laughed. "Grant, she's joking."

"I sure as hell hope so. Don't get me wrong, I'm glad you're here and you're safe, but six months to a year might be pushing it, lady."

"Lil, can I have your password for the internet? I wanna get the application done. I probably won't get the job, but I won't know unless I try."

"Cass, what are you going to do with all your belongings if you get the job?"

"Well, I was thinking about that when I was packing. I thought, if I get it, I'll have a yard sale right away to get rid of everything."

"We can do that; it won't take much to put that together. It's the right time of the year."

"I was thinking after the sale I could just load up my car and hit the road. It will be an adventure with endless possibilities, the world will be my oyster as they say."

"What about your job here?"

"I've spoken with my manager. If it doesn't work out then all I have to do is call her and tell her that I would like to come back and she will have something for me. I think the best thing for me is to go someplace new and start fresh with a clean slate. Okay enough stalling. I'm going to go and apply for that job now."

"Something smells good!"

"Thanks Grant. I'm off today and thought I would make you guys a wonderful dinner."

"Did you send in your application for that job?"

"I'm just waiting to hear back from them."

"Do you think you'll like it there, I thought you hated the cold?"

"I don't know, but there is nothing keeping me here really. I can do what I do anywhere. I just know I need a change. It's now just a waiting game. As for the cold they have battery heated socks and gloves so I should be okay as long as I can keep stocked up on batteries" Cassandra laughed.

"I hope everything works out for you."

"Sure you do. You just want to get rid of me."

"Yes, that's true, but really, I hope you get it if that's what you want."

"Thanks. I do too, and yes, I really do want this job."

Liliana got home and everyone sat down for dinner. "Cass this is really good."

"Thanks Lil. I got some news about the job I applied for a few minutes ago."

"Really?"

"Ya, they're interested. They wanna have a chat tomorrow at noon. I sent my personal references so they're going to contact them before our chat. I called my clients to let them know to expect a call."

"We'll keep our fingers crossed for you."

"Thanks guys. I'll take all the luck I can get."

"Have you told your family about what you're thinking of doing?"

"I don't want to say anything until there is something to say. I think I'll miss Aunt Sam and Uncle Joe the most. I get to see them all the time now. Once I move, I won't be able to, other than on the computer for live chats."

"Hey, what are we chopped liver?"

Cassandra laughed, "No, Grant, chopped liver you are not. Just think, if I get the job I'll be out of your hair."

"Fly, little birdie, fly." They all started to laugh.

"You both are gonna miss me when I'm gone."

"Miss your cooking, yes, but you not so much."

"GRANT!"

"What? I'm joking."

Cassandra smiled and told Grant sure he was.

Cassandra crawled into bed and prayed: please let this happen. As she lay there quietly in bed, her body and her mind relaxed. A faint whisper rolled through her thoughts—everything will happen as it should—and she drifted off into a peaceful sleep.

"Morning, Lil."

"Morning, Cass. How did you sleep?"

"I slept well for the first few hours, then I woke up and started thinking about my interview today and wondered if me moving across the country is the right thing to do. I was also thinking about what they might ask in the interview and that I should try not to make a complete ass out of myself."

"You'll be just fine. Just speak from the heart. You're a good person and they will see that. I'm sure that with your references they'll want to hire you on the spot."

"That would be nice. I wonder how long I'll have to get there, as well as settle everything here."

"One step at a time Cass. One step at a time."

The day flew by quickly. Cassandra looked at her watch— crap, she thought, I'm late. As she entered her room, she could hear her phone ringing; she thought to herself, *Of all days, to forget her phone at home.* "Hello."

"Cassandra?"

"Please call me Cass. Everyone does. Cassandra is what my grandmother calls me when I'm in trouble."

"Yours does that too, does she? So does mine. I'm Natalie and I only get called that when I'm in trouble. We must be related, then." They both laughed.

"Must be," Cassandra said, feeling a little more relaxed.

"Well, Cass, my family and I are very impressed with your application. I did call your references prior to our meeting today I wanted to make sure you were the right candidate for the position and your references were great. I didn't want to waste either of our time. With that being said, your clients speak very highly of you."

"Thanks. I've a great group of people I see on a weekly basis, and I don't mind at all. I understand completely. You want the right person to take care of your mother."

"So, first of all, Cass, let me tell you a bit about what we're looking for. We would like someone who can live in the house with our mom. Her name is Agnes Bailey. She is seventy-five years young. She is able to be left alone, but needs help getting in and out of bed. Mom will need help with her personal care and getting to and from appointments. We are looking for someone who can cook her healthy meals and maybe do a little baking. Cass, our mom is pretty easy going—she really likes her independence, so we want her to feel like she still has that. My mom has a dog. Will that be a problem?"

"No, I like dogs and they usually like me."

"That's good. Her name is Coco and really the only responsibility you'll have in regard to her, is letting her out in the backyard, feeding her, and maybe playing with her a bit. Coco is a good dog and my mom loves her dearly. Cass, we don't expect whomever we hire to be on the go, doing chores around the house every second of the day. As long as the house is clean and our mom is well taken care of, your day will be pretty easy for the most part. We have a young man who comes three times a week to clean up Coco's deposits in the backyard, as well as a wonderful lady named Jayne who takes Coco for long walks twice a day. There's a cleaning lady, whose name is Sandra, who comes in every two weeks to do the dusting and washing the floors. She's worked for our family for years. Usually when she comes, my mom likes to go out for the day—Sandra and Jayne coordinate when she is coming. Jayne will take Coco for the day so Sandra can move around freely and everyone is out of her way. It makes it easier for her to do a proper cleaning. As for your hours of work, you will work Monday to Friday and every other weekend. On the weeks where you work the weekend, you will have Fridays off. As for your salary, we've checked with other agencies and we feel that eleven hundred per week would be fair, since all your accommodations would be included. We will also have the accountant deduct all applicable deductions. We also feel that every six months the person we hire should get two full weeks off to recharge; during this time Agnes will go into a Respite care program where she and Coco can stay. Agnes has agreed to this. In the event Agnes passes away, you'd be given ample time to move out. Also, you will be given a six-month severance package, as well as a personal recommendation for any future employer—that's if everything works out as well as we all hope it does. All of this would be stated in the contract. The first contract will be for three months, to make sure everyone is happy and things are going well. At the end of three months we'll sign a lengthier contract, say for one year, and continue to renew it on a yearly basis. So, Cass, do you have any questions for me?"

"Yes, just a few."

"Okay, ask away,"

"Where would I be staying during my time off?"

"There's a granny suite at the back of the house that would be yours. It's a fairly good size living space and has its own bedroom, bathroom, and living room as well as a small kitchen. You have your own private space in the backyard. There's a small deck that's separate from the main house. There's a phone system in place so that if Agnes needs you all she has to do is buzz you. I have already spoken to her and she understands that she can't buzz you during the night unless she truly needs help. Agnes isn't like that, but I've spoken to her about this anyway. Anything else?"

"Yes. If there is an issue, whom do I speak to?"

"I have power of attorney, I make all necessary decisions regarding her, so if there's a problem or a concern, you just need to call me."

"How soon would whomever you choose for this position need to be there?"

"We would like the candidate to be here by September first,"

Cass thought to herself, *Okay, that's slightly over a month.* She would have to get everything here settled, and would still have time to get there. "Just one last question: when would the chosen candidate know if they are hired?"

"Well, Cass, as far as I'm concerned, the job is yours if you want it."

"SERIOUSLY? Yes, I want this job!" Cassandra yelled. "Sorry Nat." They both laughed.

"That's okay. Well, Cass, you do what you need to do to get here for September first. Agnes is away until the fifth, but I would like you here before she gets home, so you have time to settle in and get acquainted with the house and the area."

"That's perfect, Nat. This will give me enough time to tie up loose ends here and plenty of time for me to get there."

"I'm glad you're on board Cass. I really think you and Agnes are going to be great friends."

Natalie gave Cass her cell number and asked Cass to please text her address, so she could get the contract sent off to her. She would send two copies for her to sign. One to send back and one to keep for her own records. Natalie asked Cass to courier one signed copy back as soon as possible so that the accountant could get everything set up for payroll, so Cass would be covered in case something happened on their end.

"I will Nat. I'll send it back the next day if that's okay?"

"That would be great if you could do that, but please make sure you read it fully before you sign it, just in case there's a mistake."

"Thank you so much for choosing me, Nat."

"You're very welcome, Cass, please take care and we will chat soon"

"Sounds great."

Cassandra sat down and sent out a group message telling her parents and her aunt and uncle that she was calling a family meeting and that it was mandatory that they attended. She told them she would like them to meet her at Misty's Bar and Grill at 6 pm this coming Saturday. She assured everyone that all was good, she just had some great news she wanted to share with them all.

"Lil, I called a family meeting for this Saturday and I need you and Grant to be there."

"Okay what's going on?"

"I have something I need to talk to you all about"

"Okay. When and where?"

"Misty's Bar and Grill at six."

"I'll let Grant know—he'll be happy he likes that place."

"I know, it's my favourite place too."

That night when Cass went to bed, she felt good about what was happening in her life.

Cassandra got up and went to work and thought to herself, *Today is the day everything is going to become real.* Once those papers get here, she would know that this was really happening and that this really wasn't a dream.

"Anyone home?"

"Ya, in the kitchen, how was your day?"

"Long. One of my clients sliced her head open, so they had to take her to the hospital. I spent a good hour doing paperwork and notifying my supervisor."

"That must have been scary for her."

"It was. She said she hit the back of her head. I checked it and everything seemed to be okay, till after her shower, when I was blow-drying her hair, I found the gash at the front."

"Cass, an envelope arrived for you. I signed for it. I hope that was okay."

"Of course it is, I was expecting it." Cassandra grabbed her envelope and went down to her room, ripped it open, and started to read it. She got through the first page when her cell rang and startled the crap out of her.

"Hello?"

"Hi Cass, it's Nat. Sorry to bother you, but I was wondering if you received the envelope yet?"

"Yes, I just got it. I'm going to go through it right now and will run it over to UPS and send it back to you today or first thing tomorrow."

"That would be great. Would you happen to have your police check and abstract driving clearance yet?"

"Yes. I ordered them the day I applied for the position with you. I'm pulling them out right now. I'll include them when I return the contract."

"That's great. You're well prepared, I like that. Cass, take care and we'll see you soon."

"Natalie could you please send me a quick message to let me know you've received everything back?"

"Of course."

"Great, bye for now."

Cass hung up the phone and decided she needed to see the one person she knew who dealt with all sorts of contracts on a daily basis—her friend Barb.

2

......

Cassandra went to the Misty's Bar and Grill early, to make sure she could get a table big enough for everyone. She also needed to have a drink before her parents showed up.

"Welcome to Misty's Bar and Grill."

"Hi, can I please get a table for seven in a quiet area, please?"

"Sure, right this way. How is this?"

"Perfect!"

"Can I get you a drink while you wait for the rest of your party?"

"Yes please, I'd love a mango meltdown and could you also make sure this is all on one bill and give it to me at the end of the evening."

"Of course. Let me get you that drink."

Cassandra sat there watching the front entrance, looking for the first of her group to arrive. A few minutes passed and the waitress came back.

"Can I get you another drink?"

"Yes, please." She noticed her mother and father walk in. Cass stood up and waved at them and thought to herself, *Here we go.*

She gave her mom and dad a big hug.

"You look good Cass."

"Thanks, Dad. Are you enjoying your visit?"

"Yes, it was long overdue."

"What have you's been doing?"

"Yesterday we went to the old stomping grounds, saw the old farmhouse, our old house."

"Whenever I go out that way, I can't pick our house out. I know the old farmhouse, but I'm not sure which is the one I grew up in."

"Here's your drink. Can I get you both anything?"

"We'll wait till everyone else is here, thank you."

"What time did you tell everyone to be here?"

"I told them six, but it's not quite six yet."

"So, do you want to give us a heads up as to what this is all about?"

"No, Mom, we'll wait till everyone gets here."

"You know, Cass, waiting is not one of your mother's strongest attributes."

"I know, Dad." They all laughed. Cass hoped this get-together would go well. She took a sip of her drink and looked towards the door and saw the rest of the group walk in. She stood up and waved. Sam noticed her first, and pointed over to where they were sitting. Everyone made their way to the table. Cassandra greeted everyone.

"Please have a seat, all, and let's get our drinks and dinner ordered—then I'll tell everyone why I've asked you here tonight."

Everyone placed their order; the waitress headed for the bar to get their drinks.

"I would like to thank you all for coming, not that I gave you much choice," she said, with a chuckle. Cassandra hoped she wouldn't get a lot of questions, that she might not have all the answers for. "I was offered a job in Lethbridge, Alberta, and I have accepted it." Everyone sat there quietly, just staring at Cassandra. Her mom was the first to pipe up and say something:

"Really? Why there?"

"It's a good opportunity. I think a change will do me good and the offer is too good to turn down."

"What will you be doing?"

"I'll be taking care of a lovely lady named Agnes—she's seventy-five years young and needs a little help. She'd like to stay in her home as long as possible."

"You could do that here."

"You're right, I could, but I won't get an amazing deal like this here."

"Why would you say that?"

"Well, the pay is fantastic. I would have to work two months here for what I'll make there in a month. I'll get two weeks' vacation every six months to recharge.

They've given me my own apartment at the back of the house. I'll work two weekends a month, and everything is paid for. It's a three-month contract and, if all goes well, at the end of the three months a new contract will be signed for one year."

"I have another question,"

"I knew you would, Mom, ask away."

"What happens if she passes away? You'll have given up everything here—your job, you'll lose your full-time position and your benefits. Do you think that's a wise decision?" Liliana and Grant both looked at Cassandra and smiled.

"If Agnes passes while I'm there, they will give me ample time to move out, as well as a six-month severance package and a glowing recommendation for my future employers."

"Well, that sounds a little too good to be true."

"Mom, I had a lawyer look at my contract and she told me that if I didn't take the job, she would. Aunt Sam, Uncle Joe, what do you think?"

"Well, Cass, is this something you really want?"

"Yes, Aunt Sam."

"Well then, all I can say is—you go, girl, you only live once."

"Cass?"

"Yes, Uncle Joe."

"I agree with your Aunt Sam. If this is what you want to do then you need to do it. Go start your new life and be happy. We'll miss you like crazy, but if this will make you happy then you need to do it."

"So, what now?"

"Well, Dad, I've taken a leave of absence from my job. I spoke with my manager, Vicky—she's been very helpful with everything that has gone on and she told me if it didn't work out I would always have a job with them. So next Saturday I have decided to have a yard sale to sell everything I have left, and then Monday morning I will hit the road. Natalie wants me there by September first, so I can get settled and acquainted with the house and the town. Agnes is away until the fifth. Then I start work."

"You're going to drive there alone?" asked her Mom.

"Yes, I am."

"Cass, do you think that's wise? You get lost easily. Lethbridge is a long way from Brantford." Everyone laughed, they all knew that Cassandra was prone to getting lost. Cassandra laughed too.

"Mom, that's half the adventure."

"Just promise us you'll be safe."

"I promise, Mom." The waitress started serving their meals. Cass thought to herself, *Thank you, saved by dinner!*

"So, Cass, do you need help with your yard sale?"

"Yes please, Aunt Sam. I'll take all the help I can get."

"Your mom and I can stay an extra few days to help you out as well, we can head home Monday as well."

"That would be great, Mom and Dad. I'd appreciate that—it will give us a little more time together."

Cass was glad she was able to have this time with her family: once she moved, she didn't know when she would be back again.

3

......

The remainder of the week went by quickly. When Cass woke up, she looked outside. It was a beautiful sunny morning, a good day for a yard sale.

Everyone showed up as they promised and helped get everything set up. Cass told Grant that there were boxes left on the shelf, possessions she didn't want to get rid of. Grant told her that was fine, he would find a place for everything once the sale was done.

The day went by quickly. It was already one o'clock when Cassandra looked at her phone. She couldn't believe that everything was almost gone.

"Excuse me."

"Yes."

"I see your sale is wrapping up and you have some items left."

"Just a bit, can I help you with something?"

"My name is Reverend Felps. I'm with the Baptist church on Farringford Drive."

"Yes, I know the church. I go past it all the time."

"The church is having a community yard sale next weekend. We're raising money for a little girl that needs a special wheelchair which is very expensive. The family needs some help raising the money so I was wondering if you'd consider donating the rest of your items on the table to our yard sale?"

"Of course, I'd love to help you out."

"Guys, the yard sale is over, can we box everything up? I'm going to donate the rest of the items to Reverend Felps's yard sale that they're having next week."

"Thank you so much for your donation."

"Grant, can you help me grab the boxes that say, "not for sale?" I'm going to give them to their yard sale as well."

"Are you sure?"

"Yes, I'll go through them quickly and take out what I absolutely can't get rid of. There you go, Reverend Felps."

"I noticed these boxes have "not for sale" on them. Are you sure you want to part with these items?"

"I have gone through them and taken out what I can't part with. I wish there was more I could do for your sale, but I'm moving to Alberta on Monday and need the funds I have gotten for my trip."

"No, the donation of these items is just fine. What is your name?"

"Cassandra."

"Where are you going?"

"I'm moving to Lethbridge Alberta for a new job."

"Wow, that's quite the move Cassandra."

"Yes, it is."

"If you wouldn't mind, I would like to say a little prayer with you?"

"That would be very nice, thank you."

"Excuse me, everyone, could we all gather here for just a minute, I would like to say a little prayer for Cassandra's journey. Dear Lord, please watch over Cassandra and keep her safe on her journey. Please give her good weather, guide her through the trials and tribulations she will encounter, stand beside her, so she doesn't feel alone, and most of all, Lord, if she finds herself lost, guide her to safety. In the name of the Lord Jesus Christ, Amen."

"Thank you all for your help today. I've ordered pizza. It'll be here shortly, so let's clean up, then we can sit and relax before you all take off."

"Cass, when are you leaving in the morning?"

"As soon as I get up. I'd like to be on the road by nine the latest."

"I thought you were gonna wait till Monday."

"I was, but that was because I thought we would have to have a two-day yard sale, but now that everything is gone, I'm gonna head out a day early."

They enjoyed the remainder of the afternoon together, chatting and laughing, no one wanting to leave, but it was getting late and they knew it was time to say their goodbyes.

"Thanks for all your help, Aunt Sam. I love you guys."

"We love you too."

"Give my love to Uncle Joe and Macie."

"Cass, your Dad and I are gonna head out as well. We're going to pack up and get ready to head home."

"Love you, Mom. Safe travels home." Cassandra's father had tears in his eyes. "Hey you, none of that, I'm gonna be fine."

"You're my little girl, it's my job to worry."

"I'll be fine. I'll message you every night when I'm tucked away for the night, I promise."

"Cassandra, your mom and I want you to take this."

"Dad, no I'm fine."

"Don't argue with me girl, take it!"

"I love you, Pops."

"Be safe, Cass. Promise me you won't take any stupid risks. If you're tired, get a room for the night, promise me you will."

"I promise, Dad."

"I expect a message every night and every morning until you get to your destination."

"I promise. I love you all very much, I have my phone so you can call or text me anytime."

Cassandra hugged everyone goodbye. She held on tight as she knew it would be some time before she would see them all again.

4

......

Cassandra woke up and looked at the clock. It was six-thirty: she knew she wouldn't be able to go back to sleep so she thought she would get up and sneak out before anyone else got up. Saying goodbye was going to be too hard.

"Good morning, Cass, why are you up so early?"

"I couldn't sleep, and you?"

"I couldn't sleep either. You know, Cass, I had this sinking feeling you might get up early and try to sneak out the door before anyone got up."

"You know me only too well."

"Well, we have known each other for thirty years, I probably should by now."

"That's true," Cass said with a smile.

"Do you have all your stuff together?"

"Ya, I'm just gonna go and put my stuff in the car then I'll be back."

It didn't take Cass long to load what she was taking with her. She went back into the kitchen.

"Do you have everything?"

"Yes I did a once over to make sure."

"Do you have your passport?"

"Yes, it's in my purse. Lil, I stripped the bed and put the bedding in the washer. The room is clean so you won't have to do anything."

"Thanks Cass, I appreciate that. Your Aunt Sam said to give you this before you left. She said to tell you to never mind bitching about it, to just take it."

"Damn her, I told her I was okay I didn't need anything."

"Look, they love you."

Cass shook her head. "I know."

"So, do you have your GPS set up?"

"Yes, here are the directions I plan on taking, as long as I don't get lost." They both laughed.

"Cass, like that's not going to happen."

"It's possible Lil, it's possible."

"You keep telling yourself that if it makes you feel better," Lil laughed, "because we both know it's more likely that you will get lost at some point."

"Lil, I'm gonna go."

"Was it something I said?"

"No," Cassandra laughed, "please tell Grant thanks for everything."

"I will. I love you, girlfriend. Stay safe and please keep in touch." Liliana put her arms around Cassandra, gave her a big hug and reminded her that they were just a phone call or text message away. Cassandra hugged Liliana tight, knowing it would be a long time before she saw her friend again.

"Thanks, hun." Cassandra got into her car quickly. She knew if she didn't go now she wouldn't go at all. She rolled down her window, looked at her friend, and, with tears in her eyes, backed out of the driveway, looking one last time at Lil. Cass yelled "Ciao Bella," blowing her a final kiss. Then she turned her head and told herself, *You got this,* and drove off into the proverbial sunset.

As Cassandra drove into the unknown, tunes blasting, tears flowing down her cheeks, she pulled over at the nearest coffee shop and thought to herself, *What the hell are you doing, girl? You can't go halfway across the country for a job, what were you thinking?* She started to turn the car around and suddenly stopped. Cass put the car into park and called the one person she knew who would help her figure this out.

"Hi, Uncle Joe, can I please speak to Aunt Sam?"

"She's still sleeping, Cass, what's wrong?"

"I don't know if I can do this."

"Do what?"

"Move halfway across the country."

"Why don't you think you can do it?"

"Uncle Joe, I won't know anyone. I'll have no support system, no friends, what am I doing even thinking this is remotely possible?"

"Okay Cass, take a deep breath, sit back and listen to me. YES! You can do this and how do I know this? because you are Cassandra Elizabeth Taylor. You are your mother's daughter and Sam's niece. The three of you have been through hell and back and all of you are still standing. They didn't raise a weak girl—give yourself some credit, you are stronger than you think. You lasted five years with that loser Tom. You put up with all his lies, drinking, and cheating ways. You lost almost everything you worked so hard for. You are not a weak person: a weak person wouldn't be sitting in her car ready to go on the road trip of a lifetime. You are not curled up in a ball saying poor me, are you?"

"No."

"You got up and put your big girl pants on. Then you dealt with all the mess that loser left you with AND you are not alone, we are all here for you, all you need to do is pick up the phone and dial our number. You still know how to do that right?"

"Yes."

"Good. So you can't use that as an excuse, can you? As for friends, you still have them, they're just not with you—and Cass you will make new friends. You are a wonderful lady with a great personality, you're fun to be around and you'll have new people in your life before you know it. I believe in you, we all do. You can do anything you put your mind to. Will it be hard, yes, of course it will, change isn't easy. BUT, just think of all the new experiences you are going to have. You're going to make a brand new life for yourself and you will thrive in your new life. Change isn't easy, but sitting in the same situation you're not happy with isn't good for you either. So, Cass, this is what you're going to do, are you listening to me?"

"Yes Uncle Joe."

"Good, you're going to wipe the tears from your eyes, give your head a shake, put the car in to drive, and get back on the road and get your butt to Lethbridge. They need someone like you to stir things up and make their lives a little more interesting and there is nothing wrong with that."

Cassandra started laughing "Thanks Uncle Joe. I needed that. I love you."

"I know, what's not to love, right?" They both started laughing.

"We'll chat soon, Uncle Joe."

"Okay, Cass. Drive safely and remember, if you need us, all you have to do is call."

"Thanks, Uncle Joe." Cassandra knew her uncle was right, so she did as she was told. She wiped her tears away, gave her head a shake, turned the car off, and went into the doughnut shop for a drink and something to eat and a restroom break. *After all, priorities first,* she thought to herself.

Refreshed and feeling better about everything, she got back into her car, put it in drive, turned up the tunes, and started to sing.

Cassandra couldn't believe what beautiful countryside Canada really had. She just hadn't noticed it before now. She truly was lucky to live in this beautiful country. She looked at the clock and thought wow she had already been driving for five hours. She decided she'd better stop and grab a drink and have another restroom break.

Cassandra looked at the GPS, and she was about three hours from Milwaukee. She decided she would get to Milwaukee and stop for the night. It was almost five when she decided she had done enough driving for the day. Cass pulled into the Sunset Inn parking lot on North 6th Street and looked at her surroundings. She thought to herself, *Uncle Joe was right.* She could do this and dammit she *was* doing this.

Cassandra went into the inn and got a room at the back where she could park her car right in front of her room. She grabbed her bags and took them inside. It wasn't much of a room, but it was a place to lay her head and keep her safe.

The first thing she did was hop on the internet and send her parents a short message telling them where she was, the address and the room number. She knew these were the things her parents would want to know. She also texted Liliana and told her she'd arrived in Milwaukee safe, and had not gotten lost once. *Yet*, she said to herself with a chuckle. She texted Sam and Uncle Joe to let them know where she was and that she was stopping for the night. Sam messaged her right back "Everything okay?"

"Yes, it's all good. Uncle Joe was there and set me straight."

Cassandra decided she would run to the restaurant up the road, come back to her room and have a nice hot shower and put her snuggles on and just veg out for the night. She decided she would stay an extra day or two and check things out—she might as well check out the places she was driving through. You never know what you will find.

She woke up around ten feeling much better than she had the previous day: a good night's sleep was all she had needed. She knew now that the decision she'd made about moving to Lethbridge was the right decision for her.

She checked her messages and sent one back to her parents telling them she was planning on staying for an extra day, just to check out what Milwaukee had to offer, and she would try and catch them later that night for a video chat.

She got dressed and went down to the front desk and told them she was going to stay an extra day. She asked Evelyn, the lady at the front desk, where she could go to get something to eat. Evelyn suggested that she go and check out the public market. They had many different food vendors to choose from.

"Thanks, that sounds great, I think I will."

Cassandra looked up the address. It was in the third quarter neighbourhood. She programmed the address into the GPS and off she went. She found the market easily enough and, boy, Evelyn was right—all the different food vendors, fresh loaves of breads and cheeses. It was like nothing she had ever seen before. Cass decided to just get a couple of fresh rolls and different cheeses and a drink. She found a bench and just enjoyed the beautiful weather.

She couldn't remember the last time she'd actually done something like this, or if she ever had. She finished her meal and found that her favourite cheese was the Havarti—it was mild but creamy, and she enjoyed it very much. She would have to make a note to pick some up when she got to her destination.

Cassandra put the empty wrapping into the garbage and went looking around the market. She left around two. There was still much more to see, but she decided she would just drive around and see if anything caught her eye. Cass drove around and came upon the Harley Davidson museum; she thought what the heck, she liked motorcycles so this could be interesting.

She took her time looking at all the bikes and learned a few things she didn't know. She looked at her watch and it was going on five, she decided to grab an early dinner—she wanted an early night she intended to get up and do some more exploring.

Cass went back to the inn and thought she'd better try and reach her mom and dad for a chat. There was a message waiting for her: "Hey Cass, we forgot we have a church meeting to go to, so can we chat in the morning." She sent them a message, telling them she would try to get them when she got up, between eight and nine. She was in for the night and she loved them both.

Cass closed her computer and lay down and she was asleep within minutes. She woke up feeling refreshed and rested. She opened up her laptop and called her parents, "Good morning Mom."

"Good morning, sorry about last night."

"That's okay. I went to bed right after I sent the message and went to sleep." Cassandra told her Mom and Dad all about the previous day.

"Sounds like you enjoyed your day."

"I did. I might come back one day and spend a few days here. There's so much more I would like to check out."

"When are you getting back on the road?"

"I was going to stay another day, but I think that as soon as I get up tomorrow, I'll have a shower, grab some breakfast, and then I'll get on my way. It's about seven and a half hours to Minnesota from here so I thought I would drive there and take a break for a day. Then, from there, it's about another day's drive and I'll be in Lethbridge."

"Be careful, Cass."

"I will, Mom. How are you guys?"

"We're fine—we'll be a lot better when you get there. Your dad and I worry about you."

"I'll be fine."

"We know that, but you will always be our Baby Dumpling and we will always worry."

"Mom, I'm thirty-four years old."

"Cass, it doesn't matter if you're one hundred and six, we will always worry about you."

"I know, and I love you guys too. You guys have a great day. I'll talk with you tonight."

The next morning Cassandra loaded up the car and off she went. She finally saw the sign, "you are now entering Minnesota." She decided she had driven enough for the day and saw a sign for St. Ann's Hotel. She pulled in and parked the car and went inside to get a room where she could once again park the car just outside her room. She decided to go to the diner across the street. She walked in and grabbed a seat at the counter. The waitress gave her a menu. She looked through it and she ordered what she wanted and told the girl she would like it to go. She got her order and went back to her room and jumped in and had a quick shower. Then she got on the computer and called her parents.

"Hi, guys."

"Where are you?"

"I'm in Minnesota, I'm staying at St. Ann's Hotel. I picked up some supper and am going to lay back and relax."

"How long do you plan on staying there?"

"I'm gonna get back on the road first thing in the morning and I'll arrive some time tomorrow evening. I talked to Natalie yesterday and told her when I thought I'd be there. She said, "great"—just send her a text message when I'm about an hour away. Mom, I'm gonna say goodnight. I'll talk to you both tomorrow night."

"Okay, BD, have a good night. We love you too."

Cass shut down the computer and thought, *Thirty-four years old and they're still calling me their Baby Dumpling.* She laughed to herself. When she was younger it was Sweet Polly Purebred; *Baby D is better,* she said to herself.

She picked up her dinner, curled up in bed, turned the TV on, and started to watch some movie that had already started. She started eating her dinner and when she looked up she saw a little mouse come around from behind the dresser. It stopped in the bathroom doorway. Cass said to the mouse, "I'm sitting right here." The mouse looked up at her and scurried back behind the dresser. She thought, *Oh boy, just what I need.* She went back to eating her dinner and looked up again and there he was standing on the dresser. Cass was shocked that this little mouse had such big kahunas. "I'm still here." He looked at her and scurried away. She leaned over the bed, picked up her shoe, looked at the crock and thought, *Ya, like this piece of rubber's going to do anything.* She put it down beside her, finished her dinner, made sure there were no crumbs, and put the container in the garbage can. Cass finished watching the show and was just going to get up to go to the bathroom when there was her little friend again. He was on the rim of the garbage can. She picked up the shoe and threw it. The shoe hit the can and the mouse fell in the can and couldn't get out. Cass picked the can up, opened the balcony door, went outside, shutting the screen door behind her, and put the can on its side. The mouse scurried away. *OK,* Cassandra thought, *if I see one more mouse I'm out of here.*

She woke up looking at the clock and it was nine in the morning. She looked around and didn't see her little friend anywhere so she got up, got dressed, and went across the street to the diner for some breakfast.

After her breakfast, Cass loaded up the car, checking her bags to make sure she wasn't bringing any unwanted travellers with her. All was good. She got into the car and off she went. Eight more hours and she would arrive at the place she would call home for the next little while.

It was six-thirty when she realized she'd forgotten to text Natalie, so she pulled over. "Hi Nat it's Cassandra."

"Hi, how are you making out? Where are you?"

"I'm just coming into Lethbridge. I'm sorry, I completely forgot to call you—I just wanted to get here."

"That's okay. I'm actually at the house so we should see you in about a half hour."

"Yes, that sounds about right."

"See you soon, then."

"I can't wait," Cassandra laughed.

"No doubt." "See you soon." Cassandra found the house and when she saw it she thought, *Oh my God, such a big house for one person.* From the look of the outside, she was glad that Sandra was the one cleaning it. She got out of the car and stretched her legs, thinking to herself, *Home sweet home.*

Nat came out the front door and smiled. "You made it."

"Yes, thankfully. I don't think I could have driven another mile."

Natalie laughed. "Well let's get your bags and I'll show you to your apartment." Natalie took her around to the back of the house. "The driveway you came in is for the main house; this is your driveway and this is your garage."

"Wow, thank you, are you sure you won't need it?"

"No, this will be yours to use—it's better for your car to be out of the sun. It gets really warm here and my mom can't stand a warm car. Not only that, we have a lot of birds and it will save you from washing it all the time. Let's go in and check out your space.

Well … how do you like your new home for the next three months, and hopefully longer?"

"Wow, this is mine! Who else stays here?"

"Just you."

"Seriously?" Natalie laughed. "Sorry, I wasn't expecting it to be this big."

"Well, if you would like a roommate, I'm sure I could find you one."

"Oh no, no—I'm good." They both laughed.

Natalie showed Cassandra where everything was located. She showed her the main house; it was gorgeous. Cass had never seen a house like this before. It was beautiful, but it didn't look like a palace. It had nice things, but it made you feel at home as soon as you entered.

"Please make yourself at home. Sandra will come next Saturday to clean the house and get it ready for my mom's arrival. This binder is for you. In it is a list of foods Agnes likes and dislikes, as well as her pet peeves. I thought this might help you."

"Thank you so much, this will be a great help."

"Cassandra, through this door is the main house. This door is unlocked—go through it and get yourself acquainted. There is an elevator that has its own generator in case of a power outage—it's over here. I'll take you up and show you Agnes's room. She has an adjoining bathroom."

"Wow, this is beautiful."

"The other two rooms are guest rooms. I will be upfront with you: there are cameras throughout the house. Agnes has been living here alone and this was the only way we could keep an eye on her."

"Okay, no problem. What about the apartment I'll be staying in?"

"No, there are no cameras in there, however there is one facing your entrance into the main house. It's not there for you, but since it was empty, we felt for mom's safety, if someone broke in, we could get them on camera."

"I think that was a great idea."

"There's also one outside your entrance as well as outside the garage. This is the alarm code. Please don't keep it out in plain sight."

"I won't. I'll figure something out so only I know what the numbers mean."

"Here are your keys to your apartment and to the front door—please only use the front door when you are with Agnes."

"No problem."

"Well, you have a week to familiarize yourself with the layout of the house and where things are. I have this journal for you and wrote all of Agnes's upcoming appointments in it."

"Great, I appreciate that."

"I'd like you to record any pertinent information. For example, if you go out record where you went, just in case something happens, then we have a record of it. Also, record anything you think I should know, such as, if my mom is having an off day or if she has an outburst—those kinds of things."

"Sure, not a problem."

"Also, in the journal there are the times for her medication. All her medications come in a blister pack, so it's just a matter of giving them to her. Please make sure she takes them. She hates it, but… doctor's orders. Cass, if there's nothing else then I will leave you. You have my number, so call me or text me if you have any questions."

"I will, thank you Natalie. Oh, where is the nearest grocery store?"

"There are maps in the binder on how to get to the places you will frequent on a regular basis, with the address for your GPS."

"Awesome, thank you."

"I picked up a few things for you and put them in your refrigerator."

"Thank you so much."

"You're very welcome. I didn't think you would want to get back into the car right away. Cass, my mom will be home Monday, around eleven."

"Okay, I'll be ready for her arrival."

"Cass."

"Yes."

"Thank you."

"For what, Natalie?"

"For moving here and giving up everything and moving away from your family and friends."

"Well, it's all about new beginnings. Thank you for hiring me. I hope this works out for all involved."

"I think I'm a pretty good judge of character, and Cass, I think this is going to work out great for everyone. The house is yours, treat it like your home."

"Thank you."

Cassandra watched Natalie leave, waved goodbye, then went to her car. She moved her car into her driveway, went in, found the code to open the garage door, and parked the car. She looked at her car thinking, *Well, Oscar, we're home, get some rest.* She laughed to herself, lowered the door, and went in to unpack and chat with her parents.

5

......

Cassandra woke up early. She wanted to make sure everything was in place when Agnes arrived at eleven. She had a shower, got dressed, and went into the main house. She decided she would bake some homemade cookies. When she rolled into the house, the first thing Agnes would smell would be something good, and she would know that she was home.

Cass looked at the list of things Agnes liked, and peanut butter and chocolate chip cookies were her favourite. Cass thought to herself, *a lady after my own heart*. In no time, the cookies were done and the kitchen was cleaned up, Agnes should be arriving anytime now. Cass went to the door and turned the alarm off. She didn't want to forget it and have it go off accidentally—not the kind of first impression she had in mind.

Cass was pacing back and forth—now the panic was setting in, and her head was full of thoughts like: *what if she doesn't like me? what if she doesn't like the cookies or how I cook?* Cass decided there was time for a quick call to Lil.

"Lil, it's me, I'm freaking out here. Agnes is due any minute now—what was I thinking? What if she doesn't like me? What if she doesn't like my cooking? Oh my God, what did I do? I gave up everything, drove across Canada, and this may all blow up in my face." The phone was silent. "Lil, are you there?"

The voice on the other end said, "Dear, I think you have the wrong number."

Cass stopped. "This isn't Liliana?"

"No, dear."

Cass felt terrible. "I'm so sorry, I must have dialed the number wrong."

The lady on the other end said, "That's okay, I hope everything works out for you." Cass chuckled and told her she did too.

Just as Cass was hanging up the phone, she heard the sound of a car door shutting and voices coming up the pathway. She said to herself, *Here we go.*

Cass went and opened the door and greeted Agnes with a smile. "Hello Agnes, I'm Cassandra. Can I give you a hand with all that?" She took the bag that was on her lap and took Coco's leash.

"This is Henry, he's my neighbour. Natalie couldn't pick me up so Henry came to get me from the resort."

Coco started barking at her and wouldn't stop, so she bent down, put her hand out, "Hi there, Coco. I'm Cass. Nice to meet you." Coco sniffed her hand, smelling every inch, she acted like she'd found the pot of gold at the end of the rainbow. She gave Cass's hand a bunch of kisses and started wagging her tail. Cass thought to herself, *Thank God for cookie dough.*

"Well, I think you have a friend for life there. It smells great in here"

"I thought I would break the ice with homemade cookies."

"Well, that works for me," Agnes said with a big grin. "Let's try one and see how they taste."

They headed towards the kitchen and Cass put Agnes's bag by the elevator as they passed by. She came in behind them and put both plates of cookies onto the table. "Can I get you something to drink, Agnes?"

"Sure, I'll have a glass of milk"

"Henry, can I get you some milk as well?"

"No thanks, I need to get going."

"Oh Henry, sit down and have some cookies and milk, we won't tell your wife." Agnes said in a whisper, "His wife, Kathleen, is a bit of a health nut."

"Oh," said Cass, and they all chuckled.

After a few cookies, Henry excused himself and headed home. Agnes and Cass talked and talked. When Cass looked at the clock on the wall she realized they had been sitting there for a couple of hours, chatting and eating cookies. Cass looked at Agnes, "We'd better get you upstairs so you can lie down and rest. You look like you're getting tired."

"I'm a little tired." Cass wheeled Agnes into the elevator.

"Agnes, do your clothes need to be washed?"

"Yes please, Cass."

"Well then, let's get you settled and I'll get your laundry on the go."

"Cass, can we have a late dinner tonight? I think I ate too many cookies."

"Sure, no problem," Cass chuckled.

Cassandra started getting their dinner ready. She was making homemade pasta sauce and started chopping all the vegetables. She pulled out the crock pot, grabbed the Roma tomatoes, peeled them, took the seeds out, and ran them through the food processor. She then put everything into the crock pot, turned it on medium, and then proceeded to get the laundry going.

It was five o'clock when Agnes buzzed. "Yes Agnes?"

"Can you please come and help me?"

Cassandra got her into the chair, wheeled her into the bathroom, and started to run the bathwater. She helped Agnes get undressed, transferred her onto her bath chair and lowered her into the water. "How's the water?"

"Perfect." Cassandra left her soaking in the tub and went and fixed the bed so it would be ready when she wanted to retire for the evening.

Cass helped Agnes out of the tub, helped dry her off, and got her dressed into her evening clothes. Once she positioned her comfortably in her wheelchair, she wheeled her into the bedroom.

"Just give me a minute, Agnes, so I can clean up the bathroom." There wasn't much to do but hang up the towels and clean out the tub. She went back into the bedroom and wheeled her into the elevator.

"Something smells really good," Agnes said.

"Well, I hope it tastes as good as it smells."

They had dinner around six-thirty. Cass thought to herself, *Agnes must have liked her dinner, as she ate everything on her plate.* "Can I get you any more Agnes?"

"No thanks, that was wonderful. However, the next time maybe add a little more garlic in the sauce—other than that, it was perfect."

"Good, I'm glad you enjoyed it. Would you like a tea?"

"That would be nice."

"Let me take you into the living room and get you settled into your chair. Then I'll go and put the kettle on."

Cass went into the kitchen and put the kettle on. She filled the sink with hot, soapy water and put the dishes in to soak.

Cassandra went to the blister pack to get the pills Agnes needed to take after dinner. She got a glass of water and took in her pills. "Here are your pills."

"I'll take them later."

"No, you need to take them now."

Agnes looked at Cass and said, "So it's going to be like that is it?"

Cass looked at her, with a big smile on her face. "Yes—yes, it is."

Agnes frowned, "I see you have been talking to my daughter Natalie."

Cass snickered, handed her the pill, and gave her the glass of water. "Make sure you swallow all of them."

Agnes grimaced, "I'm not sure I like you anymore."

Cass smiled. "Would a couple of cookies with your tea help you with that?"

Agnes smiled. "Well, it just might." They both laughed.

It was a great day, Cass thought, while she was finishing up washing the dishes and cleaning up the kitchen. She went back into the living room and curled up on the couch. Coco came and curled up beside her. They chatted and Agnes told her about her stay at the seniors resort. She told her how she had rescued Coco from a puppy mill four years earlier and that it had, thankfully, been closed down. Agnes told her there had been a little over two hundred and twenty-seven dogs saved that day, but unfortunately, some of them had been ill and had to be euthanized. Coco's mom was one of the ones that lost her life due to human greed as Agnes put it. The pictures in the paper were deplorable; no human or animal should ever have had to live under those conditions. It was just terrible.

Coco lay beside Cass, without a care in the world. Cass thought to herself, well Coco's life might have started off rough, but she was doing pretty darn good now.

Cassandra looked at the clock and it was almost midnight. She looked at Agnes. "I don't know about you, but I'm whipped, let's get you up to bed." Cass took Agnes to the bathroom and went downstairs to let Coco out one last time. She got Agnes tucked away, said goodnight, and went down and let Coco in. Coco took off upstairs like a bat out of hell. Man, that dog could move. Cass set the alarm and made sure everything was locked up. When she went into her apartment, she left the door open part way, just in case she needed to get to Agnes quickly.

Cass woke up at seven-thirty and got ready for her day. She went into the main house and upstairs to check on Agnes. Coco lifted her head when she peaked in. Cass whispered, "Come on you, let's get you outside." Agnes stirred.

"What time is it?" she asked.

"Go back to sleep, it's only just past eight."

"No, I'm ready to get up."

"Let me get Coco out and I'll be right back." Cass helped Agnes freshen up and get dressed. Just as Cass was pushing her out of the bedroom, the phone rang. She picked it up and handed it to Agnes.

"Hello, yes we're home. Well, she's outside right now so if you want to come over—say around ten—and get her, that would be great. Okay, Jayne, see you then." She turned to Cass. "That was Jayne, Coco's walker. She's a very nice lady, she's from England, and was married to a guy, but she left him. He was a real douche bag."

"Agnes!"

"What? He was."

"I'm just shocked those words coming out of your mouth."

"Just repeating what I was told," she said, with a smirk on her face.

"What would you like for breakfast?"

"Nothing, right now."

"Well, you need to have something—you have morning medication to take. How about some scrambled or poached eggs on toast?"

"Poached eggs on toast sounds good, but we can skip the pills for now?"

"Well, that is your choice, but if you don't take your morning pills then I guess there will be no banana bread for a snack today."

"So, that's how it's gonna be? You're going to withhold my sweet treats from me? My question for you, Cass: will this be store-bought or are you baking from scratch?"

"Always from scratch."

Cass made breakfast, turned the alarm off, and got the paper for Agnes to read while she was having her breakfast. The doorbell rang and startled them both. Coco ran to the front door barking away, Cassandra went and opened the door.

"Good morning! You must be Jayne, Coco's walker?"

Jayne replied, "It's not just Jayne. I'm Jayne Norton, the sexy dog walker." They both laughed.

"Well, I'm just Cass—come on in. Coco missed you."

"Hi Jayne."

"Hi Agnes, come on in for a minute."

"How are you doing, hun? How was your vacation?"

"I'm good and my vacation was wonderful!"

"I'm glad to hear that."

"So, this is Cass?"

"Ya," Agnes said with a grin.

"What's wrong with Cass?"

"Well, where do I begin? She woke me up at eight this morning, she made me this horrid breakfast, and she is threatening to withhold all baked goods if I don't take my medications. Like, really? I'm seventy-five years old and am being held hostage in my own home."

Jayne laughed. "Really, you like getting up early and I don't see anything left on your plate so it couldn't have been that bad, and if you don't want to take your pills then don't—that just means more treats for me and Coco."

Cassandra laughed. "Oh great, now I have two of you ganging up on me," Agness said with a frown.

The three ladies chatted for a bit, then Jayne got up from the table and told them it was time for her and Coco to leave and do their thing.

"Cass, I think I'm ready to get into my chair in the front room now."

"Okay then, let's get you settled." Cass went upstairs, straightened up Agnes's bedroom and came back down. The banana bread was ready to come out.

She cut one loaf in half so it would cool quicker—that way she could send some home with Jayne when she brought Coco back.

The day went by quickly and before she knew it was time to get Agnes settled in bed for the night. "Can I get you anything, Agnes, before I turn in?"

"No thanks, I'm good."

"You have a great sleep and I'll see you in the morning. I'll let the girl out once more before I lock the house up."

"Sleep well, Cass."

"You too, hun."

"Cass?"

"Yes, Agnes"

"I'm glad you're here."

"Me too. Sweet dreams."

Time went by quickly; with all of Agnes's appointments and their other outings during the week there was never a dull moment and Cass loved every minute of it. She was glad she'd taken the chance and came to Lethbridge. It had been the change she needed in her life.

Natalie came by every few days, just to visit with her mom, as did her brother, John, and sister, Jasmine. They were a nice family. Jasmine was a little flighty, Cass thought, and John a very simple man—what you saw was what you got. Agnes was always trying to set them up. Cass would just smile, shake her head, and say, "Thanks, but no thanks. I'm quite happy with my life just the way it is, for now.

Cass didn't sleep well that night, and when Agnes brought up John again she snapped at her. "Look, if you don't stop trying to set me up with John, I'm going to have to quit. John's a nice man, but he isn't the kind of man I'm looking for, and in all honesty, I'm not interested in dating anyone, so please, Agnes, just stop!" Agnes was shocked at Cassandra's abruptness.

"I'm sorry, Cass, I wasn't trying to offend you, I just think you and John would be a good pair. You would be good for him. I won't bring it up again."

"Agnes, I'm sorry. I didn't sleep well last night and I have a headache that just won't go away."

"Can I do anything?"

"No, but thanks for asking. If you're good, I'm going to lay down for a little bit. Ring me if you need anything."

"Okay, dear, you get some rest."

Cass woke up and looked at the clock. *Shit, it's six o'clock.* Cass had slept the whole day. She got up and went to check on Agnes. "Agnes, I'm so sorry. Why didn't you ring me? You must be dying to go to the bathroom. Here, let's get you into the washroom. I'm so sorry, I can't believe I slept all day."

"Cass, I'm okay. Jayne helped me to the bathroom and got me some lunch. I'm good, how do you feel, dear?"

"I feel much better, I still have a headache, but not as bad."

"Good, I'm glad. You need to rest once and a while—you're always doing something. You need to relax a bit."

"Well, this is my weekend off and I think I'm going to do just that. Now, what would you like for supper?"

"Well, let's have an easy night and just order a pizza in."

"That sounds good to me." They ate their dinner and watched a movie, Cass cleaned up their dishes and put the leftover pizza in the fridge. "Would you like a cup of tea and maybe a slice of banna bread and butter before you go upstairs and call it a night?"

"Yes, that sounds great."

Cass woke up later than usual. She went upstairs, "Good morning. Sorry I'm a little late getting up this morning."

"How are you feeling, dear?"

"I feel much better, my headache is gone. So, what would you like for breakfast this morning?"

"Just some toast today, I think. I'm not really hungry."

"Would you like some peanut butter and honey on it and a nice cup of tea?"

"Sounds perfect." Cass wheeled Agnes to the table and went and turned off the alarm. She picked up the paper for her to read while she ate her breakfast. As usual, the day went by quickly, and before Cass knew it she was getting Agnes settled into bed for the evening. Agnes asked Cass what she was planning on doing on her weekend off, and Cass told her not much. She and Jayne were going to go out Saturday night, so who knew what trouble Jayne would get them into?

Cassandra was lying in bed when her phone rang. "Hello."

"Good morning, Cass. Did I wake you?"

"No, Nat, I was just lying here trying to figure out what I'm going to have for breakfast."

"Well, we have that covered. Why don't you get dressed and come into the kitchen?"

"I'll just have a quick shower and be right in."

Cassandra came into the kitchen and sat down at the table. "This looks good, Nat. Waffles are my favourite."

"That's what Mom said. Cass, I don't know if you've realized this or not, but we're overdue in our contract signing—you've almost been here six months."

"Really? Wow, time has flown by."

"So, my question to you is: will you stay permanently?"

"Well, as much as I have enjoyed my time here, I'm gonna have to say yes to that." Agnes threw her napkin at Cassandra and they all laughed.

"I brought the contract with me; we can deal with that after breakfast."

"Sounds good to me. Now, let's eat those waffles."

When breakfast was finished, they began to talk about the contract. "Cass, I took the initiative and made the contract for two years, if you're okay with that. The contract reads the same as the last one—except we've added a bonus for every year you are here.

"Well, I'll do the two-year contract, but you don't have to do the bonus. I make a good wage here."

"No, we've talked about it and we feel that you deserve it, with all that you do for Mom. You go beyond what is expected of you."

"Well, thank you, that means a lot. Your mom is great to be around and we have fun together. This really isn't work, in my mind."

"Well, thank you. My mom thinks very highly of you."

"Well, the feeling is mutual."

6

......

Cassandra was busy in the kitchen when she looked at the clock and thought she'd better go see if Agnes was ready to get up. She peeked her head inside the door. "Agnes, would you like to get up now?" She went into the room and put her hand onto Agnes's arm. She was so still. Cass felt for a pulse. Her biggest fear had happened—there was none. With tears in her eyes she dialed 911 and hopped on top of Agnes and started CPR.

"911, what's your emergency?"

"I need an ambulance to 1217 Winding Way. Please hurry, my client, Agnes Bailey, has stopped breathing. I've started to perform CPR."

"Please stay on the line. Is the door open, so the attendants can get in?"

"Yes."

"Who am I speaking with?"

"Cassandra. I'm her live-in caregiver."

"Cassandra the EMTs are five minutes out. Are you okay?"

"Yes, please tell them to hurry."

"They're coming as quickly as they can."

Just then Coco jumped onto the bed "Coco get down! JAYNE, get up here now."

"What's going on?"

"It's Agnes. Get Coco out of here please."

"Coco, come on—oh my God, Cass."

"Jayne, look at me! Put Coco outside and get my cell phone—it's on the counter in the kitchen—and bring up the journal that's sitting next to it." It seemed like an eternity when finally Cassandra could hear voices in the hallway downstairs. "We're up here!" Cass yelled.

The EMTs rushed into the room. "Thank God you're here. Her heart stopped."

One of the EMTs took over doing compression's, while the other hooked Agnes up to the defibrillator. "Everyone, stand clear!" The machine zapped Agnes... but nothing. "Raising to two hundred!" The machine zapped her again. "We have a heartbeat, a steady pulse, and sinus rhythm. Let's get her on the stretcher."

"Agnes, I'm here."

"Can you tell us what happened?" Cassandra explained that Agnes hadn't been feeling well and had wanted to stay in bed and get some more sleep.

"I brought her breakfast about nine-thirty. She didn't eat much and when I came back up at ten, she was sleeping peacefully. I take her vitals daily. They are in this journal."

"Keep that, they may ask for it at the hospital. Let's get her out of here."

"Where are you taking her?"

"Chinook Medical Centre."

"I'll follow you. Jayne, please take care of Coco." Jayne looked at Cassandra with fear in her eyes. Cass put her arms around her. "She'll be fine. She is a tough old bird. I'll call you later."

Cassandra followed everyone out of the house, jumped in her car, and headed for the hospital. She called Nat on the way—the phone rang four times before she picked up. "Nat, it's Cassandra."

"Cass, I'm in a staff meeting, I can't talk right now. I'll call you back."

"Nat! You need to listen to me."

"What's wrong?"

"Agnes is on her way to Chinook Medical Centre. Nat, her heart stopped."

"It what?"

"Natalie, just go there I'll explain everything when you get there."

"Where are you?"

"I'm right behind the ambulance."

"I'm on my way."

Cassandra kept a look out for Natalie; she saw her getting off the elevator and waved. Natalie rushed down the hall. "Where's Mom?"

"She's down the hall—the doctor is in with her now. Natalie, she wasn't feeling well this morning. I took her vitals; they were a little high, but no more than any other time when she's had a restless night. I went back up at ten to check on her and she was sleeping peacefully. When I went back up at noon, I found her unresponsive. I checked for a pulse. There wasn't any so I called 911 and started CPR until the EMTs arrived."

"Who is here with Agnes Bailey?"

"We are. How's my mother?"

"Your mother has suffered a heart attack. She's stable at the moment. We're sending her up to ICU—you can see her once we get her settled."

"Nat, you go. I've called John and Jasmine. I'll send them in when they get here."

"Thanks for everything, Cass."

"You're welcome, just go I'll wait here."

Not long after Natalie went in to be with her mother, John and Jasmine rushed in. They rushed right past Cassandra. Jasmine gave her the kind of look that could freeze a person dead in their tracks and entered into the ICU without a word to her.

It seemed like an eternity for Cassandra before Natalie came out and told her that Agnes was doing well.

"Thank God. Can I see her for a minute?"

"Yes, of course you can. My apologies Cassandra, you should have come in with us."

Cassandra put her hand on Natalie's shoulder. "It's okay, Nat."

The two of them walked back into Agnes's room Cassandra went to Agnes's side. She started to caress her arm. "Agnes, it's Cass. I'm here."

Agnes opened her eyes. "You look like shit, Cass."

"Why thank you, that's the nicest thing you've ever said to me." They both laughed a little.

"Coco?"

"She's fine. I'll go home and feed her and get her outside. Then I'll be back up later with some of your personal items."

"Take care of my girl, Cass."

"You know I will—you just concentrate on getting better."

"I will."

Cassandra leaned over and whispered, "I love you, Agnes," and gave her a kiss on the cheek. In a weak voice, Agnes told her that she loved her too.

Agnes had been in the hospital for almost a week when she suffered a massive heart attack. This time she wasn't able to be revived. She passed away with all her family around her and Cassandra at her side. The funeral was held the following week; it was a small service with family and close friends. Agnes had once told Cass that if people didn't want to see her when she was alive, they didn't need to bother when she was dead.

Cassandra sat at the foot of her bed wondering what she was going to do now. The family had told her to take her time in figuring things out, so there was no rush for her to leave.

Jayne took Coco to live with her—the family agreed to pay all her expenses if Jayne would do this for them. Jayne loved Coco and it was what Agnes would have wanted.

The phone rang and brought Cassandra out of her thoughts. "Hello."

"Cassandra Taylor?"

"Yes."

"This is Mr. Wilson, I'm Mrs. Bailey's attorney."

"Yes, how can I help you?"

"We're having the reading of Mrs. Bailey's will tomorrow at ten. It requires your attendance, please."

"Why's that?"

"Agnes added a codicil to her will and you have been named in it."

"Oh, I wasn't aware of this. Natalie didn't mention it."

"I'm not sure if she was aware of this."

"Oh," was all Cassandra could say. She'd never expected this, so she was a little shocked.

"See you at ten Cass?"

"Yes, I'll be there."

"Have a great day." The line went dead.

Cass couldn't sleep; she tossed and turned all night. At six-thirty she'd had enough and got up to have a shower. She'd been doing a lot of thinking and had decided that she was going to stay in Lethbridge. Jayne had offered her a place to stay until she found a job. Cassandra had saved all her money, so she had the time to find the right job. Cass decided that she would take Jayne up on her offer and move in with her at the end of the month. She would tell Natalie when she saw her later that morning.

Cassandra arrived at Mr. Wilson's office at 9:45, went in, and sat down in the waiting room.

"What are you doing here?" Jasmine said abruptly, surprising Cassandra from her thoughts.

"Mr. Wilson called me yesterday and asked me to be here for ten."

Everyone sat there in silence. Cass got up and sat next to Natalie. "I just wanted you to know that I'll be moving out of the apartment by the end of the month."

"Are you sure, there's no rush?"

"I know and I appreciate that, but it's too hard to be there when your Mom's not."

"Where will you go?"

"Jayne said I can move in with her till I find a job and a place of my own."

"I hope you'll stay in touch with me."

"Of course I will, we're family, you have my cell number." Natalie smiled; they'd become close since Cass had moved in with her mother.

"Cass, before I forget, here is your letter of reference."

"Thanks, I was going to ask you about it later. Nat, I have no idea what this is about. According to Mr. Wilson, Agnes saw him when I was away and she was at the lodge."

A tall lady with the reddest hair Cass had ever seen walked into the waiting are "Good morning everyone, can I have everyone follow me into the conference room, please." Everyone took a seat. "Can I get anyone anything?"

Cass looked up. "Could I please have some cold water?" The receptionist left the room and returned a few minutes later with her water.

"Thank you."

"You're very welcome. Mr. Wilson will be in shortly."

Everyone sat there quietly. Cassandra thought she was going to be sick: her stomach was doing somersaults. She had no idea what Agnes had done. Jasmine and John just sat there, glaring at her. Cass looked at Natalie and she gave Cassandra a reassuring smile.

Mr. Wilson entered the room, sat down, and opened the folder in his hands. "Good morning everyone, I would like to thank you all for rearranging your schedule for today. We're here for the reading of the Will of Agnes Bailey. This is her Last Will and Testament." Mr. Wilson went through the will and demands in regard to her estate. Cassandra couldn't believe the grumbling going on from John and Jasmine; she thought Agnes had been very generous with her three children, as the two of them barely came to visit her during Cassandra's employment.

"Before I read the codicil to her Will, this is for Natalie, John and Jasmine: 'If any one of my children makes any kind of attempt to fight my last request you will automatically be disinherited and your share of the estate will go to a charity of Cassandra Taylor's choosing.'"

Both John and Jasmine's mouths dropped open; Natalie sat there smiling, and winked at Cassandra. Cass was stunned and sat there in shock.

Mr. Wilson started. "This is the reading of the codicil to Agnes Bailey's Will. Cassandra, Agnes wrote this letter to you requesting that it be given to you to read at your leisure, along with this envelope which contains the information to a bank account that has already been set up in your name. Agnes had the funds transferred from the estate a few weeks ago, in case anyone decided to go against her will." Mr. Wilson looked at John and Jasmine. "All the information for the account is inside the envelope; we at the firm have a copy, in case any issues arise."

Jasmine blurted out, "Well, how much is in the account?"

Mr. Wilson gave Cassandra a sympathetic look. "It's completely up to you whether you wish to disclose that information."

Cassandra looked at everyone and simply said, "If Agnes had wanted you to know how much she put into this account, she would have told you." She looked over at Natalie and Nat just smiled and nodded her head.

Mr. Wilson spoke up and told them that this concluded the reading of Agnes Bailey's Last Will and Testament.

John stood up and glared at Cass, "You have till the end of the day to be out of OUR house or I'll personally throw you out myself."

"THE HELL YOU WILL!" Natalie stood up and said, with authority, "According to Cassandra's contract—that we all agreed upon and signed, if I might remind you both—she has six months to vacate the premises. If I were the two of you, I'd shut the hell up. The house can't be sold until such time as Cassandra moves out."

Both John and Jasmine stormed out of the office. Cassandra sat there stunned; she couldn't believe what had just happened. Natalie sat down next to Cass. "Are you okay?"

Cassandra looked at Natalie. "I never asked her for anything." Natalie smiled and put her hand onto Cassandra's. "I know. My mom and I talked about all of this and she had me help her write that letter in your hands. Cassandra, you have to know how much you meant to my mom. She wanted to make sure you were taken care of— those two have been spoiled far too long and Mom wanted someone who would do some good with her money to have a portion of her estate. They are financially okay. They're just greedy and want it all—as if they did anything to deserve it. Cass, do me a favour please, when you go back to the house, lock your door to the entrance to the main house and don't go back in there for any reason. Cass, I'm trying to protect you from those two." Cassandra nodded her head. "Cass, you take all the time you need to move—don't you dare rush on their account."

"Natalie, thanks for everything"

"No, Cass, thank you for making the last two years great for my Mom." The two of them hugged and left the office.

Cassandra went back to her apartment and did what Nat had asked of her; she locked the door separating the two dwellings and for the remainder of her time there she never went near that door again.

Cassandra wasn't ready to open the letter from Agnes so she tucked it away where it would be safe until she had the courage to read it. She knew there wasn't anything bad in it, she just wasn't ready to read the last message from her dear friend.

Cassandra finally opened the envelope with all the banking information, and was shocked. She didn't think she was reading it correctly. Had Agnes really left her 1.5 million dollars? She didn't think she was reading it correctly—she had never seen that many zeros in her life.

She went to the bank the next day and they confirmed, yes, that amount was in an account under her name. She sorted out what she wanted to do with her funds: they were to be locked into a high interest savings account for two years so she wouldn't spend it foolishly—not that she would, but just in case. They assigned a password to the account that only Cassandra and the manager knew.

She went back to the apartment, shut the door, and curled up in bed and cried. She cried for the loss and for the generosity of her friend. To know that she had impacted someone's life that much amazed her.

She cried for the loss of the place she had called home. A place where she finally felt that she belonged. Living in Agnes's home was the first time in a very long time she'd felt happy, safe, and at peace with her choices.

7

......

Cassandra woke up and lay there trying to decide what she was going to do. It had been three weeks since Agnes's funeral and Jayne was almost ready for her to move in with her. They were both looking forward to the company—they were good friends and Cassandra was happy with what they had decided to do.

Cassandra's phone rang, "Hello."

"Cass?"

"Hi Mom, how's it going?"

"Cass, you need to come home as soon as you can."

"Mom, what's wrong?"

"It's your father he has been in a car accident. Cass, it's really bad."

"I'm gonna call the airport and see when the next flight out is. I'll call you back as soon as I find out."

Cassandra called and was told the next flight wouldn't be until tomorrow at eleven forty-five. It was going to be a nine-and-a-half-hour flight, with at least an hour at the airport. Then a one-hour drive from the airport to the hospital—that would mean she wouldn't get there until about 3 a.m. Thursday. *That's no good*, Cassandra thought.

She grabbed her GPS and programmed it for the quickest route. It would take her thirty-one and a half hours to get there—that would be six hours quicker than flying.

Cassandra called her mom back.

"Mom, I'm on my way."

"When does your flight land?"

"I'm not flying, I'm driving."

"Cass, you can't—that's too far."

"Mom, I can't get a flight till tomorrow around lunch and it's a ten-hour flight. I can be there way before the plane gets there. I'll call you later."

"Cass, please be careful."

"I will."

"I love you, Cass."

"I love you too, Mom. Tell Pops I'm on my way."

Cassandra hung up the phone, grabbed her suitcases, and started throwing all her belongings inside. She looked around to make sure she had everything and remembered she needed her passport and her personal papers. Among those papers was the letter Agnes had left her.

She grabbed her bags, left her house keys on the counter, and locked the door. She grabbed her two suitcases and threw them in the car, set the GPS, and pulled out of the driveway. As she was driving, she thought, *Damn, I didn't set the alarm*, so she pressed her phone button in the car and told it to call Nat's cell. The phone rang and on the third ring Natalie answered.

"Hi Cass, how are you?"

"Natalie, my father was in an accident so I'm heading to their place right now."

"How are you getting there?"

"I'm driving—I couldn't get a flight till tomorrow—can you please tell Jayne what's going on?"

"I will, Cass, please be careful."

"I will. Look, I left the house keys on the counter. I have all my personal stuff, but there is still food in the fridge, not much, but I don't want you to have a surprise. I also forgot to set the alarm in my rush out the door."

"It's okay, you just get to your parents' place safe. I'll take care of everything."

"Natalie, if you find any personal items please get them to Jayne."

"I will, Cass. Please keep us posted."

"I will. I promise. I'll talk to you soon." She disconnected the call and headed for the interstate.

Cassandra looked at the clock and noticed she had been driving for five hours and figured she had better stop, have a bathroom break, and grab something to eat, then hit the road again. She took the next exit and pulled into a truck stop called Lucky's Diner. Cass filled up the tank and went in to grab a bite to eat.

"Hi there, what can I get you?"

"Can I please just get an order of chicken fingers and fries to go, and can you please put a rush on it?"

"What's the hurry?" Cass heard a voice say as two gentlemen sat down next to her.

"I have a family emergency and I need to get home as soon as possible."

"Where are you going?"

"I'm heading to Williamsport, PA"

"That's quite the drive. Can I ask what route you're taking?"

"I'm not sure, to be honest, I'm going the route the GPS is telling me to go, but I'm not quite sure if it is actually the quickest way."

"Mack, Rick—how are you boys doing?"

"Good, Maggie, and how about yourself?"

"Well ya know, same old same old. Hun, your order will be up in just a minute."

"Thanks so much. I'll pay for that now please."

Mack looked at Cass and knew it must be something really bad that was happening in this girl's life. He walked up to Cassandra and put his hand on her arm. "Is there anything we can do to help?"

"Sure—can you get me to Pennsylvania quicker?"

"Well Cassandra, let's go see what we can do."

"Rick."

"Ya, Mack."

"Go get the map out of the truck. We need to find her a quicker way to Williamsport."

"On it."

"Let's go and see what directions your GPS is telling you to take."

Cassandra looked at the waitress. "You're safe with these two, hun. They'll help you if they can."

"Thank you." And off she went.

Cass got her GPS and Mack took a look and Rick showed up with the map. "Rick, this is the direction it's sending her." Mack read them off as Rick looked on the map. Then they all looked at the map.

"Mack, if she went down here, she would miss the tolls, and then went down this way it would cut at least a half a day off her trip."

"Cass, do you have a pen and paper?"

"Yes." Cass went to get a pad and paper.

"Okay Cass, write this down." Mack told her exactly where she needed to go. They showed her on the map so she could see what they were talking about.

"Thank you both so much, you don't know how much this means to me and my mom."

"Can I ask what's going on?"

"My father was in an accident and is in ICU—other than that I don't know."

"Cass, here's my cell number. If you get into trouble, call me and we'll help you out as best as we can." Cassandra hugged both men and thanked them again.

It was going on eleven. Cass had to pull over and get a few hours' sleep. She saw a sign for a rest stop. She didn't have it in her to drive any further, so she pulled off the highway and backed the car into a spot. She put up the windows, made sure the doors were locked, and closed her eyes. Just as Cassandra started to doze off there was a knock on her window. She looked at the man standing outside her car and thought, *Shit*. She reached for her keys. She was going to turn the car on and gun it, before this creep tried to break in and do Lord knows what. He must have sensed what she was thinking.

"Excuse me, would you be Cassandra?"

She looked at him. "Who wants to know?"

"I'm Big Daddy. Mack and Rick put a message out for us boys to keep an eye out for ya."

"Yes, that's me."

"Good. Look, I want you to pull your car over there, next to that big red rig. Please back it in."

Cass had this feeling, now that she was more alert, that this man meant her no harm. Big Daddy came to her side of the car.

"Look, I'm heading in the direction you're going, let's get a few hours of sleep and we'll get on the road at four. About half an hour up the road there's a twenty-four-hour waffle house. We'll pull in there have some breakfast and get gassed up and back on the road."

"Thank you."

"No problem, dear, get some sleep."

Cass watched Big Daddy climb up into his rig and shut the door. She closed her eyes thinking, *Hold on Pops, I'm coming.* She woke up at three forty-five and had to use the restroom. She looked around and didn't see any movement from the other vehicles that had also parked there for some rest. She quietly opened the door and got out of the car and was just about to shut the door when she heard a deep gruff voice.

"Good morning."

Cass froze dead in her tracks. She turned her head slightly and there was Big Daddy "Shit. You scared the crap out of me."

"Sorry, I thought you saw me."

She gave a nervous chuckle. "No, I didn't, I was just heading to the bathroom."

"Okay—go, and then let's hit the road."

"Sure, I won't be but a minute." Cassandra took off to the bathroom. She knew it was early, but she called Mack.

"Hello."

"Hi, it's Cassandra I hope I didn't wake you?"

"No, we're just getting a coffee. Is everything okay?"

"I have a question."

"Shoot!"

"Do you know a guy named Big Daddy?"

"Ya, he called us last night and said he found you."

"I was just checking," Mack laughed.

"You're safe with him, Cass."

"Good to know. I have to run before he wakes up the whole parking lot—we'll chat soon, and thanks, Mack."

"You're welcome, drive safe."

Cassandra hurried out of the bathroom. Big Daddy yelled out his window, "Get behind me and stay there!" Cass gave him a thumbs up and they were off—and true to his word, about half an hour up the road there was Jake's House of Waffles. They pulled in, gassed up, and went inside.

Cass and Big Daddy walked in and sat down at a booth and started looking at the menu, when a waitress named Ellen came over. "Hi Big Daddy, it's been a while."

"Ya, Pickle, it has—how have you been holding up?"

"Not bad, and yourself?"

"Fair to middlin." Ellen shook her head like she knew exactly what he was talking about. Cass, on the other hand, had no clue.

"And who do we have here? Another lost puppy?"

"Ya, she's a friend of Mack's and Ricks."

Ellen looked at Cass. "Hi, I'm Cassandra. My friends call me Cass."

"Nice to meet you. So what can I get you?"

"Can I please have the chicken and waffles."

Big Daddy ordered his breakfast and asked Ellen if she could rush the order as they needed to get on the road as soon as possible. It wasn't long before Ellen brought them their breakfast. They started to eat and Cass excused herself, went up to the till, and told Ellen that she wanted to pay for both her and Big Daddy's meals.

"Sure." Ellen gave her the bill. Cassandra gave her thirty-five bucks and told her to keep the change.

"Really?" Cassandra nodded her head. "Hey, thanks!"

"No problem," Cass said with a smile. She went to the bathroom and back to their table.

"Can I ask you something?"

"Sure."

"Why do you call her Pickle?"

"Well, when she was having her babies, when ever you looked at her she was eating a pickle—so that's what a few of us started calling her and it kinda stuck."

Ellen came over to see if they wanted anything else. "Just the bill, Pickle."

"It's already taken care of." Ellen nodded towards Cassandra.

"You didn't have to do that."

"I know I didn't, it's done. Let's get going, I have someplace I need to be to in a hurry."

"Yes Mam." With that, Big Daddy stood up. "See you later, Pickle."

"Drive safe, Big Daddy. Cass, I hope everything works out."

"Thanks Ellen."

"Call me Pickle. All my friends do."

Cassandra smiled and nodded. "Thank you, Pickle." With that they were off.

Big Daddy looked at Cass. "When we get on the highway, you stay behind me. When I blow my horn and flash my right signal that means the next exit is where you get off, okay?" Cass nodded her head "Just stay on that road, don't get off, and in about two hours you'll see a sign for Williamsport."

"Big Daddy, thank you so much."

"Give me your phone." Cass did as she was asked. "Here's my cell—call me and let me know how you're doing."

"I will."

They went to their vehicles and hit the road; Cass got behind Big Daddy and kept up with him. They drove for a while, then she heard a horn blow long and loud. She looked at the right signal light and it was blinking, then it stopped. She saw the cut off and started to veer to the right. She honked her horn and waved like a crazy woman. Big Daddy blew his horn and they parted ways.

When Cass finally saw the sign for Williamsport, she pressed her phone on the steering wheel: "Call Mom's cell." Her mother answered. "Hi Mom."

"Cass, where are you?"

"I'm thirty minutes from the hospital."

"Good, we're on the fifth floor ICU."

"Okay, I'll see you shortly."

Cassandra rushed into the hospital, went to the information desk, and asked the receptionist where the ICU fifth-floor elevators were and how did she get to them. The lady behind the desk was on the phone. Cass assumed she was talking to a friend because she could hear the voice on the other end laughing—the girl behind the desk was ignoring her. Cassandra smacked her hands on the counter. She had no time for this shit and in her loudest voice, "EXCUSE ME! How do I get to the elevators to the fifth-floor ICU?"

The lady behind the desk dropped her phone and looked stunned. She pointed and shyly said, "Down the hall, go to the end of the hall, turn left, and the elevators are on the right."

"Thank you!"

When Cassandra got to the fifth floor a nurse was coming out of the ICU. "Excuse me, but I'm looking for my dad—I was told he was in the ICU on this floor."

"What's his name?"

"William Preston"

"Follow me. When you need to enter again, just pick up this phone and the nurse inside will buzz you in."

"Okay, thank you." The nurse let Cass in and took her to her father's room.

"Mom, how is he?"

"Oh, Cass." Her mom rushed over and put her arms around her daughter and cried. They held one another for what seemed like an eternity to Cass.

"Mom, look at me. What's going on?"

"Your father was hit by a poor man that was having a stroke. He was thrown to the pavement and hit his head hard. They've done a CAT scan and there's a pool of blood on the right side of his head, between his brain and his skull. They put him on medication, but the meds aren't working. Your father was supposed to be monitored closely, but something happened. We're not sure, but during the time we went downstairs to grab a coffee and a bite to eat, your father had a heart attack. The nurse came in to check on him and his heart had stopped. They don't know how long your father's heart had stopped before he was revived. They called a code blue and they got his heart going again. On his way up here to ICU he suffered another heart attack. While they were doing CPR, they broke a rib—as you know is common when doing this—but his rib punctured his lung. They felt their only option at this time was to put your father in an induced coma and on life support. They have a cooling blanket on him; they're going to leave it on him for the next twenty-four hours. They're trying to lower his body temperature to between thirty-two and thirty-three degrees Celsius. They're hoping by doing this it will lower the brain swelling by slowing down the blood flow, and are hoping that when they bring him out of this he'll start to breathe on his own. They did another CAT scan a little while ago—we're just waiting for the results. They say we probably won't hear anything until tomorrow morning."

"I thought Aunt Sam and Uncle Joe were here?"

"They were. They went back to the house to get some rest."

Cassandra looked at her mom. "Why don't you go home, have a shower, get a few hours of sleep and something to eat. I'll stay here with Dad."

"Are you sure? You must be exhausted."

"Of course, Mom. I'll call you if there's any change."

Cassandra sat there, just listening to the monitors humming and beeping. When she looked at the clock on the wall, it said eight. She stood up, stretched her legs, when a nurse walked in and looked at Cass.

"Hi, I'm Lisa, William's nurse."

"Hi Lisa, I'm Cassandra—this is my father. How's he doing?"

"There's no change, Cassandra. Can I get you anything?"

"Yes—is there someplace close I can get something to eat and drink?"

"I'm sorry, no. The coffee shop in the hospital is closed now."

"Okay, thanks."

"I can get you a bottle of cold water and a couple of packs of cookies?"

"That would be great."

Cass sat down and the thought of Mack and Rick popped into her mind. She pulled out her phone and the piece of paper she'd written their number on and gave them a call. "Mack, it's Cassandra."

"Hello there, how's your dad?"

"Not good, I'm afraid."

"How is your mom holding up?"

"I just sent her home to get some rest. They have my dad on life support and in an induced coma."

"Cassandra, I'm so sorry."

"I just wanted to call you to let you and Rick know I made it here—and when you talk to Big Daddy, please pass on my thanks and let him know I arrived safely."

"I will, Cassandra. Can I ask you a question?"

"Sure, Mack, what is it."

"When was the last time you ate?"

"What?"

"When did you eat last?"

"Why? What does that have to do with anything?"

"You need to eat. Your parents need you now more than ever. You need to be strong."

"There's nothing open now. My father's nurse, Lisa, brought me in a bottle of cold water and a couple of cookies. I'll be fine."

"What hospital is your father in?"

"Williamsport Medical Centre why?"

"I was just wondering."

"Okay, look Mack I'm going to let you go. I'm sorry, I just don't have it in me to talk right now."

"I understand, Cassandra. Keep us posted."

"I will, and hugs to you and Rick. Mack, thank you for all that you both did to get me here so quickly."

"No thanks necessary. We were in the right place at the right time. Everything in life happens for a reason, please remember that. We may not know now why things happen the way they do, but in the end, the answer becomes clear to us when the time is right."

Cassandra hung up and called her mom. Her Aunt Sam answered.

"Cass, is everything okay?"

"Ya, there's no change. Where's Mom?"

"She's sleeping. Do you want me to get her?"

"No, let her sleep—you guys get some rest too. I'll stay here with Dad."

"Did you want one of us to come up and sit with you?"

"No, that's okay Sam. I'm just going to curl up in a chair and close my eyes."

"Okay kiddo, we'll see you in the morning."

"See you then. I love you."

"We love you too."

Cassandra pulled her chair up to the side of her father's bed and put her hand on his. She thought, *Okay Pops, let's get some rest so tomorrow morning you can wake up and we can get out of here. How does that sound to you?* Cassandra drifted off to sleep, praying that when she woke up this would all have just been a bad dream.

"Excuse me, excuse me!"

"What's wrong?" Cassandra felt someone rubbing her shoulder.

"Sorry to startle you—nothing's wrong, but there's a gentleman outside who says he needs to see you."

"Who?" She looked at the nurse, whose name tag read: Jessie.

"A guy calling himself Big Daddy."

"What?"

"That's what he said his name was."

"A big, scruffy-looking guy? Sort of looks like a scruffy bear?"

"Yeah that's him."

"I don't believe this—thanks, I'll go see him. Pops, I'll be right back."

Cassandra walked to the doors, opened them, and sure enough there was Big Daddy. "What are you doing here?"

"Well I got a call from Mack and Rick and they told me what was going on. They were worried about you so they called me, and we decided: if Mohamed won't come to the mountain to get something to eat, then the mountain will come to Mohamed. I brought you some chicken and biscuits. Hope you like extra crispy?" he said with a big smile.

Cassandra walked towards Big Daddy. He put the food down, opened his arms, and she walked right into them. She put her arms around this bear-like man and hugged him so tight, like her life depended on it, and just cried. With tears rolling down her face, all he could make out was, "thank you so much."

Cassandra stood there sobbing like a baby and Big Daddy just stood there and held on to her. He spoke softly in her ear. "You cry, dear, get it all out—Big Daddy's here and he ain't going anywhere."

Cassandra finally got control of her emotions and wiped her eyes. "Thanks, I so needed that."

Big Daddy just smiled and said, "You okay now?"

"Ya, I'm good. Why are you here? I don't understand. You all have known me for, like, five minutes—why would you all help me out like this?"

"Well, it's like this, we all have kids and we all hope that if one of our kids needed help like you did, there would be people out there that would help them out. It's all about paying it forward, and it just so happened I was in the neighbourhood."

She looked at him with so much love for her newfound friends. "You all don't know how much this means to me." She pulled away and told him she didn't want to leave her dad much longer, and asked if he would like to come into his room with her, to meet him, and have a chat. "I know you guys are busy with your job?"

"Nope, I would like to meet your dad and sit with you for a while. I can't drive anymore till seven tomorrow morning, so me and my rig are parked till then."

"Great, come with me. I'll buzz them to let us in."

"Yes."

"It's Cassandra, my dad is William Preston. The nurse let them in… Hey Pops, I'm back. I want you to meet someone—this is Big Daddy. I told you about him, he brought me some dinner. We're just going to sit by the window and have a visit and a bite to eat."

"What's the prognosis for your dad, Cass?"

"Not good, I'm afraid. He was hit by a guy that was having a stroke and my dad hit his head really hard on the pavement—a pool of blood has formed around the area that hit the pavement, between his skull and brain. The medication isn't working. He had two heart attacks and they punctured his lung while doing CPR during the second heart attack."

"Cassandra, what's that machine at the foot of his bed?"

"They put a cooling blanket on him till tomorrow morning. It's to slow his heart rate down, which will slow the flow of blood to his brain. They're hoping by doing this it will relieve some of the pressure on his brain and he'll be able to breathe on his own when they bring him out of the comma. We won't know anything till tomorrow when the doctor comes in to let us know what the scan says."

They chatted for a bit while Cassandra ate her dinner. Big Daddy told them about his daughter, Becky, and all the crazy stuff she did while growing up. Cassandra looked over at her father "See, Pops, you thought I was a wild child." Cass told Big Daddy about some of the wild things she did in her younger days.

He laughed, "I think you and my Becky are kindred spirits."

Nurse Lisa came in; she had a worried look on her face.

"Is everything okay?" Cass asked.

She looked at Cass with a weak smile, "Everything's fine."

Cassandra knew at once that something was wrong. She got up and put her hand on Lisa's arm and asked her, "What's going on?"

Lisa looked at her, "I'm just tired."

Cassandra knew she wasn't being honest but decided to let it go—she would find out soon enough, though she knew deep down in her heart she wasn't going to like what they were going to tell them.

Big Daddy left shortly after one in the morning. He gave Cass a big hug and said, "Keep smiling and keep thinking good thoughts and please keep us posted."

"I will. Thank you so much for dinner. Let me give you some money."

"Don't be silly—you just take care of yourself. Your family is going to need you now more than ever, so stay strong girl, and know that you have three truckers that have your back if you need us."

"Thank you so much. I'll keep you all posted. Please stay safe Big Daddy."

As he was getting onto the elevator, he asked her, "If you're in trouble, who you gonna call?"

She looked at him with tears in her eyes, "Big Daddy."

He put his finger in the air. "You got it, girl," and the doors closed. Cassandra stood there staring at the door and thought how lucky she was to have met these amazing men.

8

......

Cassandra was in a deep sleep, but in the distance she could hear voices. She wasn't sure what they were saying. They were whispering gradually she started to wake up and realized it was her mom and Aunt Sam talking. Cass sat up, stretched, and asked what time it was. "Sorry, kiddo, we didn't mean to wake you."

She told them it was okay and stood up and stretched her legs. "I'll be back. I need to use the bathroom anyway."

"Oh, what, no hug?"

"Aunt Sam it's either a hug or pee on the floor—your choice," she smiled.

"I can wait."

"Good choice," Cassandra said with a weak smile. She returned from the bathroom and walked over to Sam. "Hi there, I've missed you." They both hugged one another and all Cass could think of was, *Sam, please don't let me go.* Sam knew exactly what her niece was thinking. They were very close; some would say they were like mother and daughter. She held onto Cass until Joe came into the room.

"Hey, where's my hug?" Cass looked up and walked over to her uncle as he put the drinks down. He opened his arms and Cass walked into them, and with tears in her eyes, cried, "I have missed you both so much."

"We've missed you too, Cassie girl."

They all sat down and started catching up on everything. Cassandra told them about Agnes's passing and about the will—she didn't tell them how much she was left, no one needed to know that information.

Nurse Lisa came back into the room one last time to check on William. She said that she was going home and that the doctor would be in around eight-thirty. He would take a look at the scan and come in to talk to them. Cassandra followed Lisa out of the room. "Excuse me, Lisa." Lisa turned around and Cass again put her hand on her arm. "You have seen the scans, haven't you?" Lisa shook her head, and the look in your eyes told Cass everything she needed to know.

"I'm not a doctor. I can't tell you what the scans are showing—you'll have to wait until he comes in to speak with all of you."

Cass put her arms around Lisa and whispered into her ear, "Thank you all for what you've done for my family. You are an amazing group of people. Just know that, whatever the outcome is for my family today and for all the other patients in ICU, whether it be good or bad news, please know you all have made a difference in their lives and in ours. Thank you all, from the bottom of my heart."

Cassandra let Lisa go. She turned around and returned back to her father's room to sit next to he dad. She waited with the rest of the family for the doctor to arrive with the news she knew they didn't want to hear.

It was eight forty-five when the doctor came in and introduced himself to Cassandra. "Hello I'm Dr. Madison."

"Hello I'm Cassandra. I'm William's daughter."

"I've taken a look at the scans that were taken yesterday. Let's all have a seat so we can discuss them, then you can decide how you would like to proceed from here. I'm afraid the news isn't good. The human brain has many cracks and crevices and unfortunately when looking at the CAT-scan this morning we are unable to see any of them. In the past twelve hours William's skull has filled with more fluids, and unfortunately, there is no longer any brain function."

Cassandra looked at the doctor. "Why couldn't you have drilled a hole in my father's skull to drain the pressure from his brain?"

"Unfortunately, that wouldn't have been an option for your father, with his heart attack and a punctured lung. He wouldn't have been able to withstand the surgery, since we don't know for sure how long his brain was without oxygen. We just can't be sure about the amount of damage that was done."

"What happened there? I was told he was supposed to be monitored at all times, so why wasn't he?"

"I'm not sure, but I assure you that we are looking into it."

"I'm sure you are. So then, what you're telling us is that there is no hope for my father and you want us to pull the plug?"

"Cass!"

"What, Mom?! That's what he's saying, isn't it?"

"I'm sorry, but yes, unfortunately, that's what I'm saying. We can leave him on life support, if that is what you want, but what will happen is the pressure from the blood surrounding your fathers brain will eventually squish his brain down into his spine, and he will eventually die. There is really nothing more that can be done."

Cassandra glared at the Doctor. "I think you all have done quite enough."

"I'm truly sorry. I'll leave you so that you can discuss where you want to go from here."

Cassandra watched Dr. Madison leave the room. She wanted to go after him and tell him that it was all his fault that this was happening—he and his staff didn't do their job and that they damn well better fix their screw up and bring her father back to them—but she knew, deep down, there was no coming back from this. Someone screwed up and they were going to have to live with that mistake, but she also knew that the death of their patient was just as hard on them, as the families who lost their loved ones.

Everyone sat in silence, Cassandra couldn't believe this was happening. She had just spoken to her father a little over a week ago and now he was all but gone. With one flip of a switch, her father wouldn't be there anymore; how was this even possible?

Cassandra was lost in her own thoughts, when she felt a hand on her shoulder—she looked up and saw her mother staring down at her. "Cass I think we both know what we have to do."

"I know. I'll go and get the nurse in a few minutes." Cassandra sat there thinking of all the things they did together, as a family and just her and her dad. She thought about all the trouble she had put her parents through and how their love for her had never wavered. They both knew she was just trying to find her place in this world.

She got up, walked out of the room, and went to the nurse's station, with tears rolling down her face. "Hi, I'm William's daughter, Cassandra. Can you please let Dr. Madison know we would like to speak with him."

"Of course, I'll page him right now."

"Thank you." Cassandra went back into the room and leaned close to her father's ear. "I love you, Dad, always and forever," as she kissed his cheek for the last time. Cass went over to her mother and put her arms around her. "I'm so sorry, Mom."

"Me too, Cass, me too."

Dr. Madison came into the room. Cassandra looked at her mother and said, "We're ready to let my father go." He looked at Cass and she could see the sadness in his eyes.

"If anyone wants to step out while we unhook everything… it can be a little much for some people to see."

Cass looked at the doctor. "I'm not going anywhere." She sat down beside her father and took his hand in hers and held onto it for what would be the last time.

Cassandra was watching the nurse disconnect all the bags, full of different kinds of medication, and unplugging all the machinery.

"Excuse me, would you like us to turn the volume off on the monitors?"

"Yes, please. How long will this take once everything is disconnected?" Cassandra asked.

"It varies with every person; it could take a few minutes to a few hours. I'm going to give William a shot of morphine to make sure he has no pain during his final moments."

The room was quiet while everyone stood around the bed. Cass stayed seated next to her father and watched his chest go up and down. It was getting slower and slower with every breath he took.

"Cass, is he gone?"

"No, not yet Mom."

Williams breathing was becoming slower with each breath that he took. They sat there, Cassandra with her Dad's hand in hers. She felt a hand on her shoulder. She turned and gave her uncle a weak smile. "It's really slow now, Uncle Joe. I don't think it'll be much longer now."

At 12:45 pm, William Preston passed away peacefully with his family at his side. Cassandra stood up and walked over to her mother and embraced her and whispered, "He's at peace now." They held onto each other and cried. "Mom, let's get you home. We don't need to stay here any longer."

Cassandra walked into the house with her suitcase, went up to her room, and shut the door. She sat on the window seat and stared at the floor, not sure as to what she should be doing now.

Nobody said much for the rest of the day. Thankfully, no one had found out that her father had passed away—or if they did, they wanted to give them some time to process and deal with everything that had just happened.

Cassandra went and had a hot shower, then went down to see her mom. She walked up behind her and put her arms around her and just held her until she stopped crying. Cass ordered them pizza for dinner and they made small talk, but no one was really into talking—or eating, for that matter. Cass cleaned up the kitchen, then excused herself, saying goodnight to everyone with a hug and a kiss. She went to her room and crawled into bed and drifted off into a restless sleep.

All that kept running around in her head was that her father was supposed to have been watched closely. She felt someone hadn't done what they were supposed to do—and her father had died because of it.

Cassandra woke up the next morning and headed downstairs. She could hear someone moving about. "Mom, how did you sleep?"

"I got a little, you?"

"Not much. What do you need me to do today?"

"Nothing really—the funeral arrangements have already been made. Your father just wanted to be cremated and have a celebration of life."

"When will that be? Everybody will wanna be here."

"Well, I spoke with our minister and he's available next Saturday, which is the seventeenth."

"I'll call everyone and let them know. If there isn't anything I can do, I'm going to go sit outside for a bit, to make some calls. Where are Sam and Uncle Joe?"

"They went out to pick some groceries up. I think they just wanted to get some air."

"Call me if you need me." She hugged her Mom and headed outside.

Cassandra went and sat on the bench her father had built for her when she was a child, under the oak tree. She thought, *Dad, I'm not sure how we're going to do this—so please help me, help Mom.* She was deep in thought when her phone rang.

"Cass, it's Big Daddy. How are you?"

"Not good, Big Daddy—my dad passed away yesterday afternoon."

"Cassandra, I'm so sorry to hear that. What can I do to help?"

"Bring my father back," she said with a little laugh. "Nothing, Big Daddy, but thanks for the thought. Could you please do me a favour?"

"Anything."

"Can you please let the boys know what happened."

"I'll call them as soon as we hang up."

"Thank you, I appreciate that."

"Will there be a funeral?"

"No, we're gonna have a celebration of life on the seventeenth. I'm not sure where it'll be yet."

"Cassandra, can you please let me know. I may be in the area and if I am, I'd like to come and pay my respects."

"Thank you, but you don't have to do that."

"I know I don't have to, but if I can, I want to."

"Okay, Big Daddy, I'll let you know. I have to go. Okay, I'll talk to you soon."

"Okay, Cass. Take care of yourself."

"Please don't forget to call the boys."

"I won't."

"You stay safe, Big Daddy."

"You stay strong, Cassandra."

"I'll try. Bye for now."

Cassandra called everyone and told them the news about her father's passing. She told them that as soon as she found out where the celebration of life would be held, she would let them know.

"Cass, your mom wants you."

"Okay, I'm coming Uncle Joe."

"You needed me, Mom?"

"I'd like you to pick a passage that you would like the minister to read at the celebration of life."

"You pick what you want, Mom—that's not my thing."

"PLEASE! Cassandra, I'd like your help with this."

"Sorry. Give me dads Bible and I'll look for one."

"Cass, I was thinking of having your dad's celebration in the backyard."

"That would be nice, but what if it rains?"

"Then we can have it in the house, it's big enough."

"Okay—what do you want to do about the food?"

"The minister talked to the women's auxiliary; they agreed to put something together. The gathering will be from one to four next Saturday."

"Okay, what can I do to help with the arrangements?"

"Nothing, Cass—just please find the passage."

"Yes, ma'am. Mom, do you need some money to help with all of this? I can help you."

"No, hun, your dad and I had already taken care of this."

Cass took her father's Bible outside and sat under the oak tree. She thought to herself that this was her favourite place to sit with her father. "I'm truly going to miss our chats under this tree Pops." Cassandra opened up the Bible and started skimming through it when her phone rang.

"Cassandra, it's Mack."

"Hi Mack."

"Cass, Big Daddy called and told us about your father. How are you holding up?"

"Doing the best I can. My mom wants me to pick a passage out of the Bible for the minister to read and I have no clue what to look for—this has never been my thing."

"I've always liked Isaiah forty versus twenty to thirty-one: 'Do you know? Have you heard? The Lord is the Everlasting God, the creator of the ends of the Earth, he will not grow tired or weary, and his understanding no one can fathom. He gives strength to the weary and increases the power of the weak. Even youths grow tired and weary, and young men stumble and fall, but those who hope in the Lord will renew their strength.

They will soar on wings like eagles; they will run and not grow weary; they will walk and not be faint.'"

"That's beautiful, thank you. I think my father would really like this."

"Big Daddy said your family is having a celebration of life for your father."

"Yes. It's next Saturday the seventeenth, between one-thirty and four-thirty."

"What's your parents' address? We would like to send your family some flowers… and before you say anything, we know we don't have to, we want to."

Cassandra gave him the address and they said their good-byes. She went back into the house and told her mom she had found a passage to read, with the help from a friend. When she showed her mom, her mom responded with, "Your father would love this."

The days went by quickly and before Cassandra knew it, it was Saturday.

She got up, had a quick shower, and got dressed. Everyone was busy getting ready for the celebration. She walked over to her mother and put her arms around her. "How are you holding up?"

"I'm doing okay. I'm so glad you're here."

"Where else would I be?" Cassandra's mother patted her hand. "Mom can we go outside to talk for a minute?"

"Sure."

They went outside and sat under the old oak tree. "I was wondering what you're planning to do with Dad's ashes?"

"I'm not sure—that was the one aspect of all this your dad and I couldn't make up our minds about. Do you have any ideas?"

"Well, I was thinking as I was sitting here under the tree. This would be a great spot to put some since it was our favourite place to spend time together, when I would come home for a visit."

"I think that's a great idea."

"What about the rest?"

"Set them free. Let the breeze take Dad where it may. You know how he liked to travel."

"I like that idea too."

"Cass, when are you heading back?"

"In a few weeks, I'm in no rush."

Her mom held her hand. "Good, I'm glad to hear that."

Cassandra looked at her watch. "We should go get ready; it's noon and people will be showing up soon."

At twelve-thirty, the cars started pulling in and by one-thirty the backyard was full of people. Cassandra was talking to some of her dad's friends from church when she felt a hand rub her back. She turned around and there were Natalie and Jayne. "Oh my God, when did you guys get here?"

"We flew in last night."

"Why didn't you call me? I could have picked you up from the airport."

"No, we didn't get in until late."

Cassandra gave both ladies a hug and then introduced them to her father's friends. "Please excuse us. Ladies, come with me, please." She hooked her arms into theirs and went to find her mom. "Excuse me, Mom, I'd like to introduce you to two special ladies—this is Natalie and Jayne." Everyone embraced. "Excuse me for a minute, guys. Liliana and Grant have just arrived."

Cassandra walked over to her dearest friends and gave them both a huge hug. "I'm so glad you could make it."

"We wouldn't have missed this. How are you holding up?"

"I'm okay. I've missed you guys so much."

"We've missed you too."

"How long can you stay?"

"We're here till Monday,"

"Good. Come with me, let me introduce you to friends of mine. Natalie, Jayne—this is my friend, Liliana, and her husband, Grant."

"We've heard a lot about you both from Cassandra."

"Cass has told Grant and myself all about you two as well."

While everyone was chatting Cassandra pulled Jayne aside. "How's Coco?"

"She's fine. She misses her mom, but she's doing well. I try to keep her busy. We're going on a lot of walks and she's having a ball playing with other dogs at the dog park."

"Cass, when do you think you'll be coming home? Or *are* you coming home?"

Cassandra put her arm around her friend. "I'll be home in a few weeks."

"Good, I'm glad. We miss you."

"I miss you guys too."

Everyone seemed to be having a nice time visiting and talking about all the good times they'd had with her father. Cassandra heard stories about her father she had never heard before. Things were winding down. Cass looked at her watch and it was three-fifteen and people were starting to leave. She headed over and sat back under the oak tree. She was in deep thought, thinking about her future, when she felt a hand on her shoulder. She looked up, and there were three very familiar faces. She got up immediately and hugged Rick, Mack, and Big Daddy. "I had a feeling you were all going to show up."

"We hope that's okay."

"Of course it is, you're welcome here anytime."

"How long can you stay?"

"Just for this evening—we have a couple of rooms in town."

"Let me introduce you to my family." They all walked over to where everyone was standing. Cassandra's mom turned around and she saw the three men standing next to her daughter. "I know who you are," Faye said with a smile on her face.

"Mom, this is Mack, Rick, and—"

"Big Daddy," her mom finished. They all laughed.

"It's so nice to meet you all. I just have one question for you, Big Daddy."

"Yes ma'am."

"What is your name?"

"It's Marvin, ma'am."

"Well, it's nice to meet you guys. I'm Faye. Why don't we go inside and get you boys something to eat and we can introduce you to the rest of the family."

Cassandra led the boys into the house "Excuse me, everyone, I'd like to introduce you to three of my friends, this is Mack, Rick, and Marvin."

Cassandra's Aunt Sam turned around and noticed the three gentlemen standing with Cass, she walked over to where they were standing.

"It's nice to meet you's. Now we've heard about Mack and Rick, but Marvin we haven't heard about you."

"Aunt Sam, this is Big Daddy."

"It's nice to meet you all. Thank you for helping our Cass; it means a lot to us that you all helped our girl out."

"There's no thanks necessary—like we told Cassandra, it's all about paying it forward."

"You're so right, Marvin."

"You boys are staying for supper?" asked Faye.

"No, we don't want to impose."

"You're not imposing. You're staying for supper and I don't want to hear another word about it."

"I'm Cassandra's Uncle Joe, and I can tell you, from years of experience, you won't win with Faye, so you might as well pull up a chair and relax."

They had a very nice evening eating, chatting, and getting to know each other. Faye stood there looking at the wonderful blessings that had come into their lives in the form of new friends. She put her arms around her daughter. "We are truly blessed here today." Cassandra looked at her mother and then at everyone seated around the table. *Yes, we are*, she thought and hugged her mother back.

9

......

It had been three and a half weeks since her father's celebration of life. Everyone had returned home and life had moved on, but not for Cassandra—she felt lost and knew it would never be the same again. There was an ache in her heart she believed would never be filled.

Cassandra promised Jayne and Natalie she would be returning back home to Lethbridge soon. She just wanted to make sure her mom was going to be fine there by herself.

Cassandra came downstairs and there was a note on the table. "Gone into town, have some legal matters to take care of. I'll be back soon."

Marvin called to see how were doing and he asked that you give him a call, when you have a minute. Cassandra stood there in the quiet, listening for any sign of life, other than her own. This was the first time she had been alone since she had arrived, three and a half weeks ago. She decided that now was as good a time to read the letter Agnes had left her.

Cassandra went upstairs and retrieved the letter from its hiding place in her suitcase. She sat on the bench under the oak tree. She carefully opened it, she didn't want to damage any part of this special gift that had been left for her.

My dearest Cassandra,

You have been a shining star in my life and have brought me more joy than I could ever have imagined possible. The first day I met you, I knew you and I would become great friends and we did (the cookies and banana bread might have had something to do with it but I think they were just an added bonus)." Cassandra smiled. "Please don't cry for me, my friend—I have lived a long and joyful life. I was fortunate to have the life I had and was blessed with a wonderful husband. The man of my dreams, who knew how to make money and take care of his family and our three great kids (well, one and two are a work in progress). With that being said, as you now know, I have included you in my will. I have done this for two reasons: the first reason is you deserve to have someone help you, to make your life a little easier and I pray I have done this for you. Cass, please do something that truly makes you happy with the money. Enjoy your life, my dear. Find happiness, and most of all find love—not all men are like Tom. He was a douche bag; see, even in death I can shock you and make you smile at the same time." Cassandra laughed. "Cass, there is someone out there for you, someone that is going to brighten your day whenever they walk into a room. Someone who will make you smile whenever you think about them or hear their voice. Someone that will hold you in their arms every night and make you feel loved and safe. Please keep your eyes and your heart open. I promise you, this will happen, or I will raise proper hell here in Heaven. This isn't goodbye, my dear— this is until we meet again. Live, Laugh, and most of all Love, my dearest Cassandra.

With all my love, Agnes. Xoxoxo

PS, The second reason I left you this money was that I knew it would piss off John and Jasmine. They are my kids and I love them dearly, but I did not do them any favours helping them out as much as I did. Maybe in some way I'm hoping that they will see the light and realize money is a great thing to have, but it feels so much better to have when you work for it and earn it yourself.

Cassandra folded up the letter and put it back into the envelope. She looked up into the sky above, thinking, *Agnes, I hope you know how much you mean to me and how much happiness you brought into my life. Until we meet again my friend, I love you too, always and forever.*

Cassandra took her letter and put it safely back in the pocket of her suitcase. She wanted to keep it safe. She would cherish this last gift from someone who meant the world to her for the rest of her life. She wished she had had a relationship with her own grandmothers like the one she had with Agnes.

Cass got her phone and thought she better call Big Daddy before her mom got home. It was time for a conversation about her getting back to her own life, even though she felt guilty for just thinking about it. Big Daddy picked up the phone. "Hello."

"Hey Big Daddy, how are you?"

"I'm good Cass, how are you doing?"

"I'm good."

"You don't sound to good."

"I was just thinking I'm gonna have to sit down with mom today and talk about me heading back home in a few days, and I'm not sure how she will take it."

"Faye is a strong woman—she will be fine. I think she's a little worried about you."

"Me? Why?"

"I think she's worried that you won't leave and get on with your life."

"Big Daddy, I miss my Dad so much. I'm worried that if I go, my mom will be so lonely."

"She has friends there Cass. Look at all the people that came to pay their respects. She will be fine. Cass, you have to remember it's not your job to take care of your mom now that your dad is gone. It's your job to live your life to the fullest and enjoy each day the best you can—that's what they want for you."

"I know you're right." Cassandra changed the subject, "So everything is good with you? How are Rick and Mack?"

"They're both good."

"I texted them last week but didn't get an answer, so they must be busy."

Big Daddy laughed. "Ya, they're busy, but Mack forgot his phone was in his pocket and it ended up in the washer and dryer—dumb ass." They both laughed. "Do you have a pen handy?"

"Yep, I do."

"Here is his new number—for some reason his sim card stopped working. I wonder why?"

Cassandra wrote down the number and chatted for a few more minutes. She heard a car door shut, so she said her good-byes, and promised she would keep in touch.

"Good afternoon, sleepy head."

"Hi, Mom."

"Did you see my note?"

"Yeah. I just got off the phone with Big Daddy."

"Everything okay?"

"Ya, he just wanted to check in to see how we were doing."

"Those three men are the best thing to come out of this tragedy"

"They sure are, Mom… Mom, can we talk?"

"Sure we can, what's on your mind?"

"I was thinking it's time for me to head home so I can find a job and get settled in with Jayne."

"I was wondering when you were gonna go."

"I can stay longer if you want."

"No!" Cass was a little shocked when her mom said it with such conviction. Faye smiled at her daughter, "I think it's time we both get on with our lives."

"I feel guilty for even thinking about that."

"Why? Do you think your father expects us to sit and mope and waste what time we have left on this earth? Your father is in an amazing place; he is happy and all he would want is for us to be happy as well."

"I'm gonna miss being here. I'm going to miss chatting with Dad under that oak tree."

"Cassandra, I have something for you." Faye went and opened the cupboard door and pulled out a small package. Faye handed it to Cass.

"What is it?"

"Open it up and find out." She did as she was told and inside this tiny box was a little urn. "It's some of your father's ashes—I thought you could take a little bit of him with you so he would be close to you."

With tears in her eyes and a lump in her throat, Cassandra whispered, "Thanks, Mom."

Cassandra woke up at seven-thirty, had a shower, and got dressed. She had packed her suitcases the night before, so it was just last-minute things to pack up. She took her bags downstairs.

"Do you have everything?"

"Yes, I was just checking around to see if I left anything."

"I packed a little something for you to nibble on while you're driving."

"You made your homemade trail mix—thanks. I spoke with Big Daddy and we're going to meet tonight at Jake's House of Waffles for supper. Mack and Rick are going to try and meet us there too."

"Well, that will be nice. Make sure you give them my best and remind them if they're in the neighbourhood I expect a visit."

"I will, I promise."

"Do you want some breakfast before you go?"

"No thanks, I just want to get on the road. Mom, are you sure you're going to be okay?"

"I will be fine—you just make sure you're careful driving home."

"I will, I promise." Cassandra gave her mom a big hug and a kiss. "I love you."

"Back at ya, kiddo."

With that, she got into the car, looked at her mom, blew her a kiss, and headed down the driveway. She drove to the top of the hill, turned right, and could see her mom waving goodbye. Cass honked her horn twice, cranked the music, and drove, singing, "Life is a Highway," thinking to herself, *No truer words were ever written.*

Her heart was still aching, but she felt better about everything since her talk with Big Daddy. She knew, deep down, her mom would be alright and she would too. It was just going to take some time. Big Daddy was right: her mom was one of the strongest women she knew.

Cassandra made it to Jake's House of Waffles in good time—she actually beat all the guys, so she gassed up and went in to see Ellen/Pickle. She got a booth in Pickle's section. A few minutes had past when she came over. "What can I get you?"

"Hi, Pickle." Pickle looked up from her order pad and just stared at Cassandra. She had that look where she sort of knew the face, but was thinking, *Give me a minute.* Cassandra looked at her friend and knew she needed a little help—after all, she had only met her once.

"Big Daddy," Pickle's eyes widened.

"Cass, right?"

Cassandra smiled. "Yes, it's me."

"Oh my God, girl! How are you?"

"Can you sit for a minute?" Pickle sat down and looked at Cass.

"Daddy was in a week ago. I'm sorry for your loss Cassandra."

"Thanks—it's been hard, but I'm doing okay."

"I'm glad to hear that. And your mom?"

"I think she's glad I'm going home."

Pickle smiled and shook her head. "Well, what can I get you?"

"Just water with some ice, please. I'm waiting for the boys. They're supposed to meet me here."

"All of them?"

"That's what they said yesterday when I talked to them. I'm early."

"Well, let me get you that water."

Cassandra sent Jayne and Natalie a message letting them know all was going well and that she was stopping to have some dinner with the boys, then she was going to find a room for the night.

Cass and the guys had a great visit. She gave them her mom's message and they all promised that if they were in the area they would stop in and check on her. Mack and Rick were the first to leave. She hugged them and wished them safe travels. They all promised to keep in touch. Then it was just her and Big Daddy. Pickle had cashed out and had gone home for the evening. Cassandra and Big Daddy chatted for a bit longer. Then Big Daddy said, "I hate leaving, but I need to get back on the road."

Cassandra stood up and gave Big Daddy a big hug and whispered into his ear, "You three guys are the best thing to happen to me in all this. You are truly my guardian angels. Thank you."

He hugged her and told her it was their pleasure. "You stay safe, Cassie girl, and keep in touch."

"I will."

They said their goodbyes. As Big Daddy was walking to his truck he turned and yelled, "Cassandra!" She turned around. "When you're in trouble, who ya gonna call?"

She yelled back with a lump in her throat, "Big Daddy." He turned around, gave her a thumbs up and got into his rig and pulled away. He blew his horn and Cassandra waved goodbye like a crazy lady, laughing until he was out of sight. She didn't care what anybody thought of her, she knew her dad would be looking down on her and saying, *That's my girl.*

Cass got into her car and decided she would drive a little longer. She had gotten her second wind and knew she wouldn't be able to sleep. She had been driving for almost two hours when she came upon a detour sign. She couldn't turn around and go back so she had no choice but to follow it. She drove for about another hour when she came upon a sign that said there was a hotel about ten kilometres up the road. Cass thought to herself that would be a great place to stop and get some sleep. She was about half way there when her car started to sputter. She pulled over to the side of the road and it died. "Shit." She tried to start the car, but to no avail. She got her phone—no bars. *Darn,* she thought to herself, *what the hell am I going to do now?*

She could walk the rest of the way but decided that probably wasn't the brightest thing to do, with bears and such, she decided to stay put until morning. It was the safest thing to do under the circumstances.

Cass started to doze off when a car came up behind her and started flashing its lights. Cassandra looked up and thought to herself, *Thank you, the cavalry has arrived.* There was a knock on the window. She lowered her window just enough to speak through it. "Are you okay, ma'am?" The man lowered his flashlight so she could see. She looked at the man and saw a police badge and a name tag that said Officer Pope. "I'm fine. My car, on the other hand, is another story."

"Well let's get you and your stuff into my car. I'll take you into town and have someone come and get your car."

"That's okay I can wait for the tow truck, if you can call them and let them know where we are."

"Unfortunately there's no reception out here for both cell phones and my car radio." Cassandra didn't think anything of it. She didn't know the area and since there was no cell reception, it was possible that his radio wouldn't work either. She hadn't heard anything from his radio that was on his hip.

"Ma'am, it isn't safe for me to leave you here." She wasn't getting any bad vibes from the officer, so she rolled up her window and got out of the car.

"Thanks so much for helping me."

"No problem, ma'am, it's what I'm here for." Cassandra followed Officer Pope to the back of his car. He opened his trunk to put her suitcase's inside, and that was the last thing that she remembered.

10

....

Cassandra started to come to. Her head was killing her. What the hell happened? The last thing she remembered was Officer Pope helping her put her suitcase's in the trunk of his police car. Cassandra froze. *Oh my God, what did she do?* She started screaming for help. The first holler for help gave her an electric shock. Every time she screamed there was a shock, and every time it was worse than the one before. She started to panic. There was something around her neck. She grabbed at her neck, trying to get the collar off. She dug her fingers around the collar and started tugging and pulling at her neck until she could feel blood running down her throat. It wouldn't budge. It was fastened on with some kind of lock.

Oh my God, who would do this to her? Why would anyone do this to another human being? She was in complete darkness. She tried feeling her way around. Suddenly there was a heavy scraping noise on the floor. Cass froze. She moved her right leg. It felt so heavy, and when she moved it she heard the scraping noise. She bent over and found she had a chain wrapped around her ankle. "Oh my God, oh my God," is all she kept repeating to herself. "What the hell is going on?" she screamed. She tried with everything she had in her to get that chain off, but it was no use. Whoever put it on didn't want her to be able to get it off. Who would do this to her? It couldn't be Pope, he was a cop. He was there to serve and protect. Her head was pounding and the side of her face was killing her. She couldn't think straight. She grabbed the chain and followed it; she found it attached to what she thought was a bed. Cassandra lay on the bed and curled herself up into a ball and repeated, "This is just a dream this isn't real," until she dozed off, totally exhausted from the ordeal she now found herself in.

Cassandra woke up not knowing what time it was—or what day it was, for that matter. She heard footsteps coming towards the door so she curled up as tight as she could on the bed and lay there as still as she could. She thought to herself, if she didn't make a sound or move, then whoever it was would leave her alone.

The door opened and a figure walked into the room. She heard another door open and a light switch being turned on. There wasn't much light, but it was enough for her to see, and she could sense that whoever it was, was still in the room, but she still didn't budge.

"I know you're awake!"

"Why are you doing this to me?" she whispered. There was no answer.

"If you want to stay alive, you will follow these simple rules. DON'T scream. I think you have found out what will happen if you do. DO what I tell you when I tell you, and don't try to get away. The only one that will be hurt will be you. Follow my rules and you will be fine. There is a bathroom here—use it. Keep yourself clean. I don't want you smelling up this room.

And if you think this is a way for you to get out of here, you're sadly mistaken. It will only cause you more pain. Do you understand?" Cassandra didn't say a word. He raised his voice, "I ASKED YOU A QUESTION: DO YOU UNDERSTAND ME!"

"Yes, I understand," she whispered.

"Good. Go clean yourself up. I'll be back shortly with some water and something for you to eat."

"Can you please take this chain off? It's hurting my leg." The door shut and she heard whomever it was walking away.

She lay there, not knowing what to do. She whispered, "Big Daddy, I need your help," and started to cry.

She wasn't sure how long she'd been lying there, when suddenly the door opened. She didn't hear the footsteps this time coming down the hall. "I told you to get cleaned up—you obviously don't know how to follow rules, but you will."

Cass closed her eyes really tight, then she felt him literally pick her up and throw her to the floor. "Get yourself into that room and get cleaned up and don't have me tell you again!" he hollered.

Cassandra started to get up and felt a blow to her midsection. "Stupid bitch," he growled. She went down again. The voice told her, "Next time you will listen to me when I tell you to do something."

Cassandra crawled to the bathroom. "Take those clothes off, you won't be needing them."

"Please don't do this. Let me go. I don't know who you are, I won't go to the police." He laughed. It was such an evil laugh, it made her cringe.

"It wouldn't matter if you did sweetheart—I run the police." Cassandra's heart sank.

"I can't take my pants off with this chain on my leg." There was no response. With one tug she was on her back, and she heard the jingling of keys. The chain dropped onto the floor. She felt her pants being pulled off and a voice came to her, "Cass—kick. Kick as hard as you can." She did just that and her kidnapper went down, moaning, on the floor. She heard that voice again, "Cass, RUN, RUN!" She scrambled to her feet, pulling her pants up as she ran. She saw a door and frantically she tried to open it. When the door started to opened, her head hit it with such force that all she felt was excruciating pain, then darkness, then nothing.

"Stupid, stupid girl. I warned you what would happen if you tried to get away." Cassandra just whimpered. She could hear him, but she was so sore all over—it hurt too much to move. She just lay there, still, and the darkness came again.

When Cassandra started to come to, she could feel cool liquid all over her body. She didn't know how long she had been out cold. Slowly, she got up and went into the little bathroom. There was a small mirror over the sink. She looked at the reflection and she didn't even recognize the person looking back at her. She let out a gasp.

"That's what's going to happen to you if you pull that shit again, do you understand?" Cassandra jumped she hadn't heard him come in.

She closed her eyes and in a shaky voice said, "Yes."

"Good. Get in the shower and get cleaned up. I expect you showered and in the other room by the time I get back."

Cassandra did what she was told. The water hit her body and the pain was almost unbearable. She looked down at her feet. There was a sea of red water flowing down the drain. She put her hands to her face and cried, "Please Pops, Agnes—help me, please."

She finished her shower and went back into the other room and sat on the edge of the bed. When her kidnapper came back into the room she could hear him walk towards her, and out of nowhere she felt his hand hit her face so hard she saw stars.

"You are nothing but trash, you don't deserve a bed, you sit and sleep on the floor—do you understand? Unless I tell you otherwise. Do you hear me?

She put her hand to her face and whimpered, "Yes."

"Good, then we won't have to have this conversation again."

Cass curled up in a ball on the floor. She heard him leave, but she didn't move. She stayed exactly where she was. A short time later, she heard the voice again, "Here is some food and water for you. I have to go to work. I have cameras all over, so I will be watching you. If you do anything that will make me mad, you will regret it. Do you understand?"

"Yes."

Pope left and locked the door. She just lay there, too afraid to move, afraid he would beat her again. She had never experienced such brutality like this from anyone.

Cassandra didn't know how long she had been lying there—it hurt too much to stand, so she crawled to the bathroom. When she was finished, she crawled back out and found some food in a bowl on the floor and some water. She sat there and picked at the food. It tasted terrible, she couldn't eat it, she refused to eat it, and the water… no way. Cass carefully got up again and took a drink from the sink. She had a feeling she knew what was in the dish—she would be damned if she would be this scumbag's dog. No way in hell.

She curled up in the corner of the room and lay there, telling herself, *Cass, you went through tough times before. You can make it through this.* As she drifted off she told herself, *You will survive, there is no other option, you are stronger than you think, you can get through anything, bide your time, Cassie girl, play the game, you got this.*

Cassandra was startled awake. "You haven't eaten. What game do you think you're playing? Get over here now and eat this!"

Cass whispered, "I can't. I tried. It made me sick."

"I don't care what it makes you feel. It was good enough for Benny so it's good enough for you, or do you want me to feed you?"

"No," she whispered. She crawled over to the bowl, put some in her mouth and almost threw up.

"You make a mess and whatever ends up on the floor will be your dinner. Do you understand me?"

"Yes."

"I expect this gone by the time I get back." He shut the door and locked it.

Again she heard his footsteps fade down the hallway. She couldn't eat this; she would be sick. Her mind was racing—what the hell was she going to do? She started to cry. She looked up and turned towards the bathroom. She took a handful of food and put it in the toilet. She swished it around and flushed it down the toilet. Cass waited to hear if she could hear him coming back, she didn't. She took more of the food, put it in the toilet again, and swished it around and flushed.

Cassandra went back to the bowl and sat down when she heard him coming back. She put her hand back in the bowl and put what was left in her mouth, just as he was opening the door. "Well, that's my girl, you ate your dinner—isn't life better when you do what you're told?"

"Yes," Cassandra whispered.

"You go get some rest. I will be back in a while to spend some time with my girl." He left, shut the door and locked it.

Cassandra knew what was coming next, she wasn't stupid. She lay curled up on the floor and thought, *You can do what you want to me, I will get out of here. I do know one thing I didn't know before, there are no cameras in here.*

Cassandra didn't know why, but a calmness came over her. For what ever reason she didn't feel alone anymore. She felt loved—like everything was going to be okay. She whispered, "Pops, Agnes, are you there?" She felt their arms wrap around her, even though she knew no one was there. Cass thought, *I must be going crazy,* but she knew in her heart of hearts they were there with her. *Please help me.* Then the door opened. She closed her eyes and imagined that she was under the big oak tree at home, talking to Agnes and her dad.

11

....

Cassandra didn't know how many days or weeks had passed since Pope found her in her car on the side of the road. She wondered if her family and friends were looking for her. She had no clue as to how long she had been missing. Cass wondered if her mother was okay and if the boys were checking up on her like they'd promised they would. She didn't know if it was night or day. The only light she ever saw was the bathroom light and the light from the hall, when Pope opened the door.

She was startled from her thoughts when she looked up and Pope was standing there in the doorway, with some items in his hands. She hadn't seen him standing there watching her. "Stand up!" he said in a loud voice. She did as she was told. He held up a nightgown. "I think you will look lovely in this. Go and have a shower and put this on and don't take too long. You've been a good girl, so here are some bathroom items to make things a little better for us both." She looked into his eyes and glared at him. He laughed in her face. She took the nightgown and toiletries from his hands and went into the bathroom. The bag he'd given her had a hairbrush, deodorant, toothbrush, toothpaste, and body spray. This was all her personal items from her suitcase.

Cass came out of the bathroom; Pope was standing there with a smirk on his face. "Sit down on the bed." She did what she was told. He brought in a small table and two chairs. "You have been so good, so tonight you're going to have a treat. Sit in that chair." Cass got up and sat down. He looked at her. "If you move off that chair while I'm gone, you know what will happen?" Cassandra nodded her head. She sat there. She didn't even move a muscle. When he came back, he had two plates; whatever it was smelled delicious. She had refused to eat the dog food he had been giving her. *It may be good for dogs, but I'm not one of them*, she'd thought to herself. She didn't know how long it had been since she'd had real food, but right now liver and onions would be amazing, even though she hated it.

Pope put the plate down in front of her. She couldn't believe that he had put real food on her plate. She had roasted chicken, baked potato with all the trimmings, a salad, and a biscuit. Cass looked at the food; it looked so good. Her mouth was watering, but she didn't want to touch it. She was afraid if she did he would go off on her and not allow her to eat. Cassandra looked up at Pope.

"Let's have a nice Sunday dinner together."

Cassandra stared at him. *So, it's Sunday maybe*, she thought to herself. She stared at him while he started to eat his dinner. He looked up at her. "May I please eat with you?"

Pope looked up with a smile on his face—it went from ear to ear. How she wanted to wipe that smug look off his face. "Yes, you may Cassandra."

Cass went to pick up the fork and she stopped herself. "May I please use this fork to eat my dinner?" Again Pope looked at her with that wicked smile that almost made her throw up in her mouth. She might have if she'd had anything in her stomach to throw up.

Cassandra ate her dinner slowly and thought to herself, *If you eat too quickly you might make yourself sick.* Pope got up and Cassandra froze. "Finish eating your dinner. I'll be back in a few minutes."

Cassandra took her biscuit and the remaining chicken off the bone, went into the bathroom, got some toilet paper, and wrapped them up. She tucked them between the bottom of the toilet tank and the wall and quickly went back to her seat to finish her potato and salad.

Pope came in and looked at her with anger in his eyes. "You got up from the table."

Cassandra looked scared; she lowered her head. "Yes, I'm sorry. I dropped some food on myself. I just wanted to clean up, I didn't want to stain this lovely nightgown. I'm sorry I disobeyed you." He walked over to her and she braced herself. She thought for sure he was going to hit her, but he lifted her head ever so gently and thanked her for wanting to look nice for him. Then he took his hand away. "I'll take these dishes away and bring dessert," he said. Cassandra sat there and didn't move a muscle. He brought in dessert. She looked at Pope and asked him if she could please use the spoon. He replied with a yes, and she ate her pie. It was raisin pie and Cassandra hated raisins, but she wanted to eat as much as she could. She knew she had the chicken and biscuit hidden, but she didn't know when she would get real food again.

Pope told her to get up from the chair and sit on the bed. He took the dishes and removed the tables and chairs, then came back and sat next to her. He started to caress her back and leaned over and kissed her. It was all Cassandra could do not to be sick. He told her to lie down, so she did as he said. Pope did what he wanted to her and Cass cried silently and thought to herself, *When will this ever end?* She lay there next to him and didn't move a muscle. Pope was trying to show affection, but it made her skin crawl every time he touched her. In her head she was screaming, *You're raping me, you sick son of a bitch, and you think talking sweetly to me and caressing me is going to make this all right? You're a sick bastard!* She wanted to scream this in his face, but she knew what the outcome would be.

Pope got up. When he was finished with her, he headed for the door. He looked at her. "You were such a good girl today so you can sleep in the bed tonight." Cassandra looked at him and said thank you.

As he was about to shut the door, Cass shouted, "Pope!" He looked at her—she saw the irritation in his eyes. "Thank you for the nice evening." She almost got sick saying those words. He nodded and closed and locked the door.

The next morning, Pope came into the room in a hurry. He put her dish on the floor. "I thought you might like something different this morning." Cassandra looked at the dish and it looked like oatmeal. She said thank you and as he was just about to leave said, "Excuse me, Pope." He looked at her.

"What do you want I'm late?"

"Could I please have something to read? If that's okay with you?"

"Why do you need something to read?"

She swallowed the lump in her throat, "I thought it would give me something to discuss with you." He thought for a minute and walked away. When he came back, he threw a book at her.

"I expect you to have a minimum of six chapters read by the time I get back." Cassandra looked at the book then back up at Pope.

"Yes sir."

After Pope left, she looked at the book he had given her. It was called *Behind the Red Door*. She picked up her breakfast and went into the bathroom, sat on the floor, and started reading and eating her oatmeal. The oatmeal tasted good; she ate it slowly, she wanted it to last as long as possible. Cassandra didn't like the book Pope had given her. It didn't make sense to her as it jumped all over the place, but she realized by chapter four that some of the things he did to her he'd gotten from this book. It made her skin crawl.

She decided that she should have a shower before he got home. Cass cleaned herself up, washed her dish, and ate a little bit of the chicken. She was so hungry. All of a sudden, she was in complete darkness. The light had burnt out in the bathroom. She felt her way across the floor, put the book on the bed, and curled up on the floor and dozed off.

Cass didn't hear Pope come in until he grabbed her by the hair. He picked her up and threw her onto the bed and violated her with such force she truly thought she was going to die. When he was finished with her, he pulled up his pants and left. Cass pulled herself up off the bed and curled back up onto the floor and cried.

A short while later, Pope came in with a bag of food. He looked at her, walked over and said softly, "Cassandra."

"Yes," she whispered.

"I'm sorry for earlier. I had a really bad day—please, Cass, forgive me."

She whispered, "I do."

"I brought you some takeout—come sit on the bed and eat with me."

She could hardly move, she was so sore, but she struggled to her feet and made her way over to the bed. She ate her meal and thanked him for the wonderful dinner.

"So, Cassandra how many chapters did you read today?"

Cassandra swallowed, "Four."

He looked at her. "Four? I told you I expected six chapters read." She put her head down waiting for him to hit her again.

She mumbled. "The bulb burnt out," and pointed to the bathroom.

"Oh, I see, I'll have to replace it." He got up, walked out of the room, then came back and replaced the bulb.

Days had gone by. Pope would give Cass a new book every time she finished one. Each night they would talk about what she had read. One day, out of the blue, Pope brought in a brown lounge chair. He told her he was so proud of her and that she deserved something special. He wanted Cassandra to have a comfortable place to sit while she read her book during the day. He would turn the light on in the bedroom when he brought her breakfast. She knew she could have done it, but again, she didn't want to take the chance.

Cassandra still slept on the floor every night. She didn't want to take the chance of setting him off. She would curl up on the floor between the chair and the bed.

As the days passed, things got better. One day, Pope surprised Cassandra by coming in and taking the plywood off the window, so she could get some light and fresh air into her room. He looked at her, "Cassandra, I'm trusting that you won't start yelling out the window when I'm not home." He walked over to her and made an adjustment to the collar. "I have turned the power up higher. Do you remember how much this hurt before?" She nodded and told him yes. "Well, this is much higher now. I will look when I come home and I will know if you've been screaming." She knew this collar would leave a mark, so there was no way she would take that chance, especially when she never knew if he was home or not. Cass knew how vicious he could be and had no desire to be beaten ever again. This was her life as she knew it, at least for now.

Pope hadn't beaten her in a really long time—he'd even stopped feeding her dog food. She had oatmeal every morning and some days he would make her eggs and toast and maybe even a little bacon or sausage.

They ate dinner together every night. He brought the table back into the room and left it there. It was too heavy for her to pick up, so there was no fear of her using it as a weapon against him. The chairs he would bring in with him when they ate together and would take them out when he left.

He gave her some clothing: mainly just sexy nightgowns, and a hoodie, she had told him that sometimes it was cold in the room. The hoodie was way too big on her and went down passed her knees, but nonetheless, she didn't have to sit around naked all the time.

Cassandra came to the end of another book. When she went to close the book she noticed something was stuck under the cover. She lifted the cover and a paper clip had been stuck to it—or had Pope placed it there to see what she would do? She sat there and thought. She needed to do something so that people would know she had been here if she ever got free—this thought never left her mind. She wanted to leave evidence so people would know she had been there. Cassandra hid the paperclip in a little hole she found in the mattress. She needed to give this some serious thought as to what she should do. She didn't want to take the chance of being caught. She had to make sure he wasn't home; she needed to do this right.

One morning Pope came into her room. "Good morning, my love. Here is some breakfast."

"Thank you, Pope." She noticed he had a cooler bag in his hand.

"Cassandra, do you remember the meeting I told you about?" She nodded her head. "Well, it's today, so I don't know what time I'll be home—so here is some lunch and snacks for you to have while I'm away."

"Thank you for thinking about me; I know you've had a lot on your mind with this meeting."

"Cassandra, do I need to worry about you today?"

Cass got up and walked over to him and put her arms around his neck. She kissed him, then looked into his eyes, "No, Pope. I promise I will be good."

He looked at her and knew she meant it. He kissed her with so much love and passion, "I love you, Cass."

She looked into his eyes. "I love you too." She smiled at him, he smiled back at her and took the keys out of his pocket and bent down and unlocked the chain. He moved it and placed it under the bed.

"Have a good day, Cass."

"You too, Pope. I hope your meeting goes well." He looked at her and smiled, then turned around, left, and locked the door behind him.

Cass heard a car start. She wasn't sure if it was his or not so she picked up her breakfast, sat down in her chair, and ate her meal quietly, deciding what she was going to do.

She knew it had been a few hours since he had left her room, the sun had already started moving to the back of the house. She went over to the mattress and got the paper clip. Cassandra now knew what she needed to do. She bent the clip and stuck the paperclip under her fingernail to make it bleed; a small amount of blood came out of her finger. She wiped it behind the toilet tank, then she moved the bed and carved, "I was here," and her name. Cass took some hair from her brush and stuck it inside the book—one strand in the seam of one of the pages. She placed another in the side pocket of the chair. Then she licked the inside of the book so that there would be DNA there, as back-up, just in case the hair fell out or Pope found it.

Next, she pricked her toe and got some more blood and wiped it on the hinge of the bathroom door. She bent the clip back and put it back into her hiding place in the mattress. Suddenly, she heard footsteps coming down the hall. Quickly, she went and sat in her chair and pretended she had just finished the book she was reading.

Pope came in and was not in a good mood. Cassandra looked at him and asked how his day was and he just glared at her. She was terrified. The look on his face was something she hadn't seen in a very long time. He came towards her and grabbed her by the hair. She gasped. He threw her to the floor and started hitting her and screaming at her. She tried to protect herself from the blows, but it was no use—there wasn't a part of her body he wasn't hitting. Cass finally passed out from the sheer pain of it all.

When she woke up, he was gone and the chain was attached to her leg. She crawled to the bathroom, crawled into the shower, and turned on the water on. Cass knew if she didn't clean up and he came back, he would do this all over again.

She was sitting in the corner by the chair when she heard Pope stumbling down the hall. He unlocked the door and entered the room. She could smell the booze on him clear across the room. "Get on the bed!" It was all Cassandra could do to get up—her eyes were swollen from the beating he had given her earlier. Everything was fuzzy. Everything was sore, but she managed to get herself over to the bed and lay down. He took his clothes off and climbed on top of her. He whispered, "Cass, I love you. I'm so sorry, please forgive me."

"It's okay, you had a bad day. I love you too."

Pope must have thought he'd done what he wanted to do because he rolled off her and passed out. Cassandra lay there, her mind racing, thinking to herself what the hell had just happened. Things were really good, she did everything he asked of her. What had she done to make him so angry that he would do this to her again? Cassandra lay there wondering if he really passed out or if it was a trick to see what she would do.

A familiar voice came into her head again. "Cassandra get up and get the keys you need to go NOW!" The voice got louder and louder. She couldn't think straight; she knew deep down if she didn't get out now, he would eventually kill her.

Quietly, she got up. She was in so much pain. The voice in her head said, "Cass, you have to do this now. Please, Cass, go, go NOW!" She found his pants and ever so quietly pulled the keys out of the pocket. She held each key and tried to unlock the lock on her leg. It was difficult—she couldn't see well and her hands were shaking out of sheer fear. Finally, she heard a click. The lock opened. She quietly laid the chain on the floor and got up and went to the chair. She grabbed her hoodie, quickly put it on, and headed for the door. Pope rolled on his side and moaned. Cass froze... then he started snoring. She quietly shut the door behind her, felt around the door and found the lock. She didn't know how, but she managed to lock the door. Cassandra felt her way down the hallway. She knew she had to get out and get out now.

She found the front door and felt for the lock. Her heart sank. There were four or five locks on the door. She started to panic. She didn't know what to do. How was she going to get out of here? The keys were in the other room. She should have brought them with her—why hadn't she taken them with her? *Oh, Cass, why didn't you bring the keys?*

All of a sudden she heard him screaming and banging on the door. "Let me out of here, Cassandra. I will beat the holy hell out of you when I get out of here, open this door now you *bitch*!" Cass froze; she didn't know what to do. The voices started hollering in her head, "RUN, CASS, RUN NOW! IF HE GETS OUT, HE WILL KILL YOU. YOU HAVE TO GO. GO NOW!"

Cass knew it was do or die. She searched for something to break the window with. She felt around, tripped over the table, and landed next to a chair. Pope's voice was getting louder and louder. The adrenaline started to kick in; Cass picked up the chair and went to the window and started hitting it. She hit it over and over again and finally she heard the window crack. She hit it faster and faster. Every muscle in her body was aching, to the point where she didn't think she could swing the chair one more time, but she did, repeatedly, until the window finally smashed.

Cassandra swung the chair a few more times to try and clear as much of the glass out as she could—all the while, Pope was screaming at the top of his lungs. She threw the chair out the window and climbed out, feeling her skin slice as pieces of the glass cut into her body. Cassandra didn't care; all she knew was she had to get out of there. She fell on the hedges below the window and rolled off onto the grass. When she looked up she saw a light and the number ninety-nine, or what she believed was ninety-nine.

Cassandra got up and ran towards the street. She didn't know which way to go, something told her to go left, so that's what she did. Cassandra ran—she didn't stop until she came to the corner and looked at the street sign under the light. She could barely make it out, but she thought it said Weber Street. She started running again and kept running until she couldn't run anymore. She came upon a well-lit street, and stuck close to the front of the buildings walking as fast as she could.

Cass could hear voices but couldn't see anyone. She cried. "Help me please!" but no one did.

Cassandra suddenly froze in her tracks. She heard sirens coming in her direction she thought to herself, *Oh my God, he's gotten out, he's going to find me and kill me.* She started to run as fast as her legs could carry her as the sirens got louder and louder. She came to the corner of a building and followed it around. She hugged the wall as tight as she could and stood as still as she could. Cass literally became one with the wall. The sirens went past the building and she told to herself, *Come on, girl, you have to find someplace to hide.*

Cassandra inched her way down the wall and felt her way around. She bumped into a large metal box that seemed to move when she pushed on it. She pushed it a little bit and crawled in behind it; she laid down against the fence and prayed, *Please don't let him find me.* Cassandra curled up in a tiny ball and thought to herself, *You're free. You're safe.* At least that's what she hoped. Then everything got dark and quiet and she drifted off.

12

....

"Sid, you're in early."

"Ya, I couldn't sleep. This damn bike of Tiny's has been driving me crazy. I'm trying to figure out the new design, but I think I finally have it. I just need to check a few things out to see if they're able to be modified, then I think we're good to go."

"Good. Can you do me a favour and put the delivery away first and then get rid of the boxes? Max is coming sometime today to empty the recycle bin."

"Sure, Ryder, I'll do it right now."

"Thanks, brother."

"I hope some of these rims that came in are for Ross's bike. It's been on back order for a few weeks now."

"Ya, me too. I warned him this might happen. These are a specialty rim and needed to come from Barracuda in Germany."

"We need to get Tiny's bike done soon. They have that charity ride in a few weeks for Toys for Tots."

"I'll get the stock put away and clean up the boxes, then finish Big John's bike. Should only be another hour or so to finish it, then I'll get onto Tiny's bike."

"Sounds good to me. I have to get some stuff done in the office, if you need me."

"Sid?"

"Ya."

"Make sure Dean gets on that paint job as soon as he gets in. We need that bike finished today and out of here."

"Will do."

Sid turned on the tunes and got to work putting all the parts away. He found the rims that they had been waiting for to finish Ross's bike. It was gonna look bad-ass when it was done, he thought to himself.

Sid bundled up all the boxes and took them out to the bin, flipped the lid open, and made a loud bang. The bang was so loud it startled Cassandra and she cried out. Cassandra thought for sure Pope had found her, she laid there and tried to be quiet. Sid picked up the cardboard boxes and threw them in and closed the lid again. Cassandra whimpered as Sid started to walk away. He thought he had heard something, he looked around, but didn't see anything. Cassandra moved. She tried to get in closer to the fence. Sid headed back into the shop but stopped. This time he knew he'd heard something. It was faint, but he had heard something moving behind the dumpster. Sid walked back by the bin. "Hello, is someone out here?" There was nothing—he turned around and was about to walk back when he heard that sound again from behind the bin. He gently moved the bin, just in case it was an animal that had gotten itself stuck and couldn't free itself. When Sid moved the bin, he looked down. *What the fuck?* he thought, as he shoved the bin away from the fence. "Lady, are you okay? Can you hear me?"

"Please don't let him find me."

"Who?" Sid didn't know what to think. He knew he shouldn't move her, but he picked her up anyway. She was as light as a feather. Cassandra cried out in pain. "You're safe hun, I've got ya and no one's gonna hurt you anymore." He carried her into the shop. "Ryder get out here, RYDER!"

"What's going on—what the hell, who's that?"

"I don't know. She was hiding behind the bin."

"Get her into the office and lay her on the couch. I'll call 911."

"No!" Cassandra moaned and tried to get out of Sid's arms, "Let me go, please. He'll find me and kill me—please don't call, I'm begging you."

"Okay, calm down, lady. Who did this to you, your old man?"

"No."

"Then who?"

"I can't tell you."

Sid spoke to Cass in a low and calm voice. "Hun, if you don't tell us what's going on, we won't know how to help you. My name is Sid and this is my friend, Ryder. What's your name?" She looked at Sid and then towards Ryder. Cass couldn't make out his face, but something inside her told her that if she was going to put her trust in anyone, it should be these two guys. She had a feeling that they wouldn't do her any harm, but she had been wrong before.

"Cassandra."

"Hi Cassandra, looks like you found yourself some trouble."

"That's putting it mildly," she said.

"Cassandra, we need to get you to the hospital."

"No, please no hospital," she whispered. "If you do that, they will call the police."

"And why is that a bad thing?" Ryder asked in a tone that she knew only too well.

Cass looked towards Ryder. "Because the man that did this to me is the police."

Sid looked at Ryder and then back at Cassandra. "Cassandra."

"Please call me Cass."

"Okay, Cass—are you sure this was a cop that did this to you?"

"Yes, I'm sure."

"Sid? Ryder? Where is everyone?"

Cass grabbed Sid. "Please don't let him find me, please."

"You're safe… that's Dean."

"Please, no one can know I'm here. Please, he'll find out."

"Calm down Cass, it's gonna be alright."

"Sid, stay with her. I'll get Dean going on what he needs to do then we'll figure out what we are going to do with her."

"Sid?"

"Yes?"

"What day is it?"

"What?"

"What's the date?"

"It's May 19, 2019."

"It can't be."

"Cass, that is the date." Cass started to cry. "What's wrong?"

"You don't understand."

"What don't I understand?"

"I have been missing for almost a year. My mom, my family and friends—they must think I'm dead."

"Cass, it's all going to be okay. We'll figure it out, I promise."

Ryder came back into the office. "We need to get her out of here."

"I'll go. I don't want to cause you any trouble." Cass tried to stand up, but she couldn't lift her own body weight.

"Sit down. You're not in any shape at all to go anywhere by yourself."

"Please—I'll be fine. I don't want to cause you any trouble."

"Too late for that," Ryder said.

Cassandra put her head down and whispered, "I'm sorry."

Sid looked at Ryder and shook his head. "Brother!"

"Okay then, what are we gonna do with her? She can't stay here."

"I'm gonna call Tiny and Shelley. They'll help us figure out what to do."

"Sid, we got shit we have to get done today!" Ryder said in a tone that surprised even Sid.

"Ryder, it will get done. Cass, excuse my friend here."

"I'm sorry to bring this to your doorstep."

"It's okay. You picked the right doorstep to bring it to."

"Your friend doesn't think so."

"Ah, he's an old softy—he just hasn't had his first pot of coffee yet." Ryder grunted. Cassandra let out a little laugh and then winced in pain.

"Cass, we have to get you checked out."

"Really, I'm good—this isn't the first time this has happened to me."

Sid just stared at her and then looked over at Ryder "No? Well I promise you one thing, it won't fucking happen again. Cass, I'm gonna make my call."

Cass put her hand on Sid's arm "Please don't leave me here alone with him."

"It's okay Cass, no one's gonna hurt you." Sid pulled his phone out of his pocket and made his call.

"Tiny, I need you and Shell to come to the shop right now."

"What's going on?

"You'll see when you get here, just hurry."

"Sid, you okay?"

"I'm good. I have a friend here that isn't though and we need help!"

"We're on our way."

"Thanks."

"Sid, the cops are here."

Cass tried to get up, "I have to get out of here."

"Cass, you're not going anywhere."

"Sid, you don't know this guy."

"Ya, that might be so, but he doesn't know us. Just stay here."

"Sid!"

"Cass, you have my word nothing is going to happen to you. I'll be right back." Sid stood up and left the office and shut the door behind him. Cass started to panic. She struggled, got to her feet, but the pain was so bad she almost fell down. She grabbed onto the arm of the couch and looked around the room. She saw what she assumed was a desk and felt her way around it. She was right, she moved the chair and knelt on the floor and crawled into the little space under the desk. Cass pulled the chair back in as close as she could and sat there and didn't make a sound.

Cassandra felt like she was going to pass out from the pain of being curled up in such a small space. She kept telling herself, *You can do this, the alternative is you dying if he finds you.* She knew this time Pope would kill her if he ever got his hands on her again.

"What's going on?"

The two officers looked at Sid. "Who are you?"

"I'm Sid, who the hell are you?" The taller of the two officers stepped forward and Sid stepped forward. Rider put his hand out on Sid's chest and shook his head no.

"We're looking for a lady that assaulted a police officer. She was spotted in the area."

"When was this?"

"Earlier this morning."

"Do you have a picture of her?"

"No, we don't, but her description is, that she is white, about five-five, long shoulder-length blonde hair, blue eyes, about one hundred and seventy-five pounds."

"Sorry, boys—we can't help you."

"Do you mind if we look around?"

Just then Tiny and Shelley walked in. "Ryder, Sid—what's going on?"

"Apparently there is some woman going around beating up cops."

"Really? I want to meet her and buy her a drink."

"Look, we're going to have a quick look around. There shouldn't be any problem with us doing that, right?"

Ryder stood up from the table he was leaning against. "Do you have a search warrant?"

"Why, do we need one?"

"Ya, I'm afraid you do. Come back when you have one. Until then, get the hell off my property!" Both cops looked at the boys. All three of them were over six feet tall and had more muscles than half the police force, and they also knew that they belonged to one of the local clubs.

"We'll be back."

Sid piped up, "We'll be here. We close at five." The two officers left and got in their car and pulled out of the parking lot. Ryder looked at Sid,

"You know they're going to be back, right?"

"Ya, we need to get her out of her now before they come back with that search warrant."

Tiny piped in. "What the hell is going on?"

"Come with me." Sid headed toward the office, opened the door, and looked at the couch. "Cass, where are you?" Sid turned around and looked at Ryder. "Where the hell did she go?"

Ryder went to the front door. It was still locked. He went back to the office. "She has to be here—the front door is locked."

"Cass, where are you? They're gone, it's okay to come out." Cassandra pushed the chair away from the desk and crawled out. She tried to stand, but she couldn't

"Sid," she whispered, "I can't get up."

He went over to the desk. "Cass what are you doing under there?"

"I was hiding in case they came in."

When Sid helped her to her feet, she cried in pain and grabbed the top of the desk for balance. "Cass, this is my brother, Tiny and his wife, Shelley."

Cassandra turned around. "Holy shit, what the hell happened to you?" shouted Tiny. Just then Cassandra's legs gave out from under her. Sid caught her, picked her up, and carried her over to the couch. He placed her on it as carefully as he could.

"Tiny, we can talk about all that later. Right now we have to figure out how we're going to get her the hell out of here before the cops come back."

Shelley went over and sat next to Cass. She took her hand in hers. "Hi Cass, I'm Shelley."

Cassandra just melted and started to cry. "I'm sorry, I'm so sorry."

Shelley pulled her close. "It's okay, sweetie, you're safe. We'll figure something out."

"When we get her out of here, we can take her to our place," Shelley said.

"Okay, but how do we do that?" Ryder snapped.

"Can we get her on a bike?" Tiny asked.

"She can't walk, how do you expect her to ride a bike? And besides, she wouldn't be able to handle the vibration of the bike."

"Ryder!" Cass froze.

"Dean, what's up?"

"Max is here to empty the bin, but Tiny's bike is in the way."

"We'll be right out."

Sid piped up. "Max, he can get her out of here."

"How?"

"We'll get her into the cab of the truck and meet him down the road."

"There is no way in hell she could handle the pain of getting up there. They would hear her screaming a mile away."

Ryder shook his head, "What if we get him to block the alley so we can get her out—we'll use Dean's car."

"Sid, we can't get him involved. He's on parole."

"Shelley, wait here with her."

"Sure, Ryder."

The three boys went outside; Max got out of the truck. "Hey boys, ya know you have company out in the alleyway."

"Ya, we figured as much."

"We have a problem, Max."

"How can I help?"

"We have a lady we need to get out of here, unseen. Can you block the alleyway so they can't get by?"

"Of course I can, Ryder—anything you need, my friend."

"So now what?" Ryder asked.

"Hold on, let me make a call."

"Tiny, we don't have time."

"Ryder, just hold on a minute." Tiny made his call. "Cliff's in the area, he'll be here in a few minutes—we need to get her outside so we can get her into the trunk of his car as soon as he gets here."

"Shelley isn't going to go for that."

"Sid, there isn't any other option. Sid, go get Cass, please. Max, go do what you came to do. I'll move my bike."

Sid went back into the office. "Cass we're going to get you out of here."

"How are you gonna do that?" Shelley asked

"Come on, we have to go now."

"Sid, how are you going to get her out of here?" Shelley asked again.

"Shelley, we have to go now." Sid picked Cassandra up, carried her out of the office and headed towards a car with the trunk open.

"You're not putting her in there?" Shelley hollered.

"We have no choice," Tiny said.

"What's going on?" Cass asked in a low voice.

Sid carried Cass over to Cliff's car and placed her inside the trunk as carefully as he could. "Cass, listen to me. We need to get you out of here. There's an unmarked car down the alley, which means they'll be back with a search warrant. We have no choice. You're in the trunk of Cliff's car." Cassandra started freaking out: she tried to push Sid's arms away, she tried to roll so she could get out. She put up such a fight—she was fighting for her life once again.

"Cass!!" Ryder yelled. She froze. "Listen, darlin', we have no other way to get you out of here. We need you to go now. You have my word it's just till we get you someplace safe." It broke

Ryder's heart to see the poor girl going through this. She'd already been through so much. She was beaten and broken and Ryder didn't know if she could ever come back from it.

Ryder put his hand on hers. In a voice that surprised everyone, "Look Cass, as soon as it's clear, they'll pull into someplace safe and get you out. Please—this is our only option and we're running out of time." Cass calmed down. She laid down in the trunk and didn't say another word. Ryder looked at her with tears in his eyes, then turned and walked away.

"Cass, it's Tiny. Shelley and I will be right behind you." Cass nodded her head.

"Guys, you need to go now." Sid gently shut the trunk lid. "Ryder and I will see you soon." Max backed up, blocked the alleyway, and the police were none the wiser. Cliff took off and, as promised, Tiny and Shelley were close behind.

"Sid, let's get back to work. We have to act like it's just another day at the office."

So that's what they did. Neither one of them could concentrate on what they were doing. Ryder was in his office, looking at the picture of his late wife, Christina, thinking, *Watch over her, baby—she's broken and needs our help.*

Ryder came out into the shop to do some work. "Tiny just called, she's safe."

"Good I'm glad."

Just then three cruisers pulled into the parking lot. The officers that were there before walked up to Sid and slapped the search warrant on his chest. "Here you go."

"By all means, search away... but you won't mind if I film this, just in case you guys decide you're going to toss the place." The cop just glared at him. The police weren't there long. They found nothing—no trace that Cassandra had ever been there. They left, and Sid hollered, "You boys have a nice day now."

They finished their day and were just closing up shop when Dean came up to Ryder. "There's an unmarked car down the alleyway Ryder, what's going on?"

"It's better if you don't know."

Dean nodded his head, "See you tomorrow, boss."

Ryder nodded his head, "See ya tomorrow."

"Sid?"

"Ya."

"There's an unmarked car down the alleyway. We have to be careful—they're going to be watching us. They know we know more than we're letting on."

"I wonder, Ryder, what's really going on here"

"I don't know, brother."

13

Ryder and Sid closed up shop. They decided it would be a good idea for them to go in different directions. They had to be smart about this they needed to make sure they weren't being followed. God only knew what would happen to Cassandra if this guy got his hands on her again.

Sid called Tiny and told him what was going on with the unmarked car in the alley. They all agreed that everyone needed to be extra careful until they figured this all out.

It was seven-thirty when they rolled into Tiny's driveway. Tiny had the garage door open, waiting for them both. When they pulled in, Tiny shut the door behind them. "Are you sure you weren't followed?" They both said yes. "Let's go inside and talk," said Tiny.

Shelley was making dinner for everyone. "Shell, how is she?"

"She's sleeping, Sid—she's in the back bedroom."

"I'm gonna go and check on her."

"Sid, please don't wake her, she needs all the rest she can get."

"I won't, I promise." Sid opened the door quietly, went in, walked over to the side of the bed, and sat down next to her.

He brushed the hair away from her eyes. "You're safe, Cass, you have my word no one will ever hurt you like this again." Cassandra moaned, but didn't wake up. Sid didn't know why, but he felt a connection with this lady he had just met and knew nothing about. He knew one thing: that he would protect her with his life.

Sid slowly got off the bed so as not to wake her—Shelley would kill him if he did. He turned around and left the room. He shut the door quietly behind him.

"How is she doing?"

"She's sound asleep. I don't get it, Ryder, how can any man do this to a woman—what possible pleasure can there be in doing this? I get it when two guys go at it—they're guy's and they can defend themselves—but to do this to a woman? I just don't get it."

"I don't know what to tell ya, Sid, not everyone lives by the code we do.

"Okay boys, supper's ready, so come fill your plates then we can sit and get you both caught up with what happened since we left the shop."

Everyone got what they wanted and sat down at the table. Ryder was the first one to ask, "So how is she, really?" Tiny told them that they got her back to their place without any problems. He called Doc Charles and he had them sneak her into the back of the clinic. He took x-rays of her ribs, arms, and legs, and told them she had three cracked ribs. He said she was fortunate. With the severity of the assault, they all should have been busted. He also took some blood to test her for STDs, as well as a pregnancy test. They should have the results in a few days.

Doc Charles told them that she had a lot of healed breaks and said she must have gone through hell—he was amazed she was still alive. He told them that she needed to stay in bed and should only be allowed to get up to use the bathroom, but shouldn't be left alone. The doc said he would come over in a few days to check up on her. He also gave Shelley a prescription for pain meds. He said she was going to need them, once she started to come around.

"So what do we do now?" Shelley asked.

"Good question," Tiny said. "What are we gonna do?"

Ryder suggested they call Josh. Sid looked at Ryder. "Seriously? He's a cop and she told us a cop did this to her. He should be the last person we call."

Tiny looked at Sid. "Brother, Josh has always been good to the club. He has helped us through some difficult shit and he can be trusted. I know you don't know much about him, but both Ryder and I do."

Sid looked at Shelley—he trusted her judgment. "What do you think?"

"I think we don't have a choice. Sid, this guy needs to be caught. Cass won't be safe until he is. And he could do this to someone else, who might not be as lucky as she was."

"I don't like it," Sid said.

"What other choice do we have?" Ryder asked. "Sid knew they were right, but still he didn't like it one bit.

"We need to get that collar off her neck." Shelley said.

"Let's wait till morning when she wakes up. We should talk to Josh before we decide to do anything."

They ate in silence, everyone thinking about what had happened that day and wondering what would unfold in the days to come. They could all agree on one thing: they needed to keep Cass safe.

Ryder went out back to make his call. He walked back into the house a few minutes later. "We're all set. I spoke to Josh and he's agreed to come to the Roadhouse to talk. He'll be there in about an hour, so we should head over there soon. Shell, can you stay with Cass?"

"Of course." She looked at Sid—she knew her brother-in-law felt something for this girl. "Sid, I promise I'll keep her safe."

"I know you will, Shell." The three of them went out the back door into the garage, hopped on their bikes, and headed to the Roadhouse. Shelley locked up the house and pulled out her little Glock forty-two that she named Bubba. She knew how to use it and would drop the first person that came into the house without an invitation.

The boys grabbed a booth at the back of the bar. They wanted to make sure they could have a private conversation. They got their drinks and sat there deep in their own thoughts, when Tiny saw Josh walk in. He nudged Ryder's arm and nodded towards the door. The bar suddenly got quiet, they knew Josh was a cop and this wasn't just any bar. This was the bar where a lot of club members came to unwind and have a good time—everyone knew everyone, and everyone watched each other's backs. This was a safe place for them to go and not have to worry about outsiders coming in and bothering them. Ryder greeted Josh, "Thanks for coming. We have a table in the back. Can I get you something to drink?"

"No thanks, I'm good." Everyone went back to what they were doing and talking about. They knew this was personal business and all was good.

"Tiny, how's it going?"

"Okay—and you, Josh?"

"Not bad, just wondering what this is all about?"

"Josh, this is my brother, Sid."

"Hi, how's it going?" Sid just nodded his head. "So why did you wanna see me?"

Ryder looked at Sid and Tiny. "You called him, brother."

Ryder nodded. "We had a couple of your boys in blue come to the shop, looking for a lady who apparently assaulted a cop."

"Really? I haven't heard anything about that."

"Well, they went and got a warrant to search the shop." Josh nodded his head, "Seriously, you expect us to believe you've heard nothing?"

"Sid."

"No, Ryder—they stick together, and you're sitting here expecting us to believe that…" Sid pounded his fists on the table, "bullshit."

Josh looked at the three of them, "Look, I have no clue as to what you guys are talking about. I haven't heard of any cop being assaulted. Ryder, Tiny—we've always been on the up and up whenever we've had dealings, so what's different now?"

"Look, we found a lady who was brutally assaulted and she claims a cop did it."

"Does she know his name?"

"Ya, she does, but she hasn't told us—she claims that she was held hostage for almost a year."

Ryder continued to tell Josh everything that had happened, from the time they'd found her that morning, until now.

"Where is she now?"

"She's safe."

"So, what is it you want from me?"

"We want to know what we should do next—we need to find this guy before he finds her… or finds someone else and does the same to them."

"Ryder, how bad is she?"

"Josh, I have never seen anyone this bad in my life. This lady's been through hell and back."

"I need to see her."

"Not gonna happen," Sid blurted out.

"Look guys, you either trust me or you don't. I think I have proven that I'm a fair and honest cop with your club."

"Ya, you have. Please excuse Sid," Ryder said, "he's very protective of her. He found her and he promised her he would keep her safe. Hell, we all made her that promise."

"Look this is what you need to do. I need you to get a medical report from a doctor with a copy of the x-rays, as well as photos of her entire body. You need to take them tomorrow while the bruises and swelling are at their worst. They need to be dated pictures. I need a written statement from both of you, with today's date. I'll also need a statement from this lady. I need to know everything: from how she met this cop to what happened while she was captive—everything she can remember. I'll get in touch with someone that I trust in the DA's office and see what he suggests we do next. Talk to her and see if she'll agree to meet and talk with me as soon as possible. If she is that bad off, a video of her telling me what happened would be better—but be careful, guys. If the cops were brave enough to get a warrant and the news hasn't gone through the station, there could be higher-ups involved. I just don't know at this point." Josh got up from the table, "I'll wait to hear from you, but in the meantime, get me what I asked for. Ryder, I'll call you as soon as I hear something from my end."

Ryder shook Josh's hand, "Thanks for your help."

"I'll do everything I can to help you with this." Josh turned around and left the bar.

Sid turned to Ryder and looked him straight in the eyes. "I sure hope you know what you're doing."

"Do you trust me, brother?"

"I trust you with my life."

"Then trust me when I tell you Josh can be trusted. Look, it's getting late—we should all go home and get some sleep. Sid, I'll see you at the shop tomorrow. We have to keep acting like it's just another day."

Sid nodded his head in agreement. "Tiny, I'm gonna stay at your place tonight."

"I figured you might."

Shelley was sitting in the backroom in her rocking chair with Bubba in her hand resting, on her lap. Tiny and Sid walked in the back door. They looked at Shelley and looked at her lap. "I see you brought your friend out to play tonight."

Shelley laughed. "It's been a while, but I wasn't taking any chances."

"How's she doing?"

"Cass is good, Sid. She was up a little while ago and I was able to get her into the bathroom. She had a little something to eat and was asking where you and Ryder were. I told her you would be back shortly."

"I'm gonna go sleep in the room with her. Goodnight." Sid walked into the room and shut the door quietly behind him.

Tiny looked at his wife. "He's falling for her."

"I know." Shelley shook her head. "What did Josh have to say?"

Tiny told Shelley everything and she said she would take the pictures in the morning, when Cass woke up. "I spoke to some of the boys at the bar tonight—I told them we have a friend in trouble staying here for a while. They're gonna come around throughout the day to make sure all is good, while we're at work."

"Tiny, I can't leave her here alone—she needs someone here with her."

"I know, Shell. I have Cherry coming in to cover for you."

"Good, I'm glad. Do the boys know what's going on?"

"I didn't get into specifics, other than she is family to us and she needs our help."

Sid sat in the chair in the corner of the room watching Cassandra sleep. He couldn't imagine the hell she must have gone through. He dozed off. Sid woke up startled, with Cassandra screaming. He bolted out of the chair and went to her side. He put his hand on her. "Cass, it's Sid, you're safe."

"Sid."

"Ya, darlin', it's me."

"I'm scared."

"You're safe. Close your eyes and try to get some more sleep."

"Will you please stay with me?"

"I'm not going anywhere—you have my word." Sid lay on the bed next to her and put his arm around her. She froze. Sid could feel her entire body go stiff.

"Cass, I want nothing from you. I'm sorry I just wanted to make you feel safer—I'll go sleep in the chair."

"No—stay, please," she whispered. She took Sid's hand in hers and held onto it like it was her life preserver. She wouldn't let it go because if she did she was scared she would drown. "What's going to happen to me now?"

"Darlin', it's late, let's get some sleep—we'll talk in the morning."

"Okay." Cass felt safe in Sid's arms; she drifted off, telling herself she was safe and she could relax, at least for tonight.

14

Cassandra opened her eyes. She could tell it was early morning, but she wasn't sure what time it was; the sun was just coming up and the light was starting to come through the window.

For a split second, she froze. There was someone lying next to her. And then she remembered where she was and who was lying next to her. She could hear Sid snoring softly as she pushed herself deeper into his body. This was the first time in a very long time that she felt safe and she wanted this feeling to last forever.

Cass felt a connection with him, but she wasn't sure if it was real or because he had found her and was protecting her. Cass lay there still, trying not to wake him. She closed her eyes and tried to go back to sleep, but she couldn't. There wasn't one part of her body that wasn't hurting.

She pulled away and tried to get up on her own, but when she tried to stand, she couldn't.

"Where are you going?" Sid said groggily.

"I'm sorry, I didn't mean to wake you. I was trying to get up to use the bathroom, but my legs don't seem to want to hold me up."

"I'll help you."

"It's okay, I'll try and wait—get some more sleep if you can." Sid got up and came around to her side of the bed. He gently put his arms around her and picked her up and carried her into the bathroom. It hurt like hell, but she really had to pee badly and was glad he didn't listen to her and go back to sleep.

Cassandra was wearing one of Tiny's T-shirts. It went past her knees so there were no panties to try and wrestle down. He gently set her on the toilet. "Call me when you're done."

"I'm sorry to be so much trouble."

"You're no trouble at all."

"Liar" she whispered. Sid had a smile on his face, but unfortunately she couldn't see it.

"Look, you're here because we want you here and want to help you—all of us do. If I'm going to be honest, there's something about you that makes me want to get to know you better. Cass, before you start panicking, I want nothing from you and I expect nothing in return—no one here does—all we want is to be your friend and help you get out of the mess you've found yourself in. Let me know when you're done, okay?" She nodded her head.

When she was finished, Cass called Sid. "Let me get you back into bed."

"Can I please sit up for a while in a chair? My body is killing me." There was a knock on the bedroom door—Cass looked at Sid, the door opened, and Shelley poked her head in.

"Good, you're up. I was just coming to see if you were. Good morning, Cass. How are you feeling this morning?"

"I'm hurting all over"

"Well, why don't we get you some breakfast? I have some pain meds that Doc Charles prescribed for you, and you need to take them with food."

"Can I come out there please?"

"You need to stay in bed!" Sid snapped.

"Please, just for a little bit. I can't stay in this room all day… please?" Cassandra started to cry.

"What's wrong? You were fine a minute ago. You're safe."

Cass couldn't stop herself; everything came flooding back— being locked in that room and the repeated abuse. She started to have a panic attack and couldn't stop it from happening. She grabbed at her chest.

Sid got really scared for her—he didn't know how much more stress her body and mind could handle. He carefully picked her up and carried her out of the room. "Shelley, there is something wrong with Cass." He sat her down on the couch in the sun room. Shelley rushed in and sat down next to her.

She looked at Cass and then at Sid. "She's okay, Sid—she's having a panic attack."

"Are you sure, Shell?"

"Ya, sweetie, I'm sure. Cass, take slow deep breaths, in and out, in and out, there ya go, keep taking slow deep breaths, you're going to be fine, just calm yourself down, that a girl."

Cass started to feel better. The colour started to come back into her face, even through all the bruising, you could see a difference in her skin colour.

Just then, Tiny walked into the room. "What's going on?"

"Cass is having a panic attack—she'll be fine, you guys need to get to work."

"We need to talk to her Shelley."

"Tiny, it can wait till tonight." He knew by the tone in his wife's voice there was no way she was going to allow any conversation to happen until Cass calmed down.

They needed to get to work and they needed to keep everything as normal as possible. "Let's go, Sid—we both need to get to work. Shelley, there will be a conversation tonight—and remember what you need to do today."

Shelley nodded her head, "I'll take care of it, Tiny. You boys have a good day and we'll see you tonight. Tiny, make sure the gate is locked in the backyard, please."

"I will. Call me if you need me." Shelley nodded her head.

Sid walked over and knelt in front of Cass. He put his hand on hers, "Are you okay?" Cass nodded her head yes. He leaned in and whispered in her ear. "I'm sorry. Everything's gonna be okay, I promise." Sid stood up and gently put his hand on the side of her face. "Get some rest. I'll see you after work."

"All of you, please be careful," ordered Shelly.

"We will." With that, Sid and Tiny headed to the garage. Tiny checked the gate to make sure no one could get in, and then they both were off.

Shelley looked at Cass, "How about some breakfast?"

"I'm good, thanks—you don't need to go to any trouble."

"It's no trouble. What would you like?"

"A piece of toast will do me for the day, thank you."

"You need more than a piece of toast, my dear." With that, Shelley got up and went into the kitchen and made Cass some eggs and toast. She brought the plate in with a cup of tea and placed it all on a tray on Cassandra's lap. "There you go, I want you to eat all of that and take these pills with your meal." Cassandra ate most of her breakfast, but she wrapped her toast and some egg in a napkin and hid it under her shirt, just in case this was all she was going to get. After all, she didn't really know these people, and they could be just like Pope. They could just be waiting for her to get better before they did what they wanted to her. She'd felt safe once before, with Tom, and look what happened there … so she wasn't taking any chances this time around. As soon as she could get around on her own, she was out of there.

Shelley came back into the sun room. "You ate everything! Would you like me to get you anything else?"

"No thank you, I'm fine."

"Cass you didn't take your meds?"

Cass lowered her head. "No."

Shelley came and sat next to her. "Why haven't you taken your pills? Doc Charles prescribed them for you."

She looked at Shelley. "I'm afraid to."

"Why, sweetie? We're not trying to hurt you."

"I don't want to make you mad, Shelley."

"Why would I get mad? It's just you and me here. Talk to me and tell me what's going on in that head of yours."

Cass looked at Shelley and tears swelled in her eyes. She swallowed the lump in her throat and said that in her heart she felt she could trust them, but in her head… that was another story. Her mind was telling her to get ready to run, before *they* got a chance to hurt her too.

"But Cass, why would we want to hurt you?"

She looked at Shelley. "Why would Pope?"

Shelley sat and stared at Cass, with tears swelling in her eyes. "I'm so sorry for what you went through, Cass—nobody should have gone through what you did." She took Cassandra's hand in hers and the two just sat there.

Cassandra looked at Shelley. "I'm getting tired, would it be okay if I lie here and get some rest?"

"Of course you can, but you really need to take your meds, Cass. Please. They're to help you with the pain, nothing more."

Cassandra took her meds and closed her eyes and drifted off. When Shelley came back into the room with a throw cover to cover Cass up, she noticed the napkin sticking out from under her T-shirt. She picked it up and thought to herself, *What the hell?* She opened up the napkin and found part of Cassandra's breakfast folded up inside. Shelley refolded the napkin, put it back where she found it, and left the room in tears.

Shelley was in the kitchen cleaning up the dishes when the phone rang. "Hello."

"Hi, baby, how are things at home?" Shelley couldn't answer him. "Shell, what's wrong?" She just started to cry. "I'm coming home."

"No, it's okay, I'm fine."

"You're not fine. What the hell is happening there? What the hell did Cass do to you?"

Shelley looked towards the backroom at Cass sleeping. "Tiny?"

"Shell, what's going on baby?"

"I asked Cassandra if she wanted some breakfast. She told me that a slice of toast would be good for her for the day. *The day*, Tiny! I made her some scrambled eggs, toast, and tea, and when I went back in she had eaten everything."

"And that upset you—why? Shelley I'm confused"

"No, Tiny. When I went back to put a blanket on her, what upset me was I just found half of her breakfast wrapped up in a napkin hidden under her shirt. Tiny, I think she's afraid we won't feed her again. What did that bastard do to her? I could kill him."

"You're not the only one. Have any of the boys been by today?"

"Ya. Mitch stopped by a few minutes ago and said he would drive by a little later. He said he didn't see anyone lurking around. I have Bubba tucked into my waistband, so I'm ready in case there's trouble."

"Has Sid checked in yet?"

"Ya—just a quick hello to see how she's doing."

"Did you tell him about the food situation?"

"No, I hadn't found it then."

"Okay, I have to go. Shell don't forget the pictures."

"I won't, Tiny, though I may need help in taking them—she wasn't able to walk this morning, her legs were too weak."

"Okay, babe, wait till one of us gets home and we'll figure out how we're gonna do it"

"Okay, Tiny. I love you."

"I love you too, Shell."

The rest of the day went by without any problems. Cassandra woke up around one o'clock to use the bathroom; she was able to stand and walk, with a little bit of help from Shelley.

"I'll leave you here for a few minutes and come back and help you to the couch."

"Thank you."

Shelley left Cassandra alone. Cass looked around the bathroom. She hid her eggs and toast behind the toilet tank—it was a good hiding spot and it kept the food slightly cold. She finished what she was doing, washed her hands, and slowly made her way out of the bathroom.

"Hey!! You were supposed to call me—here let me help you."

"I'm fine."

"How is your sight today?"

"It's still blurry, but I can make shapes out. Shelley, can we please get this collar off, or do you want me to keep it on?"

"Cass, as soon as the boys come home it will come off, okay."

Cassandra nodded, yes, and found her spot on the couch. "Shelley what time is it?"

"It's one-thirty—are you hungry?"

"No, I'm good."

"I have some chicken salad I need to get used up before it goes bad… help me finish it up, please. I'll make us a nice cup of tea with it. How does that sound? Then maybe we can have a chat if you're up for it?"

"I wish I could help you do something."

"Well, why don't you come into the kitchen and sit down at the table and keep me company while I'm making our lunch?"

Cassandra got up from the couch and felt her way into the kitchen. The phone rang. It startled Cass. She looked towards Shelley.

"Hello? Ya, hold on a minute. It's for you."

Shelley put the phone in Cassandra's hand.

"Hello?"

"Hi Cass, it's Sid. How are you doing?"

"I'm okay, how are you?"

"I'm good. Did you eat today?"

"Yes. Shelley is making us a sandwich and a tea for lunch."

"Good, I'm glad you're eating something. I have to go, Cass—we're swamped here I just wanted to check in with you."

"Will I see you again?"

"Of course you will. I'll be over after work."

"Sid."

"Ya?"

"Please be careful."

"I will."

Shelley and Cass ate their lunch. Cass asked if it was okay to have a couple more pain pills, the others were starting to wear off and her body was starting to really hurt again. Shelley got up and handed the meds to her. Cass told her about her job with Agnes and her family and friends. She told her about her father's passing and about meeting Big Daddy, Rick, Mack, and their friend, Pickle.

Shelley laughed and asked, "Why the funny names?" She told her Big Daddy got his name because he looked like a big, cuddly, teddy bear and he was like a father to everyone. She told Shelley about how she'd met the boys and what they'd done for her when her father was dying. She told her about Pickle and why the boys gave her the name; they both laughed.

The afternoon went by quickly—the girls talked about their lives. Shelley tried to get Cass to talk more about what happened, but she wouldn't go there; Shelley didn't want to push the matter, so she let it go. She knew that when the boys came home they were going to want to talk, and, unfortunately, Cass wouldn't be able to say no. The one thing she did know now was the bastard's name—and when the boys came home they would too.

"Shelley, can I please use your phone? I need to call my mom to let her know I'm alive." Shelley sat and stared at Cass—she wasn't sure what she should do.

"I'm sorry Cass, but we need to wait for the boys to get home. I'm not sure how they want to handle this. Remember, Cass, we need to be careful. We don't know what we're up against or what consequences this could cause if the wrong people found out you were here. We don't know if someone is listening, and we don't want to put your family in any danger."

Cass thought about what Shelley had said for a minute and knew she was right. If anything happened to her mother or anyone else she cared about, she knew she wouldn't be able to live with herself. It was bad enough she was putting all of them in danger.

Mitch stopped in again like he promised, and then left. It wasn't long before they heard the rumbling of motorcycles coming up the driveway. The boys came in through the back door. Tiny went straight in to see Shelley and gave her a kiss and asked her how she was doing. She told him about their afternoon and that Cass had asked if she could please get the collar off and call her mom.

"What did you tell her?"

"I told her she would have to wait till you all got home."

Sid sat next to Cass and asked her how she was feeling and how her day had gone. Ryder stood there watching Sid and Cass together. Ryder knew Sid had feelings for her, but for some crazy reason, so did he. There was something about Cass that made his heart race when he saw her or even thought about her.

Tiny and Shelley came into the room and sat down. "Cass, we need to have a serious conversation with you."

Everyone saw the fear in her eyes. "Have I done something wrong?" Sid took her hand in his and told her no she hadn't done anything wrong.

Ryder spoke up. "Cass, I'm Ryder—do you remember me?"

Cass nodded her head. "Yes, of course I do. You're the grumpy guy." Everyone had a laugh—even Ryder laughed at what she had said.

Ryder came and sat in the chair next to her. "Look, darlin', we had a chat with a friend of ours who belongs to the police force." Cass instantly started to panic—they could see the fear in her eyes. Sid piped in and told her that this was someone who they trusted wholeheartedly, who had always been upfront and honest with Ryder, Tiny, and other members of their club.

"Cass, you need to trust us on this."

She didn't know what to do. Her heart said to put her trust in them, but her head was telling her to run, run like hell.

Shelley got up and went over to Cass. She knelt in front of her, putting her hands on her knees. "Please listen to your heart this time it's telling you the truth." The boys stared at Cass and Shelley and then at one another. They knew something had happened today between these two ladies. They weren't sure what it was, but there seemed to be a new bond forming between them.

"What do you want to know?"

Ryder looked at her and said, "Everything." Cass sat there holding onto Sid's hand as if her life depended on it and in her mind it did. Ryder put his hand on Cassandra's arm "Cass, we would like to have our friend Josh come over and talk to you— would that be okay with you?" She wanted to say no, she didn't want to do it—but she was afraid that if she didn't, they would kick her out… and then what would she do? She wasn't ready to be on her own just yet.

"Can I please get this collar off and maybe have a shower first? Would that be okay?"

"Of course you can," Shelley said.

"Shelley?" Tiny said, in a voice that scared Cass. "Cass, before we can take the collar off, Josh would like us to get pictures of all your cuts and bruises. Would that be okay?"

"Pictures of what?" Ryder stepped in.

"Cass, Josh needs us to get pictures of the collar around your neck and all the bruises and marks on your body."

Shelley spoke in a soft and reassuring voice. "You and I will go into your room and I'll take the pictures, and as soon as I get them all, we'll get that damn collar off your neck."

Cass looked at Shelley "Just you and no one else." Shelley reassured her that it would just be the two of them, Cass nodded her head okay.

Sid helped Cass to her feet. She looked at everyone and asked if it would be alright if she spoke to Josh in a day or two. "I'm not sure if I'll have it in me after we finish doing what we're going to do now."

Everyone looked at Ryder. "Cass, do I have your word you'll tell us everything when Josh is here?"

"I promise, Ryder. You have my word."

Sid took Cass by the arm and walked her to her room, while Shelley went and got her phone. Tiny gently took Shelley's hand. "Are you going to be alright taking these pictures?" Shelley said she didn't really want to—but who else could take them? Cass trusted her and that was a big deal. She didn't want to betray that trust in any way.

While the girls were in the bedroom, Ryder took the opportunity to call Josh and set up a time for him to come and talk to Cass. Josh said he wouldn't be able to come until Saturday. He suggested that they continue to keep it quiet that she was there, as he'd recently heard some chatter around the station about a woman … who he assumed was the lady they were protecting.

Shelley and Cass had been in the room for almost an hour, when Sid couldn't take it anymore. He was just about to knock on the door when Shelley opened it up. She had been crying. There was no doubt this had been hard on her. She looked at the boys and told them it was done. "What took so long?" Sid blurted out. She turned towards Sid with tears in her eyes and told him she'd gone through all the pictures to make sure they were perfect. She didn't want to have to do this again and she didn't want to put Cass through it again, either.

She looked at Ryder and Tiny. "Get that fucking collar off her now!"

Tiny went out to the garage and got a pair of bolt cutters and was just about to cut the lock when Cass hollered, "Wait!"

"What's wrong?"

"You can't touch it with your bare hands."

"Why the hell not?" Ryder snapped at her.

"Because there could be evidence on it that they can use against him. No one else has touched it, but him and me."

"Cass has a point there, brother," Tiny said.

Shelley went to the kitchen and got a brand-new pack of rubber gloves from under the sink and opened it up. She also got a large freezer bag to put the collar in. Tiny looked at Cass, "Are you ready?" She nodded her head. It took less than a minute to cut the lock off and undo the collar from around her neck. Shelley picked up everything and put it inside the bag and sealed it. She took the last remaining photograph of the marks around Cassandra's neck, that had been hidden by the collar, and handed the bag to Tiny. Shelley suggested that they lock it in the safe along with her phone's sim card, just to keep everything together and safe.

Everyone looked relieved that this part of it was now over. Ryder put his hand on Cassandra's arm and told her he was sorry for snapping at her—she had startled him when Tiny was about to cut the collar. He'd thought that they were hurting her in some way. He told her that he'd spoken to Josh and he wasn't able to come until Saturday.

"Can I please have a shower now?"

Sid put his arms around Cass. "Darlin', you can have whatever you want."

"I just want a shower—and maybe a pair of shorts to put on would be nice." They all laughed and Shelley told Cass they would get her what ever she wanted.

15

Cassandra tried to fall asleep, but every time she started to drift off she would start to dream about Pope and all the things that he had done to her. She was having these nightmares all the time now, but she didn't say anything to anyone. They had enough to deal with.

Cassandra was worried about meeting Josh the next day and telling him everything that had happened to her. She honestly didn't know if she could do it, but she also knew that they had a right to know, since they were risking their safety to protect her. Cass was afraid that they would never look at her the same way again. She was mostly worried that Sid would look at her differently, and though her vision was still blurry, she could feel that he and Ryder cared about her in a different way than the others.

She got up and found her way to the kitchen to get herself a drink of warm water—maybe a glass would help her sleep. She wished Sid was there. She figured that he must have gone home by now to be with his wife or his girlfriend.

Cassandra found a cup on the counter and was able to find the faucet. She turned on the hot water.

"Are you okay?"

Cass jumped. "Holy shit, you scared the crap out of me!"

Sid came up behind her and put his hand on her back. "Sorry, Cass."

"I thought you went home. Your wife or girlfriend must be getting upset with you for spending all your time here."

"There's no one at home waiting for me."

Cass turned around and looked into his eyes—what she could make out, anyway. "Why not, if I'm not being too personal?"

"I was with someone for four years, and she decided a life with me wasn't what she wanted."

"I find that hard to believe."

"Well, she wanted someone rougher and tougher than me. Since then, I haven't found anyone I have wanted to take a chance with. Until now," he said, almost in a whisper.

Cassandra moved closer to Sid and put her hands on his chest. "Sid, you don't want me, I'm damaged goods. I'm no good for you, or anyone else for that matter."

Sid put his arms around her. "I know I've only known you for a short time, but I would like a chance to find out. I'm not pushing for anything and I'm not pressuring you into doing anything. I know you have a lot you have to deal with, but will you at least think about it?"

She looked up at Sid. "I'm scared."

"I promise I won't hurt you, Cass." She knew he wouldn't: both her head and her heart told her that and she knew he would keep his promise. "I don't want to rush you, Cass." He assured her that they could take it as slow as she needed to.

Cass looked at him, "You may change your mind after you hear what I have to tell all of you. You may not want me at all—and if that's the case, know that I truly understand."

"I want you, good or bad"

"How can you be so sure about that?"

"Cass, if I'm honest with myself, I fell for you hook, line, and sinker the day I picked you up from behind the dumpster."

"Sid, you don't know what you're saying. How could you possibly have these kinds of feelings for someone like me?"

"You obviously don't see what I see?"

"And just what is it that you see? Because all I see is someone whose only purpose in life is to satisfy other people's needs and wants—be it financial, sexual, or just as someone's punching bag. People like me haven't been put on this earth to have a good life, like others. We are here for the sole purpose of taking other people's crap, so that others who are not as strong as we are don't have to. That's my purpose. That's what I see, and so far life hasn't proven me wrong."

He looked at Cass and asked her if that was really how she saw herself.

"Yes it is."

Sid placed his hands on her face and lifted it upward. "Well let me tell you what I see. I see an amazing woman who has gone through hell and is still standing. A woman who hasn't curled up in defeat and given up. I see a woman who will fight with her last breath to survive and who cares about the people around her. I see a woman who deserves so much more in this life, and if you will give me a chance I will prove it to you. Cass, I believe, with everything I know to be true, that things happen for a reason, and maybe one of the reasons is that we would meet. There's a bigger picture here and we just may not see it right now, but when the time is right, we will."

Cassandra just stared at Sid—she remembered hearing those exact words, more or less, once before, from Big Daddy.

"Cass, how do you feel? And please be honest with me, I need to know."

Cassandra looked up at Sid. "I know when I'm with you I feel safe and when I'm not, I'm scared. I'm worried that this is some kind of survivor thing and I have these feelings because you saved me."

"Do you really believe that?"

"I don't know, and that scares me even more."

"Cass, all I know is I don't want to lose you."

"I don't want to lose you either, but I don't want to hurt you and I'm scared that I will. I'm scared that I'm truly damaged, Sid."

He lowered his head and gently kissed her. Cass felt more love in that one kiss then she had ever felt in her entire life and she didn't want it to ever end. She never wanted to lose that feeling again.

She heard Agnes in her head. *Cass, he's the one for you—take a chance, live love, and laugh, my dear friend.*

Cass pulled away from Sid and said she was tired.

"Let's get you back into bed." He walked her to her room; she crawled back into bed and he covered her up. "Goodnight Cass." Sid headed for the door.

"Sid."

"Ya, darlin'?"

"Please don't go."

"Are you sure?"

"Yes, please stay." Sid crawled into the bed next to her and asked her to lift her head. She did as he asked her and he laid his arm out so she could lay her head down. He pulled her close to him and she snuggled back into his body. *A perfect fit,* she thought to herself. Cassandra closed her eyes and slowly started to drift into a peaceful sleep. She could have sworn, as she drifted off, that she heard Sid say, "I love you, Cass."

Cassandra had the best night's sleep. She hadn't slept this well in a very long time. She was all alone in her bed when she woke up and thought to herself, *Was last night just a dream? Did Sid really tell her that he wanted to be with her, did he actually kiss her?* Oh, that kiss. It fired up her body in ways she never knew existed. As bad as her body felt, all she wanted to do was be with Sid in every way possible—even after what had happened with Pope.

Cassandra couldn't fall back to sleep. She didn't know what time it was, but she decided she would get up anyway. She walked out of her room and heard voices coming from the kitchen. "Good morning, everyone."

"Good afternoon, Cass."

"Really, it's afternoon?"

"Ya, darlin', it's twelve-thirty."

"Why didn't someone wake me up. I'm so sorry."

"There's nothing to be sorry about."

"You guys have things to do and I have just wasted your day."

"Cass, it's fine. Ryder just got here and we're waiting for Josh. He should be here soon. Would you like me to get you something to eat?"

"No thanks, Shelley, I couldn't eat anything right now. I'm going to have a quick shower and get dressed." She was thankful that they had gotten her some clothes. She was also thankful that these four amazing people were the ones that had found her. She had been lucky. Anyone else might have dumped her off at the nearest hospital—or worse, called the police.

Cass was getting dressed when there was a knock on her door and Shelley stuck her head in. "Josh is here."

"Oh." Cass sat on the bed and looked towards the floor.

Shelley came and sat beside her. "Are you okay?" Cass told her she was scared to talk to Josh. She was afraid of what might happen when they found out what had happened while she was locked up.

"Cass, none of this is your fault."

"I know, but I gave up. I stopped fighting. I just did what I was told."

"You listen to me." Cass nodded her head. "You did what you had to do to survive. You didn't give up. If you had, you would still be there and not here with us."

Cass knew she was right, but she was still worried about what would happen once they heard everything. Shelley got up and walked towards the door and turned towards Cass. "Cass, this is the day you're going to take your life back and it is also the day that Pope is going to lose the hold he has on you. Today is the beginning of the end for him."

Cassandra got up from the bed and walked over to Shelley and put her arms around her. "Thank you for all that you all have done for me and thank you for being my friend. I know that all this hasn't been easy on any of you." Shelley hugged her back and told her that they were all glad that they were the ones that had been chosen to help her through this. She was family now and they would always be there for her, just as they knew she would always be there for them.

Cassandra walked out of the bedroom with Shelley at her side. They walked into the kitchen. Sid stood up and pulled the chair out for her to sit on, next to him. He leaned over and whispered into her ear, "You've got this Cass." She turned, looked at him, and smiled.

"Hi, my name is Officer Josh Wilks. Can I ask you what your name is?"

Cass looked at everyone at the table. Sid took her hand. "It's okay."

"My name is Cassandra Taylor."

"Hi Cass, your friends here have told me a little about what has happened to you. Would you mind if I turned on my video recorder and ask you some more questions?" Cassandra nodded her head yes. "Can you please tell me your full name for the record?"

"Cassandra Elizabeth Taylor."

"Can you tell me the name of the person who abducted you?"

"His name is Pope; it was the only name I saw on his name tag on his shirt."

"Can you tell me, from the beginning, what happened—and please try not to leave anything out, we need every bit of information you can give us."

Cass proceeded to tell them that she'd been on her way back home to Lethbridge, Alberta. She'd met some friends at Jack's Waffle House for dinner and then they'd gone their separate ways. She said there had been a road closure that had directed her to take a detour—she'd driven a while when her had car started acting up and had finally died at the side of the road.

"Cass, can you please tell me the day that this happened."

"April 16, 2018."

"And what day did you escape?"

Ryder spoke up. "We found her in the yard on May 13, 2019."

"Cassandra, did you know how long you were held captive?"

"No, I had no clue. I never saw a paper, or a calendar, and when I did get free it was all about getting out of there." Josh asked her to go on. Cassandra told them about Pope helping her put her suitcase's in his trunk and how that was the last thing she remembered, until she woke up chained to a bed, with a shock collar around her neck, in a dark room. The only light she'd seen was a little shadow from under the door.

She told them about the sexual assaults, the beatings, and the lack of food. She told them that she had tried to escape once, shortly after her kidnapping, but he'd caught her and bashed her head onto the door and she'd lost consciousness. When she'd woke up, she'd barely been able to move—he'd beaten her up pretty badly. She'd decided she couldn't go through that again so she'd decided to bide her time and do as she was told. He'd told her that there were cameras watching her at all times, but she'd found out later he'd lied.

"When did you find this out?" The day he tried to feed her dog food, she told him. She'd said she couldn't eat it and he'd threatened her so when he'd left the room, she had flushed almost everything down the toilet.

"Where was the bathroom?" She told Josh it was in the room she'd been imprisoned in, but she hadn't known it was there, at first. She told them she'd had no clue how long she'd been there. When things had started to get better, he'd given her books to read and had fed her real food. It wasn't the greatest, she said, but it was better than the dog food.

Ryder stood up and walked out of the room and went outside. Tiny got up and went to see if he was okay. "Why don't we take a break?" Cass sat there and wasn't sure she could continue.

"Ryder—you good, brother?"

"He fed her fucking dog food, what kinda sick son of a bitch would do this to another person? Everything that he put her through—no wonder she doesn't trust anyone. Who can blame the poor girl? I get my hands on this Pope guy, I'll kill him myself."

"He'll get his, you have my word Ryder—his day will come. Let's go back inside. I'm sure Cass wants to get this over with."

Josh finished listening to everything Cassandra had to say, and by the time they were finished, Cass was exhausted. Josh sat there and stared at her; he was in awe of this woman who had been through such hell—that she could even function, was beyond him.

"Cass, I have just a few more questions—is that okay?" Cassandra nodded her head yes. "Do you know where you were held captive?"

"Yes, but I don't want to tell you."

"Why's that?"

"Because I'm afraid somebody here will take the law into their own hands and I don't want anyone to go to jail over me. I'm not worth it."

"Cass, nobody will do that."

"I'm sorry, but I won't take that chance."

"Will you write it down in my notepad?"

"As long as you promise not to share that information with anyone here."

"Cass—" said Sid.

"I'm sorry Sid, but I will not be the reason any of you lose your freedom. I care about all of you too much to allow that to happen." Josh handed Cass his notepad and pen, Cass got up from the table went to the counter and wrote down, "99 or 66 Weber Street," as best as she could. She shut the notepad and handed it back to Josh. She explained to Josh that she wasn't certain which house number it was, as her vision was poor because of the beating she had gotten earlier.

Josh asked Cass if there was anything else she could tell them that would prove she had been there. She told him that in the bathroom that she'd used they would find her blood on the back of the toilet tank and on the hinge of the bathroom door. She told him that she had stuck a paper clip under her nails to make them bleed. They could find a message carved in the floor under the bed in the corner that said her name and "I was here." She'd also put a strand of her hair and licked the inside cover of a book called, *Rumour Has It.* She'd also placed hair in the pocket of a brown recliner chair.

Everyone sat there stunned at everything she was telling them. Cass looked straight at Josh and told him that that was everything she could think of and asked if she could please call her mother to let her know that she was alive and safe.

"Cass, I can't let you do that quite yet."

"Look I know this has been hard on you—hard on everyone—but if you call your mom right now, before we know it is safe, it could put her life in real danger." Josh looked at everyone. "I shouldn't be telling you all what I'm about to tell you. I need your word that what I'm about to say stays here and doesn't go any further." Everyone agreed that what was said would be kept between the six of them. Josh cleared his throat. "In the past eight-teen months there has been a spike in female abductions. There have been several instances where bodies have been found in different stages of decomposition. We have heard rumours of an underground group that have been abducting women as a game, and the objective of this game is to see who can make their victims last the longest before they break or they die. Cass, I believe you were one of these victims and the fact that you escaped puts the group in jeopardy. They will do whatever they have to keep their secret, and if that means hurting your mom or anyone here, they won't hesitate. I think one of the reasons you're still alive is that Pope actually fell in love with you."

Cassandra was stunned at what Josh had just said. She glared at him with so much anger in her face. "In love with me? Are you fucking serious?" she hollered.

Josh looked Cass, with sadness. "Cass, as bad as you had it while you were held captive, some of these women had it a lot worse. I don't want to get into the grim details, but let me say this—they were tortured severely they even lost body parts. It's my belief they were still alive when this happened… what would be the thrill in doing it if they were already deceased?"

Cassandra sat down; all the anger deflated from her body. "I'm sorry Josh. Those poor women."

Josh nodded. "Guys, look, the fact of the matter is that some of these men may belong to the force, so this makes it that much more dangerous for you and everyone around you. We need to take this slow, so that no one else gets hurt." Ryder asked Josh what he wanted them to do with the pictures and the shock collar. "Hold onto it and keep it safe till we figure out what our next move is."

16

It was a little over a week since the meeting with Josh. Everyone was on edge and wondering if he was actually going to be able to help Cass. Josh finally called Ryder and told him he needed to see him as soon as possible. He told Ryder he only wanted to talk to him alone, not with anyone else, because he knew none of them would like what he had to say. Ryder agreed to meet Josh at Al's Diner after work, and he promised Josh he would say nothing to anyone until after they had spoken.

Ryder arrived at the diner and found a table in the back dining room. He asked Brenda, the waitress, who he knew, not to seat anyone near them if possible. She said it shouldn't be a problem it was a quiet night. Ryder ordered a drink and sat there and waited for Josh to arrive.

Josh walked in a few minutes later and walked over to the table. "Are you sure we're okay talking here?"

"Ya, we're good, what's going on?"

"I spoke with my friend at the District Attorney's office and, with everything we have, he feels it's time to go to a judge and get a search warrant—so the shit is about to hit the fan." Josh explained what they felt was the best plan of action in this situation. Ryder sat there and listened to everything Josh had to say. He agreed with everything and told Josh that he would take care of it and call him later that evening, after he'd spoken to everyone. Josh got up from the table and said this had to happen in the next few days. Ryder said he understood—he actually had an idea about how they could pull this off. He would get back to him. Josh shook Ryder's hand. "I'll be waiting for your call."

Ryder took his phone out of his pocket and called Tiny.

"Hey Ryder, what's up?"

"We all need to get together now, back at your place."

"What's going on?"

"I'll tell you when I get there. Can you call Sid for me? I have a few calls I need to make, then I'll head over."

Ryder looked through his contacts and found who he was looking for. He dialed the number and a voice answered on the other end. "Ryder, my brother, it's been a while. How are you?"

"I'm good, David. I need your help, brother."

"Tell me what ya need."

Sid pulled into the driveway. Tiny had left the garage door open for him, he pulled in and shut the door behind him. He had no intention of going home tonight—good or bad news, he knew he didn't want to leave Cass.

Sid walked into the kitchen and Cassandra looked up from doing the dishes. He put his arms around her and she turned towards him and put her arms around him. She whispered into his ear, "Are you okay?"

"Ya, darlin', I'm fine. How are you feeling today?"

"Today is a good day. I can see clearly—no fuzziness anymore. My body doesn't hurt as much and I didn't have any nightmares so it's a good day."

Sid leaned over and kissed her gently; all he wanted to do was make love to her, but he knew she wasn't any where near ready for that.

Everyone was sitting at the table, chatting, when Ryder walked in. "Hi everyone. I spoke to Josh today and he gave me a heads-up as to what's going on and about to go down. I need you all to listen to what I'm about to say and please don't interrupt me. I promise, after I tell you everything we can talk about it."

"This sounds serious?"

"It is." They all looked at one another. Sid put his arm around Cass and pulled her closer to him. He had a feeling he wasn't going to like this at all.

Ryder told them all that Josh finally had all his cards in place, and the District Attorney was ready to go in front of a judge for a search warrant on the address that Cassandra had given them. Apparently, he had spoken to the judge with a hypothetical situation and the judge had told him exactly how he should handle it. Ryder explained that the judge thought it would be best if they got Cassandra out of town. Since they didn't know how many people were involved, they felt that once they presented Pope with the search warrant, his friends would start searching for Cass like all their lives depended on it, which it did. Pope and his friends would be coming after all of them with everything they'd had. It turned out that Pope wasn't a cop, but a reserve police officer, so God only knew how many friends he had who were willing to help him out of this mess.

"So here is what we're going to do. The bike ride for Toys for Tots is this coming weekend. I've called some of the boys from the club and explained we need help and what we need to happen. We will have twenty guys coming here, with a passenger and saddlebags on their bikes. All the passengers are going to be dressed in the same clothes—so Shell, you're gonna have to get Cass some black jeans, a black T-shirt, and a black jacket. Everyone is going to show up here at noon and come into the backyard. Sid, you're gonna have to get someone to ride with you."

"Cass will ride with me."

"No, she won't. She'll be coming with me."

"What? Why the hell not?"

"Sid, let me finish." Sid sat there glaring at Ryder; Cass took his hand in hers and squeezed it and gave him a reassuring smile that all was going to be okay.

"On Friday, I'll bring my saddlebags. Shelley, can you please load them up with Cassandra's clothes and personal belongings. Once everyone is here, all the passengers will put their helmets on and walk out with us. We'll all get on our bikes and head towards the meeting place for the ride. We'll get into the lineup, and when we reach the highway, ten of us will get off at different exits and come back around and get in line. However, I won't. Cass and I will be going somewhere else. I have a good friend that I trust with my life, and he is willing to help us out and keep her safe. Once we're there, I'll call Josh and they will execute the warrant."

"Where are you taking her?"

"I can't tell you that, Sid."

"Why the hell not?"

"Sid, it's for her safety and everyone else as well. The fewer people that know, the safer she'll be and the safer we all will be."

"And what? We can't be trusted?"

"Sid, I get why Ryder wants to do it this way."

"Really, Cass? Then please explain it to me."

"If you knew where I was, would you be able to stay away for as long as this might take to deal with? You and I both know that you would want to come and see me every chance you could, and I am not strong enough to tell you no. I know you would be careful, but some way, somehow, someone could follow you to where I am—and that would put you and me in danger, and Ryder's friend in danger as well."

Sid stood up and said NO, that there had to be another way. There was no way in hell he would let her go anywhere without him. It just wasn't going to happen. He walked out of the kitchen and went outside for some fresh air. Cass got up and Ryder looked at her. "No, darlin', let him be alone for a while—he has to figure this out himself."

Cass looked at Tiny and Shelley and they both agreed with Ryder, she sat back down and asked Ryder if they were sure there was no other way. She was finally feeling safe—safe as she could be, with all that was going on.

Cass was starting to feel her life falling in around her. Once again with all the uncertainties: would this ever end? and would she ever see Sid again or any of them again? Would she ever be able to let her mother know that she was alive? All this was running through her head when she felt someone put their arms around her. When she looked up, she saw Sid. She looked into his eyes. He looked like he had been crying and just like that her heart broke into a million little pieces. It killed her knowing that this was affecting him this way—because of her, he was hurting bad enough to bring tears to his eyes.

Sid looked at Ryder. "Promise me she will be safe and no harm will come to her."

"You know I can't promise you that Sid, but what I can promise you is that I will do everything humanly possible to keep her safe."

Sid looked at Cass. "Baby, this is up to you. If you say yes then I'll go along with this, but if you don't, then we will figure out something else. This is ultimately your decision."

She looked at Ryder. "Are you sure there are no other options?" Ryder looked at her with more compassion than she had ever seen in his eyes since the day she met him. He put his hand on top of hers and held it gently.

"Cass, I wish there were."

Cassandra looked at everyone and then back at Ryder and said okay—if this was their only option, then she would go along with it. She excused herself from the table and went to her room and shut the door behind her.

They talked for another hour about what needed to be done, then Ryder looked at everyone. "So, we're good with this plan—can I call Josh and tell him it's a go?" Everyone looked at Sid.

"Ryder—I love her, brother." Ryder put his hand on his arm and told him he knew that and that he would protect her with his life, he had his word on that.

"Call Josh then, before I change my mind."

Sid got up from the table and went to Cassandra's room. Cass laid there crying softly. Sid curled up in bed next to the woman he wanted to spend the rest of his life with and pulled her so close to him. They laid there and didn't say a word. They both knew what the other was thinking; no words were necessary.

17

....

The remainder of the week went by quickly. There wasn't a lot that anyone could do but go about their day and wait for Saturday to come. No one was looking forward to that day, least of all Sid and Cass. They had all met in the most unbelievable way and what they all realized was that in this short time their family had grown, and one of their own was in trouble. They knew they would all move heaven and earth to keep anyone of their family members safe.

Shelley got the clothes Ryder had asked her to get, as well as some odds and ends she thought Cass might need during her time away.

"Shelley, can I please talk to you?"

"Of course Cass, what's up?"

"I just wanted to say thank you for everything you've done for me, and that you all mean the world to me. I'm sorry for all the trouble I've caused you."

Shelley put her arms around Cassandra and held her tight. "You listen to me, Cassandra Taylor. You're a gift to us all. We are glad you came into our lives. It's unfortunate you had to go through what you did to get here, but don't you ever doubt you helped us, as much as we helped you." Cassandra pulled away from Shelley with a puzzled look on her face. "Come and sit with me for a minute, there's something you should know about us. Cass, almost three years ago Ryder's wife, Christina, died of a brain aneurysm. She was Tiny and Sid's sister and my best friend. Ever since she passed away there's been a void in our lives. It's like we all stopped living and have just been going through the motions since. I believe with all my heart that Christina brought you into our lives. We're feeling alive once again. Cass, we needed something or someone to bring us back to life again and Christina brought us you. You are family in every sense of the word. Please don't ever forget that. When this is all over, we want you back home with us. You are now a part of our family."

They both had tears in their eyes. "Shelley, promise me something."

"If I can."

"Promise you'll watch over Sid—he's going to have a hard time with this."

"Do you love Sid? I've been watching the two of you and I see something there."

"Would it be okay if I did, Shelley?"

"More than anything—we haven't seen him this happy in a very long time. The circumstances are unusual, but we're all happy to see the two of you together."

The saddlebags were packed and everything was set in place for the next day. The toy ride was finally here; no one had much to say during dinner their family was about to be torn apart, and no one knew for how long.

Cassandra broke the silence. "I just want to say thank you all for everything you've done for me. I'm thankful for whoever guided me to your shop, Ryder, and brought you all into my life. You are all my family. I hope when all this is over it'll be alright if I come back here."

Sid looked at her and told her that if she didn't, he would come and find her and bring her back. "I'm not losing you, Cass." She smiled and told him, "Good," because she didn't want to lose him either. She didn't want to lose any of them. They were too important to her to let that happen—she loved all of them.

Cassandra got up from the table and walked over to Ryder. She put her arms around his neck and told him that included him, even though he was a grumpy old man. Everyone laughed, including him. He gently patted her arm and told her that she brought out the grumpy in him.

Ryder excused himself he had some things he needed to do before tomorrow. Tiny and Shelley went to the Roadhouse so that Sid and Cass could have some time alone. No one knew how long it would be before Cass would be able to come home, and they knew she and Sid needed this time together.

Cass and Sid sat out on the back deck in her favourite spot on the swing chair. Neither one of them said anything. They were just happy being together—words weren't necessary. Even though they had only known each other for a short time, they knew each other pretty well. Better than some couples that have been together for years.

Sid finally broke the silence and asked Cass if she was still sure she wanted to do this—if she had changed her mind they could hop on his bike and take off right then and never look back. She looked at Sid and asked him what kind of life would that be, always looking over their shoulder. She was tired of hiding. She wanted her life back, whatever life that might be. She didn't want to live like this anymore. "I want to see or talk to my mom whenever I want to; I don't want to always be worrying that my friends and family are in constant danger." She snuggled in closer to Sid. "Sid, as much as I don't want to leave you and everyone here, we have to stop Pope. I don't want him to do this to anyone else because I was too scared to stand up to him."

Sid knew she was right. He just hated the fact that she was going, because there was always the chance she wouldn't come back. After all, she could change her mind about them all once she was away for a while.

"Penny for your thoughts."

Cass looked at Sid with a look of confusion on her face. "A penny for *your* thoughts," she replied.

He looked at this amazing lady sitting next to him and he knew exactly what he wanted. He stood up and knelt in front of her. "Cass, I'm in love with you and I don't want you leaving here tomorrow without me telling you that."

"Sid—"

"Let me finish, okay, Cass, I fell in love with you the day I met you. You were scared as hell you had been through more hell then I have ever known and you were still a fighter. You won me over and I don't want to lose you." Sid took his skull ring off his finger. "I know this isn't the kinda ring a woman wants when being asked to marry a guy, but it's all I have right now. I love you—I love you more than I have ever loved another human being and I don't want you leaving here tomorrow without you knowing that. Will you please marry me? I promise when you come home, I will have a better ring for you."

Cass looked at Sid and looked at this amazing gift this man was offering her. She knew he meant every word he said. She looked at Sid and looked at the ring he had offered her. "Yes, of course I'll marry you—and there isn't anything wrong with this ring. It's beautiful. A little big, but beautiful."

Sid slid the ring on her finger and leaned in and gave her the most amazing kiss—at least in her mind it was. "It's getting late, we should call it a night." They entered the house and went into Cassandra's room. They curled up next to one another. Cass scooted back into Sid's body and thought to herself, *This is a perfect fit*. As she drifted off into a peaceful sleep, she knew that this was where she was meant to be, and this was the man she was meant to be with. She'd gone through hell to meet him, but in her mind it was worth it, if it meant when all this was over she could spend the rest of her life with him.

18

Cass woke suddenly and looked around the room in a panic. For a moment she had forgotten where she was and that she was safe. She'd just had another one of her terrible nightmares. She always felt helpless and more scared after having one, and she hated that feeling.

She knew it was early. The sun was just starting to peek its way through the blinds. She thought of the night before. Had it all really happened or had it just been a dream? She looked down at her finger and saw Sid's token of love sitting there in all its glory. She was amazed that this man beside her, who, she felt, could have any woman he truly wanted, had chosen her to spend the rest of his life with—even after knowing everything that had happened to her.

There was no way she would be able to go back to sleep, so she quietly got up and hopped into the shower. She got dressed and walked out into the sun room, quietly shutting the door behind her. Cass went into the kitchen and decided to make breakfast for everyone. She got the bacon and sausage in the oven, cracked all the eggs to make scrambled eggs, and decided she would make homemade biscuits as well. She wanted everyone to have something good to remember, since she didn't know when they would be together again.

"Something smells good."

"Morning, Tiny."

"Sid not up yet?"

"No. I thought it would be better if he slept in—less time to think about what's happening today." Tiny nodded his head just as Sid walked into the room.

"Morning all." He walked over to Cass and put his arms around her. "How come you didn't wake me up when you got up?"

"I wanted to make everyone a nice breakfast before you all woke up. I wanted a little time alone to think."

Everyone sat down at the table and was just about to eat when the doorbell rang. Cass looked at Sid with concern in her eyes. Sid gave her a reassuring smile that told her she was safe and it was okay; he got up from the table and went to see who was at the front door. Ryder walked into the kitchen. "Sorry to startle you all."

Cass looked at Ryder and smiled, "Grab some breakfast." Nobody said much during breakfast everyone was deep in their own thoughts. "I have something I want to say." Everyone stopped eating and looked at Cass. "I know I keep saying this, but I want to thank all of you again for what you've done for me and what you are about to do for me today. I want you all to know I love you dearly and I'm so grateful you are all a part of my life. The only good thing to have come out of all of this, is all of you. As strange as this is going to sound, if Pope hadn't done what he did, we would never have met. This is the only silver lining in all of this mess."

Sid told them he also had something he wanted everyone to know. "I've asked Cass to marry me when all of this is over and she said yes." Everyone stared at both of them. Shelley told them she was thrilled and couldn't wait to help Cass with the wedding plans, and that she would love nothing more than to be able to call her her sister-in-law. Tiny got up and walked around the table and gave his brother a hug and told him he was really happy for them both. Ryder just sat there looking at Cass. When she looked over at him, she saw a look in his eyes—she wasn't sure what it was, but it made her feel sad and she didn't know why. Ryder stood up and congratulated them both, then excused himself. He said he had a few calls to make.

The morning went by quickly and before they knew it, people started to arrive. Ryder suggested that it would be best if Cassandra went to her room. He felt it was best that no one saw who she was—it was safer for everyone that way. Sid followed her, shutting the door behind him. He walked over to the window, where she was standing, and put his arms around her. "Cass, please listen to Ryder when you go. Okay? He will keep you safe. Promise me."

"I will, if you promise me you will stay safe and be here when I come home." He pulled her closer to him and they held onto one another. "I don't want to go, Sid."

"I know, baby. I don't want you to either, but this is what we have to do to keep you and everyone safe."

"Is it too late to hop on your bike and just disappear?"

Sid laughed. He lifted her head up so he could look into those baby blues that he loved so much. "I love you, Cass. Please don't forget that, and promise me you will stay safe and do what they ask. And promise me that as soon as it's safe, you'll come home to me."

Cass looked at Sid with tears streaming down her face. She promised him she would do everything she had to do in order to come back home to him—come back home to them all.

"I love you more than I ever thought possible, Cass."

"I feel the same way, hun. Please stay safe, Sid. If you're okay, then I'll be able to get through this."

Sid leaned over and kissed her and didn't stop. There was a knock on the door, Tiny opened the door and said it was time. He came over to Cass and put his arms around her and told her to stay safe. They would be here waiting for her to come home. She hugged Tiny tightly and whispered, "Thank you for everything."

Shelley walked in and Cass pulled away from him. She looked at Shelley and both women grabbed onto one another—neither one wanted to let go. Cass whispered, "Please watch over these guys. You know if you don't, all hell will break loose and I won't be around to help you kick their asses." They all laughed. "Seriously guys, watch out for each other. As long as you are all safe, I can get through what's coming next. Just remember, I love you all.

Ryder walked into the room with a helmet and told them it was time to get going. They had a long ride ahead of them. Cass went to Sid and kissed him one last time.

"Cass, if you get scared, just look at this ring and know I'm there with you and everything is going to be okay."

Ryder handed Cass the helmet. "Put it on," he said, and turned around and walked out of the room.

Everyone was waiting outside. Ryder thanked them for the help they were about to give them today. Someone piped up, "We're all family, brother. When a member needs help, we're here—no questions asked."

Ryder, looked at Cass and Sid. "It's time." Cass grabbed onto Sid and didn't want to let go. Sid held her tight and told her he loved her and he would see her soon.

Everyone headed for their bikes. Sid's bike was in front of Ryder's, and Tiny's was behind. Cass got on behind Ryder and closed her eyes. She didn't want to see Sid. It was hard enough knowing that at any minute she would be seeing him for the last time. For how long, nobody knew, and she knew she couldn't handle that. So, not seeing him separate from the group, she felt, was better for her state of mind.

Cass put her arms around Ryder's waist. All around her she could hear the thunder of the bikes starting up. Then they were moving. It was happening; her heart was pounding so fast she thought she was going to pass out. Ryder must have known something was up. He gently patted her hand with his and left it on hers for a moment and gave her hand a squeeze. Cass held onto Ryder and laid her head on his back, She kept telling herself it was going to be okay—*You'll be back before you know it.*

Cassandra wasn't sure how long they had been driving. The noise of all the bikes around them was actually calming. She knew by the slight motion of the bike that they were leaving the group. She could feel the bike lean a little to the right. She opened her eyes and held on tighter. With tears rolling down her face she said "I love you, Sid," into the wind, hoping that he would hear her words. Ryder patted her hands and gave them a gentle squeeze.

They drove all day, stopping only for bathroom breaks. It was starting to get dark, Ryder decided to pull into a motel. He told Cass not to take her helmet off. She nodded. She sat quietly on the bike. When Ryder came back out, he hopped on and drove the bike to the back of the building, where he unhooked the saddlebags, and went inside to their room. Cass took her helmet off. Once she got inside, she stretched, and looked at Ryder. "Can I please call Sid?" She knew Ryder would say no, but she had to ask.

"I'm sorry, Cass—you know you can't."

"I just thought I would take a chance at you saying yes." Ryder gave her a weak smile and told her to go and have a shower and he would order them some dinner. She grabbed the saddlebag and went into the bathroom. The hot water felt good running down her body, her butt was sore from sitting for so long on the back of the bike. Cass finished, and got dressed. Ryder told her that the pizza would be there shortly, so he was going to grab a shower—and she was not to answer the door if anyone came knocking.

A short time later there was a knock on the door. Cassandra went into the bathroom Ryder didn't want anyone to see her face. They ate their dinner quietly. Cass wasn't very hungry. She was worried about Sid and everyone at home.

"I'm going to gas the bike up so we don't have to do it in the morning. I want to hop back onto the highway as soon as we get up. Keep the door locked and don't answer to anyone."

"I won't, I promise."

"Finish that pizza. I'll be back soon," Ryder got up and left, shutting the door behind him. Cassandra really didn't want any more to eat so she wrapped the rest of the pizza up in some paper towel. She didn't know who this person was she'd be staying with, or where she'd be staying, and she figured they might not want to spend much money on food for her—so this would give her a little to eat for a day or two. She knew only too well how to ration out her food.

Cassandra curled up on one of the beds. She was so tired it didn't take her long before she was sound asleep. Cass was startled awake by someone pounding on their door. It was a man's voice. She panicked. Pope had found them! When she looked around the room, Ryder wasn't there. *Oh my God, they got Ryder.* She jumped out of bed, looking for somewhere to hide. She saw the closet door, got inside, closed the door, and curled up into a ball. She lay there and didn't make a sound. The pounding continued. Her mind was racing and the fear was once again digging in deep; she wanted Sid, she wanted Big Daddy, but no one could help her now. She was all alone.

Finally it went quiet, but she wouldn't move. If she stayed completely still and quiet, maybe Pope wouldn't find her and he would just leave. She was exhausted and eventually she drifted back off to sleep.

Ryder came back, opened the door, and flicked on the light. Where the hell was Cass? He called her name and checked the bathroom, but she wasn't there. Where the hell had she gone? He'd told her not to leave the room. He started to panic. He looked at the chair, the saddlebags were still there. He looked inside the bag and found the pizza wrapped up in a piece of paper towel. *What the hell,* he thought to himself. Ryder knew he shouldn't, but he called Shelley. "Shell, it's Ryder." She could hear the concern in his voice. She asked him what was wrong and he told her that he had gone out to gas up the bike, stopped for a drink at the bar, and when he came back, Cass was gone.

"What do you mean—she's gone?"

"Just what I said. I told her not to leave the room and she isn't here."

"Ryder, she has to be, she wouldn't have left. She promised Sid she would do what you told her to."

"Shelley, I don't know what to tell you. The bags are here, she even wrapped the leftover pizza up and put it in the saddle-bag—what the hell is going on?"

Shelley told Ryder that Cass had done the same thing when she first came to stay with them. She told him that when Cass got scared, she would hide. Once she'd found her sleeping in the closet. "Ryder, did you check the closet?"

He walked over and called Cassandra's name and gently opened the door. There she was, curled up sound asleep. "She's here."

"Thank God."

"Shelley, don't tell Sid."

"Okay, but please remember she is going to be that scared girl you found behind the bin. You've taken her from the place she felt the safest, so it's going to be hard for her to trust and feel safe right now."

Ryder asked how everything was at home and Shelley told him all was good—as good as it could be. The charity ride was great and everyone made it home safe. Shelley asked when they would get to where they were going. He told her by the follow-ing night, if everything went according to plan. Ryder hung up the phone and sat on the end of the bed, staring at Cass. He wondered what the hell had happened in that room to have scared her so much. He got up and went over to the closet and gently picked her up and laid her on the bed.

"Ryder?"

"Ya, darlin', it's me."

"I'm scared."

"You're safe, Cass, I promise you."

"Please don't leave again."

"Cass, why were you hiding in the closet?"

She told him what happened—about the guy pounding on the door and him not being there. She thought maybe Pope had got him and the only thing she could think of was to hide and maybe he wouldn't find her. Tears were rolling down her face—she was shaking with fear and Ryder didn't know what to do. All he wanted to do was hold her close to him and let her know everything was going to be okay. He loved her and would protect her with his life. Ryder told her he was sorry he hadn't been there, but he was there now, and he would make sure she stayed safe.

He got her to lie back down. He was just about to walk away, "Please don't go. Stay here with me, please."

He knew he shouldn't, but he didn't care—he had feelings for her, though he would never cross the line and hurt Sid. He knew Cass wouldn't either, but he wanted to be close to her just this one time. He lay there next to her, put his arms around her, and whispered, "You're safe, Cass, I promise." She snuggled into him, and as she drifted off, she thought to herself, *A perfect fit.*

Ryder was up at the crack of dawn, sitting on the edge of the bed watching her sleep. He wanted to give her a little longer—they had another six hours or so before they reached their destination. Cassandra started to stir and he just sat there looking at this lady who had stolen everyone's heart, including his. He hadn't felt like this since Christina was alive. He was in deep thought, when he heard, "Good morning."

"Morning, Cass." Cassandra looked at Ryder. He looked so tired—and something else. But she couldn't put her finger on it so she asked him if he was okay. He told her that he was fine, but as soon as she was ready, he wanted to get going—they had a long ride ahead of them.

Ryder grabbed the bags. He thought about saying something about the pizza but decided he wouldn't say anything. He thought about what Shelley had said the night before and decided it was better to just let it go.

They drove all day, making only a couple of stops along the way. Finally Ryder stopped in front of a little house. He got off the bike and looked at Cass. They had arrived. Cass got off the bike and took off her helmet. She looked at Ryder and he could see the fear in her eyes, so he put his arm around her and assured her that she would be safe here. He trusted his friend with everyone and everything that was important to him.

Cass looked up at Ryder, "I'm important to you?"

Ryder looked down at Cass. "More than you know."

19

....

Ryder rang the doorbell. Cass stood by the bike, not knowing what to do, and thinking—should I just stand here or should I run? How did she know this guy wasn't another Pope? She trusted Ryder, but she had been wrong before, and after last night she wasn't sure about anything. She shook her head and told herself to stop it. She trusted Ryder and she knew he wouldn't leave her anywhere that would put her in harm's way, she was being foolish.

Ryder rang the doorbell again and Cass could hear two dogs barking from inside the house. Suddenly the front door flew open and a tall, lean man, with tattoos everywhere, opened the door. Cassandra thought to herself, *That one on his head must have hurt like hell.* She had a few tattoos herself, so she knew how painful they could be in certain spots. She stared at this man with the mean look on his face.

"Who the hell is ringing my doorbell?"

Ryder looked at the guy standing in the door. "Who the hell do you think?"

The guy stepped forward and Cass thought for sure they were going to come to blows. "Brother, good to see you—it's been too long." They both embraced and said their hellos.

Cassandra stood by the bike, not sure what to do, when Ryder motioned for her to come over to them. But she found her body wouldn't move. Ryder walked over to her. "It's okay, darlin', I promise you." He put his arm around her waist and guided her to the front door. "Cassandra, this is my good friend, David." Cass looked into the man's face and backed into Ryder. She was scared. David could see the fear in her eyes, and his facial features softened.

"Hi, Cass. It's nice to meet you. Why don't you come in? You must be tired.

Ryder guided her into the house. The two dogs were waiting inside to greet everyone. Cass loved dogs, but the bigger one scared her. "This is Bruiser and Willow." Cass looked down at the two dogs: Willow was a tiny girl, but Bruiser, on the other hand, was a big boy. He was nothing but pure muscle. If he wanted to, he could probably rip her apart. Bruiser came over to her and she grabbed Ryder's arm and went behind him for cover. David chuckled, because everyone knew that Bruiser was a big mush pot and just liked being loved—he told her that Bruiser wouldn't hurt her, he just wanted to say hi.

They all went into the living room and sat down. If Cass could have sat any closer to Ryder, she would have been sitting on his lap. "Sorry, brother—Cass had a hard night last night and she's a little off her game. She usually isn't this scared."

"That's okay. New surroundings can be scary. How long you staying, Ryder?"

"I'm gonna head back tomorrow."

Cass looked at Ryder, almost in tears. "Can't you stay a bit longer, please? You can't leave so soon Ryder—please." Cassandra pleaded with him.

He looked at her and he knew he couldn't leave her until she was a little more comfortable with her new surroundings. "I can stay for a couple of days, but Cass, I have to go back Wednesday."

Cass looked at David and then back at Ryder. "Okay."

David and Ryder talked. Bruiser came back over to Cass and laid his head on her knees. Ryder was about to say something, when David shook his head—so the boys just kept talking. Cassandra started to feel a little more comfortable with Bruiser. She started to rub his head, and you would have thought Bruiser had died and gone to heaven. He crawled up on the couch next to her and laid his head on her lap.

"Looks like you've made a friend for life." Cass smiled a little and told David he had two beautiful dogs.

Ryder got up from the couch and Cass grabbed his arm. "I just have to go make a quick phone call."

"Can I talk to Sid?"

"You know you can't."

"But if *you're* gonna call him..."

"Cass, I need to call Josh." Ryder knelt in front of her, "Darlin', as soon as Josh gives the okay you can call whoever you want. The reason we came to David's is so you would be safe."

"Am I?" Ryder looked at her. "Am I really safe here? I don't mean to be ungrateful or disrespectful, since David has opened up his home, but you know David—I don't."

"Do you trust me?"

"Yes, you know I do."

"Then I'm asking you to trust David: he's a good person and he is the only other person I would trust to keep you safe, other than our family back home." Ryder got up to make his call and David sat there, looking at Cass.

"Can I ask you a question, David?"

"You can ask me anything."

"Why did you let Ryder bring me here? Do you know why I'm here?"

"No, I don't. Ryder called me and said a friend of his was in trouble and needed a safe place to stay—so I told him to bring you here."

Cass continued to ask David questions and he answered every one of them. She started to feel a little more comfortable with him—not too comfortable, but at least she wasn't feeling like she was going to crawl out of her skin with fear.

Meanwhile, Ryder made his call to Josh. "Hay Josh, it's Ryder. I just wanted to let you know that you can do what you need to do."

"Are you sure she's safe?"

"Ya, she's far away. They can't get to her where we are."

"Good, I'll head over now to get my search warrant. I'll call you when it's done."

"Josh, she wants to talk to Sid and I know she wants to call her mom."

"Ryder, you know we need to get all the evidence we can and make sure he is arrested, before we can even think about that happening. I'll let you know as soon as it's okay for her to make those calls. Remember, we still don't know who is helping him out."

"I know. We'll wait to hear back from you, then."

"I'll call you as soon as I have news."

Ryder went back into the living room to tell them that Josh was on his way right now to get the search warrant and he would call them as soon as he could. He said he would let them know when it was safe for Cass to call Sid and her mom.

David stood up and told Cass he would show her where she would be sleeping while she was there. Ryder went out to his bike to bring in the bags. Her room was on the main floor just off the living room. It had its own small bathroom with a shower. "I hope you'll be comfortable here."

"Thank you, it's very nice—and I promise I won't cause you any trouble."

David looked at Cass. "I didn't think you would," he said with a smile. "I know this has to be scary for you, Cass, but you have my word I don't want anything or expect anything from you while you're here. I would, however, like to help you deal with all that has happened to you. Maybe in a better way, so that when things get stressful for you again, it won't be so hard on you. Stress and fear can play havoc on our bodies and on our spirit."

"I would like that too. I hate being scared all the time and I hate what it does to Ryder and everyone back home."

"If it's okay, David—could I have a shower and get cleaned up?"

"You do whatever you want, Cass. This is your home for now." David turned around and was about to leave the room.

"David?"

"Yes."

"I have no money to give you for board. Will you be expecting me to do other things for payment?"

David looked at her with a questioning stare. "Like what, Cass?"

She looked towards the floor and said, in almost a whisper, "Sleep with you or your friends."

David walked towards her and she backed up, until there was no place left for her to go. "Cass, you don't have to do anything you don't want to do. I don't expect you to sleep with me or anyone else, unless it's something you want to do."

"I don't want to. I'm going to marry Sid when this is all over with, he is the only man I want to sleep with."

"Well then, Sid is one lucky guy." David said with a smile.

"No, I'm the lucky one."

David smiled at Cass and told her that all he expected from her was to keep the house clean and be good to his dogs—and if she liked to cook, well that would be great too.

Ryder walked into the bedroom and placed the saddlebag on the bed. Cass got her clothes out and put them away. She took the pizza out of the bag and placed the two pieces behind the toilet tank, just in case things weren't as they seemed. It was one thing to say those things when Ryder was there, but when he went home, things could be a whole lot different.

Cass had a shower and laid down. She was tired and all she wanted to do was talk to Sid. She wanted to hear his voice so he could reassure her that everything was going to be okay—but since she couldn't, a little sleep was the next best thing.

"Ryder, so what's going on with her?"

Ryder told David everything, he thought David had the right to know what he was getting into. David sat there and listened to everything Ryder had to say. He began to understand a little more why she was acting the way she was acting. It was now making sense to him. Ryder told him about what had happened the night before: how he'd found her in the closet and how she'd hidden the leftover pizza in the bag. "David, if this is going to be too much for you, let me know and I will figure something else out."

"No, this is the best place for her. I'll keep her safe and try to help her heal. She has a long road ahead of her, but here is a good place for the healing to start."

Bruiser started barking and running back and forth, trying to get into the house. "What's up with him?"

"Something's wrong." They both looked at each other—Cass? Both guys headed for the door; they could hear crying coming from her room. Bruiser bolted through the door and went straight for Cass. She was curled up in the corner by the bed. Bruiser went and laid by her feet, waiting for her to touch him.

"Bruiser," she whispered. He got up and went to her side. She was shaking like a leaf.

"Darlin', what's wrong?"

She looked up at Ryder and David. "I had a bad dream. Ryder, call Sid please."

"Cass, you know we can't."

"I'm begging you, please call him and make sure he's okay, please Ryder. I won't ask for anything else. Please, I need to know he's safe. I need to know they're all safe."

David walked out of the room and came back a few minutes later and handed a phone to Ryder, "Call Sid. It's a burner—we can toss it after the call."

"Cass, this is a one-time-only. It's not safe. You're putting everyone in danger, even David and the pups."

"Please, Ryder. I won't ask again, I promise." Ryder looked at her and knew she needed this more than anything. He looked at David and asked him if he was sure.

"Ryder, dial the number or I will."

"Sid, it's Ryder. Cass needs to talk to you."

"Is she okay?"

"She's having a hard time. Sid this is a one-time call—this can't happen again. Cass, here you go. You have two minutes, no longer." Cass nodded her head.

"Sid, are you there?"

"I'm here baby—you okay?"

"No, I had a dream that Pope and his friends found you guys. Are you sure you're all okay?"

"Cass, we're all good. We miss you like crazy."

"I miss you all. I wanna come home. Please come and get me."

"Soon, baby, soon. Cass, I love you and you need to stay where you are until it's safe. Can you do that for me?"

"Okay, Sid. I hate these nightmares—they're so real and it scares me. Sometimes I don't know if they're real or not."

Ryder told Cass she needed to hangup now.

"I have to go, Sid. I love you. And tell Shell and Tiny I'm okay."

"Cass, just remember they're just dreams—they're not real. I love you, baby."

"I love you too, Sid."

Ryder took the phone and hung up. Everyone turned in for the night. Cass couldn't sleep—she tossed and turned, and finally she got up and went into the living room, where Ryder was lying on the couch. "Are you awake?"

"What's wrong, Cass?"

"Can I sleep with you, please?"

Ryder sat up. "Darlin', there isn't enough room here for the two of us."

"Then come in my room—please, just for tonight?"

He got up and walked Cass back to her room and got her back into bed. He knew he shouldn't crawl in bed with her again, but he couldn't say no to her. He loved her too and he wished he didn't, but he did. He put his arms around her, and as they both drifted off he told her that he loved her.

Ryder spent the next two days getting her ready for him to go home. He took her shopping to get anything else she might need during her stay at David's place. He and David showed her around the area. Cass was feeling a little more comfortable at David's, so much so that she took her pizza out of it's hiding place and threw it in the garbage.

Ryder knocked on her bedroom door. "Can I come in?"

"Of course you can." He sat on the side of the bed and asked her to join him.

"I have to go home tomorrow, but before I do, I want to give you this. It's a prepaid Visa card with two-thousand dollars on it, so if you need something, you get it."

Cass took the card and told Ryder thank you, but she didn't need it. He didn't have to do this for her, he'd already done so much for her. Ryder told her that he knew he didn't have to, but he wanted to. He explained to her that he cared about her and wanted her to know that when he left, she didn't need to stress out about things such as having enough food. He didn't want her to feel that she was dependent on David for anything.

"Cass, all I want you to do while you're here is heal and stay safe. Please don't do anything that will draw attention to yourself, and promise me that you'll be careful."

"I promise. Would I be able to go out of the house alone? The beach is just down the road and I would love to go down there—or if David will let me take the dogs for a walk?"

"I can't see why not. Just promise me when you do leave the property, you wear the sunglasses we got you—just as a safety precaution."

Cassandra promised she would and asked if he had heard from Josh yet. He told her he hadn't, but as soon as he did he would let her know.

David came home from work early that night and they all sat in the backyard They had a nice dinner and chatted. David handed Cass a cell phone. "I got you this today: it has my number programmed in it, in case you need to get in touch with me. You need to have this on you at all times, but you have to promise you won't call anyone else."

"You didn't have to do this. But thank you, and I promise I won't call anyone."

It was getting late and David said goodnight. He told Ryder if he didn't see him in the morning, to have a safe trip home and to keep them posted as to what was going on. "Cass, there's a key to the house on the kitchen counter, in case you want to go out or take the dogs for a walk." She thanked David and told him to sleep well.

"Are you going to be okay Cass?" Ryder asked.

She looked at Ryder and put her hand onto his and told him not to worry, she would be fine. She was going to do as he asked and use this time to heal—so that when she came home, all the bad stuff would be behind her and she could move on with her life with all of them.

Ryder suggested they go to bed he needed to be up early and get back on the road.

Cass went to her room and Ryder went and laid down on the couch. How he wanted to go in and curl up behind her one last time, but he knew he couldn't. She belonged to Sid, and he wouldn't do anything to jeopardize that. He finally drifted off to sleep when he was woken up by the sound of a phone ringing. He sat up and realized it was his cell. "Hello."

"Ryder, did I wake you?"

"Who's this?"

"It's Josh, sorry for calling you so late, but I wanted to let you know that we have arrested Pope."

"What? When did this happen?"

"A few hours ago."

"Josh, I need to wake Cass up—she needs to hear this from you. Hold on a minute," Ryder got up and knocked on the door. "Cass, are you awake?"

"What's wrong?"

"Josh is on the phone." Ryder went and crawled into bed next to her. "Go ahead, Josh, I have you on speakerphone."

Josh told them both that at 6:45 that evening, Pope had been arrested and had multiple charges against him. Josh told them that so far he had been charged with kidnapping, unlawful confinement, rape, assault, and battery. They were trying to get him to flip on his friends, but he didn't think that would happen any time soon… but they would keep trying.

"Cass, we searched his home and found all the evidence you said you had left. You were a smart lady—everything was exactly where you said it would be. We also found your personal items hidden up in the attic: all your clothes and your purse with your ID."

"Josh, can I come home? Can I call my mom?"

"I'm sorry, Cass, you have to stay put for a little while longer. It has been brought to our attention from a reliable source, that there are people looking for you, and until we're able to determine if the threat out there is real, you need to stay put. I'm sorry—it's not what you want to hear, but that's the best I can give you right now."

"Is everyone at home going to be safe or are they in danger?"

"No one's name has come up other than yours. I've spoken to Tiny and Sid, so they're aware of what's going on and they'll keep an eye out." Josh said his goodbyes and said he would call as soon as he knew anything else.

Cass and Ryder lay there, processing everything Josh had told them; neither one said anything. Cass curled up next to Ryder and he put his arm around her as they both drifted off to sleep.

Ryder woke up early, grabbed a shower, and got ready to head home. Cass was already up. She had woken up early and had a coffee waiting for him with some breakfast. "How long have you been up?" Ryder asked.

"Not long. Come sit and eat—you need something before you go."

He sat down and ate his breakfast and asked her if she was going to be alright, and if she needed anything else before he left. She told him that she'd be fine: she was just going to take this one day at a time and wait for him to call her and tell her when it was finally safe to come home.

Cassandra walked Ryder out to his bike. She put her arms around him and told him to please stay safe, and if he could get a message back to them to let them know he got home, she would appreciate it.

Ryder started his bike and looked at Cass. "You good, darlin?' she leaned in and kissed his cheek. "I am, because of you. Be safe." She gave him one last hug and then he was gone.

20

....

Life went on after Ryder left. He got a message to them, through a club member, that he'd made it home safe and would talk to them soon.

A few days after Ryder had left, David wanted to know how Cass was holding up. She told him she was just trying to make it through each day without having a meltdown.

Cass was enjoying sitting on the beach. It was peaceful and it helped her to relax. Listening to the water rolling in and out—and just the calmness around her—made her feel better. She was glad that Ryder had brought her here. He was right, this was the best place for her.

Over the next few weeks, David and Cassandra had long conversations. She found him so easy to talk to, as he listened to everything she had to say and he wasn't judgmental. He allowed her to feel the way she was feeling, but he also helped her to see that there were better ways to deal with her feelings. This seemed to make her feel better about the situation and, most of all, better about herself. She still had the nightmares, but for some reason they didn't seem as scary as they once had.

Every day, she woke up and did her morning meditation that David had taught her. It brought her a kind of peace that she had never known. She was thankful for that—she hadn't felt this good in a very long time. Cassandra knew she owed David more than she could ever repay, but she knew that somehow, one day, she would. He was a gift that she would cherish for the rest of her life. She was becoming Cassandra again and she was glad.

Four months had passed since she'd come to stay with David. True to his word, he never asked anything of her that she wasn't comfortable doing. Almost every day she and the pups would go to the beach and play in the water, and then, when Willow was tired, they would come home. Bruiser could have gone on for hours. He loved to chase the waves in and out, but they would come home and continue to play in the backyard until he was tuckered out and didn't feel like playing anymore.

Cass would tidy the house and cook meals every day. Sometimes she and David would cook together, depending on what time he was able to get home from work. Life was good. She thought about everyone, every day, and couldn't wait until they were together again. Most of all, she missed Sid and Ryder. Sid was truly the love of her life and she couldn't wait until they could finally be together, but Ryder had become someone very special to her. She knew in her heart that she loved him as well, but she also knew Sid was the one her heart ached for. She just had to keep reminding herself that this is how it had to be for now.

There were days when Cass would go to the beach by herself and leave the dogs at home. She wanted a little time to just sit there and listen to the water roll in and out and enjoy the beauty that was around her. There was a feeling of utter peace that she felt deep inside herself.

It was a Friday afternoon and Cass was starting to head home from the beach when she noticed a guy walking towards her. She kept on walking, but changed her direction. Something was off and she wanted to see if he was trying to get to her. The guy got closer and for some reason she started to feel uneasy. There was something off about this guy. She pulled her phone out and pressed David's number. He answered on the third ring. "Hi Cass how's it going?"

"David, I'm on my way home from the beach and there is a guy walking towards me on the beach who's making me uneasy."

"Why?"

"I don't know, but every hair on my body is standing on end."

"Is there anyone else close by, like a group of people?"

"Ya."

"Head over to them now and stay on the phone."

"I will." She could see the guy following her, through the corner of her eye; she kept on talking to David. Cass got to the group of people that were sitting around a bunch of surfboards.

"Excuse me."

"Hey, what's up?" They all turned and stared at her.

"I'm sorry to interrupt your conversation, but there is a man over there that is making me really nervous. Would it be okay if I stayed with you? My friend is on his way to get me."

They all looked at the guy, standing alone and staring in their direction. A few of the guys got up and were about to head over and confront him.

"Please don't. He could be dangerous."

They looked at her. "We got this, girl."

"NO!" Cass said in a panicked voice. They stopped and looked at her. "I'm sorry. I've recently gotten out of an abusive situation and I don't know if he is a friend of my abuser—if he is, he is dangerous. Please... my friend will be here in a few minutes."

One of the guys replied, "I'm Ridge. Come and sit with us till your friend gets here."

Cass kept her sights on the guy, who was walking back and forth like he was looking for someone. "Where are you on the beach?" she heard David ask. She looked, and told him just left of the cabana hut. He told her he was almost there and to stay put. A few minutes later she saw David heading over to where she was, so she stood up. Ridge asked her if she was okay and she told him yes, that this was who she was waiting for.

"Cass, you okay?" She nodded and introduced him to the group. David had seen these guys around the beach before, when he did a little surfing, David asked her if she recognized the guy who was following her. She told him she didn't—she didn't even remember seeing him on the beach before. David told her to stay with the group. He was going to see what the guy wanted. Cass asked him if they could just go home. David looked at her—she knew that look, so she sat back down.

The guy saw David coming and suddenly turned and started walking in the other direction. Cass was scared. David caught up to him and put his hand on his shoulder. They had words, and David turned around and headed back to Cass. "Ridge can you do me a favour?"

"Anything, bro."

"Keep an eye on this guy till I get her out of here."

"Sure thing."

"Let's go."

Cass got up and thanked them all for their help. Ridge told her that it was no trouble, and that anytime she was on the beach she was welcome to come and join them. She thanked them and then headed to the car with David.

She sat quietly in the car—David looked deep in thought. She didn't want to make him any angrier than he already seemed to be. "Did they find me?" David didn't answer her she knew there was trouble ahead. She just wasn't sure how much trouble there was going to be.

They seemed to be taking a different way home, it was taking too long to get back to his place. It was only a twenty-minute walk from his place to the beach. Cass sat quietly in the car. Finally, they arrived back at his place. David was just about to get out of the car when she put her hand on his and stopped him dead in his tracks. He turned and looked at her. "Did they find me?"

He didn't want to scare her—she had come so far since she'd arrived—but he also didn't want to lie to her either. "I think so."

"How? I've been so careful. I always have my sunglasses on, I haven't called anyone. How could they have found me?" David told her he didn't know, but he had a gut feeling that trouble was about to come knocking on their door.

When they got into the house, David sat down and stared at his phone. "We need to call Ryder," he heard her say. He shook his head, no. "You call him or I will, David." He sat there looking at her. She didn't know it, but inside he was beaming, full of pride. He thought to himself, *Had this happened two months ago she would have curled up on the floor in the closet, but look at her now*—she was standing there, trying to take control of her life and he couldn't have been more proud of her. David asked for her cell phone and she handed it to him. He dialed Ryder's number.

Ryder looked at his phone when it started to ring, but there was no number showing. He had no idea who was on the other end.

"Hello"

"It's David."

"Why are you calling? Is everything okay?"

"I think they found Cass."

"What?"

David repeated himself and told Ryder that he believed they'd found her. He wasn't sure if they knew where she was staying, but they knew what area she was in.

"How the hell did that happen?"

"I don't know, but it has. Now we have to figure out what we're gonna do."

Cass thought to herself, *Enough of this shit*. She took the phone out of David's hand, which shocked the hell out of him. "Ryder, it's Cass. Come and get me, I'm coming home."

"You can't—we'll figure something out."

"You and Sid come and get me or I will find another way of getting back to you. I have lots of money left on the Visa card. I'm done hiding and that's the end of this conversation."

Ryder and David were both stunned at what had just happened. Cass handed the phone back to David and said she was going to pack her bags and they'd better figure out what the hell they were going to do, and do it fast.

A short time later, David went to Cassandra's room. He stood there staring at her and watching her pack her bags. "I'm proud of you, Cass." She stopped and looked at him and asked him why. He told her for one thing it took guts, taking the phone away from him the way she did. He wasn't sure if that had ever happened to him before. They both laughed. "You're not the same person you were four short months ago. You have changed, and you have become stronger and more sure of yourself."

She walked over to David and hugged him. She whispered into his ear, "You are the reason I'm the way I am now." She pulled away from him and stuck her hand out. "Hi David, I'm Cassandra Elizabeth Taylor. It's nice to meet you." They both laughed and David said it was nice to meet her too. They sat down on the bed. "So what are we going to do now?"

"Ryder and Sid will be here the day after tomorrow and we'll figure it out when they get here. Ryder is going to call Josh and let him know what's going on."

"David, I'm done hiding, I'm taking my life back—and that starts today."

21

....

Cassandra stayed home; she could no longer go to the beach. It wasn't safe any longer. They had noticed a few cars that looked similar, passing the house all day and into the evening. David figured they were trying to catch a glimpse of her so they could find out what house she was living in. She hated that this was happening and she hated that David and the dogs were in danger now because of her.

Ryder called and said he had spoken to Josh and he'd agreed to let Cassandra come home. He didn't like it, but Ryder had told Josh that they didn't have a choice—she was coming home whether they liked it or not. Josh explained to Ryder that there had been a break in her case, that Pope was finally starting to name names—Josh said that hearing Cassandra was in danger was all it had taken. Josh explained to Ryder that Cassandra still couldn't call her mother, even if she was coming out of hiding. Ryder told Josh that he agreed and promised she would wait for the time being.

The day seemed to drag on. It seemed like the entire day was running in slow motion. Cassandra tried to keep herself busy, but there wasn't much to do. David threatened that if she didn't stop pacing, he would tie her to a chair. They both laughed and she told him that, like her mother, patience had never been one of her strongest virtues.

She decided, that before David grabbed the Duck Tape, she would go outside and sit under the apple tree. She imagined she was sitting under the big oak tree at home. She started to take slow deep breaths to calm down her inner spirit. She was so grateful that she had listened and learned from what David had taught her. She was a much better person for it and she knew she had truly become the person that Sid deserved—but most of all the person she deserved to be again.

Cassandra was speaking with her inner self and the universe around her. She was constantly working on healing and forgiving. She still had a long way to go, but she was proud of how far she had come, She was deep in all these thoughts, when the sound of a couple of motorcycles slowing down in front of the house brought her back to the present.

Cassandra jumped up and ran for the front door. She peeked through the blinds and saw two guys she cared deeply for getting off their bikes. She saw Sid's face first and she flung the door open, ran outside, and jumped into his arms. She didn't care who saw her; she was with Sid now, and that was all that mattered.

Sid held onto her and wouldn't let her go. He looked at the lady he loved and missed more than anything as he bent over and kissed her. She kissed him back with more passion then either of them had expected. Ryder interrupted their reunion and told them they needed to get into the house. Cassandra looked at him, then back at Sid—she smiled and said okay. Ryder and Sid looked at one another. She agreed with Ryder, no questions asked. Sid smiled and thought to himself, *Who is this woman and what did she do with Cassandra?* This wasn't the lady that had left, a little over four months ago. Cass took Sid's hand in hers, turned around and headed into the house. There was no way in hell she was letting him go, now that she had him there.

She introduced Sid to David, to Bruiser, and to Willow. Bruiser wasn't sure about Sid. He had become very protective of Cass and he wasn't sure Sid could be trusted, but he saw how happy she was around him and must have decided he was one of the good guys because in a short time he'd warmed up to him, like they'd known each other for years.

When they were all in the house, Cass walked over to Ryder and put her arms around him and said thank you. He put his arms around her and whispered into her ear that there wasn't anything he wouldn't do for her. She hugged him back and told him she knew that. She also told him that being with David had been exactly where she needed to be and she was sorry that she'd given him such a hard time. "I want you to know that I'm where I am now, both mentally and physically, because you took charge and made me do what no one else wanted to do. You and David mean the world to me. I love you both and will be forever in your debt."

Ryder leaned over and kissed her forehead, and told her as long as she was happy and safe that's all that mattered to him. She looked into his eyes and told him that's what she wanted for him as well—he deserved that and so much more.

Ryder and Sid got Cass caught up on what was going on back home. Sid told her that Shelley was excited that she was finally coming home where she truly belonged. Shelley told Sid to make sure he told Cass that she would be living with her and Tiny until the wedding, and she wouldn't take no for an answer. She missed Cass and wanted her close by for a little while longer. They all laughed.

Ryder told everyone what Josh had told him and reminded Cass again that she still couldn't call her family, because if these people found out that she had been in touch, it could be dangerous for them all. Cassandra agreed immediately with Ryder. He looked at her, "Who are you and what did you do with Cass?" They all laughed and then she got up, walked over to Ryder, put her hand out and said, "I'm Cassandra Elizabeth Taylor. It's nice to meet you. The Cassandra you met all those months ago no longer resides in this space. This is who I was before all this happened and it's because of all of you that I'm back. I'm sure the Cassandra you knew will try to peek her head out once in a while, but this person you see in front of you here and now is the person I am and will continue to be."

They continued to talk about everything and anything. They had a great night together, but it was getting late and it had been a long day for everyone. They said their good-nights and everyone turned in. Sid stayed up with Cass and they talked for a few more hours. Finally they just curled up in each other's arms and drifted off to sleep.

Tiny and Shelley arrived a couple of days later and the first thing Shelley said was, "Where is she?" David pointed to the door on the right. Shelley stood in the doorway, staring at Cass as she packed some last-minute items. Cass could feel someone behind her. She turned around and saw Shelley. She dropped what she had in her hands and embraced her dear friend. They both cried and checked each other out to make sure the other was good, then hugged again and sat on the bed and talked for what seemed like hours. Finally they got up and went into the living room with everyone else. Cass walked over to Tiny and gave him a big hug. He hugged her back, pulled away, and gave her a once over saying, "Looking' good' hun."

"I am good and I'm glad I'm finally coming home,"

"We are too, Cass—maybe now Sid will stop walking around like a lost puppy."

She walked over to Sid, put her arms around him, and looked up, "You missed me?" He smiled and winked at her, "Just a little."

David's cell rang. Whatever was being said wasn't good; he looked at everyone and said trouble had arrived at the front door.

Ryder and Sid went and looked outside and sure enough there was a group of guys in plain clothes standing by some vehicles across from the house. David made a call. He told everyone to stay in the house, some of his friends were on their way. About twenty minutes later you could hear the thunder of bikes coming down the street and pulling in front of the house. Ryder called Josh and told him what was going on and Josh told him not to do anything. He was going to make a call and would call him right back.

Ryder looked at Cass. "Stay in the house." She nodded her head, "Shelley, make sure she doesn't come out." Both ladies looked out the window and watched what was going on from the safety of the inside of the house. Both sides were sizing the other side up.

Cass was really worried that something bad was going to happen. She was afraid that someone was going to get hurt or get arrested and it would be all her fault. The guys from across

214 | SUE ADAIR

the street finally started to make their move and come over to their side. "It's certainly going to get interesting fast," Shelley said to Cass.

"We have a warrant for Cassandra Taylor and we believe she's inside this house."

"Let's see it," David said.

"See what?"

"The warrant."

"And who are you?"

David told him that he was the owner of the house. The guy handed him the warrant. David looked at it and laughed. "This is bogus and not enforceable since no judge signed off on it." David ripped the piece of paper in half and threw it at the guy. "Get back in your car and get the hell out of here."

Things started to get heated. Words were being thrown back and forth and Sid was just about to nail one of the guys, when Cass pushed Shelley out of the way, flung the door open, and hollered his name. Everyone stopped what they were doing and looked at her. "Get in the house!"

"No." She walked down the front steps and stopped just behind David. "You're looking for me, well here I am."

David grabbed her arm, "Don't go any further Cass." She looked at him and told him that it was okay.

"The warrant is phony."

"I know. I heard."

Sid walked over to Cass and grabbed her arm and told her to get her ass back in the house. She smiled and put her hand on his face. "I love you, hun, but I can't do that." She took a few steps forward and spoke to the guy who seemed to be the group leader. "What's your name?"

"Kevin"

"So—let me guess, Kevin: you and your friends here are here for Pope. Is that correct?"

"Yes, and we're bringing you in."

"I'm not going anywhere with any of you. The only place I'm going when I leave here is home."

"I don't think so, lady." Cassandra looked Kevin square in the eyes and told him she knew so. She said she wanted to tell them all a story. It all started late one night when her car broke down on a deserted stretch of road... "when your friend Pope showed up he threw me in the trunk of his car. Later, I woke up chained to a bed in a dark room with no light, and your friend Pope beat me and raped me repeatedly." Cass told them how she had been locked up in his house for almost a year. She hasn't been able to speak to family or friends to let them know she was still alive because they were afraid that some bad people would harm them if they found out.

The four guys stood there with smug looks on their faces. Cass told them she knew all about the little game that they have been playing and about the lives they'd destroyed. She said that hell would freeze over before they got their hands on her. The look on their faces told her that there suspicions were correct. All four gentlemen started looking very angry and a little nervous.

Three police cruisers showed up and Ryder's phone started ringing. All of the officers got out of their cars and walked over to the group of guys. "I'm Officer Jennings. We got a call about a disturbance in the neighbourhood—what seems to be the trouble here?"

Ryder looked at Jennings and said, "This call is for you." He passed him his phone. Officer Jennings spoke to whoever was on the other end, took out his note pad, and started writing. Then he handed the phone back to Ryder.

Officer Jennings turned to Kevin and his buddies. "Gentlemen, can I please see some ID." The guys just stared at him. "Gentlemen, I won't ask again—ID please." The other officers gathered around Kevin and his friends. They looked at each other, and one by one took out their identifications and handed them to Officer Jennings.

"Gentlemen, I'm glad you are all here. I'm informing you that there are arrest warrants out for all of you. Please place your hands behind your head." They looked at one another and did what they were told, they knew it was all over now. As they were being cuffed, Officer Jennings read them their rights and asked them if they understood—they all responded with yes. One by one they were loaded into the cruisers and were taken in to answer for their crimes.

It was finally over Cass thanked everyone for their help. She turned around and walked into the house, got her bag, and came back outside. Cassandra walked up to her family and told them it was time to go home.

She hugged David, thanked him for everything and told him she expected him and his dogs to be there when she and Sid finally tied the knot. He promised that they would be there. Cass gave Willow a big hug and put her arms around Bruiser and thanked him for all his help, "I love you, Buddy boy—you are my lifesaver." She kissed the top of his head.

Sid placed her bags into the truck, handed her a helmet, and said, "Let's go home." And they did just that.

22

....

Time went by quickly, now that she was home. Cass was staying with Shelley and Tiny, just like Shelley wanted her too and to be honest, she wanted to be there as well. This was her home—however she did spend weekends with Sid, at his place.

She woke up every morning and performed her meditation faithfully—she'd missed it one day and had found it completely threw her off, she wasn't able to keep focused. She was on edge all that day and for a person with her demons, that wasn't a good thing.

Cassandra spoke to David almost daily, and when she was on edge, even after her meditation, he seemed to be able to help her calm her inner self. Sometimes all it took was hearing his reassuring voice to let her see things clearly again.

Days went by and they hadn't heard any more chatter about anyone looking for Cassandra. No one felt or saw any suspicious-looking guys around the neighbourhood or at the Roadhouse. Though she still hadn't spoken to her mom, Cassandra knew that day was coming soon; she trusted Josh and was waiting for the okay. Josh promised that before the trial started they would let her make the calls she was dying to make. She knew she could have called her mom at any time she wanted to and there was really nothing anyone could really do about it, but this voice in her head kept telling her to just wait.

Cassandra and Sid had gone back to visit David a few times. Bruiser always went crazy when she pulled in front of the house and got off the bike; David said Bruiser always knew when she was coming for a visit, about ten minutes before she got there. He would start pacing back and forth and cry—and God forbid you didn't have that door open the minute she got off that bike. He would have ripped the door off the hinges just to get to her. They had a bond that was like no other.

Sid and Cassandra spent every day together after work, but they hadn't been intimate yet. They'd tried and as much as she truly wanted to, she was just not ready for that part of their life and she felt terrible about it. She loved Sid with all her heart and she knew he loved her and would never hurt her, but the damage that Pope had caused had left its mark, and there was nothing anyone could do but wait until she was ready. Sid told her over and over again that he loved her and wasn't going any-where. She was worth the wait.

It had been three months since Cassandra had come home from David's and she was now working at the Roadhouse with Shelley and Tiny. She was their new bartender and she turned out to be really good at it. The patrons liked her and she enjoyed her new job. It was agreed shortly after she started that she would stay behind the bar. She tried waiting tables, but some of the guys got a little too touchy-feely and Cass didn't do well with that.

One beautiful Tuesday morning Cass decided to walk to work. The sun was shining, the birds were singing, and there was a beautiful breeze. It was a great day all around and she couldn't wait to complete her shift Sid was going to try to teach her how to drive a bike. She was terrified, but excited at the same time—they all made it look so easy.

Cass was in the middle of restocking the bar when she got a call from the DA's office, saying that Mr. Harper would like to speak to her in person. She told him that she wanted her family to be there, so they made the appointment for Friday at six o'clock.

Before they knew it, it was Friday. Cassandra meditated twice that day and spoke to David for their daily chat. She promised him she would let him know what the meeting was all about. Cass kept herself very busy. She cleaned the house from top to bottom, went to the grocery store, picked up some chicken that she marinated, picked up potatoes for the barbecue, and made a large Caesar salad and a couple of apple pies for dessert.

Everyone got home around the same time. Ryder was the last one to walk through the door. They sat around the table and talked about their day, just like they did almost every night when they had dinner together. Although Sunday, it was mandatory they had a family dinner—and if truth be told, it meant a lot to all of them. Family was very important to them all. When Ryder walked in, he asked what smelled so good. Cass told him the menu for supper and said they had all better be hungry there was lots to eat.

At 6 pm. on the dot, the doorbell rang. Cass got up from the table and looked at everyone—"I've got this." They were all nervous even though there didn't seem to be any need to be, but old habits were hard to break.

Cassandra opened the door "Hi, can I help you?"

"Yes, I'm looking for Cassandra Taylor. I'm Mr. Harper. We have an appointment for six."

"I'm Cass. Please come in—let's go into the kitchen, every-one's here. Mr. Harper walked in behind her and Cass intro-duced him to everyone. "Can I get you a drink or something?"

"No thanks, I'm fine."

"Please have a seat."

Mr. Harper sat down and cleared his throat. "The reason I asked to meet with you today is that I have some news about Mr. Pope. First of all, I would like to thank you personally for being so patient with the process we've had to go through. I know it hasn't been easy not to let your family know you are alive and safe, but after today, you will be free to do just that. Mr. Pope has waived his right to trial."

Cass and everyone looked stunned. "Why?" Cassandra asked.

"Well, his attorney informed him that there was so much damning evidence against him, that the judge might be a little lenient with him if he didn't put you and your family through a long court battle—a battle that he would definitely lose. The sentencing date is set for May 17. Would you like to read a vic-tim's impact statement? You have the right to address Mr. Pope. The judge will take what you say into consideration when he is handing down his sentence. Is this something you think you might want to do?"

Cassandra sat there staring at her hands. She wasn't sure what to say. She didn't know if she could stand being in the same room as Pope. She looked at Sid and the rest of her family sitting there; she didn't know if she could put them through that again.

Cassandra tried hard to swallow the lump in her throat. "I don't know," was all she could manage to say. She got up and went into the bathroom. She felt she might be sick.

Sid followed her. "Cass, talk to me." She looked at him and turned around and walked into his arms.

"I don't know if I can do that."

"Why, hun?"

"Because all of you will be there and will have to relive it all over again."

"Cass, look at me—this isn't about us, this is about you and what he did to you and you getting closure. Baby I honestly believe this is something you need to do. I think if you don't, you won't be able to close that chapter of your life and move on."

She held onto Sid as tight as she could. He told her he would support her in whatever she decided to do they all would. She looked up at Sid and nodded her head okay.

They went back into the kitchen and joined everyone else at the table. Cassandra looked at Mr. Harper and said she would like to read a victim impact statement. She looked at everyone. "I'm sorry to put you all through this again. If this is something any of you can't go through again, please know I understand."

Ryder put his hand on hers and squeezed it. He told her they would all be there. They needed to be there so they all could shut that door for the last time. Both Shelley and Tiny agreed. Shelley reminded her that they were family and family was always there, no matter what. Cass looked at Mr. Harper. "My family?" she said with a smile.

"You're free to get in touch with any family members, when-ever you want. We have spoken with Mr. Pope and he has assured us that there is no longer anyone looking for you. With his group now all locked up, waiting for their day in court, Mr. Pope is now on his own."

As much as she hated Pope for what he had done to her, she felt bad for him. She had all these amazing people in her life and he had no one, and to her that was sad.

"Cass, if there is anything I can do to help you just call this number." He handed Cass his card, "I'm going to leave you all now—there is a lot for you to process. Please don't hesitate to call me, Cassandra."

Mr. Harper got up from the table. Tiny walked him to the door while everyone sat there in silence. Cass looked at Sid, "Can we please go for a ride?"

"Sure we can."

Cass looked at everyone. "I mean all of us." Ryder told her, whatever she wanted.

23

....

It had been a few days since Mr. Harper had come to Tiny's and told everyone the good news—that it was finally over and Cassandra was free to contact her friends and family whenever she wanted to. It's what they had all been waiting for since the ordeal began. They were relieved that it was finally over and they could move on. But what should have been the most exciting time for Cassandra, now wasn't. She hadn't slept much since that day, her nightmares had returned—these dreams were different from the ones she had had before, but terrifying to her, nonetheless.

Cassandra was having a really difficult time trying to figure out how she was going to tell her family and friends that she was alive and safe. She should have been excited and relieved that it was all over, but to her, the nightmare was still going strong. It was just a different kind of nightmare now.

She tried to go to work, but she just couldn't do her job. Her mind wasn't able to handle what she needed to do, and the thoughts that were running through her head interrupted her duties. Tiny told her to take as much time as she needed—her job wasn't going anywhere.

No one could come close to imagining what she was going through. How could they? It was easy for someone to say, "just pick up the phone and call," but it wasn't that easy. She had been missing for almost two years and nothing about any of this was easy.

Cass was no longer Pope's hostage. She now was a hostage in her own mind. Fear can be a powerful thing and why she was so scared now, she didn't know—and that scared her even more. She tried to meditate, but not even that was working. She didn't know what to do and she felt like she was spiralling out of control and was going to crash. She was scared that Sid and the rest of them would say they had had enough—really, who could blame them?

Being held captive and chained to a bed and abused in the most brutal ways changes a person; even the happiest of times can bring fear flooding back. It was like the roller coaster she'd been on while she was with Pope.

There were days that were good and days that were terrifying—so even though Cass knew that she was safe and free, the fear was always with her. She just hid it well from the others.

Cass was sitting in the backyard, deep in her thoughts, when Shelley came and told her there was someone here to see her.

"Can you please tell whoever it is, I'm just not up to talking to anyone right now."

"No, I can't, Cass. It's Josh."

She got up and went into the house. They hadn't seen Josh in a while and she was scared that he had bad news to tell them.

"Hi, Cass, how are you doing?"

"Terrible."

Josh could see that things were not good for her and he felt bad for what she had gone through and still was going through.

Shelley excused herself and told them she would be upstairs if they needed her.

"Can I get you something to eat or drink?" she asked Josh.

"No thanks, I'm good. I just wanted to stop in and check in on you to see how things were going. Have you called your family yet?" Cass shook her head, no. "Can I ask why?" Cassandra looked at Josh with red, swollen eyes and told him she didn't know how.

"I have been gone for such a long time, maybe it's best if I don't."

"You really don't mean that, do you? Do you honestly think they have given up hope on you coming back to them?"

Cassandra told him she knew he was right and everyone told her the same thing, but she just didn't know how to do it. "Well, maybe this will help." Josh handed Cassandra all her personal items that had been found in the attic at Pope's place. He told her that her suitcases were in the front room and that they had found her car, or what was left of it at, a chop shop that they'd raided. "Your phone is in that bag. Maybe it will help you figure out what to do now. Please let me know if I can help." Cass looked at Josh and then back at her phone and she asked him if he could stay for a little bit. She wanted to call Sid. Josh said he would stay as long as she needed him.

Cassandra called Sid, but he didn't answer so she called Ryder.

"Hi darlin', what's up?"

"I'm looking for Sid—is he there?"

"Everything okay?"

"No. Josh is here and I just need him to come home."

"I'll send him home now."

"Ryder, can you please come too?"

"We'll be there shortly—we're just closing up shop."

"Please drive safe."

"Always, darlin.'"

Cassandra called Shelley down and asked her to phone Tiny and ask him to come home. She needed to talk to everyone.

In no time, everyone was walking through the front door. Shelley came down from upstairs. Sid came over and put his arms around Cass and asked her if she was okay. She looked into his eyes and said, "No," with a weak smile.

"Can everyone please sit down." They all looked at Cass. They were really worried about he—she looked so tired. She looked like she did the day they found her, minus the bruises and swelling.

"Baby, what's going on?"

Cassandra looked at Sid. "Josh brought my belongings back from the evidence locker. My wallet, my cell, and all my personal effects. I need your help in trying to figure out how to call my family. I've been racking my brains since Mr. Harper told us I could call them. I've been trying to figure out the best way to do this and I just can't. I'm lost on how to do this. I know it should be easy, but for some reason it isn't and I don't know why. Please help me figure this out. I need to do this before I go crazy."

They sat there talking back and forth when finally Shelley said she had a thought. "Josh, can you call Cassandra's mom and tell her that Cass has been found and that she has asked that everyone come here. She feels seeing everyone at one time would be easier for her because she could explain what happened to her once, rather than multiple times?"

"I can do that. How does that sound to you, Cass?"

"Someone needs to be there with my mom when that call comes. She can't be alone." Tiny spoke up and asked about any friends or family that lived close to her mom. No one did, but Cass thought of one man that was always in the area… and that was Big Daddy.

Cass picked up her cell and sat there staring at it. It was deader than a door nail—of course it was, what was she thinking? It hadn't been used in forever. Sid gently took the phone from her hands, went over to the counter and plugged it in. The light came on: it was charging.

A few minutes passed. Cassandra got up and went over to her phone. Her entire body was shaking. She unlocked the screen and looked into her contacts and found his number. She wrote it down and went back to the table.

Everyone was looking at her, no one was sure what to do. They were waiting for her to say something, but she couldn't. She was so scared that she was shutting down and they could all see it; they knew the signs, they had seen them before.

Ryder, being Ryder, took charge. He took the piece of paper from Cassandra's hand and dialed the number. The voice on the other end said, "Hello." Cassandra burst into tears the minute she heard his voice and got up from the table and ran into the other room. Sid followed her.

"We've never met. My name is Ryder Stone. Can I ask if you are behind the wheel?"

"Who are you and what's this about?"

"Do you know a Cassandra Taylor?" There was silence on the other end.

"Who the hell are you?"

"I don't want to get into this while you're driving. Can you please call me back when you've pulled over someplace safe? It's about Cass." The line went dead.

Cass and Sid came back into the room and she looked at Ryder. "I don't know, darlin'—the line went dead."

Cassandra's legs gave out from under her and Sid caught her just before she hit the floor. He placed her in the chair next to Ryder and she sat there shaking and sobbing. Sid had his arm around her and told her that it was going to be okay. Everyone had tears in their eyes and their hearts were breaking, watching Cass fall apart again.

Ryder's phone rang. He looked at it and everyone looked at him. "It's him." He put it on speaker.

"Hello, this is Big Daddy, but you can call me Marvin. What's this about and how do you know our Cassandra?"

"My name is Ryder and I'm a friend of hers."

"What do you mean you're a friend of hers. She's been missing for almost two years. What kinda game are you playing?"

"It's no game I can assure you. Cass is here with me and my family."

"Bullshit. Cassandra would have contacted her mother if she was able to. I'm hanging up now—don't call my number again or I'll call the cops, you sick son of a bitch."

Out of nowhere, Cass blurted out, "Big Daddy it's me, Cass!" The phone went quiet again. "Are you there? Please say something."

"Who the hell is this?"

"It's me, Cassandra."

"Bullshit." Cass started to cry. "I'm hanging up. You people are sick to pull something like this."

"How are Rick, Mack, and Pickle?" There was silence. "You once asked me if I was in trouble who was I gonna call? and I said, "Big Daddy," and you gave me a thumbs up. You brought me dinner when I was at the hospital when my dad was there; you brought me chicken and said that if Mohamed wouldn't come to the mountain for dinner then the mountain would come to Mohamed. You brought me extra crispy chicken and biscuits." Still nothing. "Please, Big Daddy, I need your help." They could hear something, so they knew he was still on the line.

"Cassandra, is that really you?"

"Big Daddy, it's me. I need your help—I'm begging you."

"Cass, what's going on? Where are you? Where have you been?"

"I promise I'll explain everything, but I need a favour... please?"

"I'll do anything, Cass, you know that. What do you need me to do?"

Cass started to cry and couldn't control herself—it was all too much for her. She was talking to Big Daddy; someone she'd thought she would never speak to again.

"Marvin, this is Officer Josh Wilks. I was the officer in charge of Cassandra's case. Up until a few days ago, it wasn't safe for Cassandra to reach out to her family and friends, but she is now able to do so. We were wondering if you would be able to go to her mother's home, so that someone could be there when I call her. Cassandra doesn't want me to call unless someone is there with her mom."

"I'm actually close to there now, but my time for driving is almost up—I won't be able to get there until tomorrow."

"Can you tell me where you'll park your truck and I'll have someone come and get you. We understand this is a lot to take in, but Cassandra doesn't want to wait any longer."

Marvin explained to Josh where he would be parking and what time he would be there. Josh told him someone would be waiting there for him when he arrived. Josh asked him to please not call anyone else and tell them—for Cassandra's sake. They needed to do this in a way that was going to make it easier for her.

Marvin agreed. He asked if he could speak to Cass once more before they hung up. Josh told him he was sorry, but Cass couldn't talk anymore—the phone call had taken everything out of her.

"Is she okay?"

"She's been through a lot, but she's getting there."

"Please tell her I'm on it."

Josh told them that it was going to be a few hours before the phone call to Cassandra's mom happened, so Sid took Cass to her room and convinced her to lie down and get some rest. Sid curled up behind her and pulled her close and held her tight while she cried. She finally cried herself to sleep. She was exhausted and Sid was scared for her.

Josh excused himself and made a few phone calls. He came back to the table and told everyone that the arrangements had been made for someone to pick up Marvin. "So what now?" Tiny asked.

"Well, we need to figure out where everyone is going to go to be reunited."

Shelley spoke up "They will come here; this is where Cass feels the safest." They all agreed.

Sid walked in as they were talking. Ryder looked over at Sid. "How is she?"

"She's sleeping. She's exhausted she cried herself to sleep. I'm really worried about her." He looked at Ryder and asked him if he would call David and see if he and Bruiser could possibly come there—she was going to need them all.

Ryder got up from the table and put his hand on Sid's shoulder. "I'll call right now, brother." A short time later, Ryder returned and told Sid they were on their way.

Sid sat there rubbing his hands together. Shelley could see that this was really tearing him up inside. She knew that Sid had never loved anyone as much as he did Cassandra. She got up and put her arms around him and asked how he was holding up. He shook his head and the tears started to roll down his face. "I'm so worried about what all this is doing to her. I know that this is a good thing, but still—how much can one person take? I'm afraid this will break her and I'll lose her altogether."

"Sid, we're not going to let that happen. Cass is a fighter—look at how far she has come. This is just a little set back. It's just one small ripple in a very big pond. We're all here for her and we'll help her deal with this. We're family, remember, and that's what we do."

Sid leaned his head into Shelley and told her, thanks.

"I have a question for all of you." Everyone looked over at Josh. "Are we going to wake Cassandra up for the phone call to her mom?"

Sid said, "No."

"We saw what hearing Marvin's voice did to her—hearing her mom's voice could throw her over the edge. So no, were not."

Tiny looked at Sid and asked him if he was sure that that was the right thing to do. "Look, I know you all love Cassandra just as much as I do," said Sid, "but she is my old lady and this is my call and I'm saying no." Sid got up from the table and went back to check on Cassandra.

It was eight-thirty when Ryder's phone rang again. It was Marvin, telling them they were just pulling into Cassandra's mother's driveway. "I'll call you back in a few minutes," and then the phone went dead.

At eight-forty, Ryder's phone rang again and he put it on speaker. "Mr. Wilks, I have Mrs. Preston with me."

"Hello Mrs. Preston, my name is officer Josh Wilks. I'm calling you in regard to your daughter, Cassandra."

"Oh my God—have you found her? Is she alive?"

"Yes, ma'am, she's safe."

"Where is she? Can I talk to her?"

"I'm sorry, ma'am, but that isn't possible right now. Your daughter's been through an ordeal and it took everything she had just to speak to Marvin for the short time that she did. She is with a family that loves her very much."

"I don't understand—why is she with these people?"

"Ma'am, I promise you, you will know everything when you come here."

"Cass has asked me to speak to you on her behalf and to make arrangements to have her closest family and friends come here to see her. She would like to see everyone on the same day. What she is going to tell you will be very difficult for her to talk about and for you all to hear, so she would rather not have to repeat her story."

"This family that she is with—who are they? Are they with you now?"

"Yes, ma'am, they are."

"Please call me Faye. May I please talk to them?"

Everyone looked at each other. Tiny nudged Shelley's arm and Shelley looked at him. "Um … Hi Faye, this is Shelley"

"Hi Shelley. How is it that my daughter is with your family?"

"Faye, two of my family members found Cass. She was in a terrible state when they did."

"What happened to her?"

"I'm sorry, Faye, this isn't my story to tell. I can tell you that we all love your daughter very much. We've kept her safe all this time and will continue to keep her safe."

"Is she in danger?"

"Not any longer. We found out a few days ago that the threat no longer exists. She was given the okay to contact you and to let you know she is safe and alive."

"So, why did it take a few days to call me? I don't understand."

"Faye, all I can say is Cass has been through hell and back and this has shaken her to her core. I promise you everything will become clear when you talk to her."

"Shelley, please keep her safe."

"Faye, when you meet my family you will see and understand why this has been the safest place possible for her to be. We won't let anything happen to her, you have my word—there isn't anything we won't do to keep her safe."

"Thank you. So now what do we do?"

"You have Ryder's cell number—when you know when all of you will be able to get here, please call him and we'll make arrangements on our end. Can you please make sure you call Cassandra's friends Jayne, Nat, and Liliana? She'd like them to come. And please, Faye, only Cassandra's closest family members. This is what she wants. Faye, please don't take offence for what I'm about to say, but we are very protective of Cassandra. She has become part of our family. I realize you are all her family, but there will be guidelines you all must follow for this visit and anyone not following them will be asked to leave immediately—and if they won't go, they will be removed. Cassandra is our number-one priority; her health and mental state is our only concern. Please understand that Cassandra has been with us since she was found and we'll protect her at any cost, even from her family members."

"Shelley, how bad was it?"

Shelley started to tear up remembering how Cassandra was the day they met. "Faye—think of the worst thing that could happen to you and then multiply it by a million and that probably wouldn't be enough. All I can say is she must have come from strong people because I think it's the only reason she survived this ordeal."

"Shelley, I'll be in touch with you as soon as I have the information"

"Okay, Faye. Take care of yourself and we will see you soon. Faye, please don't give Ryder's number to anyone."

"I won't. Please just take care of my daughter. I'll talk with you soon."

24

....

David arrived a few days later, with Bruiser and Willow in tow. Cass hadn't said much to anyone since they contacted her family—she didn't come out of her room much either. She wouldn't let Sid near her and had barely eaten anything. They were worried. Nothing they did or said seemed to help her feel any better.

Sid was beside himself. He was mad and frustrated and all he wanted to do was get his hands on Pope and kill him, make him pay for what he did to her. It wasn't fair, she deserved to be happy again. He felt bad for feeling the way he did, but he wondered if they would ever get past this and be happy together, or if this is what their life would be like.

The morning David arrived he walked in on Tiny and Sid arguing about Cass. Things were getting heated and almost came to blows, but instead Sid put his fist through the wall out of sheer frustration. Ryder guided Sid away so that they all could cool down. Everyone was on edge and it was beginning to show.

"Where is she?" David asked.

"Her room," Shelley said. David walked to the door and he quietly opened it. He looked at Bruiser and said, "Cass?" Bruiser was up and in the bed next to her in a split second. She didn't even open her eyes. She put her arms around Bruiser and whispered, "Thank you." David closed the door and went and sat with everyone at the kitchen table.

Ryder and David embraced "Brother, thanks for coming." David backed away and put his hand on Ryder shoulder, "Anytime... What's going on?"

Ryder explained everything: how Cass had turned from this lady who was on top of the world and was now back to being the scared little girl they'd found hiding behind the dumpster. They couldn't understand the drastic change in her and she wouldn't talk to them about it.

"May I speak freely?" David asked, and Tiny told him to go right ahead. "Look guys, to us it seems like this should be a piece of cake, that calling her family and being reunited with them should be one of the easiest thing for anyone to do, but we need to see it from Cassandra's point of view." Shelley asked what he meant. "We need to remember what she has been through—it wasn't just about the physical abuse, it was also about the mental abuse that he inflicted on her. The time I've spent with her makes me believe there were things that happened to her that we know nothing about and she herself may not remember because she blocked it from her mind to protect herself. I've spoken to a friend who counsels people who have gone through Traumatic events, and she said that to save themselves, a person might make themselves believe that it was a bad dream, that it really didn't happen, or just block it out completely. Doing anything else could do more damage to them then they could handle mentally.

She told me that no doubt there was some manipulation to break down her self-esteem, to make her feel worthless. He was making her believe that she was trash and nobody wanted her. Even her family and friends didn't want her. If they did, why wouldn't they have come and gotten her? And that could be part of the reason she stopped fighting and trying to get away. Cass is suffering from PTSD and even though the ordeal is over and she's about to be reunited with her family for the first time in a really long time, her memories or her version of what happened to her in her mind is starting to crack. The truth is starting to come to the surface and she isn't sure what version is true. She's probably afraid that if the bad stuff she blocked out actually did happen to her, nobody will want her, and Pope would have been right all along. She was trash and that's why no one came to help her. She just wasn't worth it."

Sid shook his head. "David we've told her we love her no matter what. We will do anything to help her. She's safe again. What more can we do? How do we show her it's going to be okay and, most of all, that *she* is going to be okay?"

"Deep down in her heart she knows that, but she is dealing with a lot of demons and it would be my guess, from the state she's in now, she's been hiding how she's truly been feeling."

"Why, would she do that? When we picked her up from your place, she was a new person; she said she was the Cass she was before all this happened. She's been happy."

David put his hand on Sid's shoulder, "I know, brother, but she doesn't love me like she loves all of you. With me, she could be herself and say exactly how she was feeling, even if it meant repeating the same thing over and over again."

"But she can do that with us."

"Shelley, I don't think so, because of how much you all mean to her. The look on your faces would have been something she couldn't handle. She thinks she's protecting all of you and she would rather be the one going through the suffering than any of you."

"But we *are* suffering."

"I know, Sid, but in her mind, she is protecting you and she can't see right now what she is actually doing to all of you."

"So what do we do to help her?"

"Give me some time with her—me and Bruiser."

"You're not taking her anywhere. I'm sorry, but this time whatever is going to happen, it's gonna happen here—end of discussion."

David nodded his head. "When is Cassandra's family coming?"

"They're due to arrive this Saturday." David asked Shelley to try and see if they would cancel and come the following week—he didn't think she could deal with them right now.

"Give me some time to try and get her in a better frame of mind, for her sake and everyone's."

Shelley left to call Faye and told her exactly what David had just told them. Faye agreed and promised she would call everyone and postpone their arrival until the following Saturday. She asked Shelley to please keep her in the loop as to how her daughter was doing, and Shelley promised her she would.

Shelley came back into the kitchen and told them Faye agreed and would take care of it on her end and they would see them all the following weekend. "David, I've been doing some research and talking with friends. I have a friend that makes marijuana cookies to help her father calm down at night with his Parkinson's. Do you think this is something that might help Cass? Maybe to relax her a little so she can think more clearly?"

"It's worth a try."

Shelley got up from the table and called her friend. She found out where she got the weed she used for the cookies and the recipe to make them. Shelley handed Sid the address and asked him to go and get some so she could make the cookies tonight. She looked at the men sitting around her table and suggested that if this didn't help her, they needed to call Doc Charles and see what he could come up with—because this couldn't go on any longer. They all agreed.

Ryder left. He said he was going home and if they needed him, he would come back.

Tiny headed to the Roadhouse and Sid went on the hunt for weed. He stopped Tiny on his way out the door and apologized for what happened earlier and promised he would fix the hole in the wall.

"Tiny, it's driving me crazy that I can't help her."

"Sid don't you realize you are helping her? You've been there for her even when she was pushing you away and you kept coming back. She'll remember that when things get clearer in her mind; have faith, Sid, it will get better."

A short while later, David opened the door to Cassandra's room and stuck his head in. Bruiser lifted his head up and looked in his direction and then laid it back down on her side. David walked over to the bed and sat down. "Are you awake Cass?"

"Ya."

"I want you to get up and come out to the kitchen and have something to eat."

"I'm not hungry, David."

"I'm not asking you."

Cass looked at him, not sure what to say next. She hadn't seen this side of David before. "Look, darlin', I know you're going through hell right now, but lying here starving yourself isn't going to help. I want you to get up and have a shower and come out to the kitchen."

"David, I just can't. I'm sorry."

"So what you're telling me is that you're going to let that bastard Pope win."

"What?"

"Well isn't that what you're doing? You're giving up. You're letting him win."

"That's not fair."

"None of this is fair, but you're not going to get better by just lying here feeling sorry for yourself. There are four people out there that are doing that enough for you." David told her he was giving her fifteen minutes to shower and get out to the kitchen or he would come back and throw her in the shower himself.

Sid was back from his weed run and Shelley had started to make the cookies. David told them what he had told Cass and said if she wasn't out in the time he'd allowed her, that he had every intention of following through with what he told her he would do. He needed them to support him.

Sid looked at David. "I won't let you do that to her."

"So, what you're telling me is that you want her to be like this for the rest of her life. It's up to you, Sid, but she is acting like her life is over because of what happened to her. We need to show her that that isn't true. I'm not saying all this will be easy, but we have to change things now before it's too late and she does something nobody will come back from."

Shelley told Sid she agreed with David. For the past few days, she'd been feeling that they were doing Cassandra more harm than good. "Sid, we're too close to her. We need to let David do whatever he can to help her." Sid didn't like it, but he agreed. He knew David was trying to do what was best for Cass. All they wanted was for her to get better and Shelley was right: what they were doing wasn't working.

David looked at his friends and at the clock on the wall. "Time's up." He got up from the table and went to Cassandra's room and opened the door. She hadn't moved. He went into her bathroom, turned on the shower, told Bruiser, "Out," and shut the door behind him. David walked over to the bed, picked Cass up, and put her in the shower. She screamed so loud that Sid jumped up.

"NO, Sid."

"I can't sit here while he does this to her."

Shelley gave Sid a weak smile and suggested he go take the dogs out into the backyard and get some air.

Once Cass had stopped screaming and yelling at David, he told her she had fifteen minutes to be dressed and at the kitchen table or he would be back.

"Why are you doing this to me? I thought you were my friend."

David walked over to her and put both his hands on her face and lifted it up so she could see his face. "Cass, it's because I'm your friend and because I care about you that this is happening. You may have given up on life, but I will be damned if I'm going to let Pope win and take you from us all." David turned around and walked out of the bathroom. "You're down to twelve minutes."

25

....

David spent the next week helping Cassandra get back on track. They started their morning prayers and meditation again, though this time seemed much harder for her— but she was sticking with it. She truly wanted to get better and get back to being herself once again.

Cassandra wanted to be the woman Sid deserved. He had gone through so much with her already, she felt he deserved nothing but the best, and that's exactly what she was going to give him. The fog in her head was beginning to lift—not much, but enough to give her hope that things would get better in time. She was glad Shelley had gotten the recipe for her cookies; they helped her a great deal. She was amazed how this little bit of pot in a cookie made her feel. David was right: she couldn't let Pope win. It was up to her what kind of life she wanted to live and she knew for sure the life she had now, feeling the way she did, just wasn't it.

One morning when they were about say their prayers, she told David that she wasn't sure she believed in God. He sat and looked at her for a few minutes, not sure what to say. He closed his eyes then lifted his head, and asked if she'd ever believed. She told him that until this all happened she'd believed in a higher power, but she couldn't understand why any God would let this happen to her—or anyone for that matter. David didn't have an answer for her; he told her that things happen for a number of reasons and one day she would know why.

"Cass, please have faith that something big, in a positive way, will happen because of this experience. Please just have faith—faith in the future, faith in yourself. There is a reason you're going through this and the day will come when you'll understand the bigger picture."

They talked for hours about the thoughts in her head and about what she was feeling and why she felt the way she did. They went for long walks, and a few times David drove her down to the beach just so she could hear the water roll in and out. But there were times that nothing seemed to help. Cass would get really upset and stressed, and this is where the cookies seemed to come into play. They seemed to help calm and relax her just a little, so she was able to slow down her thoughts and see things in a better light.

She was so glad that David and the dogs were there. Bruiser stayed with her all the time and Willow—well, she was more a laid-back kind of girl. If she thought you needed a little bit of loving she would come over and cuddle on your lap or lie next to you, but she was David's girl—where he went, she followed. You could see the love in her eyes she had for him. Bruiser, on the other hand, seemed to know that Cass needed him right now and it was his job to be there for her. David joked that Bruiser loved her more than him, but they both knew that wasn't true. He just knew somehow that he had a job to do and that job was to help his girl, Cass, feel better—and by doing that, that would make David happy. So in turn, it made Bruiser happy. Nonetheless, she was glad they were all there.

Sid stayed away. He and David had a heart-to-heart talk and David thought that some time apart might help her deal with everything that was going on in her head.

As promised, Shelley kept both Sid and Faye posted daily on what was going on and how she was doing. They were both grateful for that—they both would do whatever it took to help Cass get better.

Cassandra seemed to be getting a little better each day, though she had a very long way to go. In no way was this going to be a quick fix. This was going to take time—and probably a long time, David told her—but he was willing to stick it out and help her work through her problems, as long as she was willing to give it everything she had.

David stayed in constant touch with his friend, Sarah, who dealt with people in Cassandra's situation. She helped guide him through the minefields when they arose. It was a slow process, but this time the end product was going to be a much happier and healthier Cassandra, and that's all anyone really wanted.

Cassandra woke up early Thursday morning and for some reason thought of the letter Agnes had written to her. She had forgotten all about it. She went to the closet and pulled her suitcase down from the top shelf and laid it on her bed. She unzipped the small zipper on the side and stuck her hand inside—and the letter was still there. She pulled it out and held it in her hands and knew right then she needed to see Sid.

"Hello?"

"Sid, it's Cass—did I wake you?"

"No, baby, I was just getting up. Are you okay?"

"I'm doing better. I would love to see you if you have the time."

"I have all the time in the world for you."

"Can you please come over after work?"

"Is this a good thing or a bad thing?"

"I'm hoping it's a good thing. I miss you and just really want to see and talk to you—is that okay?"

"Of course it is. I'll see you later this afternoon. Cass, I love you."

"I love you too, Sid."

Cassandra hung up the phone, put her suitcase back in the closet, and put the letter carefully away in her dresser drawer.

Later that morning, before they started their morning routine, she told David she had called Sid and said she wanted to talk. David asked if she was sure she was ready for that. She looked at him—this was the clearest her head has been in a very long time. Yes, she was positive this is what she needed to do. As for what was going to happen on the weekend when she was supposed to see her family … that she wasn't as sure of.

David looked at her. "Good, I'm glad. I was hoping you were going to do it soon. Good for you, Cass. You're working hard at getting better. Just remember we still have a long road to travel, so please take it one day at a time. Please don't promise anyone what you aren't able to give."

"Well, you're in a good mood today, brother."

Sid looked up at Ryder. "Cass called me this morning and wants to see me."

"How's she doing?"

Shelley says she's doing better. She's had good days and bad, but the good days seem to be outweighing the bad."

"Have you seen her?"

"No. David asked me to stay away for a while."

"Oh I didn't know that."

"Ya—even Shelley and Tiny have tried to stay clear of them both while they're doing their thing."

"I miss her too, Sid."

Sid stood up and looked at Ryder. "You're in love with her, aren't you?" Ryder didn't say anything. He was caught off guard by Sid's question. "You don't have to answer that—I know you have feelings for her. I knew something changed when you came back from David's. I just have one question for you: Do I have anything to worry about? Are you going to try and come between us?"

Ryder looked up "Sid, I would never do anything to come between you and Cass. She loves you and wants a future with you. Would I love for her to be mine? to spend the rest of my life with her?

"Damn straight I would, but not at the cost of hurting you."

"The three of us have been through something that not many people can say they have ever experienced—and it changes you."

"Ryder, I know that Cassandra loves you. You can see it when she looks at you."

Ryder nodded his head. He was at a loss for words and didn't know what to say to Sid, so he said nothing.

"Ryder, I have one favour to ask of you."

"What's that?"

"Promise me you will be there for Cass."

"I will always be there for both of you, whenever you need me."

Sid looked at Ryder and shook his head. "You know what I mean."

"Ya, I do, brother, and you have my word I will be there for her." Sid walked over to Ryder and the two men embraced. "You should take off early, go home and get cleaned up. Maybe stop off at the ice cream shop and get Cass a dish of her favourite."

Sid laughed and told Ryder that she was the only woman he knew that would rather have ice cream over flowers any day. Ryder laughed. "As long as it has nuts and gooey chocolate, she's happy."

Sid arrived at Tiny's place around four, with ice cream in hand, and rang the bell. Cass answered the door. "Why did you ring the bell?" He just smiled at her and handed her the ice cream.

"You might want to put that in the freezer before it melts." She smiled, took the ice cream, and put her arms armed his neck.

"This is more important," she said. She hugged him and he hugged her back. They both just held onto each other, not wanting to let the other go, not wanting it to end. It had been so long since they had been together.

Sid finally pulled away and looked at her. She looked so much better than she had the last time he saw her. "How are you doing?"

Cassandra smiled at Sid. "I'm getting there. Can we take a ride down to the beach and take a walk?"

"Sure."

"Let me go and put this in the freezer—then we can go."

Cassandra put the ice cream in the freezer and went to her room and took Agnes's letter out of the drawer. She put it carefully in her back pocket.

They went to their favourite spot on the beach. There weren't many people in the area because there were too many rocks to walk around, but Sid and Cass didn't care. They walked hand in hand, neither one needing to say anything. They were just glad to be together.

They found the perfect rock to sit on. It was away from the water and it wasn't wet or covered in slime. Cass looked at Sid and touched the side of his face with her hand. He put his hand on top of hers and just held it there. She took it away slowly but kept holding onto his hand.

"I want to say thank you for sticking by me during all this."

"Cass?"

"Please let me say this before I lose my nerve... Most people would have given up on me and walked away. There aren't a lot of people who would have stuck around through all of this and with all that I put you through. As much as I have pushed you away, your love for me has never wavered—please don't think I haven't noticed, because I have. It's just that when we contacted my family, things in my head started to change and I didn't know how to deal with it. I know I love you more than I ever thought was possible to love another human being, and I should have been able to talk to you about what's been going on up here," she pointed to her head. "But they're not nice images, and to be completely honest I didn't want you to have them in your head. There are things that happened to me that I can't talk about, not because I don't think you can't handle them, because I know you can, but because I can't handle you knowing them. I can see the look in your eyes: you wonder why I can talk to David and not you. I'm sorry, I don't have an answer that will make any sense—all I can say is, it just is. Maybe it's because he hasn't been there since the day you and Ryder found me, or because he has been through some crazy stuff as well, or just because he has this feeling of utter calmness about him. There could be a bunch of other reasons I just can't think of off the top of my head. Maybe it's just because I couldn't handle the hurt look in your eyes. From the bottom of my heart, I wish I could talk to you—and I just wanted you to know that." Cassandra pulled the letter from her back pocket and held it with care. "I have never shown anyone this, but I would like you to read it if you want to."

Sid took the envelope out of her hand, carefully took the letter out of the envelope, and began to read. When he was finished, he just sat there looking at it. He folded it up and put it back into the envelope. Sid gently handed it back to Cass and stared into the face of the woman he loved.

Cass held onto the envelope and thought of the woman who'd written it. She cleared her throat. "The lady that wrote me this, meant the world to me, and the reason I wanted you to read it is because the man she spoke about—the one who would make me smile when he walked into a room or when I heard his name, the man that would hold me in his arms at night and let me know I'm safe and will love me through all the good times and bad—Sid, that man is you. I have felt that way about you since that day you picked me up from behind that dumpster. I will do everything in my power to make you feel like I do every time I'm with you. I know I still have a ways to go, but I have a question for you... After this weekend, which I'm sure is going to be a rough one for everyone, when it's over with, and we've had a few days to clear our heads, will you marry me? I don't want all the bells and whistles—just you and me and our family. Pope has taken enough time away from me and us and I don't want him to take any more. I really understand if you can't answer me now, but will you at least think about it? "

Sid sat there and didn't say anything, and she didn't try to make him. She just sat there quietly holding his hand, waiting for him to decide what should happen next.

"Cass, are you in love with Ryder?"

The question shocked Cass. She looked at Sid and knew she owed him the truth. "Yes, I am. I've loved him since David's. But Sid, as much as I love him, I know deep in my heart that you are the man I want to spend my life with. I can't promise my feelings for Ryder will ever change—and if I'm honest with you, I know they won't—but what I can promise you from the bottom of my heart is I will never give you anything to worry about when it comes to Ryder and myself."

He knew that Cass meant what she'd just said. She would never let her feelings for Ryder come between them, and he could see in her eyes that he truly was the one she wanted to be with.

"Cass, all those things you said about how I make you feel, I've felt about you for just as long—and it makes me happy knowing that that is how I make you feel. I agree this weekend is going to be hard, but we'll get through this together—with the help of our family. Hell yes, I'll marry you! How does next Saturday sound to you?"

Cassandra put her arms around him. She told Sid she couldn't wait to become Mrs. Cassandra Davis.

26

....

The day Cassandra had been waiting for was finally here. Today she was going to see her family for the first time in over two years and she had mixed feelings about it. Not because she didn't want to see them, because she truly did, but because she was scared of the thoughts in her head. The thoughts that kept creeping in telling her she was trash and nobody but Pope would truly want her.

David had once told her the mind can play terrible tricks on you, especially when someone as manipulative as Pope has your undivided attention and complete control over everything you do or see for a long period of time. People like Pope can make you believe in anything. David told her to trust in her heart and that feeling in the pit of her stomach that tells you if something is right or wrong.

The morning went by quickly and the closer it got to her family's arrival, the more restless she got. Bruiser wouldn't leave her side but even her best boy being there with her wasn't helping her today. She felt like a caged animal and all she wanted to do was run, run as fast and as far as she could.

"Are you okay?" Shelley asked.

Cass turned around and shook her head. "Not really. I'm afraid I'm going to freak out when everyone starts hugging and kissing me. Shell, I'm not sure I can do this."

"Well maybe it would be better if you weren't home when they arrive. Why don't you and Sid go for a ride to help clear your head. While you're gone, we can have a chat with them and lay down some ground rules."

"Would you really do that for me?"

"Of course I would."

"You guys have done so much for me. How am I ever going to repay you?"

"Cass you keep forgetting your part of our family, whether you and Sid get married or not. You are one of us and we will always be there for you, just like we know you will always be there for us."

Cass gave Shelley a big hug. "What would I do without you?"

"I don't know," she laughed.

She looked at Shelley. "I never want to find out."

Shelley hugged her back. "You never will." Cassandra went out to the garage to talk to Sid. "Excuse me."

"What's up, Cass?" Ryder asked

"Can I please steal Sid away from you all? I'd like to go for a ride, to clear my head, before everyone shows up."

"Are you okay, babe?" Sid asked

"I'm on edge big time. I don't think I want to be here when everyone gets here."

"Go get a jacket on—it's a little chilly."

"Cass, would you like David and me to clear out of here when they get here?" Ryder asked.

"Ryder, if you would rather not be here, I understand—but I'd like it if you were."

"Look, why don't you all go for a ride," said Tiny. "Shelley and I can take care of everything till you get back." "I think I'll stick around just in case they have questions that I may be able to answer," said David

"I'll go get my jacket and we can go," Cass said. "Your gonna come too Ryder?"

He looked at Cass and then at Sid.

"You should come," said Sid. "It's been a while since the three of us went for a ride together."

"I'd like that," Ryder told them both.

"Tiny, are you sure?"

"You guys go. You know Shelley will be all over this."

Riding on the back of the bike, whether it was with Sid or Ryder, always made Cass feel at peace. The warm breeze in her face, the sun shining overhead, and the rumbling and vibration of the bike running through her body, were wonderful. It was truly the only time she felt free of her thoughts about what had happened. She was just watching what was going on in the here and now and enjoying the time with the people she cared about the most.

At 1p.m. on the dot the doorbell rang. Tiny and Shelley went to the door to greet their guests.

"Hi, Shelley I'm Faye."

"Hi Faye. I can see the resemblance—you and Cass look a lot alike. Come in. This is my husband, Tiny."

Jayne looked at Natalie and whispered, "There ain't nothing tiny about that man." Natalie just smiled and nodded her head.

"Why don't we all go into the back room and have a seat," said Shelley. Everyone followed Shelley and found a place to sit. "Can I get anyone anything?" They all said no. "This is our friend, David. He has been helping Cass."

Faye told everyone it was nice to finally meet them and thanked them from the bottom of her heart for all they had done for her daughter.

"Let me introduce you to Cassandra's family. This is her Aunt Sam and Uncle Joe, this is Marvin, who you spoke with on the phone, and this is Liliana, Natalie, and Jayne.

"It's nice to meet all of you. Cass has told us so much about all of you, it's nice to be able to put a face to the names."

"Shelley, where's Cass?"

"Faye she's with the boys. They'll be back soon. We just wanted to talk to you all before they get home."

"Is everything okay?"

"Sam, she's doing better. She has a ways to go, but she's getting there. Look, Cass asked us to talk to all of you. She knows how excited you are to see her and how emotional it's going to be for everyone, but for Cassandra's sake—when she comes in please don't get up and try and hugging her or trying to kiss her. We know that's the first thing you're going to want to do, but please don't. She's afraid that if you do, she'll have a meltdown. Let her come to you. Let her get used to the fact that you are actually here."

"We're her family! She knows us and she knows we love her and want only the best for her," Sam said with an annoyed look on her face.

David stepped in. "Sam Cass that you're gonna see today isn't the Cass you know. This Cass has had to deal with some terrible things. Cassandra is suffering from PTSD. In her heart she feels one thing, but her brain is telling her something completely different and she's struggling to try and figure out which is telling her the truth."

Shelley looked at everyone sitting there and could see how much they all loved Cassandra. "Faye, when Cass first came to stay with us she would hide food because she didn't think we would feed her everyday. Some nights she slept on the floor because that's what she knew. In her words Whores don't sleep in beds, they sleep on the floor like the trash they are. When she was really scared, we would sometimes find her curled up on the floor in the closet. She lived in hell for over a year, so it's been hard for her to adjust to how life really is. All we ask is that you please just take her lead: don't touch her unless she says it's okay and please don't take it personally if she shies away. It's not you or anything you've done, it's just a part of her coping mechanisms. We all care about Cass, and we all want what's best for her—please remember she's been with us for a little over a year, so we're her normal right now." She turned to David. "… Bruiser?"

"Oh ya, I'll let the dogs in." David got up went to the back door—before he opened it, he asked if anyone was afraid of dogs. They all said they were fine. Willow was the first one through the door. "This is Willow and this is Bruiser," he said. Jayne looked at this big hulk of a dog come strutting through the door.

"He's a big boy."

"Yes, he is," David laughed. "Look, we just want you all to know that Bruiser is very protective of Cassandra. If you get too close and he feels Cassandra's fear, he'll come between you and get you to back off or push you away from her completely. He's has sort of become her service dog, in a sense—but he won't bite you, he'll just let you know that it's not cool."

"What's he looking at?" Faye asked. David looked in Bruiser's direction, "Cass should be here in a few minutes. He seems to know when she's almost home… and please don't get in his way when she does. He loves her and he will run you over to get to her, that's his girl."

Tiny laughed, "Ya, there's times when he won't let us near her. He seems to know when she needs space and when she needs his love. Poor Sid doesn't have a chance of sitting next to her when she's upset. None of us do."

Bruiser started running back and forth crying, "They're home." They heard the rumbling of motorcycles pulling in the driveway. Sid, Ryder, and Cass walked in and Bruiser met them at the door. They headed towards the back room, and Cass grabbed Sid's arm. He turned and looked at her.

"You okay?"

Cass shook her head, no.

"Ryder and I won't leave your side."

"Promise?"

Ryder put his arm around Cassandra's shoulders. "You know we won't."

Cass continued holding onto Sid's arm as they walked into the room. Shelley stood up. "Everyone—this is Sid and this is Ryder."

Everyone just sat there and stared at Cass.

"Come on hun, let's sit down." said Sid

The three of them sat on the ledge in front of the fireplace. Bruiser came and sat between Cassandra's legs. She put her arms around him and nestled her head in his neck and held onto him for a few minutes. Bruiser just sat there and didn't move. She looked up at everyone sitting there. She looked at Ryder and then Sid and then back at everyone else. "I'm sorry," she said with tears in her eyes.

Jayne got up and walked towards Cass very slowly and knelt in front of her. Cass looked up into Jayne's eyes "Hi, darlin'. I've missed you."

Cass had always loved Jayne's English accent. She smiled. "Hi Jayne. I've missed you too."

Jayne went to put her hand on Cassandra's knee but she pulled her legs away and Bruiser let out a growl. "Cass, can you please look at me?"

Cass looked back at Jayne.

"I'm sorry, hun," Jayne got up to go back to the couch.

"Jayne—it's not you, it's me. Please stay." Jayne turned around and came back and sat on the floor in front of Cassandra and gently stroked Bruiser's head. "I see all of you and I don't know what to say or do. I love you all and have been fighting to let you know I was alive and okay. I've missed you all terribly, but it scares me that you're all here."

"Why's that, doll?"

Cass looked back at Jayne. "Because right now I should be hugging and kissing all of you and there should be all these tears of joy, my heart is crying inside. I can see the hurt in your faces because that's not happening. My head is telling me something completely different then my heart and I know it's trying to trick me, but it's really hard to make sense of everything."

Cass got as close to Sid as she could and she looked at Ryder and then back at everyone else. Ryder put his hand on her knee. "It's all good, darlin'."

"Cass, why don't we just talk. Okay?"

Cassandra nodded her head okay. "How's Coco?"

"She's good; she's the boss of the dog park."

Cass laughed and Bruiser looked up and laid his head back down on her feet. "She always thought she was queen of the world."

"Yup, nothing's changed."

Cassandra looked at Shelley and Shelley asked, "Do ya need a cookie?" Cassandra nodded, "yes please," and Shelley got up and brought a canister over to her.

Cass took one and told Shelley, thanks. She started to eat it. "When I start feeling scared or nervous and I know the other things I do won't help, I have one of these cookies. It helps calm me my mind down so I can think a little clearer. It seems to slow down all that is going on in my head."

Shelley explained to everyone about how these marijuana cookies helped her friend's father with his shakes due to Parkinson's and it helped calm him. She explained how they'd talked to Cass about them and she'd wanted to try them.

"Mom... how are you?"

"I'm fine, Cass. I'm glad you're safe and you're with people who care about you as much as we do."

"I'm the fortunate one. If it wasn't for these guys and whoever guided me to them, the outcome could have been a lot different. If it wasn't for Sid and Ryder, I don't know what would have happened to me. They saved my life. Sid found me behind their dumpster and when he picked me up I knew in my heart he would be in my life forever. Ryder, on the other hand..." Cass put her hand onto his and smiled at him. "He was not so nice, but I knew deep down he was worried about me and didn't know how he could help."

"I knew you were gonna be trouble and I wasn't wrong, was I?" He winked at her and everyone laughed a little.

Cassandra smiled at Ryder. "Would you have done anything differently?"

"Not a single thing, darlin'. I'm glad we were the ones to help you. Faye, you have an amazing daughter here. She's made our lives interesting, that's for sure, and to be honest, if she wasn't here we would miss her. She is a part of our family now so I guess we're all stuck with one another."

Everyone talked for a while. Marvin got Cass caught up on the news with Mack, Rick, and Pickle, while Sam and her Uncle Joe sat there and listened and watched Cassandra, which made her a little uncomfortable. Her uncle wasn't a big talker when he was around people he didn't know. Liliana and Natalie and Jayne got her caught up on what had been happening with them. When Cass had gone missing, they'd all became a support system for one another and spoke weekly to each other. Cass was happy they'd become friends—that meant a lot to her.

Cass looked at her Aunt Sam. "You're awfully quiet, Aunt Sam." Everyone got quiet.

"We don't know what to say." said Sam

"How have you been?"

"We've been worried about you," said Sam. "And, to be honest, Cass, I'm really worried about what's going on in front of us—your relationship with Sid and Ryder."

"Sam!" Faye said, with a stern look in her face.

"I'm sorry, Faye, but I'm just saying what everyone is thinking."

Cass looked at her mother and gave a little smile and told her it was okay, "I'm going to be honest with all of you. Being anything but, will only hurt my healing process and will only add more stress and insecurity in my life, and I've enough already without adding more. The way I see it, a person may get one true love in their life, where they love each other, faults and all. I've been lucky to have found two of them—unfortunately, at pretty much the same time."

Cass looked at Sid and Ryder and they both smiled back at her and nodded to let her know it was okay. "I know we haven't known each other for very long and we come from two different worlds, but the one thing I do know in both my head and my heart is that I love both of them and I know they both love me. For different reasons, they've helped me in ways I just can't explain—and they both know this. They both know how important they are to me. They each have a place in my heart and they know that too. It's not something we've ever really talked about, but the feelings are there and we're all aware of them. Sid and I are together. We are planning to get married next Saturday and we hope you will all be a part of our special day. Ryder will always be a big part of my life and nothing anyone can say or do will ever change that. I'm not looking for anyone's approval or opinion on this—this is just how it is and will always be."

Cassandra's Uncle Joe shocked everyone by blurting out, "Now there is my Cassie girl. She isn't taking crap from anyone. She knows what she wants and she'll be damned if anyone is going to tell her she can't, not even her Aunt Sam."

Cassandra looked at her uncle with a smile on her face and mouthed a thank you. Joe just nodded and smiled at his niece.

"Ryder and I have never crossed the line, nor will we ever—and Sid knows that, too. I fell in love with Sid the first day we met. Sid is my number-one priority and the man I have chosen to be with."

Everyone sat quietly, not knowing what to say. Sid looked at Cass and leaned over and kissed the side of her head, "Cass is the love of my life, and she is right—both Ryder and myself have known how she has felt for some time and we both know how the other has felt about her. So please don't think this is something new to any of us. We both have a place in her heart and we are both cool with the relationship that we have with each other."

Ryder didn't say anything, and it didn't go unnoticed. Cass looked at Ryder and asked if he was okay. Anyone could see the love they felt for each other, "I am, darlin'. Sid's right—we both love you and we would be lying if we said we didn't, but you and he deserve a chance at happiness with each other and I'm good with that because I care about you both. I've had the good fortune to have loved an amazing woman and I want Sid to have that same chance."

Cass sat there staring at Bruiser, who was curled up at her feet. "Cass?" said David. She lifted her head and looked at him. "Maybe if you explained what happened, it would make it easier for everyone to understand what they're seeing here."

"Excuse me, Jayne," said Cass. She got up and went to the kitchen for a bottle of water. Sid got up to follow her, but Ryder said "Brother…" and shook his head, no, and Sid sat back down.

After a few minutes, she came back and sat next to her mom. Faye looked at her daughter and went to put her hand on hers, but Bruiser lifted his head and let out a growl. Faye put her hand back down in her lap and Cass looked at her mom and thanked her.

"I'm going to tell you what happened—not everything, because I don't think that will help anyone, but enough so you know why things had to happen the way they did and why my feelings are what they are. Please don't interrupt me; it's going to be hard enough for me to tell you this at all. After today I won't talk about it again, so please don't ask me to. Other than the court date coming up I'm finished with this dark chapter in my life."

Cass took a drink of water, then cleared her throat. She told them what had happened. How Pope had abducted her and how she'd found herself chained up in a dark room. How she'd tried to escape and the beating she'd got for trying. She told them about the abuse, both mental and physical, and how she'd believed that her dad and Agnes were there watching over her— she'd felt that she wasn't alone. She told them how she'd finally got free and found her way to the back of Ryder's Bike Shop: the two of them helping her, the police showing up looking for her, how they'd hidden her and got her off the property, getting her to Tiny and Shelley's house without anyone finding out. She continued by telling them how they'd all helped care for her and protect her. How Sid would sit with her every night so she wasn't alone and when she had a bad dream would be there to let her know she was safe. She told them it had been Ryder's plan to get her out of there, and to safety, at David's.

"I'm going to be honest: I don't think things would have turned out the way they did if it wasn't for Ryder. I'm in no way disrespecting anyone or making what they did to help me any less important, but when it was needed, Ryder took charge. He did the things nobody wanted to do and he took the flack because of it." Sid put his hand on Ryder's shoulder and nodded his head in agreement. "The journey to David's wasn't an easy one for Ryder. It had its problems and it sure tested his patience, but he was amazing and helped me through my fears. He stayed with me for a few days after we arrived at David's and held me when I had one of my nightmares. He kept reminding me that I was safe and he wouldn't let anyone hurt me. You have to understand some of my nightmares were not easy ones. I would wake up swinging, fighting for my life because I was reliving what had happened. Ryder gave me a credit card so I wouldn't be afraid of not getting food or whatever else I needed. *He* knew that David would have gotten me anything I wanted, but *I* didn't. I didn't really trust anyone and I thought David might be a totally different person once Ryder wasn't there, but he wasn't. He was so much more, in a good way, then I could ever have expected."

Cass explained all the help she got from David, Bruiser, and Willow. She explained why she'd had to go into hiding and why it had taken so long to arrest Pope, and why she hadn't been able to let them know she was alive and safe. She explained how Pope's friends had found her and how it had all ended, with them confronting the guys outside David's place, and all the people that had been there to help keep her safe. That day she had taken her life back and told everyone she was done hiding.

"When we were told it was safe and I could finally let you know I was alive a whole different kind of nightmares started. I'm sorry it took so long, but our concern was your safety and my mental state, I needed time to wrap my head around the fact it was over. I already put their lives in danger by them helping me—I couldn't take the chance of Pope's friends finding and hurting any of you to get to me. We just didn't know how far these people would go. This has been my life since I went missing. I'm so sorry for what you all have gone through. I wish I could have made this easier for you all in some way. I've nothing more I can tell you, other than I'm okay, I'm safe and I'm loved, and I'm so thrilled to have all the people I love back in my life and in one room." She got up and walked into the kitchen; this time, Sid followed her.

Everyone sat there, taking in everything she had just told them. No one knew what to say. What could you say after hearing everything they'd just heard?

"So, what now, Marvin asked?" Tiny spoke up. "The sentencing date is on May seventeenth and Cass has said she would like to read an impact statement before the judge sentences Pope. When that day is done, it's finished."

Cass and Sid came back into the room. Shelley walked over to her. "You okay?"

"I am." Cass looked at everyone. She asked if there was anything else they wanted to know.

Jayne looked at everyone, "I have one question." Jayne smiled, "I don't know about anyone else but I'm starving. Shall we go out or order in?" Everyone started to laugh.

Ryder stood up and said, "Let's order in. Dinner's on me tonight."

They had a wonderful evening together—everyone getting to know one another they chatted until late into the evening, when finally Faye was the first one to say she was getting tired and would like to call it a night.

Cassandra and Sid walked everyone out to their car. Sid hugged the women goodnight and shook Joe and Marvin's hand. Cass stood there smiling at everyone and said her good nights.

Sid came to her side and put his arm around her; Cassandra looked up and smiled. As the cars pulled away, Cassandra waved goodbye and they went back into the house.

27

....

They spent a lot of time together over the next week, working on the wedding plans. There was a lot of laughing, some crying, but there wasn't any further discussion about what had happened to Cass. It was over. All that mattered now was that Cassandra was back—maybe not the Cassandra they knew, but still their Cassandra nonetheless.

Cassandra was getting more comfortable with everyone and within a few days she was able to let them give her little touches, but nothing that lasted more than a couple of seconds. Everyone was okay with that. They got to know what she could handle and they respected that. Nobody tried to push her beyond her limits and she appreciated that more than they knew.

Sid and Ryder took Joe and Marvin to do some guy activities in the evening. They seemed to be having a good time together. She was glad Big Daddy was able to stay for the wedding. He told her Mack and Rick were going to try and make it but couldn't make any promises.

One afternoon, Ryder closed up shop early, so that Marvin and Joe could take Sid and him out to try their hands at playing golf, but the ladies knew better. It was so they could say they'd played golf, when what they really just wanted to do was go back to the Roadhouse for wings and beer and to watch sports and play pool.

Cass was happy that her Uncle Joe was having a good time with all the guys. They seemed to find things that interested them all, which Cassandra found interesting because they were such different people. Her new family belonged to a club and her birth family... well, they were like country bumpkins in comparison to them. She smiled to herself and thought, *Life is sure going to be interesting when we're all together.*

Everyone was busy helping with the wedding plans there was so much to do, and really not a lot of time to do it in—but it was getting done. They were having a blast together and in her mind that was all that mattered. Cass still wasn't sure who was going to walk her down the aisle. She really wanted Ryder to, but she was afraid she would hurt her mom or Uncle Joe's feelings if she didn't ask one of them. They all had been hurt enough with all that had happened.

Cass woke up early Wednesday morning; no one was up yet. She decided to go outside and curl up on the lounge and watch the sun come up. It was her favourite time of the day. After not seeing the beauty that Mother Nature had to offer her for so long, she appreciated it more than she ever had before.

"How long have you been up?" Cass looked up and Sid was standing there. She opened the blanket and he curled up next to her.

"Not long, I couldn't sleep. I didn't want to wake you so I came outside to watch the sunrise. How did your meeting go at the clubhouse last night?"

"It was okay. We're planning another event for the military families who have family that won't be home for Christmas."

"That sounds awesome—let me know what I can do to help."

"Thanks, babe, I will. And they would love the help. Maybe you and Shelley can figure something out to raise some money?"

"Did you get the marriage license yet?"

"Ya, I gave it to Shelley to hold onto and I also asked Tiny to be my best man. How are things going with you?"

"We're going to look for a dress today. The cake has been ordered—a friend of Shelley's is going to make it and the Roadhouse is catering. We have people that are coming to set up and get the backyard ready for the wedding and the party afterwards. We still need to get the rings and someone to marry us. Do you think David would become an ordained minister so he could do it?"

"I don't know. We could ask him."

"Who did you ask to stand up with you?"

"That's a hard one. Liliana is my oldest and dearest friend, but Shelley is my best friend here. I don't know Sid—it feels like whoever I ask, someone is going to be hurt because I didn't choose them. I want Ryder to give me away but Mom or Uncle Joe might be hurt if I don't ask them. And Ryder… well, he may not want to give me away with how he feels about me. I don't know what to do."

"Cass, the best thing you can do is be honest with them. Let them know how you're feeling and see what they say. I have a feeling they will all be okay with whoever you choose."

Sid put his arm around Cass and pulled her in close and told her it would all work out. He kissed the nape of her neck and that little kiss sent shivers down her spine and feelings in areas she hadn't felt in a very long time. For the first time it didn't frighten her. She rolled over and looked up at Sid and gently kissed him on the lips; he pulled her even closer and started kissing her gently, not wanting to scare her. He gently ran his hand up her back and then down her leg. She didn't want him to stop. Their kissing became more intense and her body was on fire. She couldn't believe what she was feeling. She had never been aroused like this before, every inch of her was aching inside for Sid to touch her everywhere. She wanted more and she wanted everything he could give her.

Sid moved his hand slowly up to her breast and slowly began circling his tongue around her nipple and Cassandra moaned with pleasure. "Please don't stop," she whispered with a moan and Sid was only too willing to keep going. They both had waited for this moment for so long. They continued to explore each other's body, both wanting to consume every inch of the other. Sid slowly moved his hand down her leg and gently slid it between her thighs and Cass spread them just enough so that Sid could feel the moistness between her legs.

"Oh shit. I'm sorry. I didn't know anyone was up yet. Bruiser, come on let's go." Both Cass and Sid froze—neither one knew what to do. All of a sudden, Cassandra started to laugh and Sid buried his head into her neck, fuck! And that was that—their moment was gone.

Sid looked into Cassandra's eyes. "Just my luck," he laughed. Cassandra kissed him gently on the lips and told him that maybe it was for the best.

"Really?"

She smiled. "Ya, when we do finally make love I don't want to have to stop. I want to make love to you over and over again."

"Mmm baby, I like the sound of that."

"Me too," she said, and she kissed him again.

Sid stood up and adjusted his shorts and Cass adjusted hers. They went back into the house. Cass went to her room to get dressed and Sid went into the kitchen. David turned around with a smirk on his face. "Sorry man."

Sid looked at David and grumbled, "Right," and went and made himself a coffee.

A few minutes later Cass came into the kitchen. David and Sid were at the table having their morning coffee, neither one saying a word. She went and filled up her water bottle with ice and water and sat down next to Sid.

"David, I have a question for you." He turned and looked at Cass and smiled.

"Ask away."

"Would you be willing to become an ordained minister so you could marry us?"

Sid looked at David and told him it was the least he could do after just ruining the best morning they were about to have since they met.

"Sid!"

"What? It's true." David laughed and said that Sid was right: it was the least he could do.

"What's the least you could do?" Tiny walked into the kitchen and went and grabbed a coffee, so his back was towards everyone. Cass shook her head and mouthed, "Please, no," and David told Tiny Cass just asked him to become an ordained minister so he could marry them—it's the least he could do, to help the two of them get hitched.

Sid and Tiny went to work and David and Cass went outside to say their morning prayers and meditate. They got into a comfortable position and were just about to start. "Cass I'm really sorry about this morning."

"That's okay."

"Can I ask you something?"

"Of course you can. Anything,"

"How do you feel about what almost happened this morning?"

"David, that's personal."

"No that's not what I was asking. I was just wondering if you were scared at any point. How did you feel when I accidentally interrupted you? What was going on in your head? I was concerned that it might be a little too much for you."

She sat there for a moment. "For the first time, David, I felt nothing but pleasure. There was nothing going on in my head. It was quiet and my whole body was listening to my heart."

"And how do you feel now?"

"Now? Well I feel like I want to kick your ass for interrupting us." They both had a laugh and then got down to business.

Everyone showed up around ten. Marvin and Joe were going to play golf on their own and meet back at the house for dinner later in the day.

"Shelley, can I please talk to everyone in private for a minute?"

Shelley looked at Cass. "Sure you can. I'm gonna take the pups out to do their business before we leave."

"Thanks Shell."

Everyone was looking at Cass and wondering what was going on. She sat there looking at the floor not knowing how to approach the subject, "Cass, what's wrong?" asked Faye.

Cass lifted her head and looked at her mom. "Well, I'm torn about a few things. I need to choose a maid of honour and, Lil, you are my best friend, and Nat and Jayne, you are both very important to me as well… so is Shelley. If I choose one of you,

I'm afraid the rest will be hurt that I didn't choose them. I don't know what to do."

Everyone was quiet. "Kiddo, in your heart of hearts who do you want standing up there beside you?" She looked at her Aunt Sam and then back down at the floor; she was starting to panic. They could all see it and Bruiser could feel it—he started barking at the back door.

Nat got up and sat next to Cass. She put her hand on hers to comfort her. "Cass, look at me please." Cass lifted her head and gave Nat a small smile. Nat looked at her friend and told her that this was her day and whomever she chose, they all would be fine with. They were all just happy to be there to celebrate her and Sid's special day.

Cass looked at everyone and she cleared her throat. "Shelley."

"Shelley it is, then," Faye said with a smile. They all looked okay about it, so Cass relaxed a little.

"So what is the second problem?" Just then Shelley opened the door and Bruiser came straight to Cass.

"Sorry Cass. I had to let him in; he was making too much noise outside."

"It's okay, Shell." Shelley turned around to head back outside. "Please stay."

Cassandra started stroking Bruiser and he just sat there. Nat put her hand on Cass's arm. "What else, Cass?"

"Well I would like Ryder to give me away, if he will." No one said anything.

"After spending time with your friends, Cass, I think that's a great idea," said her Uncle Joe. Cass lifted her head and looked at him and saw he was smiling. She knew he truly meant that. She looked at her Mom, who was just staring at her.

"Mom?"

Sam nudged Faye; she looked at Sam and then at Cass. "I'm sorry, Cass. I was just sitting here thinking what your dad would say."

"Mom, if this is something you aren't okay with, please tell me. I want to know how you honestly feel."

"Well, to be honest with you, Cass, I was going to tell you that I didn't like it at all. But I could hear your Dad's voice telling me to look at you and see just how much our girl wants this. Look how far she has come because of these new people in her life. Your father and I can't think of anyone better to do the job than someone who loves you as much as we do. So I'm okay with this—you ask Ryder, if he'll do it."

Cass got up and went over to her mother. Faye stood up and Cass gave her a hug that she would remember till the day she died. Cass let go of her mom and just smiled and told her thanks. She turned around and looked at Shelley and asked her if she would be her maid of honour. Shelley said, "Most definitely."

Marvin stood up. "Well, now that all that is settled, Joe and I have a serious golf game to get to and you ladies have a dress to find." So the boys went their way and the girls went theirs.

The ladies headed for the bridal boutique on Sherman. They walked in and the store was empty. Jayne piped up and said they had the shop all to themselves and Cass thought oh boy. The ladies were pulling out dresses from every direction. They were having a blast trying to find the perfect dress for that special day: the one that would make Cass look and feel amazing.

Finally, an employee of the boutique came over and introduced herself. "I'm Hope. Can I help you find the perfect dress?"

Cass introduced herself as well as her entourage. She told her she was looking for a dress for her wedding on Saturday.

"This Saturday?"

"Yes."

Hope had a worried look on her face. "I'm not sure if we can get a dress altered in that short of a time."

"I'm not looking for a traditional wedding dress. I'm looking for a dress that I can wear instead of the traditional white dress."

Hope asked them to follow her into the other room. "Cass, what style of dress are you looking for?"

"I'm not sure. I would like it to be red if possible—that's Sid's favourite colour on me."

"Okay, let's see what we can do." The ladies started looking for what they thought would be the dress that would make Cass feel as beautiful and as special as she was. Every dress they showed her just wasn't the one.

They had almost gone through the entire room and Cass was getting discouraged—she might not find something to wear—when Hope brought out a dress that Cass fell in love with instantly. It was a beautiful shade of red. It went down to just below the knee and it showed off her chest, but still left something to the imagination. "Would you like to try it on?" Hope showed Cass the back of the dress and Cass's heart sank. She looked towards the floor and said, "No," and turned around and walked out of the room.

"Did I say something wrong? I thought she would look amazing in this."

Shelley came over and looked at the dress; when she saw the back, she knew exactly what the problem was. Shelley asked Hope to put the dress in a fitting room—she would try it on. Shelley went to find Cass and found her looking out the window. "Cass, please come with me." Cass turned around and followed her into the back room. Shelley took her to the fitting room and motioned her inside. "I want you to try this dress on, please." Cass looked at the dress; it was the dress that Hope had showed her. She looked at Shelley and said she couldn't. "Cass, I have never asked you to do anything that I didn't believe you could do or handle. I'm asking you to please try this on for me."

Cass looked at Shelley—how could she say no after everything she had done for her? Shelley turned around and shut the door behind her and Cass started to get undressed. She took the dress off the hanger and stepped into it. She fastened the strap around her neck and looked at herself in the mirror. It was beautiful. She had to be honest with herself: she felt and looked amazing in it. The only problem was the back of the dress, or the lack thereof.

She opened the door and stepped out of the room and everyone just stared. "Cass, you look amazing. It was made for you." Jayne asked her to come out and look at herself in the bigger mirror. Cass refused to leave the doorway.

Shelley came and took Cass by the hand. "Please don't," Cass said. "I can't wear this."

Faye came up to her daughter. "What's wrong?"

Cass looked at her Mom and turned around and everyone saw what Cass hadn't wanted them to see. Faye touched her daughter's back then put her arms around her. "Do you know what I see when I look at you?" Cass shook her head, no. "Well, let me tell you. I see a beautiful woman who has found the perfect dress for her wedding day. You look stunning in it and Sid is going to flip when he sees you in this."

"Mom—the back?"

"What about the back?" Cass looked at her mom and was just about to burst into tears.

"Cassandra Elizabeth Taylor! You listen to me young lady: this dress was made for you and you look stunning. As for the marks on your back…" Faye lifted her daughter's face so that they were eye to eye, "… Cass, you must be proud of these scars. They are the scars of a survivor. You went through a battle that not many people would have survived, let alone walked away from—and you did. You have to embrace them. They tell everyone that you won your battle."

"I hate them. They remind me of all the bad things that happened."

Liliana came to her side and put her arms around her. "Cass, I know they remind you of all the bad things that happened, but instead of looking at them and seeing bad memories, why not see them as a few good memories?"

Cass looked at Liliana. "Seriously?!"

"Yes, I'm serious. Let me ask you this: if this hadn't happened, look at all the great people you would have never met. There would be no Sid or Ryder, or the rest of their amazing family. That includes David and his pups, for that matter. Could you imagine your life without them? We wouldn't be here right now helping you find the perfect dress and helping to plan the perfect wedding you and Sid deserve to have. Cass, as bad as this was for you, just think of the good things that came into your life because of it—that's all I'm saying. Please don't let these few marks define who you are or the life you deserve, because none of us do."

Cassandra gave Lil a big hug, turned around, and looked at herself. She knew this was the dress for her. Whoever had made it, they'd made it just for her.

She looked at Hope and told her she would take it. "Now we have to find something for Shelley— then a little something for the honeymoon," Jayne said with a wink.

28

....

Cassandra woke up early. Today was the day all of her dreams were coming true. Today she was going to marry Sid and become his wife.

She had spoken to Ryder, Wednesday night after dinner, about him walking her down the aisle. She told him she completely understood if he couldn't do this— she wasn't trying to hurt him, she knew how he felt about her. It was just that she couldn't imagine anyone but him doing it. She remembered the look in his eyes: a little hurt, but happy at the same time. He told her he would be honoured to walk her to Sid.

Cass got up and went outside and curled up under the blanket on the lounge, waiting for the sun to peek its way through the darkness. She thought about the other morning when she and Sid were lying there, starting to explore one another—and thought to herself that tonight they were going to do that without any interruptions. *There damn well better not be any interruptions*, she told herself and laughed.

Her cell phone ringing brought her back to the here and now. "Hello?"

"Good morning, babe. Did I wake you?"

"No, I couldn't sleep. I'm outside, watching the sun come up… for the last time, as a single woman."

"Really? I thought maybe you were thinking about what almost happened between us the other morning." She told him she had no idea what he was talking about. She was teasing him and he knew it. "Shall I describe what almost happened?"

"If you think you can remember," she laughed.

"Oh, I remember," he said in a deep gruff voice.

"Mmm," was all she said.

They changed the subject because they were both getting a little excited, and they didn't want to get interrupted again.

"Cass, how are you doing?"

"I'm fine—why?"

"The other morning I was worried that maybe you might have been a little scared."

"Sid, for the first time in a long time I felt nothing but complete peace and sheer happiness."

They talked to each other until the sun was just cresting the top of the trees, then decided they'd better say goodbye so that they could get ready for their big day.

Cassandra was sitting in the backyard when David came outside with the pups. "You're up early!"

"I've been up for a few hours. I was just going to do a little meditation."

"Are you okay?"

"I'm fine. Today is a good day and I want to keep it that way."

"Then let's get comfortable and do this. But before we get started, we need to talk. I think you're in a good place and it's time for me to head home." Cass got this worried look on her face. David smiled at her and reassured her she would be fine.

He promised they would talk every day and she could call him whenever she needed to talk. He told her he wanted her to get up every morning and do her morning prayers to the universe and do her meditation, without fail.

"Cass, promise me you won't hide how you're feeling. Tell Sid and everyone here what is bothering you. They can handle whatever you need to tell them." She started to cry. David got up and sat next to her. "What's wrong?"

"It's been easier dealing with all of this with you and Bruiser here. What do I do when you're both gone and nothing seems to work?"

"Cass, the first thing you do is call Sid—he wants to be there for you, you have to let him. He's going to be your husband and that's a part of what he is signing up for—and you know if you really need us we'll always be here for you, but it's time that we go home. You're not going to fully heal if you depend on us. Have faith in yourself and in Sid. Both of you can work through anything. You're stronger than you're giving yourself credit for. Just continue to do what we've been doing every morning: just take it day by day."

She knew he was right. She could handle this. She had to keep doing what she was doing and remind herself that each day was a new day full of new possibilities.

Cassandra was watching the crew getting the backyard ready when she saw her mother's reflection in the glass. "I didn't hear the doorbell," she said.

"Tiny was just going out. Are you okay?"

"Ya. I was just standing here thinking about dad and how I wish he was here to share this day with us."

Faye came and stood next to her daughter. "He is here. I feel him all around us—you don't think that he would miss the happiest day of your life, do you?" She put her arms around her daughter and just stood there, and this time Cass didn't move or flinch. "Your father and I are so proud of you, proud of how far you've come. Please promise me you will keep on track with what you're doing, and if you need help, you'll ask for it. Promise you won't hold everything in again."

"I promise, Mom." She turned to her mom. "I love you, Mom. Thank you for never giving up on me."

The doorbell rang and in came the rest of the girls. Jayne piped up and said she heard there was a wedding happening today, so they all wanted to come and help her get ready.

"Cass, come sit for a minute." Natalie told her that there were a few items that she needed before she could marry Sid. She handed Cass a small box. Cass opened it and looked at what was inside.

"Nat," said Cass, "this was your mom's."

"Yes, and now it's yours. You need something old and this was given to my mother by her mother on her wedding day. Open it up and look inside."

Cassandra's hands were shaking. Inside was a locket, with a picture of her dad and Agnes. "They will always be with you and close to your heart," Natalie said. Cassandra hugged Natalie and thanked her so much for this amazing gift, "Agnes would have wanted you to have it."

Liliana gave her a small box. Inside was a beautiful gold bracelet with the infinity symbol. "This is your 'something new.' This is for the love you and Sid have for each other—it will last forever, and I'm so happy for you both."

Faye gave her a small box too, which contained a pair of diamond earrings. She had always loved these. She remembered begging her mom to let her wear them as a young adult. Faye had told her one day, when it was a very special occasion, she would let her borrow them. And this was that day.

Jayne, being Jayne, was assigned the 'something blue.' She had a devilish smile on her face and Cass asked her if the package was safe to open. Everyone laughed. Inside was the traditional blue garter, but underneath the garter, was a pair of baby blue panties that truly left nothing to the imagination. She pulled them out of the box and held them up. "Well, I think Sid is gonna have a surprise when he unwraps his gift tonight. I can see him hanging these from his mirror in his truck."

Faye stood up. "Well, ladies, I think we need to get our bride ready for her big day."

By two o'clock all that was left to be done was helping Cassandra get into her dress. The few guests that were invited to share this special day started to arrive.

The ladies had just finished helping Cass do the final touches there was a knock on the door. Sam went and opened the door just a crack. It was Ryder. "Can I see Cassandra, please." Sam looked at Cass and she nodded her head, yes. She turned around and Ryder just stopped and stared at her. He thought to himself how he wished it was him she was walking down the aisle to. "You look beautiful."

"Thank you."

Ryder couldn't take his eyes off her. "Can I please speak to Cass in private?" Everyone left the room to give them a few minutes alone.

"Are you alright?"

"I'm fine, I just—." He couldn't finish what he wanted to say.

Cassandra walked over to him and put her hands on his chest. "If this is going to be too hard, I can ask my Uncle Joe to walk me to Sid?"

"No, darlin', it's my honour to do this. It's just I'm standing here looking at you and thinking about the day we met. I wasn't very nice to you and I'm sorry about that." He put his hand on the side of her face.

"Ryder—."

"Cass, let me say what I came in to say, please." She stared up at him. "The day we found you, you woke something up inside of me that died when I lost Christina. When I saw you, all the memories of her death came rushing back, along with all the fears and feelings I felt that day. I want to thank you for coming into my life, even though the circumstances were terrible. You brought life back into me again. You made me feel alive and that I had a purpose in life once again. I've felt lost since Christina passed. I wasn't able to help her—she was gone in the blink of an eye—but you allowed me to be a part of your recovery. You could have pushed me away, but you didn't and I'm grateful for that. I'll be honest with you—I wish it was me you were marrying today. But there is no one in this world I would rather you be with than Sid. There isn't anyone I trust more to keep you safe and make you happy. I truly wish you both a lifetime of love and happiness."

Cassandra looked into Ryder's eyes. "Ryder, I wish with all my heart I could make you both happy. If I could, you know I would—please know you will always be more than a friend to me and you will always be a part of our life and we will always be there for you when you need us. The three of us have a special bond that no one or nothing will ever break." Ryder put his arms around Cass and held her close and she put her arms around him and they stood there in silence.

Shelley stuck her head in. "It's time." Cass looked up at Ryder and he smiled at her and asked if she was ready to become a married woman. She nodded and said she couldn't wait.

Everyone rose to their feet as Ryder walked Cassandra down the aisle to Sid. Sid looked at the woman he was about to marry and thought to himself he was the luckiest guy in the world.

As Ryder placed Cassandra's hands into Sid's, he looked at his friend and told him to take care of their girl. "You have my word, brother," said Sid.

Ryder turned to Cass and kissed the side of her face and whispered, "I love you. Be happy." Then he pulled away and walked to his seat.

Cassandra looked at Sid. "Hi there."

"Hey baby, you ready to do this?"

"Hell ya." They both laughed and looked at David.

"We are all here to bring these two people together and join them in the bond of marriage. If there is anyone here who doesn't think these two should become man and wife, speak now or forever hold your peace." It was so quiet you could have heard a pin drop. "I'm told Sid has written a few words."

"Cassandra," said Sid, "you are the most amazing woman I have ever known and I'm so happy that you chose to spend the rest of your life with me. I may not always be the person you want me to be, but I promise I will always protect you from harm and stand with you through the good and the bad. I promise to give you the best of me—my heart and my soul. I will never stray from your side. You are my everything and I promise to show you how much you mean to me every single day."

Cassandra looked at Sid and mouthed, "I love you so much." David looked at Cass and asked her if there was anything she wanted to say.

"How can I even come close to topping that? Here goes nothing!" Cassandra looked at the man standing in front of her. "Sid, I can't believe that I get the chance to stand here in front of our family and friends and give myself to my greatest friend and partner in crime. I love you more than you will ever know. I promise you with everything that I am, that I will be yours—heart and soul. I will stand by your side through the good and bad and I will hold you when you need me to, and even when you don't. I'm yours and I will never stray from your side. You are my everything."

David continued with the rest of the ceremony and the words they were all waiting for were finally said: "I now pronounce you husband and wife. Sid, you can kiss your bride."

It was too late—Cassandra was already in Sid's arms having their first kiss as husband and wife. Everyone cheered.

"It is my great pleasure to introduce you all to Mr. & Mrs. Sid Davis."

It was a wonderful evening. They partied late into the night and everyone had a wonderful time. They agreed to have dinner with everyone Sunday night before everyone went home Monday morning.

Sid put his arms around his wife and asked if she was ready to go. She kissed him and told him she would follow him any-where. They said their goodbyes and were off to spend their first night as husband and wife.

Sid took Cassandra back to their place. He put the truck in the garage and shut the door and took his bride into their home. He picked her up and carried her into their bedroom, placed her feet onto the floor, took her face in his hands, and kissed her gently on the lips. She pulled away and asked him to give her a minute. She went into the bathroom, took off her dress, and placed it neatly on the counter. Then she opened the door to the bedroom.

Sid looked at her, picked her up, and laid her on the bed. He took his shirt off and she helped him with his belt and pants. He lay next to her just looking at his beautiful wife. "You look amazing, Mrs. Davis."

Cassandra snuggled in closer. "You don't look half bad yourself, Mr. Davis." Sid hovered over Cass and kissed her softly on the lips and then moved down towards her neck. He gently nibbled around her ear and whispered softly how much he wanted her. It drove Cass crazy. She wanted him so bad and he could feel the heat and excitement coming from her body, but he didn't want to rush it. He wanted their first time together to be something she would always remember. He started to nibble her neck while running his hand up and down her body, Cassandra moaned a quivered with anticipation. Sid took her nipple in his mouth and gently sucked and nibbled it while he ran his hand up her leg where is found her moist treasure spot. Cassandra spread he legs further and Sid gently slid his finger into her mound gently teasing her bud. Cassandra started moaning with anticipation. Sid placed himself between Cassandras legs and he gently entered her, gliding his shaft slowly in and out. This dove her crazy begging for more begging for everything he had to give her. Sid's penetrations became faster and faster, Cassandra begged him to please not stop, she wrapped her legs around him meeting him with every pounding thrust. Every inch of her body was screaming for more and Sid was only to willing to give his wife everything he had and all that she wanted. They both had waited for this day for so long, both of their bodies we on fires with desire, they explored each other over and over again with the most explosive orgasms either of them had ever experienced. After hours of love making they finally drifted off to sleep in each other's arms, knowing this was the only place they wanted to be.

29

Sid and Cass spent most of the next week in bed together. They did get dressed to have Sunday dinner with everyone before they left, and Cassandra would get dressed every morning to meditate. Other than that, they didn't leave the house.

They were curled up on the couch watching a movie, when Cass sat up. "Sid, I need to talk to you about something."

"Is everything okay?"

"I need to go back to Lethbridge and take care of some personal business."

Sid sat up. "For how long?"

"Just for a few days." She was thinking that maybe she would see if she could get a flight out on Wednesday and be back home Friday. Sid told her he didn't like the thought of her going there alone. "Then come with me—we can leave Friday and come back Sunday."

"I can't, Cass. We're going to be really busy getting things caught up." She curled back up against him. She didn't want to push it and decided to let it go for now.

Cass got up with Sid the next morning and made him breakfast. They ate quietly—too quietly for Cassandra's liking. "Is everything okay Sid?"

Sid looked up. "I've been thinking about what you said last night, about you going back to Lethbridge. Cass, I don't want to be the kind of husband that thinks he can tell you what you can and can't do, but if you need to do this, please be careful and don't stay away too long."

Cass got up and sat on Sid's lap. "I will be gone no more than a couple of days, I promise. I will see what arrangements I can make and will let you know what I can come up with."

"I just worry about you."

"I understand that, hun, but that's the past. We can't live in fear of the what ifs right?"

Sid asked her what stupid fool would tell her something like that. She laughed, put her arms around his neck, and whispered into his ear, "You, baby." Sid shook his head. What the hell was he thinking? She laughed and gave him a long and passionate kiss.

Cass left for Lethbridge early Thursday morning and promised Sid she would be back Friday before he was done work. She told him she might even bring him back a surprise. Jayne picked her up at the airport and lent her her car so she could do some running around. The first place she went was to the bank. She arrived shortly after lunch and asked to speak to the branch manager.

"Mrs. Davis, I'm Mr. Bowman. How can I help you?"

"I would like to transfer all my funds to my account where I'm now living please. The account is under my previous name, Taylor."

"Sure. I can help you with that."

Cassandra went into Mr. Bowman's office and explained that she had an account that was put in trust in her name. The two years had elapsed and she would like to have those funds transferred as well. Mr. Bowman looked up all the information. "Mrs. Davis," he said, "it seems that there is a password in place. Can you please tell me what that password is?" Cass told him the password and he told her that that was correct. "That's quite a sum of money you want to be transferred." Cassandra asked if there was going to be a problem, Mr. Bowman told her no, but this was going to take a few minutes to process. In no time, all her money had been transferred to her account at home.

Cass took time to do a little bit of shopping. She wanted to buy Sid a treat—and what man doesn't like sexy lingerie? She got a beautiful lacy number that had a split up the side. It showed off her curves and the fullness of her breasts.

Cass spent the evening with Jayne and Natalie. They had a wonderful evening talking about anything and everything.

"Cass, can I ask you a question?" said Jayne.

"Sure Jayne."

"This is kind of a personal question, but … you have two great guys that love you—how did you choose?"

"It was easy. I fell in love with Sid first."

"Really?"

"Don't get me wrong—I love Ryder and if it were possible I would love to have a life with both of them. In so many ways they are alike, but in other ways they are so different. It just came down to who I fell in love with first."

"Sid's okay with this?"

"I've been honest about how I feel with both of them. It's not like I was with Sid for a year and then Ryder showed up. They came into my life at the same time and it just developed slower with Ryder. I had no intentions of falling in love with him, it just happened—the heart loves who it loves. With that being said, I would never cross that line. I would never do anything that would hurt either one of them. It's just my luck to find two amazing men at the same time."

They talked for a while longer, then Natalie said her good-byes and Jayne said goodnight. She had to be up early for work. Cass told Jayne that she had a car picking her up at ten to take her to the airport and would text her when she got home.

Cass curled up in her bed and called Sid. "Hi hun," said Cass. "Were you sleeping?"

"No."

"What's wrong?"

"You're not here."

Cass laughed and told him she would be home tomorrow and she had no plans on going anywhere else anytime soon.

"I'm gonna hold you to that."

"I'm good with that."

"Did you get what you needed to do done?"

"Yes, it's all been taken care of." They talked for a few minutes longer, then they said their good nights. "I love you, hun," said Cass.

"I love you too, baby. Just make sure your ass is back in our bed tomorrow."

"Yes sir. See you tomorrow."

Her plane arrived just past one o'clock. Cass called for an Uber to pick her up and arrived home a short time later. She went straight into the shower to get freshened up and put Sid's present on. She took a picture of herself in the mirror and sent Sid the picture with a message saying, "I'm home."

Twenty minutes later, Sid walked into the house, locked the door, and went to find Cass. He picked her up and she wrapped her legs around him. He lowered her onto the bed and started to devour her. It was like it was their first time all over again. His mouth was kissing and caressing her entire body. They made love three times that afternoon and finished by curling up together. Just as Cass started to doze off, Sid pulled her close to him and whispered into her ear, "Please don't ever leave me again." Then they drifted off to sleep.

Cass took another week off to get things straightened around the house so she could be there when Sid came home for lunch. It seemed every time he came home, they ended up in bed—not that she was complaining. Sid was an amazing lover and if she was honest, she couldn't get enough of him either. Her sex life with Tom had been boring, but with Sid it was like she was a different person. She wasn't afraid to try something new or wasn't afraid to ask him to do it a bit differently, so she could enjoy it even more. Sid was very much into her needs—what she liked and didn't like—and it was the same for Cass. She wanted to make sure that at the end of their lovemaking Sid was always satisfied.

Life was good, it was better than good—everyone seemed to be doing well. Ryder even started to date a lady named Sasha … although Cass didn't think it would last. Sasha couldn't understand that there were things the guys didn't talk about, and she didn't seem to like that. Sasha didn't like how close their family was more to the point how close Cassandra and Ryder were. Sunday was always a family day and they would all go for a ride, then have dinner together. It was what they'd done from the time Cass had met them and it still continued. It was something that would never change. Family and loyalty was something they all believed in.

Cass was in the kitchen making a few pies to take to Tiny's for their Sunday dinner when Sid came out and put his arms around her. "Smells good, babe, is this for dinner tonight?"

"Ya. Why?"

"I was just thinking that maybe we could leave one at home."

Cass turned around and put her arms around him. "Well, I guess it's a good thing I have the last one in the oven for you." Sid kissed her and told her that she was too good to him. "Yes, I am." He walked away and smacked her on the ass—she turned around with a smirk and told him not to start something he couldn't finish. He walked back to her and in a gruff voice told her that he could finish if she wanted him to. She laughed. "Maybe later. We have to go as soon as the pie comes out of the oven, and that's in a few minutes."

During dinner that night, Tiny brought up the event that the club was planning for the families of the military. They still had a lot of time before the event, but they needed to get on it, there would be lots to do. Both Cass and Shelley said they were willing to help. They were talking about things to do and Cass suggested a carnival that everyone could attend—not just club members, but also their community and club supporters. They could arrange some games, maybe get some house bands to play, and sell hamburgers and hot dogs.

30

....

Everything moved rather quickly. The club was in full swing, with everyone working hard getting everything ready for the big event. They decided to get a dunk tank and asked for volunteers to be dunked. Tiny mentioned this during one of their Sunday dinners and Cass said she would do it. She challenged both Sid and Ryder to do it as well... that is if they weren't chicken. Both rose to the challenge and Cassandra said she couldn't wait to spend money on dunking them both. Ryder smiled and winked at her and told her to bring it on.

Cassandra called Jayne to see if she could come for a visit, and told her what was going on. She told her about the dunk tank and the challenge she'd made with the boys. Jayne told her she wouldn't miss it, it sounded like it would be a blast.

Cass was at work when her phone rang. It was the District Attorney's office, calling to remind Cass that the sentencing for Pope was in five days and they wanted to make sure she still wanted to read a victim's impact statement. She told the lady on the other end of the phone that she wouldn't miss the chance to read it and they would be there.

Cassandra had been really quiet since she received the call about the court date and Sid was getting worried. "Babe, are you okay?"

Cassandra was in her own little world. Sid put his hand on her knee and she looked up. "I'm sorry, hun, what did you say?"

"Are you okay? You've been really quiet since you got home."

She put her laptop down and curled up next to him. "I'm okay, I'm just working on my impact statement. Sorry I haven't been with it tonight."

"I'm worried, Cass." She looked at Sid and could see the concern in his eyes.

"I'm good, Sid, I promise. I don't feel at all like I did before. It's just that—" Cass paused for a moment. "I'm struggling as to what I'm going to say that will have the most impact with the judge."

Sid pulled her in closer. "Just say exactly how you feel."

"That's easier said than done."

The days went by quicker than Cass wanted them to. She hadn't slept well that night and today she was going to see Pope for the first and last time since she escaped.

They arrived at the courthouse for nine o'clock, and just before ten they were allowed into the courtroom to find their seat. Cass sat between Sid and Ryder, near the aisle, and Tiny and Shelley were right next to them. A few minutes later, Cass heard the door behind them open. She felt a hand on her shoulder and when she turned and looked up she saw David, her mom, and Big Daddy. She smiled and whispered, "Thank you."

Judge Snyder came in and everyone rose. Each side said what they wanted to say, then Mr. Harper stated that the victim, Mrs. Cassandra Davis, would like to read her impact statement.

Pope turned his head and stared at Cass, then turned his head back and stared straight ahead.

Cassandra got up and went to the podium. She stood there for a few minutes looking at what she had written down—none of it made any sense to her now. She started to tear up and she could feel herself starting to have an attack. She turned and looked at Sid and the rest of her family. She was trying so hard to be strong. Sid stood up and walked over to her, put his arms around her and told her she had this and that he loved her. She hugged him back and told him she loved him as well.

Sid returned to his place on the bench and leaned over and quietly said, "Ryder—he's a dead man," and Ryder nodded.

Cassandra turned around and cleared her throat. "I would like to thank the court for allowing me this time to speak and let Your Honour know just how much Mr. Pope's actions have affected me. Your Honour, because of Mr. Pope's actions I lost two years of my life, and my family went two years thinking that I might be dead and they would never see me again. It's been a rough road since I regained my freedom. Trusting anyone… well that's a hard one and still a work in progress. The people who are here with me today are my family, I trust them, but with that being said, there is still a constant voice in the back of my head that is telling me to be careful and always be ready to run. Your Honour, if you looked under our bed you will find a bag. In that bag are some clothes and personal items for a quick getaway. I trust my husband and my family with my life, but that scared lady that is still deep inside me won't stay quiet. The only way I can keep her calm and have peace in my life is to have that bag, even though I know I will never have to use it." Cass turned and looked at Sid, who had this stunned look on his face. With tears rolling down her face she told him she was sorry she had never told him about it, she was sorry he'd found out about it this way.

"Your Honour, I have put my husband and family through emotional hell and I didn't want to put them through any more—that is why I didn't tell them I am still having these kinds of feelings. Even though they have told me many times they want to know how I'm feeling, I'm just tired of feeling like I'm a burden, with all that I have put them through. Mr. Pope, will you please look at me—you owe me that much." Pope turned his head and stared at Cassandra and listened to everything she had to say.

"Mr. Pope, do you know what the worst thing about this whole ordeal was? One would think it was being kidnapped or being brutally raped repeatedly or when you almost beat me to within an inch of my life. I made it through that. But for me, the worst thing was when I was reunited with my family again. I wasn't able to let them touch me. My mother, who had just lost her husband, my father, just three weeks before you took me, had to go through two years of hell not knowing if I was dead or alive. My mother tried to hug me and I almost lost it, and still now, my family and friends know that if they touch me or hug me it can only be for a minute because that's all I can handle. I'm getting better, but my entire life is a work in progress. I have my good days and bad days, and there are times when my husband touches me in a way that you did and it makes me sick to my stomach and my skin crawl. I have to tell myself it's completely different and that Sid loves me and would never hurt me, but Mr. Pope you damaged me.

"I have put my family through hell, but they never gave up on me. God knows I gave them plenty of reason to walk away. My depression alone is something no one should have to deal with. Mr. Pope, today is the last day you will have a hold on my life. Today is going to be the last day my family is going to have to worry about whether or not I'm going to lose it. It ends here and it ends now.

"Today is the day that my husband, Sid, is going to get all of me. What you don't know, Mr. Pope, is that Sid is the one who found me hiding behind their garbage dumpster. You told me I was trash and nobody would want me—well, you were wrong. Sid not only wants me, but he loves me. And that's all I need to know.

"Your Honour, please give Mr. Pope the toughest sentence possible. If he were to do this again, I don't know if the next person would be as fortunate as I was. I was fortunate to have people in Heaven guide me and stay with me during my captivity. I was lucky that I ended up where I did, behind the dumpster, and blessed to have had it be these two amazing men and their family who were brought into my life to help me. If it wasn't for all of them, I truly don't know where I would be today. Thank you."

Cassandra turned around and walked back to her seat. Sid stood up and put his arms around his wife and whispered into her ear, "I love you and I'm so proud of you." Everyone sat quietly in the courtroom, waiting for the judge to speak.

"First of all, I would like to say, Mrs. Davis, I'm sorry for what you and your family have had to endure at the hands of Mr. Pope. If I could, I would put him behind bars for the remainder of his life, but I can't. I have to sentence him according to the law and though I agree that the sentencing isn't enough, it is the law, and I must sentence according to that.

"Mr. Pope, please stand. Do you have anything you would like to say at this time?"

"No, Your Honour."

"Mr. Pope, on the count of kidnapping I'm sentencing you to the maximum sentence of twenty years; for the multiple counts of rape, I'm giving you the maximum sentence of ten years; for the aggravated assault charges, I'm giving you the maximum of twenty years, and these will be served concurrently, with no possibility of parole for twenty-five years. Mr. Pope, I'm astounded that an officer of the law, who has seen some horrific situations in his career, would put another human being through such a terrible ordeal. I truly hope during your time in prison you will seek help and find out why you felt the need to do this, and maybe help others in some way. Court is adjourned."

Everyone rose as the judge left the courtroom. They watched as Pope was taken away in handcuffs. Cassandra thanked Mr. Harper for all that he had done for her. "Cassandra," he said, "with everything you have gone through and with Mr. Pope being a reserve police officer, you have every right to go after the city for damages."

"No thank you. I just want to move on with my life."

Cassandra shook Mr. Harper's hand and turned around and joined her family, who were waiting for her at the doors. She walked out of the courtroom a free woman—that chapter of her life was now over and she could move on.

Just as they were exiting the courthouse Pope's lawyer, Mr. Oaks, stopped them and asked if he could please speak to Cassandra for a few minutes in private. She turned and looked at Mr. Oaks. "I'm not sure what you would have to tell me that I would want to hear, Mr. Oaks."

"This is a private matter, Mrs. Davis."

Cassandra told him that anything he had to say to her he could say in front of her family, there would be no more secrets. Mr. Oaks proceeded to tell them that Pope had signed over all his assets to her. This would include the house, plus a cashier's check and his truck. All of these items were free and clear. Cassandra asked, why he would do such a thing?

"Mr. Pope feels that once he is in prison, his days on this earth are numbered. He has no family and feels that, with everything he put you through, that you deserve to have his estate now."

Cass stood there not knowing what to say. Mr. Oaks handed her his business card and told her to call him whenever she was ready to get together and sign the required papers to transfer everything over to her.

Everyone went back to Cassandra and Sid's place after court. It had been a long and exhausting morning and all Cass really wanted was to be alone. She could never have imagined this happening in her wildest dreams, but it had, and now she just had to figure out what she was going to do about it.

Everyone was talking and getting caught up. It had been a while since they all had been together. Cass excused herself and went into the kitchen. She just needed to get away from all the chatter. "You okay, Cass?"

She turned around and saw Big Daddy standing by the counter. "I was just getting a glass of water. Can I get you any- thing, Marvin?"

"No, I'm good thanks." Marvin went and sat on one of the chairs that were set up around the island in the kitchen. "Why don't you come and have a seat and you can tell me what you're thinking? I can see your brain going a mile a minute and you look like you're ready to explode."

She went and sat down next to her friend. "I don't know what to do. I have all these possessions that belong to Pope and

I don't want any of them, but they're about to be all mine. I'm confused as to what to do with them. Where do I begin?"

Marvin put his hand on top of hers and told her that if it was him, he would sell it all and use all the money she got for something good. "Cassandra, turn this terrible situation into something positive. Something that will make you feel a little good about this whole ordeal and maybe help others. Do it to honour those poor women that weren't so lucky."

She looked at Marvin. "How did I get so lucky to have you as a friend? I'm so grateful to have you in my life." She put her arms around Marvin and gave him a big hug.

"Do I need to be worried? I come into the kitchen and find my wife with her arms around another man."

"Well, Sid—if I was thirty years younger, you just might." They all laughed.

Sid came around and put his arms around Cass. "How are you doing?"

"I'm fine. just wanted some alone time with Marvin here."

"What do you want to do about dinner? The villagers are getting restless."

"Why don't we take everyone out for dinner to the Pit, that way we can just relax and you can get something for your lunch tomorrow—kill two birds with one stone."

"Sounds good to me."

31

....

Marvin stayed for a couple of days, then headed back on the road and promised he would come by for another visit when he was in the area. David went home a few days later, promising he would be back for the carnival and he would bring Bruiser and Willow with him. Cassandra told him he had better bring the dogs or he would be sleeping outside. Faye stayed for a week to spend some time with Cassandra, just the two of them.

"Cass, can I ask you something?"

"Of course you can, Mom—what's up?"

"Have you thought about what you're going to do with the items Pope left you?"

"I have. Marvin and I had a chat and what he said made sense. I just have to think about a few things. I'll let everyone know what I'm going to do on Sunday, at dinner."

Cassandra and Faye spent the last few days of their visit just hanging out. They went to the spa and took Shelley with them. They also went to the movies and down to the beach for some nice long walks. Faye was going to head home Monday morning and Cassandra was going to go back to work.

Cassandra was getting dinner ready. Everyone was coming to their place this time. It was decided that they would alternate Sundays, so this was her weekend—it wasn't fair for Shelley to do it all the time. Cassandra was making Sid's favourite fried chicken, potato salad, and homemade biscuits with apple pie for dessert.

Everyone started to arrive. Ryder walked into the kitchen and put his arms around her and gave her a big hug and then let her go.

"Hey, you! There's cold beer in the fridge."

"Thanks, darlin.'"

"Where's Sasha?"

Ryder grunted, "She won't be coming around anymore."

Cass looked at Ryder and told him she was sorry. He shook his head and told her Sasha wasn't cut out to be with him, she never liked how close the family is… 'but more to the point, how close *we* are."

"I'm sorry."

Ryder did what he always did. He shrugged his shoulders and told her it was okay; it didn't really matter. She walked over to him and gave him a hug. "Of course it does." He kissed her forehead and headed for the back door to find Sid and the rest of the family.

Cassandra called everyone to the table—dinner was ready. They all gathered around, filled their plates, and since Faye was there, they said grace. This was one of Cassandra's favourite times—having her whole family there, listening to everyone chatting back and forth, joking around, and just the love that surrounded them.

Cass made up a care package for Ryder and Tiny to take home. She always made way more than they could possibly eat and they never complained. They took it and left with a smile on their faces. Cassandra cleaned up all the dishes and put the rest of the food away.

Over dessert, she said she had something to talk to them about. She told them she had been thinking about what to do with the items Pope left her. "I want to sell everything. I want to go through it and take everything that may be of value, like coins or stamp collections. All the furniture can be given to charity—or if you guys know of a family in need, they can have it all." Cassandra told them that all the items that were in room she'd been held in would go directly to the dump. She didn't want anyone to have that garbage. "I want to sell the truck and the house, and put all the money into an account until I can figure out what I want to do with it. Big Daddy said that I should use the money to do some good, so that what we all went through becomes a positive—and I agree with him. I'm going to need everyone's help with this."

As always, everyone agreed to do whatever they could to help.

A few days later, Cassandra met with Mr. Oaks and signed all the papers that needed to be signed. She found out that Pope's parents had passed away and left him a rather large inheritance, and after all the debts were paid in full, what was left was hers to do with as she wished, and that was a considerable amount.

Saturday morning everyone met at 99 Weber Street—a place Cassandra hoped she would never have to see again. She sat in the truck, just staring at the front of the house. Sid put his hand on hers and asked her if she was going to be okay. "Baby, we don't have to do this today."

Cassandra didn't say anything. All she could see was that terrified girl on the other side of that window, trying to break free. When she'd finally broken free and crawled through the broken window she could feel the pain from the broken glass slicing her legs. She saw herself get up and run past the truck and head towards the street. Then she was gone. A calmness came over her; she knew where that frightened girl was heading and knew she would soon be safe.

Cass turned and looked at Sid. "I'm good." They got out of the truck everyone was standing there waiting. She handed the keys to Tiny and told him that when he walked down the hallway, he would see a bedroom door on the right-hand side— the bedroom in question had a small bathroom with a shower in it. She asked him to please make sure that the door was shut. She didn't want to see the inside of that room ever again.

Tiny took the keys and Ryder and Sid looked at her with a questioning look on their faces. She knew what they were thinking and told them she didn't want them to see the inside of that room either—as long as she was there, no one was allowed to go in that room.

A few minutes later, Tiny came back outside. He looked like he had been crying. He walked over to Cassandra and wrapped his arms around her and said, "He is a dead man." Cassandra pulled away and looked into Tiny's eyes and shook her head, no. Cass knew that all he would have to do is send a message to his friends, who knew inmates in the same prison as Pope, and they would take care of him.

"You have to all promise me that you will do nothing to Pope. I refuse to have anyone give him his just deserves on my behalf. That would make us no better than he is. If he dies there, I don't want it to be because of me—is that understood?" Ryder told her he couldn't make that promise to her. She walked over to him and looked up and told him if he loved her like he said he did, he would. Cassandra looked at everyone. "I can't handle the idea of someone losing their life over this, not even him." She looked at Ryder. "Please, Ryder."

"Fine." Ryder pulled away and walked towards the house.

She looked at Sid with a worried look on her face, "Nothing will happen, Cass—you have my word."

They entered the house and Cassandra stopped dead in her tracks. The look on Ryder's face told her that he had gone into the room and the look on her face told Ryder he was scaring the hell out of her. Just like that, the anger was gone and he could see what this was doing to her. He didn't want to be a part of anything that brought that look on her face ever again.

They spent the entire day going from room to room, pulling out anything of real value—which turned out to be quite a bit. They cleared a part of the living room and placed the items in that space. Shelley knew a guy that could help them figure out the value of the items and where she could sell them.

It was five-thirty when they decided to call it a day. They were going to come back on Sunday and pick up the truck and take it to a friend of Ryder's. Cass told Ryder, as long as it was a good deal they were to just sell it. They decided that all the furniture was going to go to a few families the boys knew were in need. Ryder would bring boxes over to pack everything up. They all agreed that they would come back the next weekend and sort out all the furniture—what each family was going to get. Shelley said she would call them to ask what they really needed.

It was going to take a few days to get everything in order, but Cassandra wanted it done as soon as possible. They all did, for that matter. As promised, Ryder got a stack of boxes to pack items up.

Cassandra decided to take a few days off work and go over to the house by herself. Sid didn't like it at all. He didn't like the thought of her being in the house all alone. He asked her to please wait until he'd finished work and he would go over with her, but she was adamant that this was something she needed to do and he knew there was no chance of talking her out of it.

Cassandra put all of Pope's clothes and bedding into garbage bags and dropped them off at the thrift store. She found a bunch of family pictures that she boxed up and took to Mr. Oak's office. She had the list of kitchen items the two families needed; she packed them up into boxes with their names on them.

Tiny had a friend who owned a garage and he came over and went through all the tools and took almost everything. She had offered the tools to Ryder first, for free, but he told her he didn't want anything. It took them almost a month to get everything out of the house and the garage, but it was finally done. The only room that was left, was the room that she was held in. She didn't want anyone from her family to have to deal with this room, so she asked a couple of guys she knew from the bar to come with their pickup and clear the room out.

That Tuesday, Cassandra had made arrangements for the front door and the door to the bedroom to be replaced with new ones. She didn't want anyone to see all the locks on them. The locks would only bring questions she didn't want to have to deal with. The gentleman that was replacing the two doors also agreed to paint the room she'd been held in a nice soft yellow, as well as sand and re stain the floor where Cassandra had carved her name. The cleaners would be coming Friday to clean the house from top to bottom and once they left she had a lady coming to cleanse the house of all negative energy. She wanted the new owners to feel nothing but positive energy throughout the house.

Saturday morning, the house was put on the market. Cassandra was hoping that the house would be sold quickly. The Realtor had an open house set for the day after it was listed, so she was keeping her fingers crossed.

32

It took a little longer then Cass had hoped to sell the house. She was beginning to wonder if it would ever get sold, but three weeks later, early in the morning, the phone rang. It was Wendy Parker, their Realtor. "Good morning, Cass. I hope I didn't wake you?"

"No. I was just getting up."

"Well, I have some good news for you. We have two offers on the house. One is for the asking price and one is for ten thousand above. What would you like me to do?"

Cassandra sat there for a minute, thinking about what Marvin had said to her: do something good with this money, make something positive come out of a bad situation. "Who do you believe is at their limit for funds?"

"I would say the couple that gave you the asking-price offer. They have two kids and I overheard them talking. The wife was telling her husband that there was no way they could afford any more. It was a little over their budget as it was."

"I know this is unorthodox, but could you set up a meeting with them at their home? Would you also find out if either couple is looking to flip the house?"

"I can call their agent and see if they would be willing to meet with you and see if either is thinking of doing that."

"Can you please see if you can set this up for today, preferably?"

"Sure. I'll call their agent's right now."

"Thanks. Talk to you soon." Cassandra hung up the phone and went out into the kitchen. She walked up to Sid, put her arms around him, and said, "Good morning."

Sid turned around and put his arms around her, leaned down and kissed her gently on the lips. "You had a rough night—are you okay?" Cassandra hugged him tighter and told him she was fine. She told Sid about the phone call from Wendy and what she asked her to do.

"Why would you want to do that?"

"I just had this feeling that I needed to. I don't know why, really—I guess we'll find out if they agree to meet. If they do, will you please come with me?"

"Of course I will. Baby, I'm worried about you. You haven't been yourself since you went back into that house. You barely let me touch you and you've been extremely quiet. I'm not complaining, because I know you're going through a lot and you must have a lot of mixed emotions going on in your head. I haven't wanted to pressure you, but I'm kind of feeling like you would rather I not be here. If that's the case, if you need some space, I have no problem staying at Tiny's for a while, if that's what you want."

Cassandra looked at Sid and saw the hurt in his eyes. Why hadn't she seen what she was doing to him before? He has done so much for her and all she has been thinking about was herself.

She hadn't even thought about how all of this was affecting him. She looked up at Sid. "I'm so sorry, hun, I've been so caught up in my own thoughts that I didn't even think how this was affecting you. I wouldn't blame you if you wanted to leave me. Hell, if it were me I would leave me. I don't want you to go. Please forgive me." She'd dropped the ball again—why did she keep doing this to him? She hadn't realized how much she had been hurting him ... yet again she was.

Sid told her he wasn't going anywhere. He loved her and would stand by her through whatever life had to throw at them. He just wanted her to remember that she wasn't alone—that he was, and would always be, there for her. "Cass, I want to help you, but you have to let me. You can't shut me out when things get bad. We are a team, remember? 'Through the good times and the bad'—that's what we both told each other the day we got married. Please, baby, talk to me, tell me what you're thinking, scream, yell, hit me if you have to—just not on my face, that's one of my best attributes." They both laughed. "Cass, do whatever you need to, but, baby, please let me in. I can handle whatever you have to throw at me."

Cassandra took Sid by the hand and sat down next to him on the couch. She looked at her amazing husband. "You're right, I haven't been fair to you at all and for that I'm truly sorry. This is in no way an excuse, but I was alone for so long before all this happened that having someone I can depend on is something I'm still getting used to, even after all this time. And let me say for the record that your face isn't your best attribute. It's your eyes. When I could finally see you clearly, it was the look in your eyes that made me fall in love with you more than I already had. The rest of you is just a huge bonus." She leaned over and kissed him on the cheek. "Sid you're right, my thoughts have been all over the place since we went back into that house. I'm wondering why this happened to me? what did I do so bad in this life that would justify such cruelty? I looked at the outside of the house and saw how close the other homes were. Why didn't I scream? Why didn't I do something to let the neighbours know I was there? Why didn't I fight harder? Why didn't I do so many other things? I lost a year of my life because I was too scared to do anything. I put my friends and family through hell. I put you all through hell. Why didn't I fight harder for them why didn't I fight harder for me? And why the hell did I get out of my car that night? I felt things change that day between all of us when we went to that house and I guess I am little afraid that maybe, after seeing it all, everyone's feelings towards me might have changed. I know that may sound stupid to you, but it's my insecurities rearing their ugly head, doing their best to make me distrust everyone, even the people who have shown me nothing but love and support. Please try and understand that there are still times when I can hear Pope's voice in my head telling me I'm trash and nobody will truly love me. It's been a real struggle for me at times. That look on Ryder's face is embedded in my mind. I've never seen such hatred in someone's eyes and that scares me because those kind of feelings can make a person do things they normally wouldn't do. The last thing I want is for someone else to get hurt over this. I'm worried about all of you—what this is doing to you and what it has already done to you. You're right, my mind has been going in a million different directions with worries and concerns and my own insecurities. I'm at fault here. I shut out the one person I should have been talking to—you."

Sid sat there, taking in everything she had just told him. She had finally opened up to him and now he needed to take a minute to process everything. She had bared her heart and soul to him and he knew that was a big deal for her. Cassandra just sat there, holding his hand. She knew she'd unloaded a lot on him, but in doing so an enormous weight had been lifted off her shoulders and she wished she'd talked to him sooner. David was rite, Sid could handle everything she had to tell him.

"Cass, I don't know why this happened to you. There is nothing you could ever have done to deserve this. The truth of the matter is, there are sick fucking people out there that don't give a shit about what they do to others and the aftermath that their actions cause. Baby, you did fight. You did what you needed to do to stay alive. Nobody can say that you should have done this, or that you should have done that. They weren't there in that situation and I'm so sorry that you were. What you went through … I honestly don't know if there are many people out there that could have survived that. I'm sure there are things that happened that we don't know about; just know, babe, I'm here if you ever want to talk about them. I'm not pushing you to talk about anything you don't want to—just know that if you do, I will listen to you. You're not alone. As for our feelings changing about you … it made us love you that much more. Cass, until we saw all the locks on the door and the chain attached to that bed, we could kid ourselves about this really happening—because what human being would do that to another? I guess it really made this all real—and I know how strange that must sound to you, because we knew it was real. We saw what he did to you. We saw the damage he did both physically and mentally, but it just made it more real—if that makes any sense to you?"

"It does. I know that sometimes you need to see everything in order to see the whole picture of how things were. It's one thing for me to tell you, but it's totally different when you see it for yourself."

"Cass, I'm glad you handled things the way you did. If you'd done things differently, the outcome could have been a whole lot different than it was. And I don't mean about us finding you—I mean he could have killed you and dumped your body someplace no one would find you, like those other poor women. Then what closure would anyone have gotten? You did what you needed to do to survive and there is absolutely nothing wrong with that." Sid put his arms around her and pulled her in close and just held her. He knew everything that needed to be said had finally been said.

They both felt better about the situation and each other. Sid understood his wife a little better and his wife finally under-stood that she really wasn't alone: Sid really could handle any-thing she needed to tell him. He wasn't going anywhere. And most of all, she could stop blaming herself that she hadn't done more. She came to the realization that there are things that will happen in one's life that you have no control over. There are bad people out there that don't play fair and don't care about what they do to others. She had to stop feeling guilty—thinking she hadn't done enough to try and get free. She'd done what she had to do to survive. She was alive because of the way she'd handled things, and was now living her life with the man she loved.

A little after eleven, the phone rang. It was Wendy. "Hi, Cass. The couple you wanted to meet with are Ray and Lisa Smith. They agreed to meet with us at two-thirty. "I am texting you you the address now. I will meet you there. Cass, as for either couple wanting to flip the house their Realtor couldn't say." Cassandra thanked Wendy and hung up the phone. She told Sid the couple had agreed to meet with them at two-thirty.

Sid and Cass pulled in front of the house a little after two and waited for Wendy to show up. They sat quietly holding hands, both thinking about what transpired earlier, when there was a tap on the window. It startled them both. It was Wendy.

"Is everything okay? You both were, like, a million miles away."

Cass told her they were fine. They just had some personal stuff going on.

"Shall we go in?" Cass nodded her head and headed up the walkway. Wendy rang the doorbell.

A tall man with blond hair answered the door. "Hello, I'm Ray."

"Hi, Ray. I'm Wendy and this is Sid and his wife Cassandra."

"Nice to meet you. Come in." Everyone walked in and Cass looked around. It was a small home for a family of four. "This is my wife, Lisa, and our son, Broady, and our daughter, Sadie. Lisa—this is Wendy, Sid, and Cassandra."

"Hi," Lisa said. "It's nice to meet you. Please have a seat. Can I get you anything to drink?" Everyone declined. Broady walked over to Cass and put his arms up.

"Up, please." Cass was a little taken aback by this. She wasn't sure what to do. When he said "up" again, Cass leaned over and picked him up and sat him on her lap.

"Hi there." Broady was grinning from ear to ear. He looked at Sid and touched his arm. He was curious about his tattoos. He had this serious look on his face. He looked back at Cass and then at Sid and then just snuggled up in her arms, staring at Sid's huge arm. Every once in a while, Sid would flex his biceps and make his tattoo move and Broady would laugh.

"I think you've made a new friend. Broady doesn't normally take to people so quickly. Do you have kids?" asked Lisa. Cass told them, no. "Do you plan on having kids? They seem to like you."

Cass looked at Sid. "It's not something we've ever talked about. I sort of like our life the way it is."

Cassandra looked at Sid and he smiled. "I would rather be an Uncle Sid than a dad. Fatherhood is something that never really appealed to me. I like my toys and our freedom to come and go whenever we want—and if I'm completely honest, I want Cass all to myself. I'm lucky to get near her at all when our friend brings his dogs over. Bruiser thinks she belongs to him, so he is our kid when he's around." They all laughed.

"Well," said Cass, "I guess you are probably wondering why we asked to meet you." Broady started to wiggle his way down to the floor. He walked over to his toys and started playing quietly. Sadie was asleep in Lisa's arms. "Can I ask you if this is a home for your family or is this a place you're going to try and flip for a profit."

"It's for our family—why?"

Cass told them she just had a few more questions and she would make everything clear in just a few minutes. "Do you work, Lisa, or are you a stay-at-home mom?"

"I'm hoping to be able to stay at home with my kids. I work part-time from home now."

"Ray, what is it you do for a living?"

"I'm an EMT."

"This may sound like a strange question, but what is it about the house that made you put an offer on it?"

Lisa looked at Ray and then back at Cassandra and stared at her for a few moments. "Well, it has three bedrooms and lots of space for the kids to play. We like its open concept and the fact it has a fenced-in backyard. I love the yellow colour in the one bedroom, that would be Sadie's room, it's such a calming colour. We just felt good being in the house. It has lots of storage space, and with two kids that's a big bonus. To be honest, if we get it, it will mean I won't have to go back to work full-time. Oh, and it's located in a nice neighbourhood. One of Ray's friends just lives down the street from the house so he would be able to carpool with him—so we wouldn't need to get a second vehicle we really can't afford."

Cass looked at Sid. "Can I talk to you a minute?" Sid got up, they excused themselves, and he followed Cass onto the front porch.

"Cass, what's going on?"

"I want to sell them the house, but I want to take, say, sixty thousand off the price. What do you think?"

"Baby, this is your house. You can do whatever you want."

Cassandra looked at Sid and shook her head. "No, it's ours and I want to know what you think."

"Why them? And why do you want to lower the price?"

"I think the house deserves some happiness and I think their family would be happy there. I wanna help someone, like you all helped me. I want to do something good with all this money, and meeting them—well, it just feels right. I want to make something good come out of all of this—other than meeting you all, of course."

Sid hugged Cass. "Baby, you never cease to amaze me. Let's go tell them the good news."

Cassandra and Sid went back into the house and sat back down on the couch. "Cass," said Lisa, "I'm sorry, but what is going on? All we'd like to do is buy your house. What's with the fifth degree?"

"Lisa!" Ray looked at his wife and shook his head.

"Ray and Lisa, Sid and I have decided to sell the house to you and your family. Wendy, we would like to reduce the asking price by sixty-thousand dollars."

"Are you serious?" Lisa asked.

"Yes, we are."

Lisa got up and went over to Cass and gave her a big hug and then turned and did the same to Sid. "Thank you. Thank you both so much. You don't know what this means to us."

"Lisa and Ray, my hope is that you'll have a wonderful life in this house." Wendy, can you make all the changes and get this taken care of right away?"

"Of course. I can have everything ready by morning."

"When can we take possession?" Ray asked

"As soon as the papers are signed and the money has been transferred it's yours." said Cass

They said their goodbyes and Sid and Cass wished them well. As they were walking down the walkway, they could hear a celebration going on inside the house.

Sid looked at Cass. "You made the right choice."

"Sid, can I ask you something?"

"Sure you can."

"We've never talked about it, but were you serious when you said you didn't want kids?"

He turned his head and looked at her. "Do you?"

"I asked you first."

"Well, if I'm truly honest with you Cass, no I don't. I watched my parents struggle to raise Tiny and me—always having to give up what they wanted in order to give us a great life—and I really never wanted to have to do that. Do you?"

"I did once, but no, not now. It's not just because of what happened with Pope, but what has happened throughout my life. I don't think I would make a good mom. I think I would do more harm than good to a child."

Early the next morning Wendy dropped by and had Cass sign the paperwork, and by Wednesday afternoon, the house was sold and the money deposited into the account Cassandra had opened. Everything Pope had given her had been turned into cash and was now sitting, collecting interest, waiting for her to decide what to do next. It was finally over: that chapter was closed. There was no need to ever reopen it again, as far as she was concerned.

33

....

Things finally calmed down and the nightmares finally stopped. It was as if the house and all the bad things that happened there had finally set her free. It no longer had a hold on her and everyone could see the change—most of all, Cass could feel the change.

Cass sent Ray and Lisa two congratulations baskets, one for the kids with some toys and monogrammed bath towels, and one for the parents. This one was filled with alcohol-free champagne, massage oils, and two bathrobes. She thought that after all the unpacking was done, they could probably use some quality time together.

There was a long weekend coming up and she decided she wanted to take Sid someplace nice and quiet, where it would just be the two of them. She spoke to Shelley, and Shelley gave her Rick's number. She knew he had a cabin he rented out, so Cassandra decided to give him a call. Rick told her she was lucky: the people that had booked the cabin for the upcoming weekend, a few months back, had just called and cancelled. "Can I ask you how you got my number?"

"My sister-in-law, Shelley Davis, gave it to me."

"Oh—you're Sid's wife?"

"Yes."

"You can e-transfer me the three hundred bucks and the cabin is yours from Friday to Monday."

"Would it be possible to get the cabin Thursday? I'd like to set everything up so Sid doesn't have to do anything."

"Sure, not a problem."

"Perfect. Can you please email me all the information and where I can pick up the keys?"

"If you deposit the funds today, I'll drop the keys off to Shelley tomorrow."

"How much for the extra day?"

"Nothing—it's all good."

"Awesome. Thank you so much. I'll send you the money as soon as we hang up. Thanks again." Cass hung up the phone and transferred the money, then told Shelley that Rick would drop the keys off the following day.

Cassandra called Ryder and sweet-talked him into giving Sid Friday off. It didn't take much—just a promise of one of her homemade apple pies when they got back. She knew he would say okay, but it was all worth it for four days alone with Sid.

As promised, the keys were dropped off to Shelley the next morning, along with all the information Cassandra had asked for. She made arrangements to have her shifts at the bar covered. With keys in hand, she headed off to the cabin to set everything up.

It turned out to be a two-hour drive but well worth it. The cabin was amazing. It was the last cabin on the road and the lake was right there, just a few feet from the front door. The nearest cabin was a half-mile from theirs; it was just perfect.

She put all their clothes and supplies away. She was thinking to herself, why did she pack them?—she didn't expect to see much of the outside. She laughed to herself.

She tucked the candles and the vanilla oil in a drawer. She had a very special night planned and she just wanted everything to be perfect. It was getting late, so she locked everything up and headed back home. Cassandra made it home a few minutes before Sid rode in.

Sid walked in with a big smile on his face. "What's up with you? You look like the cat that swallowed the canary."

"I don't know what you're talking about." She walked over, put her arms around his shoulders, and kissed him passionately.

"Wow. And what did I do to deserve this?"

"Well, Mr. Davis, it happens to be a long weekend this weekend and I have plans for us."

"Well, I just got an extra day off—so what might these plans be?" Cassandra told him he would have to wait and see, but they needed to get an early start in the morning, so they had to have an early night. "I'm good with that."

They ate dinner and crawled into bed early. He put his arms around her and asked for a hint as to what the upcoming weekend had in store for them. She told him he would just have to wait and see.

Cassandra woke up before the alarm went off and rolled over and whispered into Sid's ear, "Good morning … time to get up." Sid mumbled something like, the sun isn't even up yet, woman. She told him if he didn't get up now then he would miss part of his surprise—and the next four days were all about him.

"If that was true, then you'd let me sleep a little longer."

"No problem. You go back to sleep. I'll have to have a shower all by myself."

She got up, took her T-shirt off, threw it at him, and walked into the shower. Sid thought to himself, *More sleep? Or a shower with Cass?* He was up and in the shower before the water was even hot.

They made love in the shower. She loved it when he took control. He would take her to such amazing heights. It wasn't just a matter of having sex, it was about both of them having the best sexual experience with each other. He always made her body scream for more and she was willing to give him everything he wanted, so he would have the same pleasure she had.

Sid was an amazing lover. He could do things to her that drove her insane. He was taking her from behind and caressing her in ways that made every hair on her body stand on end, even the ones she didn't have. Just as they were both about to climax, the sun peeped its way into the window, casting a beautiful glow all around them and making them feel as one.

While they got dressed, Cass told him breakfast was waiting for them at Al's Diner. Sid asked what she had planned for them—she told him to just get in the truck. They locked the house up and Cassandra was just about to get behind the wheel.

"I'm driving," Sid said.

"No, you're going to get into the passenger seat, Mr. Davis, because I'm driving and I don't want to hear another word about it."

"Cassandra..." Sid said in a firm voice.

"Mr. Davis," was all Cass had to say, while giving him the look that told him it was her way or no way. He mumbled, got inside the truck, and pouted all the way to Al's.

They had a delicious breakfast. Sid was in better spirits after he ate breakfast and had his first few cups of coffee. He looked at Cassandra. "Mrs. Davis, what are your intentions with me this weekend?" He had a smirk on his face. She told him that once they got to their destination, he would find out.

"Sid, I want to do something special for you. Please don't give me a hard time about it—okay?"

He looked at his wife. "Baby, I'm yours. I'll follow you anywhere."

She smiled back. "Even if I'm the one driving?" He gave her a mischievous grin and said, ya if he had to. She smiled back and told him she would make it well worth his while.

He smiled and winked. "Darn right you will."

They finished their breakfast, then hit the road. It was a beautiful drive, the sun was shining, and they were together. Sid dozed off shortly after they left the diner; when Cassandra turned into the driveway at the cabin, she woke him. "Hun, we're here."

He opened his eyes and stretched his arms out. "Where are we?"

Cassandra gave him a devilish look. "Someplace no one can hear your pleas for help." He quickly perked up with a devilish look of his own.

She parked the truck at the side of the house and they both got out. She was reaching into the back seat to grab her bag when Sid came up behind her, "Nobody can hear us, right?" She told him the closest house was half a mile down the road. "Let's test that theory." He turned her around and sat her on edge of the back seat and pulled down her shorts and panties.

"Sid, what are you doing?"

"If no one can hear us, it doesn't matter what I'm doing." He pulled her closer to him and spread her legs a little and started playing with her mound. "Oh my God," she moaned. She lay back and her panting became heavier and heavier; she was getting wetter with every flick and stroke of his fingers. The next thing she felt was him spreading her legs further and the feeling of his smooth bald head rubbing her inner thighs. She could feel the heat from his tongue and his breath as he licked and sucked her bud. Cassandra started to moan. The more his tongue licked and sucked her, the louder she got. He suddenly stopped and she leaned up onto her elbows.

"Baby don't stop, please!"

He looked at her with so much lust in his eyes. "I want to hear you scream."

Cassandra lay back down and he started again. It didn't take long for her to get so hot. She wiggled with pleasure as his tongue started to dart in and out and then he started to nibble her. His fingers replaced his tongue. Everything he was doing to her was insane. Her moaning for more was getting louder and louder. When she couldn't take it anymore, she had the most mind-blowing orgasm she had ever had. She let out the loudest scream and shook like never before.

Before she had her bearings straight, he'd pulled her out of the truck, turned her around, and bent her over the seat and penetrated her. She gasped with pleasure. There was no warning. He just plunged his shaft deep inside her. She grabbed on to the end of the seat and met him with every thrust. They both were moaning and panting loudly. She found herself telling him, "Faster, baby, faster," and before they knew it, they both hollered. As they orgasm ed, he slowed his rhythm down and they both were able to catch their breath. He pulled out of her and she turned around. "Well, that was a nice surprise, Mr. Davis."

"Well… I wanted to see if anyone could hear us."

Cass looked around. "So far so good, but the weekend is still young and there is still time."

The next three days were amazing. They went for walks, went swimming, made love under the stars—they even took the rowboat out to do a little fishing but ended up making love instead. It was a challenge not to tip the boat, but they managed to do it.

Sunday morning, when Cass got out of bed, she cooked Sid a wonderful breakfast and served it to him in bed. They ate, talked, and laughed. It had been an amazing weekend of reconnecting—something they'd truly needed to do. They finished their breakfast and cuddled, just enjoying being with one another. A short time later, they got up and went for a walk.

The evenings at the cabin were wonderful. They heard the sound of crickets chirping and looking for a mate for the evening, and they saw fireflies flickering off and on, looking for theirs. They were sitting outside when Sid thanked Cass for this wonderful weekend. She looked at him and told him it wasn't over yet. Cassandra got up and told Sid she would be right back. She went into the cabin and changed into the lacy number she had brought, lit the candles, and put the vanilla oil on the nightstand.

She opened the door and stepped out onto the porch. Sid looked up. "Wow." Cass held out her hand and asked him to follow her. She took him back to the bedroom and undid his shorts and pulled both his shorts and briefs off.

"Please lie down on the bed, face down." Sid did as he was told. Cassandra took off her panties so he could feel her body on his skin. She reached over for the oil and rubbed it between her hands and while she was warming up the oil she was ever so slowly moving her pelvis while sitting on his butt. Sid was enjoying it; he was giving out little moans which made Cass excited.

She gently massaged Sid's arms and back and gradually moved down his body. She separated his legs a bit and as she was massaging his upper thighs, she gently slid her fingers up and down his sack. Sid groaned even more.

"Hun, roll onto your back, please." He did as he was told. He looked at Cass. "Do you trust me?" she asked. He nodded, yes. She reached over and grabbed her bandana and tied it around his head, covering his eyes. She took his hands and put them at his side, and told him to grab the sheets. He did as he was told. She sat on top of him and leaned over and whispered in his ear. "Here are my rules, Mr. Davis. You are not allowed to talk, only moan and groan. You are also not allowed to let go of the sheets—do you understand?" He nodded his head, yes. "If you break my rules I will stop and you will have to lie here till I decide to come back and begin again. Do you understand?" He nodded his head again. "Do you need anything before I begin?" He shook his head, no—he was getting extremely excited. He had never seen this side of his wife and he had to admit he was enjoying every bit of it.

Cass could feel Sid getting aroused, and she was as well for that matter. She leaned over him and her nipples caressed his chest as she gently kissed him. She teased his tongue with hers. He tried to say something, but stopped and just moaned, grabbing the sheets even tighter.

Cass moved down Sid's body, gently kissing and nibbling her way to his large manhood that was now almost fully erect. She gently took her tongue and licked the head of his shaft and Sid almost lost it. He quivered and moaned loudly as she circled her tongue around his head and gently took his sack into her hand and massaged it. She gently moved her mouth up and down his member and Sid moaned loudly with utter pleasure. She increased her speed both with her mouth and her hands and just when he was almost ready to lose all control, she stopped. Sid cried out. She bent over him and let her nipples touch his chest and whispered into his ear, "Paybacks a bitch." He let out a big sigh but didn't say a word, in fear that she would truly stop altogether he wanted so much more.

Cassandra rubbed her body against Sid's body. She began moving back down his body and when she finally reached his manhood she gently started to pump it with her hand. In mere seconds, Sid was rock hard again. She placed the head of his shaft at the entrance of her mound and guided herself slowly over it, which made Sid moan and she stopped and pulled herself off his shaft, then again she teased him by lowering her self over the head of his shaft again then stopping she teased him a few more time and Sid couldn't take it any more, he grabbed Cassandra by the waste and pulled her down hard onto his shaft. Cassandra hollered with pleasure, she started moving faster faster and faster. Cass was smacking against his body with every thrust he gave her. He couldn't believe this was happening. He had never had an experience like this with any other women.

It was so intense that when they both finally climaxed, the only words that came out of Sid's mouth were, "Holy fuck." He wrapped his arms around her. They were exhausted.

"I love you, Sid."

"I love you too, baby." And they both drifted off.

34

Cassandra couldn't believe it had been three weeks since her weekend away with Sid. She was in a great place both mentally and physically. She couldn't recall if she had ever felt this way—even she and Sid were better together. Everything had finally fallen into place for them and neither one could be happier.

It was one week before the club's big event, so Cassandra made arrangements to take a few days off work to give them a hand. When Sid came home, Cass was on the phone getting all the information about Jayne's arrival. Jayne was telling her she was able to get a flight the next day. Cass told her she couldn't wait to see her and Jayne told her she felt the same.

Sid leaned over and kissed Cass and asked her what was going on and who was coming. "Jayne and Coco are coming tomorrow; their flight lands at one forty-five."

"I do have one question for you."

"What's that?" Cassandra asked.

"Well, what's in it for me?"

Cassandra looked at Sid with a questioning look. "What do you mean?"

"Well, you get your friend for the next little while, so what about me? What do I get?"

Cassandra looked at Sid, who had this smirk on his face. "What would he like?" she asked with a smile.

Sid walked away and came back with Cassandra's bandana. He held it up. "This please."

Cass started to laugh. She got up and gave him a kiss and whispered in his ear, "Anytime, baby."

He grabbed her around the waist pulled her in close, "How about now?" She told him to go and have a shower she would be waiting for him in their bedroom with the vanilla oil and nothing else on. He smiled and told her he wouldn't be long.

Cass arrived early at the airport to pick up Jayne and Coco. She couldn't wait to see her. It had been a while since they'd been together.

Jayne's flight was early and it took her no time at all to get through customs. "Jayne! Over here!" Cassandra hollered.

"I'm so glad you're here, I've missed you so much."

"Cass, we've missed you too." Cass bent down and said hello to Coco and gave her a bit of loving, then stood up.

"Let's get you guy's the hell out of here."

"Sounds good to us."

The club's big day had finally arrived. Cass was up and dressed before the sun was even up. She was going over her list of things she'd promised the club she would take care of today, before everyone else started to arrive.

Cassandra was making breakfast for everyone, Ryder showed up early to give Cass a hand. The doorbell rang. Sid was still in the shower so Ryder went to see who it was and was nearly bowled over by Bruiser rushing in to see his girl. "Perfect timing," he told David.

"Why, what's up?"

"Cass is making her famous breakfast burritos. Tiny and Shelley should be here any minute."

Jayne and Coco came in from outside and said hello to everyone. Bruiser and Coco sniffed around and then walked away—neither seemed impressed with the other.

It was a beautiful day and the turnout was amazing. Everyone was having a great time. Ray and Lisa brought Broady and Sadie to visit the petting zoo and ride the ponies. The club was spot on the Carnival was a huge hit for all, the dunk tank was a huge hit aswell. Jayne and Cass were having a blast trying to dunk Sid. When it was Cassandra's turn in the dunk tank, the first one to throw at her was Ryder. He missed the first two throws, but he nailed it on the third, the forth, and the fifth. Poor Cass was getting waterlogged. She hollered to Ryder, "I thought you liked me?"

"Darlin', this is just way too easy to pass up and after all, it is for a good cause." he said with a huge smile on his face.

"Just remember paybacks."

He laughed. "I think I'm safe."

There were a lot of attempts to dunk Cass and a few people other than Ryder were able to succeed. Ryder turned to Sid and asked him when he was going to take his turn. Sid told him it wasn't happening, brother, he had to sleep with her tonight. Everyone around them laughed. David even took his turn and dunked her once. He told her he felt bad for doing it, but after all this was for a good cause. Cass took it all in stride. She really didn't mind—she was having a great time—but just as she was going to get out, a familiar voice piped in, "Am I too late?" Cass looked in the crowd and there was her mom and Big Daddy. He stepped up and paid for his balls and tried to dunk her. He missed with every throw and Cass had a feeling it was intentional, but then her mom stepped in and got Cass with her first ball and everyone started to cheer.

Finally, it was Ryder's turn, and everyone stayed close because they wanted to see what happened when Cassandra took her turn at trying to dunk him. She let a few people go first, then she stepped up and bought some balls. Jayne and Faye were beside her. "Cass, darlin', you and I both know it's not gonna happen—so why don't you just walk away before you embarrass yourself?"

Cassandra looked at Ryder and, with a big smile on her face, she threw her first ball and hit it dead centre. Down Ryder went and everyone hollered and laughed. Ryder got back up on the seat, beginners luck he hollard and Cass threw her second ball and again down he went. She did this two more times with the same results, when Faye hollered, "Ryder, didn't Cass tell you she was the head pitcher for her high school baseball team?"

Ryder looked at Cass. "No, Faye, she neglected to tell us that part of her life." Cass just smiled at him and threw another ball and down he went again.

The day was starting to wind down and the sun was starting to set. They had hired a band to play for some extra evening fun. The BBQ was still hot, so people stayed and were enjoying their supper while the music way playing. People were dancing and having a great time. Cass was dancing a fast one with Big Daddy and thought to herself, wow that man has moves for a guy his age.

The next song was a slow one and Sid went and took Cass by the hand and got up close and personal with his wife. They nuzzled close together and when the song was over they just kept on dancing. They didn't care what anyone else was doing.

At midnight, the band packed up and everything was shut down and locked up. People were already talking about what they might do the next year.

35

....

Cassandra woke up early; Sid had gotten up extra early to go into the shop. He was working on a bike that had to be done by the end of the day. Cass decided she would surprise him and made some breakfast burritos and a big thermos of coffee; she was just about to head to the shop when Jayne came upstairs to make herself a coffee.

"Morning, Cass. You're up early."

"I'm taking Sid and Ryder some breakfast. Sid went in really early."

"Cass can we talk?"

"This sounds serious?" They sat down at the counter and Jayne sipped her coffee.

"Cass, I've really enjoyed my time here with you and everyone; I would really like to stay."

"I would love that. You can stay as long as you want."

"Cass, I mean I would like to move here."

"Seriously, that would be amazing. You can stay with Sid and me till you get your feet on the ground."

"Are you sure Sid won't mind?"

Cassandra sat there for a moment. "I was just thinking... Ryder has this small apartment above the shop. I can ask him if he would rent it to you. I'll ask him when I see him."

"Oh Cass, that would be great."

"There are some burritos in the oven for you"

Cassandra headed over to the shop. She let herself in and went to the back of the garage and turned down the music. She didn't want to startle Sid.

"Morning, hun."

He turned his head and looked up. "Hey baby."

"I thought you might be hungry and in dire need of some good coffee so I made you some breakfast."

"Mmm, smells good"

"Can you take a break?" He said for her, definitely.

They went into Ryder's office and sat on the couch. Cass poured him a nice cup of brew and handed him the container of burritos. Sid was halfway through his first one when Ryder walked in. "Is that burritos I smell?" Cass laughed and said yes and handed him his own container to eat. He told her she was way too good to them.

"Ryder, I have a favour to ask."

"Uh-oh! Ryder, look out," Sid said with a grin.

"Jayne and I were talking, and she said she would like to move here. I told her that would be amazing and that she could stay with Sid and me for as long as she liked."

Sid stopped eating and looked at Cass. "You what?"

Cassandra smiled and put her hand on his knee. "Ryder, I was thinking about the apartment upstairs. It's empty and maybe she could work around here till she finds a job."

Ryder looked at Cass. "It will cost you, big time."

"How big?" Cassandra said with a smile.

"Burritos and an apple pie once a month."

"Deal."

"Okay Cass, bring her around so she can see the place and we'll work something out." Cassandra got up and went over to Ryder put her arms around his neck and told him thank you.

Sid was quiet; for the rest of Cassandra's visit, he didn't say much. "Hun, are you okay?" Cass asked.

"I'm fine, just tired."

Cassandra got up and got ready to leave; she told Ryder she would bring Jayne over to see the apartment around noon. Sid walked Cass to their truck. She looked at him with a worried look on her face. He kissed her deeply. "Stop worrying—all is good."

Cassandra went home and told Jayne the good news. The two ladies went to check out the apartment and Jayne said she would take it. Ryder told her she could work part-time in the office to help cover the cost of her rent. He wouldn't charge her much, just a couple of hundred to cover the cost for the extra hydro and water.

Sid agreed to let Coco stay with them until Jayne came back with all her and Coco's belongings. Coco was getting up there in age herself, and it wasn't fair to put her through the extra drive and flight. Sid didn't mind that Coco was there. He sort of liked having her around.

Cass hired a cleaning service to come and do a top-to-bottom cleaning so that the place was move-in ready—she even stocked the cupboards and fridge with all the supplies Jayne might need. She knew the last thing Jayne would want to do was go shopping after all the driving she'd have just done.

Coco was excited to see Jayne and so was Cass. Jayne said Natalie was sad to see her go but was glad that she was going to be with Cass, and reminded her about a girls' weekend. Jayne promised they would sit down and pick a date as soon as she got settled.

Sid and Ryder helped Jayne get her belongings up to her new apartment, and Cass stayed and helped her get settled. Cassandra thought to herself life was truly wonderful.

36

....

Everything got back to normal. Jayne started to work in the office at the bike shop to help with the paperwork. It didn't pay much, but the rent was cheep, so Jayne didn't need a lot.

Cass woke up and Sid was already up and in the shower. She couldn't believe that tonight they were celebrating their second wedding anniversary already. Where did the time go? She thought back to the day Sid and Ryder had found her and all that they had gone through since then to get where they were today. They'd all been lost and broken in one way or another, and finding one another finally had made them all feel whole again. Cassandra remembered the day Sid had told her that bad things happen to good people. She thought to herself, *but out of the bad came something amazing*. She was living the life she always dreamed of, she was married to the love of her life, and Ryder and Tiny and Shelley were her family. Cass finally felt at peace.

Cass got up and made Sid a nice breakfast. When he was finished, she cleared the dishes from the table and headed towards the bedroom to get dressed, when Sid grabbed her and pulled her onto his lap. "Happy anniversary, baby."

He nibbled her gently on her neck while slipping his hands between her legs, running it upwards towards her panties "Mmm, happy anniversary, hun." She kissed him and gasped as he caressed her mound and before either of them knew it, they were naked and making love on the kitchen table.

When they'd finally finished and had enough for the time being, Sid got dressed, smacked Cass on the ass, and told her to be good. She gave him her devilish smile and told him, "But baby, when I'm bad I'm so much better."

He winked at her. "Ain't that the truth," he said, and headed to the shop.

Sid told Cass he had to work until noon, run a few errands, and would be home to spend the remainder of the weekend with her in bed. She told him she was looking forward to it.

Cassandra cleaned up and went shopping. She went to her favourite lingerie store and picked up a few new pieces for their weekend together. Then she stopped at the butcher's and grocery store for supplies. She decided to go by the florists for some rose petals. She truly wanted to make this a romantic evening, to show Sid how much he meant to her.

Cass was just getting out of the shower when Sid called and told her he would be home shortly—he just had one more stop to make, then he would be all hers. As always, Cass told him to drive safe and she would see him soon. She got dressed in an outfit she had purchased earlier in the day and made a trail from the door to the bedroom of rose petals.

The candles were in place—as soon as she heard his bike, she would light them. The vanilla oil was on her nightstand along with her bandana. She had created a monster with that bandana.

Cass looked at the clock. It seemed to be taking Sid a long time to get home. She was starting to get a little worried. She called his cell but there wasn't any answer it went to voice mail. She called Jayne and Jayne told her he had left a few hours ago. Cass called Tiny to see if he had stopped in and lost track of time. Tiny told her he hadn't seen him all day.

Cass hung up her cell. She had a bad feeling in the pit of her stomach. Something was wrong. She started to pace back and forth, when she finally heard the rumbling of Sid's bike coming down the street. She was relieved she had been wrong. She headed into the bedroom and was just about to light the candles when she heard the door open and Ryder holler out her name. Her stomach dropped and the panic set in: something was wrong. She rushed out into the kitchen, not even thinking—she barely had anything on. Ryder was standing in the doorway, just staring at her. She stopped dead in her tracks and stared right back at him.

Ryder walked over to her and put his hands on her bare shoulders. "Cass, there's been an accident. Sid is on his way to the hospital; we have to go." Cass just stood there. She couldn't move. What was Ryder telling her? Sid was fine. He was on his way home. Ryder had to be mistaken.

"Cass—look at me, darlin'. You need to get some clothes on. We need to get to the hospital, now!" She just stood there. Ryder raised his voice. "CASS!" She shook her head. "Darlin', please go get some clothes on." She looked down at what she was wearing and then back up at Ryder. "Please, we have to go." Cass turned around and rushed into the bedroom and pulled a pair of jeans on and one of Sid's hoodies. She pulled on her sneakers and out the door they went.

Ryder was weaving in and out of traffic, trying to get to the hospital as quickly as he could, when he heard sirens coming up from behind. There was no way in hell he was going to stop. The officer must have called in for backup because the next thing Ryder knew there was a cruiser beside him, telling him to pull over. Ryder slowed down and hollered that he needed to get to Hope's Medical Centre. It was life and death. The officer told him to get behind him and that it had better be life or death. The other police cruiser pulled in behind Ryder and they were given a police escort. Cassandra was oblivious to everything going on around her; she just held on tight and was thinking about Sid and praying he would be alright.

A few minutes later they pulled into the medical centre parking lot, with the cops following them into the centre. They rushed up to the desk where the nurse was sitting taking information from a guy who was in there because he had sliced his hand open when he was trying to open a can of pork and beans.

"Excuse me," said Ryder. The nurse looked up at Ryder with an annoyed look on her face and told him to have a seat, she would be with him shortly. "Look," Ryder said in a very loud and stern voice, "my brother was brought in from a serious motorcycle accident. This is his wife." The nurse quickly stood up and told the guy she was speaking to that she would be right back.

"Follow me," she said. Ryder and Cass were right behind her and so were the four police officers.

Cass was in shock and her mind was racing. It just couldn't be Sid, it had to be someone else, it was all a big mistake she kept telling herself. Ryder went and spoke with the officers and then came and sat next to Cass. He put his hand on top of hers and just left it there.

The officers were sticking around. Cass didn't even notice them standing there. "Tiny?" was all that Cass could manage to say.

"They're on their way."

It seemed to take forever for the doctor to come out, but when he did, the look on his face told them it wasn't going to be good news.

"Hello, I'm Doctor Scott." They both stood up.

"I'm Ryder and this is Cassandra, Sid's wife."

"Mrs. Davis."

"Please call me Cass."

"Cass, I'm sorry to tell you this but your husband is in really bad shape. We've stopped the bleeding from his right leg, and we're just about to take him downstairs for a CT Scan and x-rays of his leg, pelvis, as well as his lungs. We are doing blood work as we speak to make sure his levels are normal. Thankfully, he is breathing on his own. If all goes well, when his tests are all finished, he'll be brought back up to our trauma centre so he can be monitored to make sure there is no internal bleeding and to make sure that his neurological status doesn't change within the next twenty-four to forty-eight hours. I'm sorry, but that's all I can tell you right now."

"Can we please see him?" Cass whispered.

"Of course you can, but just for a minute—we need to get him downstairs."

They followed Dr. Scott to the cubicle where Sid was located. Cass went to his side and put her hand on his hand. "Sid, baby, I'm here. You're going to be okay, just stay strong for me. I love you Sid."

Sid opened his eyes just a little. "I love you," he said. "Promise me you'll be okay."

"What do you mean?"

"Baby, I..."

"Sid Davis, don't you fucking dare give up on us. You fight, dammit. Do you hear me! Fight! I'm not living this life without you; do you understand me?"

Sid gave a weak smile, "Yes ma'am."

Dr. Scott said they had to go, as they needed to take Sid down for his tests.

"Ryder?"

"Yes, brother." Ryder leaned in.

"Promise me you will take care of our girl. Don't let her shut down. Love her, brother."

"You're going to be fine, Sid."

"Promise me."

Ryder took Sid's hand. "You have my word."

"We have to go now," said the doctor. They wheeled Sid down the hall quickly and onto the elevator, and then they were gone.

Ryder called Jayne and told her what was going on. She told him to tell Cass she was on her way. Cass sat down and Ryder came and sat next to her. "Jayne is on her way."

Cass nodded her head. "Can I please use your phone?" He handed it to her and she dialed her mom's number. Tiny and Shelley arrived and Ryder got up to tell them what had happened and what Dr. Scott had just told them.

Faye answered on the third ring. "Hi Ryder, how are things?"

"Mom..."

"Cass, what's wrong?"

"It's Sid. He's been in a terrible accident."

"Is Ryder there? Let me talk to him, please."

Cassandra looked up. "Ryder...?" Cass held the phone up to him. "My mom." Ryder came and took the phone from Cass and walked over to the window to talk to Faye. Shelley came and sat next to Cass. "We can't lose him, Shell, we just can't," said Cass. Shelley took her hand and the two ladies sat there, tears streaming down their faces.

Ryder told Cass that her mom was on her way and handed his phone back to her. Cass stared at the phone and dialed another number. "Hey, Ryder. How are things?"

"Marvin, it's Cassandra."

"Cass, my girl, how are you? I thought we were talking Monday—or did I get my days mixed up?"

"Big Daddy—" was all Cass could say.

"Cass, what's wrong?"

"Sid was in an accident"

"Say no more, Cassandra. I'm on my way, dear. I just have to drop this load off. Where are you?"

"Hopes Medical Centre."

"I'll be there as soon as I can. Your mom?"

"She's on her way."

"Cass, I know it's hard but think positive. Positive thoughts only."

"I will," was all she could get out before she broke into uncontrollable sobs. Ryder took the phone and spoke with Big Daddy while Shelley put her arms around Cass.

Jayne walked in. "I'm here Cass," she said and sat down next to her. Jayne looked up at Shelley and said she was here for all of them. Shelley smiled and said thank you.

Tiny was standing over by the window, not knowing what to do for anyone or what to say. His baby brother was fighting for his life and there wasn't a damned thing he could do. He felt lost and was mad as hell.

"How you doing, brother?"

Tiny just shook his head. "He's my baby brother. I don't know what to do and if he dies, Ryder... This shit isn't supposed to happen to good people like Sid. He finally has the life he's always wanted. If we lose him, we're gonna lose her too."

"No, we're not. We're not going to let that happen. Cass isn't the same girl we met four years ago."

Tiny nodded his head. "I think you should call David if something happens to him; we're gonna need him." Ryder agreed and walked away to make the call.

It was hours before Dr. Scott came back to talk to them. "Mrs. Davis, I"

"How's Sid?"

"I was just looking at his CT scan and x-rays. Your husband's leg is broken in three places and his right hip has been broken as well. These things we can deal with later, but the CT scan wasn't as good as I had hoped. There is brain swelling on the right side of his brain. We've started him on three-percent normal saline. We also placed an arterial line in your husband's wrist so we can monitor his blood pressure closely, as well as a central line for his hydration management and blood pressure control. He'll have continuous cardiac monitoring and he'll be staying in the neurological ICU where he'll have hourly neurological assessments. I'm sorry I don't have better news."

"Can we sit with him, please?"

"Of course you can. Just give the nurses a few minutes to get him all set up and one of them will come and get you shortly."

Cassandra got up and walked over to Tiny and he put his arms around her. Cass looked up. "I know this is a stupid question but how are you doing?"

Tiny leaned over and kissed the top of her head. "I'm good."

"Liar."

"Cass, promise me you're gonna be okay, whatever happens. Promise me we're not gonna lose you too."

"I'm not going anywhere, I promise."

"Can anyone join this hug?" Shelley asked. Tiny put his other arm around his wife and the three of them held onto each other.

It seemed like an eternity to Cass when finally a nurse came out to get them. She looked familiar, but Cass couldn't place where she knew her from. "Hi Cass, I'm Georgie Walker. I'll be your husband's lead nurse in the ICU. Let me take you all to his room. I just want to warn you all—there are a lot of monitors, wires, and tubes hooked up to Sid."

"How is he?" asked Tiny, Cass jumped in, "This is Sid's brother, Tiny and his wife Shelley. Nurse Walker looked up at Tiny and Shelley and touched Cassandra's shoulder.

"He's stable. He's in and out of consciousness. Follow me, please. He's been asking for you, Cass."

They all entered the room; Cass took Sid's hand in hers and kissed him gently on the forehead. "I'm here Sid. I love you." Sid moaned and slightly squeezed her hand.

Sid made it through the night, which Cass hoped was a good sign. Everyone spent the night at the hospital. No one wanted to leave, in case the unthinkable happened. Nurse Walker came into the room every hour, and every hour Cass asked her how he was doing. She smiled and told her he was holding his own and there was no change in his vitals. She told Cass that he would have another CT scan in the morning to see if the swelling had gone down. If it had, they would discuss the next step—all they could do for now was sit and wait.

The doctor came into Sid's room shortly after 7 a.m. "I'm going to have to ask everyone to leave, we need to check some things out and get Sid ready to go down for another CT scan."

"Cass," said Jayne, "let's go down and get something to eat. You need to keep your strength up." Cass looked at Jayne and said no, she wasn't going anywhere.

Ryder walked over to her. "Come on darlin'. You need a break and they need to take care of Sid."

"You all go. I'm not leaving him."

"Cassandra …" Cass turned around and there was Faye standing in the doorway. Cass rushed into her mother's open arms and almost collapsed. Faye put her arm around her daughter and led her out of the room and down the hall to the lounge.

Nurse Walker came to the lounge and sat next to Cass. "Is Sid okay?" Cass asked.

"There's no change. They're taking him downstairs for his CT scan. I'm done my shift but I'll be back tonight. You need to get some rest."

Cass looked at Nurse Walker. "Where do I know you from?"

The nurse smiled at Cassandra. "I was at your wedding, with my husband, Max." Cassandra nodded her head—she remembered her now.

"Nurse Walker?"

"Call me Georgie, please."

"How long will Sid be?"

"He'll be a while. You should go get a coffee and something to eat. You all should."

Sid was brought back to his room a short time later and Cass was back at his side. "Cass, hun, you look dead tired. You need some sleep." said Shelley

"Listen," said Cass, "I know you all mean well, but I'm not going anywhere. If it was me, Sid wouldn't leave my side. And I'm not about to leave his. Please everyone, stop asking me to. Because it's not going to happen."

People were in and out; everyone was tired but nobody wanted to venture too far. Ryder picked up the two-seated chair and put it next to Cass. "Cassandra, come sit with me." She looked at him and was just about to say no, when he gave her the look that said, "I'm not asking, darlin.'"

She got up from where she was sitting and pushed her chair out of the way so the other chair could get closer to the bed, and sat down next to Ryder. He put his arm around her and she placed her head on his chest. A short time later she drifted off for some much-needed sleep.

Cassandra slept for almost two hours. When she woke up and opened her eyes, there was David standing next to Sid saying a prayer. "David, what are you doing?"

"Hi, Cass. I'm just saying a prayer for God's help."

"Why would God help us? He did this to Sid."

"No, Cass, he didn't." David shook his head.

"Bullshit!" Cass lost it and went off on poor David and everyone for that matter. She wouldn't let up—everyone tried to calm her down but she would have none of it. She was mad as hell and she knew she was losing Sid. She could feel it in her heart and she'd be damned if she wanted to hear anything about anyone's God.

Finally, a nurse came into the room and told everyone if they didn't quiet down, they would all have to leave.

"I'd like to see you try and make me," Cass snapped back.

"Cassandra!" She looked towards the door and there was Big Daddy staring at her. The look on his face completely sucked all the built-up anger and frustration right out of her and she looked at everyone and started to cry.

"I'm sorry, David. I'm sorry everyone please forgive me." David walked around the bed and put his arms around her and told her that there were no apologies needed, they all understood.

Big Daddy walked into the room with food and told everyone to help themselves. He walked over to Cass with a separate bag and told her to sit down and eat her chicken and biscuits, and he didn't want to hear one word about it. She looked at him and with a slight smile asked if it was extra crispy, and he asked her, would he bring anything but? She put her arms around his waist and gave him a big hug and told him thank you and kissed the side of his face.

Everyone was talking quietly and eating—even Cass started to eat. She didn't want to admit it, but she was hungry. Faye looked at Marvin and mouthed, "Thank you." Marvin smiled and nodded his head.

Dr. Scott came into the room. "Good evening. Something smells good."

"There's pizza. Help yourself Doc," Marvin told him.

"Cass, I just got the results of Sid's CT scan and the swelling has gone down a little, but I'm still concerned. I feel it should have gone down a lot more than what it has, so it's still a waiting game. His vitals are a little better, but it's too soon to tell. I'll come back in to check on Sid later, before I leave for the day."

Sid was stable for the moment so Tiny and Shelley left to go home to shower. Ryder said he was going to run home himself but would stop by her place and pick her up a change of clothes.

"David, where are you staying?" asked Cass.

"Downstairs at your place; my dogs are at the house now."

"Can you take my mom back to the house so she can have a little rest? The pups will want to go out and then you can come back up. I'd like some time alone with Sid, please."

Everyone left, to give Cass some time alone with Sid. Marvin went and sat in the lounge and Jayne went home to let Coco out. She said she would be right back. Suddenly the room was quiet. All you could hear were the beeping sounds coming from the monitors.

Cass gently moved the wires that were hanging down on Sid's left side and crawled in next to him and watched as his chest moved up and down with every breath he took. She whispered in his ear, "Sid, I don't know what's going to happen here. I pray with all my heart you're going to pull through. I can't imagine my life without you. You saved me and I wish I could do the same for you. I love you, baby. Please don't leave me."

Cassandra lay there for a while next to him, then got up and went back and sat in her chair. She was deep in her own thoughts when she heard a voice saying, "Excuse me." She looked towards the door. There was an officer standing there. "I'm sorry to bother you at a time like this, but I was one of the officers at the scene of your husband's accident. Could I speak with you for a moment?"

"Of course. Come in."

"My name is Officer Camilleri."

"I'm Sid's wife, Cassandra. Can I ask you what happened to my husband, please?"

Officer Camilleri told her that a young lady had run a red light and taken off. She'd been drinking. There were a lot of witnesses and they had a very good description of her and the car she was driving. "Her lawyer called and the young lady turned herself into us a few hours ago." Cassandra just stared at the officer and nodded. "The reason I'm here, is that your husband had this package in his pocket and it fell out when he was lifted onto the gurney. I put it in my cruiser and forgot about it. I apologize for that."

"It's fine. Thank you for bringing it to me. Is the girl who hit my husband alright?"

"She's fine. Just a bump on her forehead." Cass told him that was good. "How is your husband doing?"

"Not good, I'm afraid."

Officer Camilleri stood up and handed Cass his card and told her if he could do anything, to please call. He turned around and was about to leave. "Officer Camilleri,"

"Yes ma'am?"

"Thank you for all that you did to help my husband and thank you for bringing this. It was our second wedding anniversary."

"I pray you have more with your husband, ma'am." He turned and left. Cass thought to herself, *So do I.*

Everyone started coming back into the room. Marvin came and sat next to her. "What's that?" He pointed to the box in her hand.

"I don't know. It fell out of Sid's pocket at the accident site. I think this is what he was picking up for me for our anniversary."

"Are you going to open it?"

"I don't know if I should."

"I think Sid would want you to, after all it was a gift to you from him."

She unwrapped the box and inside was a beautiful gold chain with a heart pendant trimmed with small diamonds running around the entire heart. Cass took it out of the box and put it around her neck.

"Cass?" said Sid.

"I'm right here, hun."

"Hey, beautiful."

"I got your gift. It's beautiful." She leaned in closer so he could see it on her neck. "Unfortunately, yours is underneath these clothes." He smiled.

"It looks beautiful on you, baby."

"Everyone's here." Tiny and Shelley walked over to the bed.

Tiny took Sid's hand. "Hi, buddy, nice to see you're finally awake."

"Tiny, thank you for being the best brother a guy could ask for and Shelley, you've been the best sister-in-law. I love you both."

"We love you too, Sid." Shelley leaned over and hugged him and gave him a kiss on the cheek, then backed away.

"Ryder?"

"I'm right here, Sid."

"You've been like a brother to me. You're my best friend. Thank you. Take care of our girl. Love her and don't let her push her away."

"Sid, you have a long life ahead of you with Cass."

"Promise me." Ryder nodded his head.

"Sid don't talk like that. You're not going anywhere. You have to get better. I need you," Cassandra said with tears rolling down her face.

"Cassandra listen to me. You've been the love of my life and I thank the man up there every day for bringing you to me. Please don't shut yourself off, baby. Every day is a second chance. Take it. Cass, you'll never be alone. I'll always be there. I'll always love you. Promise me you'll live."

"Sid, don't talk like that. I won't let you say goodbye to me."

Sid closed his eyes and the monitors went off. Nurse Georgie ran in and called code blue and jumped on top of Sid and started to do CPR. Cassandra started screaming, "No, Sid, please don't leave me, baby, I beg you. God, please don't take him from me, please take me instead."

The rest of the nursing team ran in with the crash cart. One nurse told everyone to leave. "NO!" Cassandra yelled back at her. David came in and guided Cass out of the way and everyone else stepped back.

They were able to get Sid's heart started again. They paged for Dr. Scott who was there within mere seconds. Cass was pleading to God, to the universe, to anyone that would listen, not take him from her.

"Cass, I'm sorry but Sid is getting worse."

"He can't be. He was just talking to us. I want a second opinion."

"Cass, I've seen this happen many times. In all likelihood his heart will stop again and we'll do our best to revive him, but every time we try, it will get harder until we won't be able to revive him. Please Cass, for his sake, agree to a DNR."

"No! I won't give up on him." she yelled.

Dr. Scott walked out of the room and a short time later the alarms went off again. The nurses and Dr. Scott came back in and started the procedure all over again. Tiny went to Cass and pulled her close to him. "Cass please, for Sid's sake, tell them to stop. He's fighting to stay for you, but, hun, his body is tired and he is damaged beyond repair. Cass, this will be that hardest thing you will ever have to do. Please let my brother go."

Cassandra looked up at Tiny, who was in tears himself. She turned around and looked at the man she loved and knew in her heart she had to let him go. She walked over to the bed and just as they were about to shock him again, she told them to stop.

Nurse Georgie moved out of the way. Cass leaned over Sid. "Baby, you can go. I'll be okay, we all will. I love you more than anything. Be free and at peace, I will see you soon. I love you, Sid."

At 9:15 p.m. Sid passed away. Everyone gathered around his bed. Faye was the first to say that he looked happy and at peace. Cass just put her head on his chest and stroked his side and kept telling him she loved him.

Nurse Georgie undid all the wires and unhooked all the IVs. No one knew what to do. They were all in shock. Cass asked for some time alone with Sid, so they all kissed him and said their goodbyes. When the room was cleared out, she crawled into bed with him and held him tightly and cried until there were no more tears.

Cassandra finally got off the bed and kissed Sid one last time and walked out of the room. She never looked back. There was nothing there for her anymore. The man she loved was gone.

Faye walked over to her daughter and was about to hug her. "Please don't," Cass said. "It's taking every bit of control I have left in me not to lose it."

Nurse Georgie walked over to Cass with a bag that contained Sid's personal effects and told her she was so sorry for her loss. She placed the bag into her hands. Cass looked down and there was Sid's wallet and wedding ring on top of his clothing. She took them out of the bag and asked Ryder to please get rid of the rest, she didn't want to see them ever again. She took his wedding band and slipped it onto her thumb.

Nurse Georgie told Cass if there was anything she could do, to please not hesitate to call. She turned around and went back to the nurse's station.

There wasn't a funeral. It wasn't what Sid wanted. He was cremated and his ashes were separated into two urns: one was for Cassandra—she wanted a piece of him with her always. Faye had called Sam, Joe, and Liliana and they said to tell Cass they

360 | SUE ADAIR

were on their way. Jayne called Natalie and she told Jayne she was on the next flight out.

There was a large gathering at the grounds where they had the carnival. Tents were set up, music was playing, and people were celebrating the life of a husband, dear friend, and family member. Cassandra didn't realize just how many people knew Sid. There were so many bikes lined up in rows and they just kept coming. People were sticking around. They were friends that hadn't seen each other in a while and everyone wanted to connect—and that made Cass happy, because she knew it would have made Sid happy.

Tiny got up and thanked everyone for coming to celebrate Sid's life. He raised his beer and said, "To Sid." Everyone followed suit and shouted, "To Sid." Tiny called Cass and asked her to come over to where he was. She was reluctant. She didn't want to lose it in front of everyone. Ryder walked over to her, placed his hand on her lower back, and whispered, "You got this," into Cassandra's ear.

The four of them stood together. "We would like to take Sid for one last ride and we would like you all to join us. We're going to take him down to Riverdale. There is a small bridge in the middle of a huge field where Sid liked to go to think. This is where we want to set his ashes, free to roam" Tiny said.

They got onto their bikes and a few people drove in cars. Cass got onto the back of Ryder's bike and held onto Sid's urn with one arm and Ryder with the other. Everyone started their bikes. It was amazing to hear the rumbling of them all. *Sid would just love this*, Cass thought to herself.

They had a police escort; Officer Camilleri was leading the procession. There were so many people, they wanted to make sure everyone was safe.

They arrived at the bridge. Everyone lined their bikes in rows and Cass and her family walked onto the bridge. They quietly said their goodbyes one last time. Cass held the urn in the air and set Sid's ashes free, while all his friends and family started to rev their motors. It was like hundreds of angelic trumpets blowing. It was the send-off of all send-offs and that's what Sid deserved.

37

....

It had been a year since Sid's passing. Cassandra couldn't stand being in their home without Sid, so she packed up what she wanted and gave the rest to charity. Tiny and Shelley took what they wanted, as well as Ryder, and the rest was let go. The house was put up for sale and sold quickly. Cass moved into a small bungalow on the beach close to where she proposed to Sid. It would have been too hard for her to stay at Tiny's—after all, that's where their love story truly began.

She quit her job at the Roadhouse. She just couldn't do it any longer. She wanted to take some time and figure out what she wanted to do next. Cass spent some of her time at the beach, where she would sit on the rock where she had asked Sid to marry her. She just wanted a private place where she could talk to him. She didn't like to do it when the family was around her. It really didn't matter where she was, she could always feel him with her.

She and Ryder spent a lot of time together. Everyone knew it would happen eventually, and everyone in the family was good with it. They knew it didn't mean Cass loved Sid any less. It was just that Sid's death reminded them all that life was too short and anything could happen in the blink of an eye, as it had with Sid. They also knew it was what he wanted for them both.

Cassandra and Ryder decided to buy a house of their own. A house where neither of them had ever lived. They wanted a fresh start, a home where they could make their own memories.

It was a beautiful sunny day. They decided to go for a ride— no place special, they just wanted to do something they both loved to do together. Out of nowhere, Cass heard Sid call her name. She turned her head and caught a glimpse of a house up in the trees with a small "For Sale" sign. "Ryder, please stop. Ryder, pull over please."

Ryder pulled over. "What's wrong?"

"Please go back… but go slow."

Ryder turned the bike around and drove slowly. "There," Cassandra pointed. He stopped his bike in front of the house. Cass got off the bike and took off her helmet. "Ryder, we have to look at this house, please."

"Why, Cass?"

"I don't know, but everything in me is telling me we need to."

Ryder took out his phone and called Wendy, their Realtor. He told her where they were and asked if she could find out who owned the house and if it would be possible to see the place today. Wendy called back in less than five minutes. She told them the owner was home and to just go up to the house. She was on her way with all the information.

Ryder knocked on the door; the owner, whose name was Terry, answered and asked them to come in to look around. Cass looked at Ryder and he smiled. They both felt the same thing as soon as they walked in. They were home.

They went to the sliding doors at the back of the house and walked outside onto a huge deck. In the centre of the yard was this huge oak tree with a beautiful bench for sitting underneath. Cassandra turned to Terry and asked him if the bench came with the house. He told them if they wanted it, yes—he would sell it with the house. Wendy arrived and walked over to Cass and Ryder. "Here's the information about the house."

Ryder and Cass read it over. "Are there any other offers on the house?" asked Ryder

"Nothing… and I'm really surprised. It should have sold quickly."

Cass turned to Ryder and told him that it was Sid's voice calling her name that had made her turn and notice the "For Sale" sign. Ryder smiled and told Wendy to do what she had to; they wanted this house.

Thirty days later, Ryder and Cass moved into their new home. After everyone left, Ryder got a shovel out of the garage and both he and Cassandra lifted the bench up and moved it away from the tree. Ryder dug two holes and Cass placed her father's ashes in one and Sid's in the other. They filled them in and returned the bench back over them, to protect them.

They sat on that bench—Ryder, with his arm around Cass, enjoying the sounds of the crickets and seeing the fireflies dancing in the night sky.

"Ryder? I know what I want to do with all that money."

"What's that?"

"I wanna open up a K9 facility to train dogs for soldiers with PTSD and to help dogs as well, with the same issues. I want to name it the Sid Davis Healing Hearts Foundation. Be honest with me—what do you think?"

"I think that Sid would love that; he was all about helping our soldiers and their families whenever he could."

"Will you help me make this happen?"

"Hell ya. We all will. I know Tiny and Shelley will want to be a part of this too." Ryder pulled Cass in closer to him, both of them feeling at peace with what had happened, and what was about to happen.

Ryder leaned over and kissed Cass on the side of her head. "Let's go to bed. We have a lot of work to do to get this foundation up and running."

Cass got up, looked at the bench, and in her head said, *Dad and Sid, I love you both.*

Cassandra put her hand in Ryder's. They headed into their new home to begin their life together. As Cassandra drifted off to sleep in Ryder's arms, she heard a familiar voice: "Live, Love, and Laugh, baby."

I will, Sid. I promise.

CPSIA information can be obtained
at www.ICGtesting.com
Printed in the USA
LVHW111017290521
688874LV00010B/517/J